HUNTING ZERO

Jack Mars is the USA Today bestselling author of the LUKE STONE thriller series, which includes seven books. He is also the author of the new FORGING OF LUKE STONE prequel series, comprising three books (and counting); and of the AGENT ZERO spy thriller series, comprising six books (and counting).

Jack loves to hear from you, so please feel free to visit www.Jackmarsauthor.com to join the email list, receive a free book, receive free giveaways, connect on Facebook and Twitter, and stay in touch!

HUNTING ZERO

(An Agent Zero Spy Thriller—Book #3)

JACK MARS

CONTENTS

Agent Zero - Book 2 Summary (recap sheet to be included in book 3)

Samples of an ancient, deadly virus are stolen from Siberia and unleashed in Spain, killing hundreds in hours. Though his memory as a CIA agent is still fragmented, Agent Zero is reinstated to help find and secure the virus before a terrorist organization can release it in the United States.

Agent Zero: More memories of his former life as a CIA agent have returned to him, most notably that of a clandestine plot by the American government to initiate a pre-planned war for insidious motivations. The details of what he knew two years ago are muddied and faded, but before he had the chance to dig further he returned home to discover that his two daughters had been kidnapped from their home.

Maya and Sara Lawson: While their father was away, the girls were under the watchful eye of Mr. Thompson, their neighbor and a retired CIA operative. When the assassin Rais broke in, Thompson did his best to fend him off but was ultimately killed, and Maya and Sara were taken.

Agent Maria Johansson: Once again Maria proved an indispensable ally when she helped to secure the smallpox virus from being released. Though her newfound relationship with Kent borders on the romantic, she has secrets of her own, having met with a mysterious Ukrainian operative in the airport at Kiev to discuss where Agent Zero's allegiances lie.

Rais: After being beaten and left for dead in Switzerland, Rais recovered for several weeks in a hospital under guard and handcuffs.

With nothing but time on his hands, he engineered not only a daring and bloody escape, but also managed to abscond to the US before international borders were shut down due to the virus. From there it was not difficult to find the Lawson home, kill the old man, and kidnap Agent Zero's two teenage daughters.

Agent John Watson: As part of the team sent to secure the smallpox virus, Watson made it abundantly clear that he has a distaste for Agent Zero's daredevil tactics. Nevertheless, after their success in stopping Imam Khalil, the two reached an understanding and a mutual respect.

Assistant Director Ashleigh Riker: A former intelligence officer who has worked her way up the chain to Special Operations Group, Riker works directly under Deputy Director Shawn Cartwright on the op to secure the virus. She does not mask her disdain for Agent Zero and the license the agency gives him. After another agent attacked Zero unprovoked, he began to suspect that Riker might be in on the conspiracy—and therefore not to be trusted.

CHAPTER ONE

At age sixteen, Maya Lawson was mostly certain she was going to die soon.

She sat in the backseat of a large-cabbed pickup truck as it barreled down I-95, heading south through Virginia. Her legs still felt weak from the trauma and terror of what she had experienced barely more than an hour earlier. She stared straight ahead impassively, her mouth slightly open in a shell-shocked, blank gaze.

The truck had belonged to her neighbor, Mr. Thompson. He was dead now, likely still lying in the tiled foyer of the Lawson home in Alexandria. The truck's current driver was his murderer.

Seated beside Maya was her younger sister, Sara, only fourteen. Her legs were drawn up beneath her and her body curled into Maya's. Sara had stopped sobbing, at least for now, but each breath escaped her open mouth with a soft moan.

Sara had no idea what was going on. She knew only what she had seen—the man in their house. Mr. Thompson dead. The assailant threatening to break her sister's limbs to get Sara to open the door to their basement panic room. She didn't know any of what Maya knew, and even Maya knew only a small part of the whole truth.

But the elder Lawson girl did know one thing, or at least she was mostly certain of it: she was going to die soon. She did not know what the driver of the truck was planning to do with them—he had made the promise that he wouldn't hurt them as long as they did what he asked—but that didn't matter.

Despite her slack-jawed expression, Maya's mind was working a mile a minute. Only one thing was important now, and that was keeping Sara safe. The man behind the wheel was alert and capable, but at some point he would falter. As long as they did what he asked, he would get complacent, even for just a second, and in that moment she would act. She did not know yet what she would do, but it would have to be direct, ruthless, and debilitating. Give Sara the opportunity to flee, to get to safety, to other people, to a phone.

It would likely cost Maya her life. But she was already very much aware of that.

Another soft moan escaped her sister's lips. *She's in shock*, Maya thought. But the moan became a murmur, and she realized that Sara was trying to speak. She bent her head close to Sara's lips to hear her quiet question.

"Why is this happening to us?"

"Shh." Maya cradled Sara's head against her chest and gently stroked her hair. "It's going to be okay."

She regretted it as soon as she said it; it was an empty sentiment, something that people say when they have nothing else to offer. Clearly it was not okay, and she could not promise that it would be.

"Sins of the father." The man behind the wheel spoke for the first time since he had forced them into the truck. He said it casually, eerily calmly. Then louder he said, "This is happening to you because of the decisions made and actions taken by one Reid Lawson, known to others as Kent Steele, known to many more as Agent Zero."

Kent Steele? Agent Zero? Maya had no idea what this man, the assassin who called himself Rais, was talking about. But she knew some things, enough to know that her father was an agent of some government group—FBI, possibly CIA.

"He took everything from me." Rais stared straight ahead at the highway beyond them, but he spoke with a tone of unadulterated hatred. "Now I've taken everything from him."

"He's going to find us," Maya said. Her tone was hushed, not defiant, as if she were simply stating a fact. "He's going to come for us, and he's going to kill you."

Rais nodded as if he agreed with her. "He will come for you; that is true. And he will try to kill me. Twice he has made attempts and left me for dead ... once in Denmark, and again in Switzerland. Did you know that?"

Maya said nothing. She had suspected that her dad had something to do with the terrorist plot that unfolded a month earlier in February, when a radical faction tried to bomb the World Economic Forum in Davos.

"But I endure," Rais continued. "You see, I was led to believe that it was my destiny to kill your father, but I was wrong. It is my *fate*. Do you know the difference?" He scoffed lightly. "Of course you don't. You are a child. Destiny is comprised of the events that one is supposed to fulfill. It is something we can control, something we can dictate. Fate, on the other hand, is beyond us. It is determined by another power, one we cannot fully comprehend. I don't believe I am allowed to perish until your father dies at my hand."

"You're Amun," Maya said. It wasn't a question.

"I was, once. But Amun is no more. I alone endure."

The assassin had confirmed what she had already feared; that he was a fanatic, someone who had been indoctrinated by the cult-like terrorism group of Amun into believing that his actions were not only justified, but necessary. Maya was gifted with the dangerous combination of intelligence and curiosity; she had read much on the subjects of terrorism and fanaticism in the wake of the Davos bombing and her speculation that her father's absence at the time it had happened meant he had been a part of stopping and dismantling the organization.

So she knew very well that this man could not be swayed with pleas, prayers, or supplication. She knew there was no changing his mind, and she was aware that hurting children was not beyond him. All of it only strengthened her resolve that she had to act as soon as she saw the chance.

"I have to use the bathroom."

"I don't care," Rais responded.

Maya frowned. She had once eluded an Amun member on the New Jersey boardwalk by feigning the need for the bathroom—she didn't believe her father's cover story about the man being a local gang member for even a second—and had managed to get Sara to safety then. It was the only thing she could think of in the current moment that would allow them even a precious minute alone, but her request had been denied.

They drove for several more minutes in silence, heading southbound on the interstate while Maya stroked Sara's hair. Her younger sister seemed to have calmed to a point that she was no longer crying, or had simply run out of tears.

Rais put the blinker on and eased the truck off the next exit. Maya peered out the window and felt a small surge of hope; they were pulling into a rest stop. It was tiny, little more than a picnic area surrounded by trees and a small, squat brick building with restrooms, but it was something.

He was going to let them use the bathroom.

The trees, she thought. *If Sara can get into the woods, maybe she can lose him.*

Rais parked the truck and let the engine idle for a moment as he scanned the building. Maya did too. There were two trucks there, long tractor trailers parked parallel to the brick building, but no one else. Outside the bathrooms under an awning were a couple of vending machines. She noted with dismay that there were no cameras, at least none visible, on the premises.

"The right side is the women's restroom," Rais said. "I will walk you there. If you try to scream or call out to anyone, I will kill them. If you so much as gesture or signal to anyone that anything is amiss, I will kill them. Their blood will be on your hands."

Sara was trembling in her arms again. Maya hugged her tightly around the shoulders.

"The two of you will hold hands. If you separate, Sara will get hurt." He twisted around partially to face them—specifically Maya. He had already assumed that of the two, she would be the one more likely to give him trouble. "Do you understand?"

Maya nodded, averting her gaze from his wild green eyes. He had dark lines beneath them, as if he hadn't slept in some time, and his dark hair was shorn short on top of his head. He did not seem all that old, certainly younger than their father, but she could not guess his age.

He held up a black pistol—the Glock that had belonged to her father. Maya had tried to use it on him when he broke into the house, and he had taken it from her. "This will be in my hand, and my hand will be in my pocket. Again I will remind you that trouble for me is trouble for her." He gestured toward Sara with his head. She whimpered slightly.

Rais got out of the truck first, sticking his hand and the pistol into his black jacket pocket. Then he opened the rear door of the cab. Maya climbed out first, her legs shaky as her feet touched the pavement. She reached back into the cab for Sara's hand and helped her younger sister out.

"Go." The girls walked in front of him as they headed for the bathroom. Sara shivered; late March in Virginia meant that the weather was just starting to turn, lingering in the mid- to high fifties, and both of them were still in their pajamas. Maya wore only flip-flops on her feet, striped flannel pants, and a black tank top. Her sister had on sneakers with no socks, poplin pajama pants emblazoned with pineapples, and one of their dad's old T-shirts, a tie-dyed rag with the logo of some band neither of them had ever heard of.

Maya turned the knob and pushed into the bathroom first. She instinctively wrinkled her nose in disgust; the place smelled of urine and mold, and the floor was wet from a leaking sink pipe. Still she pulled Sara along behind her into the restroom.

There was a single window in the place, a plate of frosted glass high up in the wall that looked like it would swing outward with a good push. If she could boost her sister up and out, she could distract Rais while Sara ran...

"Move." Maya flinched as the assassin pushed into the bathroom behind them. Her heart sank. He wasn't going to let them be alone, even for a minute. "You, there." He pointed to Maya and the second stall of the three. "You, there." He instructed Sara to the third.

Maya let go of her sister's hand and entered the stall. It was filthy; she wouldn't have wanted to use it even if she actually had to go, but she would at least have to pretend. She started to push the door closed but Rais stopped it with the palm of his hand.

"No," he told her. "Leave it open." And then he turned his back, facing the exit.

He's not taking any chances. She slowly sat on the closed toilet seat lid and breathed into her hands. There was nothing she could do. She had no weapons against him. He had a knife and two guns, one of which was currently in his hand, hidden in the jacket pocket. She could try to jump him and let Sara get out, but he was blocking the door. He had already killed Mr. Thompson, a former Marine and a bear of a man who most would have avoided a fight with at any cost. What chance would she have against him?

Sara sniffled in the stall beside her. *This isn't the right time to act,* Maya knew. She had hoped, but she would have to wait again.

Suddenly there was a loud creak as the door to the bathroom was pushed open, and a surprised female voice said, "Oh! Excuse me...Am I in the wrong restroom?"

Rais took a step to the side, past the stall and out of Maya's view. "So sorry, ma'am. No, you're in the right place." His voice immediately took on a pleasant, even courteous affectation. "My two daughters are in here and...well, maybe I'm overprotective, but you just can't be too careful these days."

Anger swelled in Maya's chest at the ruse. The fact that this man had taken them from their father and would dare to pretend to be him made her face hot with rage.

"Oh. I see. I just need to use the sink," the woman told him.

"By all means."

Maya heard the clacking of shoes against tile, and then a woman came partially into view, facing away from her as she twisted the faucet knob. She looked to be middle-aged, with blonde hair just past her shoulders and dressed smartly.

"Can't say I blame you," the woman said to Rais. "Normally I would never stop in a place like this, but I spilled coffee on myself on the way to visit family, and … uh …" She trailed off as she gazed into the mirror.

In the reflection, the woman could see the open stall door, and Maya seated there atop the closed toilet. Maya had no idea what she might look like to a stranger—hair tangled, cheeks puffy from crying, eyes rimmed red—but she could imagine it was likely cause for alarm.

The woman's gaze flitted to Rais and then back to the mirror. "Uh … I just couldn't drive another hour and a half with my hands sticky…" She glanced over her shoulder, the water still running, and then she mouthed three very clear words to Maya.

Are you okay?

Maya's lower lip trembled. *Please don't talk to me. Please don't even look at me.* She slowly shook her head. *No.*

Rais's back must have been turned again, facing the door, because the woman nodded slowly. *No!* Maya thought desperately. She wasn't trying to plead for help.

She was trying to keep this woman from suffering the same fate as Thompson.

Maya waved her hand at the woman and mouthed one word back at her. *Go. Go.*

The woman frowned deeply, her hands still dripping wet. She glanced in Rais's direction again. "I suppose it would be too much to ask for paper towels, huh?"

She said it a bit too forcefully.

Then she gestured to Maya with her thumb and pinky, making a phone signal with her hand. She seemed to be suggesting she would call someone.

Please just go.

As the woman turned back toward the door, there was a blur of motion in the air. It happened so fast that at first Maya wasn't even sure it had happened at all. The woman froze, her eyes widening in shock.

7

A thin arc of blood spurted from her open throat, spraying against the mirror and sink.

Maya clamped both hands over her mouth to stifle the scream that rose from her lungs. At the same time, the woman's hands flew to her neck, but there was no stopping the damage that had been done. Blood ran in rivulets over and between her fingers as she sank to her knees, a soft gurgle escaping her lips.

Maya squeezed her eyes shut, both hands still over her mouth. She didn't want to see it. She didn't want to watch this woman die because of her. Her breath came in heaving, smothered sobs. From the next stall she heard Sara whimpering softly.

When she dared to open her eyes again, the woman stared back at her. One cheek rested against the filthy wet floor.

The pool of blood that had escaped her neck nearly reached Maya's feet.

Rais bent at the waist and cleaned his knife on the woman's blouse. When he looked up at Maya again, it was not anger or distress in his too-green eyes. It was disappointment.

"I told you what would happen," he said softly. "You tried to signal to her."

Tears blurred Maya's vision. "No," she managed to choke out. She couldn't control her trembling lips, her shaking hands. "I-I didn't…"

"Yes," he said calmly. "You did. Her blood is on your hands."

Maya began hyperventilating, her breaths coming in wheezing gulps. She bent over, putting her head between her knees, her eyes clenched shut and her fingers in her hair.

First Mr. Thompson, and now this innocent woman. They had both died simply by being too close to her, too close to what this maniac wanted—and he had proven twice now that he was willing to kill, even indiscriminately, to get what he wanted.

When she finally regained control of her breathing and dared to look up again, Rais had the woman's black handbag and was rooting through it. She watched as he took out her phone and tore out both the battery and the SIM card.

"Stand up," he ordered Maya as he entered the stall. She stood quickly, flattening herself against the metal stall partition and holding her breath.

Rais flushed the battery and SIM down the toilet. Then he turned to face her, only inches away in the narrow space. She couldn't meet his gaze. Instead she stared at his chin.

He dangled something in front of her face—a set of car keys.

"Let's go," he said quietly. He left the stall, seemingly having no problem walking through the wide puddle of blood on the floor.

Maya blinked. The rest stop wasn't at all about letting them use the bathroom. It wasn't this assassin showing an ounce of humanity. It was a chance for him to ditch Thompson's truck. *Because the police might be looking for it.*

At least she hoped they were. If her father hadn't come home yet, there was little chance that anyone would know that the Lawson girls were missing.

Maya stepped as gingerly as possible to avoid the puddle of blood—and to avoid looking at the body on the floor. Every joint felt like gelatin. She felt weak, powerless, against this man. All the resolve that she had mustered only minutes ago in the truck had dissolved like sugar in boiling water.

She took Sara by the hand. "Don't look," she whispered, and directed her younger sister around the woman's body. Sara stared at the ceiling, taking long breaths through her open mouth. Fresh tears streaked both of her cheeks. Her face was white as a sheet and her hand felt cold, clammy.

Rais pulled the bathroom door open just a few inches and peered outside. Then he held up a hand. "Wait."

Maya peered around him and saw a portly man in a trucker's cap walking away from the men's room, patting his hands dry on his jeans. She squeezed Sara's hand, and with her other she instinctively smoothed her own tangled, messy hair.

She couldn't fight this assassin, not unless she had a weapon. She couldn't try to enlist the help of a stranger, or they might suffer the same fate as the dead woman behind them. She had only one choice now, and that was to wait and hope that her dad came for them...which he could only do if he knew where they were, and there was nothing to help him find them. Maya had no way to leave clues or a trail.

Her fingers snagged in her hair and came away with a few loose strands. She shook them off her hand and they fell slowly to the floor.

Hair.

She had hair. And hair could be tested—that was basic forensics. Blood, saliva, hair. Any of those things could prove that she had been somewhere, and that she had still been alive when she was. When the authorities found Thompson's truck, they would find the dead woman, and they would collect samples. They would find her hair. Her dad would know they had been there.

"Go," Rais told them. "Outside." He held the door as the two girls, holding hands, left the bathroom. He followed, glancing around once more to ensure no one was watching. Then he took out Mr. Thompson's heavy Smith & Wesson revolver and flipped it around in his hand. With a single, solid motion, he swung the gun's handle downward and snapped the doorknob off the closed bathroom door.

"Blue car." He gestured with his chin and put the gun away. The girls walked slowly toward a dark blue sedan parked a few spaces away from Thompson's truck. Sara's hand trembled in Maya's—or it might have been Maya doing the trembling, she wasn't sure.

Rais pulled the car out of the rest stop and back onto the interstate, but not south, the way they had been going before. Instead he doubled back and headed north. Maya understood what he was doing; when the authorities found Thompson's truck they would assume he would continue south. They would be looking for him, and them, in the wrong places.

Maya yanked out a few strands of her hair and dropped them to the floor of the car. The psychopath who had kidnapped them was right about one thing; their fate was being determined by another power, in this case, him. And it was one that Maya could not yet fully comprehend.

They had only one chance now to avoid whatever fate was in store for them.

"Dad will come," she whispered in her sister's ear. "He'll find us."

She tried not to sound as uncertain as she felt.

CHAPTER TWO

Reid Lawson moved quickly up the stairs of his home in Alexandria, Virginia. His movements seemed wooden, his legs still feeling numb from the shock he'd experienced only minutes earlier, but his stare was set in an expression of grim determination. He took the steps two at a time to the second floor, though he dreaded what would be up there—or, more appropriately, what wouldn't.

Downstairs and outside was a flurry of activity. In the street in front of his house were no fewer than four police cars, two ambulances, and a fire truck, all protocol for a situation like this one. Uniformed cops stretched caution tape in an X over his front door. Forensics collected samples of Thompson's blood from the foyer and hair follicles from his girls' pillows.

Reid could barely remember even calling the authorities. He barely recalled giving the police a statement, a stammering patchwork of fragmented sentences punctuated by short, gasping breaths while his mind swam with horrifying possibilities.

He had gone away for the weekend with a friend. A neighbor was watching his girls.

The neighbor was now dead. His girls were gone.

Reid made a call as he reached the top of the stairs and away from prying ears.

"You should have called us first," Cartwright said as greeting. Deputy Director Shawn Cartwright was head of the Special Activities Division and, unofficially, Reid's boss at the CIA.

They've already heard. "How did you know?"

"You're flagged," Cartwright said. "We all are. Anytime our info comes up in a system—name, address, social, anything—it's automatically sent to the NSA with priority. Hell, you get a speeding ticket the agency will know before the cop lets you drive away."

"I have to find them." Every second that ticked by was a thunderous chorus reminding him that he might never see his daughters again if he didn't leave now, this instant. "I saw Thompson's body. He's been dead for at least twenty-four hours, which is a significant lead on us. I need equipment, and I need to go *now*."

Two years earlier, when his wife, Kate, had died suddenly of an ischemic stroke, he'd felt completely numb. A dazed, detached feeling had overtaken him. Nothing felt real, as if any moment he would wake from the nightmare to find it had all been in his head.

He hadn't been there for her. He had been at a conference on ancient European history—no, that wasn't the truth. That was his cover story while he was on a CIA op in Bangladesh, pursuing a lead on a terrorist faction.

He wasn't there for Kate back then. He wasn't there for his girls when they were taken.

But he was sure as hell going to be there for them now.

"We're going to help you, Zero," Cartwright assured him. "You're one of us, and we take care of our own. We're sending techs to your house to assist the police in their investigation, posing as Homeland Security personnel. Our forensics are faster; we should have a bead on who did this within the—"

"I know who did this," Reid interrupted. "It was *him*." There was no doubt in Reid's mind who was responsible for this, who had come and taken his girls. "Rais." Just saying the name aloud renewed Reid's rage, starting in his chest and radiating through every limb. He clenched his fists to keep his hands from shaking. "The Amun assassin that escaped from Switzerland. This was him."

Cartwright sighed. "Zero, until there's evidence, we don't know that for sure."

"I do. I know it. He sent me a picture of them." He had received a photo, sent to Sara's phone from Maya's. The picture was of his daughters, still in their pajamas, huddled together in the back of Thompson's stolen truck.

"Kent," the deputy director said carefully, "you've made a lot of enemies. This doesn't confirm—"

"It was him. I know it was him. That photo is proof of life. He's taunting me. Anyone else might have just…" He couldn't bring himself to say it aloud, but any of the other myriad foes Kent Steele had amassed over his career might have just killed his girls as revenge. Rais was doing this because he was a fanatic who believed he was destined to kill Kent Steele. That meant that eventually the assassin would want Reid to find him—and hopefully, the girls as well.

Whether or not they're alive when I do, though… He gripped his forehead with both hands as if he could somehow pry the thought from his head. *Stay clear-headed. You can't think like that.*

"Zero?" Cartwright said. "You still with me?"

Reid took a calming breath. "I'm here. Listen, we need to track Thompson's truck. It's a newer model; it has a GPS unit. He also has Maya's phone. I'm sure the agency has the number on file." Both the truck and the phone could be tracked; if the locations synced and Rais hadn't ditched either of them yet, it would give them a solid direction to pursue.

"Kent, listen…" Cartwright tried to say, but Reid immediately cut him off.

"We know there are members of Amun in the United States," he rattled on, unabated. Two terrorists had gone after his girls once before on a New Jersey boardwalk. "So it's possible there's an Amun safe house somewhere within US borders. We should contact H-6 and see if we can get any info out of the detainees." H-6 was a CIA black site in Morocco, where detained members of the terrorist organization were currently being held.

"Zero—" Cartwright tried again to break into the one-sided conversation.

"I'm packing a bag and heading out the door in two minutes," Reid told him as he hurried into his bedroom. Every moment that passed was another moment that his girls were farther away from him. "The TSA should be on alert, in case he tries to take them out of the country. Same with ports and train stations. And highway cameras—we can access those. As soon as we have a lead, have someone meet me. I'll need a car, something fast. And an agency phone, a GPS tracker, guns—"

"Kent!" Cartwright barked into the phone. "Just stop a second, all right?"

"Stop? These are my little girls, Cartwright. I need information. I need help..."

The deputy director sighed heavily, and Reid immediately knew something was very wrong. "You're not going on this op, Agent," Cartwright told him. "You're too close."

Reid's chest heaved, his anger swelling again. "What are you talking about?" he asked quietly. "Just what the hell are you talking about? I'm going after my girls—"

"You're not."

"These are my *children*..."

"Listen to yourself," Cartwright said sharply. "You're ranting. You're emotional. This is a conflict of interest. We can't allow it."

"You know I'm the best person for this," Reid said forcefully. No one else would be going for his children. It would be him. It had to be him.

"I'm sorry. But you have a habit of attracting the wrong kind of attention," Cartwright said, as if that was an explanation. "The higher-ups, they are trying to avoid a...repeat performance, if you will."

Reid balked. He knew precisely what Cartwright was talking about, though he didn't actually remember it. Two years ago his wife, Kate, died, and Kent Steele buried his grief in his work. He went on a weeks-long spree, cutting off communication with his team as he pursued members of Amun and leads across Europe. He refused to come in when the CIA called him back. He didn't listen to anyone—not Maria Johansson, not his best friend, Alan Reidigger. From what Reid gathered, he left a slew of bodies in his wake that most described as nothing short of a rampage. In fact, it was the primary reason that the name "Agent Zero" was whispered in equal parts terror and disdain amongst insurgents the world over.

And when the CIA had had enough, they sent someone to take him out. They sent Reidigger after him. But Alan didn't kill Kent Steele; he had found another way, the experimental memory suppressor that would allow him to forget all about his life in the CIA.

"I get it. You're afraid of what I might do."

"Yeah," Cartwright agreed. "You're damn right we are."

"You should be."

"Zero," the deputy director warned, "don't. You let us do this our way, so it can get done quickly, quietly, and cleanly. I'm not going to tell you again."

Reid ended the call. He was going after his girls, with or without the CIA's help.

Chapter Three

After hanging up on the deputy director, Reid stood outside the door to Sara's bedroom with his hand on the knob. He did not want to go in there. But he needed to.

Instead he distracted himself with the details that he knew, running through them in his mind: Rais had entered the house through an unlocked door. There were no signs of forced entry, no windows or door locks broken. Thompson had tried to fight him off; there was evidence of a struggle. Ultimately the old man had succumbed to knife wounds to the chest. No shots had been fired, but the Glock that Reid kept by the front door was gone. So was the Smith & Wesson that Thompson perpetually kept at his waist, which meant that Rais was armed.

But where would he take them? None of the evidence at the crime scene that was his home led to a destination.

In Sara's room, the window was still open and the fire escape ladder still unfurled from the sill. It seemed that his daughters had attempted, or at least thought, to try to climb down it. But they hadn't made it.

Reid closed his eyes and breathed into his hands, willing away the threat of new tears, of new terrors. Instead he retrieved her cell phone charger, still plugged into the wall beside her nightstand.

He had found her phone on the basement floor, but hadn't told the police about it. Nor did he show them the photo that had been sent to it—sent with the intent that he would see it. He couldn't hand the phone over, despite it clearly being evidence.

He might need it.

In his own bedroom, Reid plugged Sara's cell phone into the wall outlet behind his bed. He put the device on silent, and then turned on call and message forwarding to his number. Lastly he hid her phone between the mattress and box spring. He didn't want it taken by the cops. He needed it to stay active, in case more taunts came. Taunts could become leads.

He quickly stuffed a bag with a couple changes of clothes. He did not know how long he would be gone, how far he would have to go. *To the ends of the earth, if necessary.*

He switched out his sneakers for boots. He left his wallet in his top dresser drawer. In his closet, stuffed deep in the toe of a pair of black dress shoes, was a wad of emergency cash, nearly five hundred dollars. He took it all.

Atop his dresser was a framed photo of the girls. His chest grew tight just looking at it.

Maya had her arm around Sara's shoulders. Both girls were smiling wide, seated across from him at a seafood restaurant as he took their picture. It was from a family trip to Florida the previous summer. He remembered it well; he had snapped the photo mere moments before their food arrived. Maya had a virgin daiquiri in front of her. Sara had a vanilla milkshake.

They were happy. Smiling. Content. Safe. Before he had brought any of this terror down upon them, they were safe. At the time this photo was taken, the very notion of ever being pursued by radicals intent to harm them, kidnapped by murderers, was the stuff of fantasy.

This is your fault.

He flipped the frame over and tore open the back. As he did, he made himself a promise. When he found them—*and I will find them*—he would be done. Done with the CIA. Done with covert operations. Done with saving the world.

To hell with the world. I just want my family to be safe and kept safe.

They would leave, move far away, change their names if they needed to. All that would matter for the rest of his life would be their safety, their happiness. Their survival.

He took the photo from the frame, folded it in half, and tucked it into his inside jacket pocket.

He would need a gun. He could probably find one in Thompson's house, just next door, if he could manage to slip in without the police or emergency personnel seeing—

Someone cleared their throat loudly in the hall, an obvious warning sign meant for him in case he needed a moment to compose himself.

"Mr. Lawson." The man stepped into the bedroom doorway. He was short, soft in the middle, but had hard lines etched in his face. He reminded Reid a little of Thompson, though that could have just been guilt. "My name is Detective Noles, with the Alexandria Police Department. I understand this is a very difficult time for you. I know you've already given a statement to the first-responding officers, but I have some follow-up questions for you that I'd like to be on the record, if you would please come with me down to the precinct."

"No." Reid took up his bag. "I'm going to find my girls." He marched out of the room and past the detective.

Noles followed quickly. "Mr. Lawson, we strongly discourage citizens from taking any action in a case like this. Let us do our jobs. The best thing for you to do would be to stay somewhere safe, with friends or family, but close by..."

Reid paused at the bottom of the stairs. "Am I a suspect in the kidnapping of my own daughters, Detective?" he asked, his voice low and hostile.

Noles stared. His nostrils flared briefly. Reid knew his training dictated that this sort of situation be handled delicately, as not to further traumatize victims' families.

But Reid was not traumatized. He was angry.

"As I said, I just have a few follow-up questions," Noles said carefully. "I'd like you to come with me, down to the precinct."

"I reject your questions." Reid stared back. "I'm going to get in my car now. The only way you're taking me anywhere is in handcuffs." He very much wanted this stout detective out of his face. For a brief moment he even considered mentioning his CIA credentials, but he had nothing on him to back it up.

Noles said nothing as Reid turned on his heel and strode out of the house to the driveway.

Still the detective followed, out the door and across the lawn. "Mr. Lawson, I'm only going to ask you once more. Consider for a second how this looks, you packing a bag and running off while we're actively investigating your home."

A white-hot jolt of anger ran through Reid, from the base of his spine up to the top of his head. He very nearly dropped his bag right there, so much was his desire to turn and deck Detective Noles across the jaw for even remotely implying that he might have had a hand in this.

Noles was a veteran; he must have been able to read the body language, but still he pressed on. "Your girls are missing and your neighbor is dead. All this happened while you weren't home, yet you don't have a solid alibi. You can't tell us who you were with or where you were. Now you're running off like you know something we don't. I have questions, Mr. Lawson. And I *will* get answers."

My alibi. Reid's actual alibi, the truth, was that he had spent the last forty-eight hours running down a crazed religious leader who was in possession of an apocalypse-sized batch of mutated smallpox. His alibi was that he just got home from saving millions of lives, perhaps even billions, only to find that the two people he cared most about in this entire world were nowhere to be found.

But he couldn't say any of that, no matter how much he wanted to. Instead, Reid forced his rage down and held back both his fist and his tongue. He paused alongside his car and turned to face the detective. As he did, the shorter man's hand moved slowly to his belt—and his handcuffs.

Two uniformed officers milling about outside noticed the potential altercation and took a few cautious steps closer to him, hands also moving to their belts.

Ever since the memory suppressor had been cut from his head, it felt like Reid was of two minds. One side, the logical, Professor

Lawson side, was telling him: *Back down. Do as he asks. Or else you'll find yourself in jail and you'll never get to the girls.*

But the other side, the Kent Steele side of him—the secret agent, the renegade, the thrill-seeker—it was much louder, shouting, knowing from experience that every second counted desperately.

That side won out. Reid tensed, ready for a fight.

CHAPTER FOUR

For what felt like a long moment, no one moved—not Reid, not Noles, not the two cops behind the detective. Reid clung to his bag in a white-knuckled grip. If he tried to get in the car and leave, he had no doubt the officers would advance on him. And he knew he would react accordingly.

Suddenly there was the screech of tires and all eyes turned toward a black SUV as it came to an abrupt halt at the end of the driveway, perpendicular to Reid's own vehicle, blocking him in. A figure stepped out and strode quickly over to defuse the situation.

Watson? Reid nearly blurted it out.

John Watson was a fellow field agent, a tall African-American man whose features were perpetually passive. His right arm was suspended in a dark blue sling; he had caught a stray bullet to the shoulder only the day prior, assisting on the op to stop Islamic radicals from releasing their virus.

"Detective." Watson nodded to Noles. "My name is Agent Hopkins, Department of Homeland Security." With his good hand he flashed a convincing badge. "This man needs to come with me."

Noles frowned; the tension of the moment before had evaporated, replaced by confusion. "Say what now? Homeland Security?"

Watson nodded gravely. "We believe the abduction has something to do with an open investigation. I'm going to need Mr. Lawson to come with me, right now."

"Now hang on." Noles shook his head, still thrown by the sudden intrusion and rapid explanation. "You can't just barge in here and take over—"

"This man is a department asset," Watson interrupted. He kept his voice low, as if sharing a conspiratorial secret, though Reid knew it was CIA subterfuge. "He's WITSEC."

Noles's eyes widened to the point it looked like they might fall out of his head. WITSEC, Reid knew, was an acronym for the witness protection program of the US Department of Justice. But Reid said nothing; he simply folded his arms over his chest and shot the detective a pointed glare.

"Still…" Noles said hesitantly, "I'm going to need more to go on here than a flashy badge…" The detective's cell suddenly blared a ringtone.

"I assume that will be your confirmation from my department," said Watson as Noles reached for his phone. "You're going to want to take that. Mr. Lawson, this way, please."

Watson strode away, leaving a befuddled Detective Noles stammering into his cell. Reid hefted his bag and followed, but he paused at the SUV.

"Wait," he said before Watson could climb into the driver's seat. "What is this? Where are we going?"

"We can talk while we drive, or we can talk now and waste time."

The only reason Reid could conceive of for Watson being there was if the agency sent him, with the intent of picking up Agent Zero so they could keep an eye on him.

He shook his head. "I'm not going to Langley."

"Neither am I," Watson replied. "I'm here to help. Get in the car." He slid into the driver's seat.

Reid hesitated for a brief moment. He needed to be on the road, but he had no destination. He needed a lead. And he had no reason to believe he was being lied to; Watson was one of the most honest and by-the-books agents he'd ever met.

Reid climbed into the passenger's seat beside him. With his right arm in a sling, Watson had to reach over his body to shift and he steered with one hand. They pulled away in seconds, doing about fifteen over the speed limit, moving quickly but avoiding scrutiny.

He glanced over at the black bag in Reid's lap. "Where were you planning on going?"

"I have to find them, John." His vision blurred at the thought of them out there, alone, in the hands of that murderous madman.

"On your own? Unarmed, with a civilian cell phone?" Agent Watson shook his head. "You should know better."

"I already talked to Cartwright," Reid said bitterly.

Watson scoffed. "You think Cartwright was standing alone in the room when he spoke with you? You think he was on a secure line, in an office at Langley?"

Reid frowned. "I'm not sure I follow. It sounds like you're suggesting that Cartwright wants me to do the thing he just told me not to do."

Watson shook his head, not taking his eyes off the road. "It's more that he knows you're going to do the thing he just told you not to do, whether he wants you to or not. He knows you better than most. The way he sees it, the best way to avoid another problem is to make sure you have some support this time around."

"He sent you," Reid murmured. Watson neither confirmed nor denied it, but he didn't have to. Cartwright knew that Zero was going after his girls; their conversation had been for the benefit of other ears at Langley. Still, knowing Watson's penchant for adherence to protocol, it didn't make sense to Reid why he would help. "What about you? Why are you doing this?"

Watson merely shrugged. "There are a couple of kids out there. Scared, alone, in bad hands. I don't like that much."

It wasn't really an answer, and it might not have even been the truth, but Reid knew it was the best he was going to get out of the stoic agent.

He couldn't help but think that part of Cartwright's acquiescence to help him was some measure of guilt. Twice while he was away Reid had asked the deputy director to put his girls in a safe house. But instead the deputy director made excuses about manpower, about a lack of resources... *And now they're gone.*

Cartwright could have avoided this. He could have helped. Again Reid felt his face grow hot as a surge of anger rose up within him, and again he stifled it down. Now wasn't the time for that. Now was the time to go after them. Nothing else mattered.

I'm going to find them. I'm going to get them back. And I am going to kill Rais.

Reid took a deep breath, in through his nose and out through his mouth. "So what do we know so far?"

Watson shook his head. "Not much. We just found out right after you did, when you called the cops. But the agency is on it. We should have a lead shortly."

"Who's on it? Anyone I know?"

"Director Mullen gave it to Spec Ops, so Riker is taking lead…"

Reid found himself scoffing aloud again. Less than forty-eight hours earlier, a memory had returned to Reid, one from his former life as Agent Kent Steele. It was still foggy and fragmented, but it was about a conspiracy, some sort of government cover-up. A pending war. Two years ago, he had known about it—had at least known some part of it—and had been working to build a case. Regardless of how little he knew, he was certain that at least a few members of the CIA were involved.

At the top of his list was newly appointed Deputy Director Ashleigh Riker, head of Special Operations Group. And his lack of trust in her notwithstanding, he definitely didn't expect she would put her best foot forward in finding his children.

"She assigned a new guy, young, but capable," Watson continued. "Name's Strickland. He's a former Army Ranger, excellent tracker. If anyone could find who did this, it'd be him. Other than you, that is."

"I *know* who did this, John." Reid shook his head bitterly. He immediately thought of Maria; she was a fellow agent, a friend, maybe more—and definitely one of the only people Reid could trust. Last he'd heard, Maria Johansson was on an op tracking Rais into Russia. "I need to contact Johansson. She should know what's happened." He knew that until he could prove it was Rais, the CIA wouldn't pull her back.

"You won't be able to—not while she's in the field," Watson replied. "But I can try to get word to her another way. I'll have her call you when she's able to find a secure line."

Reid nodded. He didn't like not being able to contact Maria, but he had little choice. Personal phones were never carried on ops, and the CIA would likely be monitoring her activity.

"Are you going to tell me where we're going?" Reid asked. He was getting anxious.

"To someone who can help. Here." He tossed Reid a small silver flip phone—a burner, one that the CIA couldn't trace unless they knew about it and had the number. "There are a few numbers programmed in there. One's a secure line to me. Another's to Mitch."

Reid blinked. He didn't know a Mitch. "Who the hell is Mitch?"

Instead of answering, Watson pulled the SUV off the road and into the drive of an auto body shop called the Third Street Garage. He eased the vehicle right into an open garage bay and parked. As soon as he cut the ignition, the garage door rumbled slowly down behind them.

They both climbed out of the car as Reid's eyes adjusted to the relative darkness. Then the lights flickered on, bright fluorescent bulbs that made dots swim in his vision.

Beside the SUV, in the second garage bay, was a black car, a late eighties model Trans Am. It wasn't much younger than he was, but the paint job looked glossy and new.

Also in the garage bay with them was a man. He wore dark blue coveralls that barely concealed spattered grease stains. His features were obscured by a tangled mass of brown beard and a red baseball cap pulled low over his forehead, the brim of it discolored with dried sweat. The mechanic slowly wiped his hands on a filthy, oil-stained rag, staring at Reid.

"This is Mitch," Watson told him. "Mitch is a friend." He tossed a ring of keys to Reid and gestured to the Trans Am. "It's an older model, so there's no GPS. It's reliable. Mitch has been fixing it up for the last few years. So try not to destroy it."

"Thanks." He had been hoping for something more inconspicuous, but he would take what he could get. "What is this place?"

"This? This is a garage, Kent. They fix cars here."

Reid rolled his eyes. "You know what I mean."

"The agency's already trying to get eyes and ears on you," Watson explained. "Any way they can track you, they will. Sometimes in our line of work you need...friends on the outside, so to speak." He gestured again toward the burly mechanic. "Mitch is a CIA asset, someone I recruited from my days in the National Resources Division. He's an expert at, uh, 'vehicle procurement.' If you need to get somewhere, you call him."

Reid nodded. He didn't know that Watson had been in asset collection prior to being a field agent—though, to be fair, he wasn't even sure that John Watson was his real name.

"Come on, I got some things for you." Watson popped the trunk and unzipped a black canvas duffel bag.

Reid took a step back, impressed; inside the bag was an array of supplies, including recording devices, a GPS tracking unit, a frequency scanner, and two pistols—a Glock 22, and his backup of choice, the Ruger LC9.

He shook his head in disbelief. "How did you get all this?"

Watson shrugged one shoulder. "Had a bit of help from a mutual friend."

Reid didn't have to ask. *Bixby.* The eccentric CIA engineer who spent most of his waking hours in a subterranean research and development lab beneath Langley.

"You and him go way back, even if you don't remember it all," Watson said. "Although he made sure to mention that you still owe him some tests."

Reid nodded. Bixby was one of the co-inventors of the experimental memory suppressor that had been installed in his head, and the engineer had asked if he could run a few tests on Reid's head.

He can open my skull if it means getting my girls back. He felt another overwhelming, powerful wave of emotion crash over him, knowing that there were people willing to break the rules, to put themselves in harm's way to help him—people he could barely remember even having a relationship with. He blinked back the threat of tears that stung his eyes.

"Thank you, John. Really."

"Don't thank me yet. We've barely begun." Watson's phone rang in his pocket. "That'll be Cartwright. Give me a minute." He retreated to a corner to take the call, his voice low.

Reid zipped the bag closed and slammed the trunk shut. As he did, the mechanic grunted, making a sound somewhere between clearing his throat and muttering something.

"Did…did you say something?" Reid asked.

"Said sorry. 'Bout your kids." Mitch's expression was well hidden behind his grizzled beard and baseball cap, but his voice sounded genuine.

"You know about…them?"

The man nodded. "Already on the news. Their photos, a hotline to call with tips or sightings."

Reid bit his lip. He hadn't thought about that, the publicity—and the invariable connection to him. He immediately thought of their Aunt Linda, who lived up in New York. These sorts of things had a way of spreading quickly, and if she heard about it she would be fraught with concern, calling and calling Reid's phone for information and getting none.

"Got something," Watson said suddenly. "Thompson's truck was found at a rest stop seventy miles south of here on I-95. A woman was found dead at the scene. Her throat was cut, car gone, ID taken."

"So we don't know who she was?" Reid asked.

"Not yet. But we're on it. I've got a tech on the inside scanning police airwaves and keeping an eye via satellite. As soon as something's reported, you'll know about it."

Reid grunted. Without an ID they wouldn't be able to find the vehicle. Even though it wasn't much of a lead, it was still something to go on, and he was anxious to be on the trail. He had the door to the Trans Am open as he asked, "What exit?"

Watson shook his head. "Don't go down there, Kent. It'll be crawling with cops, and I'm sure Agent Strickland is en route."

"I'll be careful." He didn't trust that the police or this rookie agent would find everything that he would. Besides, if Rais was playing this the way Reid thought he would, there could be another clue in the form of a taunt, something meant just for him.

The photo of his girls flashed again across his memory, the one Rais had sent from Maya's phone, and it reminded him of one last thing. "Here, hang onto this for me." He handed Watson his personal cell. "Rais has Sara's number, and I've got her phone forwarding to mine. If anything comes through, I want to know about it."

"Sure. The crime scene is on exit sixty-three. You need anything else?"

"Don't forget to have Maria call me." He settled behind the wheel of the sports car and nodded to Watson. "Thank you. For all your help."

"Not doing it for you," Watson reminded him somberly. "Doing it for those kids. And Zero? If I'm made, if I'm compromised in any way, if they figure out what I'm doing with you, I'm out. You understand? I can't afford to get agency blacklisted."

Reid's initial kneejerk instinct was a quick swell of anger—*this is about my children, and he's afraid of being blacklisted?*—but he stifled it just as fast as it came on. Watson was an unexpected ally in all of this, and the man was sticking his neck out for his girls. Not for him, but for two children he'd only met briefly.

Reid nodded tightly. "I understand." To the solemn, grunting mechanic he added, "Thanks, Mitch. I appreciate your help."

Mitch grunted in response and pressed the switch to open the garage bay as Reid climbed into the Trans Am. The interior was all black leather, clean, pleasant smelling. The engine turned over immediately and thrummed under the hood. *A 1987 model*, his brain told him. *5.0 liter V8 engine. At least two hundred fifty horsepower.*

He pulled out of the Third Street Garage and headed for the highway, his hands tightly wrapped around the steering wheel. The horrors that had been swirling through his head previously were replaced with a steely resolve, a hard determination. There was a hotline. The police were on it. The CIA was on it. And now he too was on the road after them.

I'm on my way. Dad is coming for you.
And for him.

CHAPTER FIVE

"You should eat." The assassin gestured at a carton of Chinese takeout on the nightstand beside the bed.

Maya shook her head. The food was long cold by now, and she wasn't hungry. Instead, she sat on the bed with her knees drawn up, Sara leaning against her with her head in her older sister's lap. The girls were handcuffed together, Maya's left wrist with Sara's right. Where he had gotten the handcuffs, she didn't know, but the assassin had warned them several times that if either of them tried anything to escape or make noise, the other would suffer for it.

Rais sat in an armchair near the door of the seedy motel room with orange carpeting and yellow walls. The room smelled musty and the bathroom reeked of bleach. They had been there for hours; the ancient bedside alarm clock told her in blocky red LED numerals that it was two thirty in the morning. The television was on, tuned into a news station with the volume low.

A white station wagon was parked directly outside, mere feet from the door; the assassin had stolen it after dark from a used car lot. It was the third time they had switched cars that day, from Thompson's truck to the blue sedan and now to the white SUV. Each time they did, Rais changed directions, heading first south, then back north, and then to the northeast toward the coast.

Maya understood what he was doing; a cat-and-mouse game, leaving the stolen vehicles in different locations so that the authorities would have no idea which way they were heading. Their motel room was less than ten miles from Bayonne, not far from the border to New Jersey and New York. The motel itself was a strip of a building that was so rundown and frankly disgusting that driving by it gave the impression it had been closed for years.

Neither of the girls had slept much. Sara had catnapped in Maya's arms, stealing twenty or thirty minutes at a time before rousing with a start and a whimper as she woke from whatever dream she'd been having and remembered where she was.

Maya had fought the exhaustion, trying to stay awake as long as possible—Rais had to sleep sometime, she knew, and it could afford them a precious few minutes they needed to make a run for it. But the motel was located in an industrial park. She saw when they had pulled in that there were no houses nearby and no other businesses that would be open this time of night. She wasn't even certain anyone would be in the motel office. They would have nowhere to go except into the night, and the handcuffs would slow them down.

Eventually Maya had succumbed to the fatigue and unwillingly nodded off. She was asleep less than an hour when she woke with a slight gasp—and then gasped again when, startled, she saw Rais sitting in the armchair only three feet from her.

He was staring directly at her, eyes wide open. Just watching.

It had made her skin crawl… until a whole minute passed, and then another. She watched him, staring back, her fright mingling with curiosity. Then she realized.

He sleeps with his eyes open.

She wasn't sure if that was more disturbing than waking to find him watching her or not.

Then he blinked, and she sucked in yet another startled gasp, her heart leaping into her throat.

"Damaged facial nerves," he said quietly, almost a whisper. "I've heard it can be quite unsettling." He gestured to the carton of leftover Chinese takeout that had been delivered to their room hours earlier. "You should eat."

She shook her head, cradling Sara across her lap.

The low-volume news station was repeating the major headlines from earlier that day. A terror organization had been deemed responsible for the release of a deadly smallpox virus in Spain and other parts of Europe; their leader, as well as the virus, had been apprehended and several other members were now in custody. That afternoon the United States had officially lifted its international travel ban to all countries except for Portugal, Spain, and France, where there were still isolated incidents of mutated smallpox. But everyone seemed confident that the World Health Organization had the situation under control.

Maya had suspected that her father had been sent to assist with that case. She wondered if he had been the one to take down the ringleader. She wondered if he was back in the country yet.

She wondered if he had found Mr. Thompson's body. If he had realized they were missing—or if *anyone* had realized they were missing.

Rais sat in the yellow chair with a cell phone resting on the armrest. It was an older style phone, practically prehistoric by today's standards—it wasn't good for anything but calls and messages. A burner phone, Maya had heard such things called on TV. It did not connect to the internet and had no GPS, which she knew from police procedural shows meant it could only be traced by the phone number, which someone would have to have.

Rais was waiting for something, it seemed. A call or a message. Maya desperately wanted to know where they were going, if there even was a destination. She suspected that Rais *wanted* their father to find them, to track them down, but the assassin did not seem to be in any rush to get anywhere. Was this his game, she wondered, stealing cars and changing directions, eluding the authorities, in the hopes that their father would be the one to find them first? Would they just keep bouncing from place to place until there was a faceoff?

Suddenly a monophonic ring tone blared out from the burner phone beside Rais. Sara jumped slightly in her arms with the high-pitched intrusion.

"Hello." Rais answered the phone flatly. "*Ano.*" He stood from his chair for the first time in three hours as he switched from English to some foreign tongue. Maya knew only English and French, and she could recognize a handful of other languages from single words and accents, but she didn't know this one. It was a guttural tongue, but not altogether unpleasant.

Russian? she thought. *No. Polish, maybe.* It was no use guessing; she couldn't be sure, and knowing wouldn't help her understand anything that was being said.

Still, she listened in, noting the frequent usage of "z" and "-ski" sounds, trying to pick out cognates, of which there seemed to be none.

There was one word that she managed to pick out, however, and it made her blood run cold.

"Dubrovnik," the assassin said, as if by way of confirmation.

Dubrovnik? Geography was one of her best subjects; Dubrovnik was a city in southwestern Croatia, a famous seaport and popular tourist destination. But far more important than that was the implication of the mentioned word.

It meant that Rais was planning to take them out of the country.

"*Ano,*" he said (which seemed like an affirmative; she guessed it to mean "yes"). And then: "Port Jersey."

They were the only two English words in the entire conversation besides "hello," and she picked them out easily. Their motel was already close to Bayonne, a stone's throw from the industrial Port Jersey. She had seen it many times before, crossing the bridge from Jersey into New York or back, stacks upon stacks of multicolored freight containers being loaded by cranes onto vast, dark ships that would carry them overseas.

Her heartbeat tripled its pace. Rais was going to take them out of the US by way of Port Jersey to Croatia. And from there... she had no idea, and no one else would either. There would be little hope of ever being found again.

Maya could not allow it. Her resolve to fight back strengthened; her determination to do something about this situation came roaring back to life.

The trauma of watching Rais cut the woman's throat in the rest stop bathroom earlier that day still lingered; she saw it whenever she closed her eyes. The vacant, dead stare. The pool of blood nearly touching her feet. But then she touched her sister's hair and she knew that she would absolutely accept the same fate if it meant Sara would be safe and away from this man.

Rais continued his conversation in the foreign language, chattering in short, punctuated sentences. He turned and parted the thick curtains slightly, only an inch or so, to peer out at the parking lot.

His back was to her, probably for the first time since they had arrived at the seedy motel.

Maya reached out and very carefully pulled open the drawer of the nightstand. It was all she could reach, handcuffed to her sister and without moving from the bed. Her gaze flitted nervously to Rais's back, and then to the drawer.

There was a Bible in it, a very old one with a chipped, peeling spine. And beside it was a simple blue ballpoint pen.

She took it and closed the drawer again. At almost the same moment Rais turned back. Maya froze, the pen clutched in her closed fist.

But he did not pay her any attention. He seemed bored with the call now, anxious to get off the phone. Something on the television caught his attention for a few seconds and Maya hid the pen in the elastic waistband of her flannel pajama pants.

The assassin grunted a halfhearted goodbye and ended the call, flinging the phone onto the armchair cushion. He turned toward them, scrutinizing each in turn. Maya stared straight ahead, her gaze as vacant as she could make it, pretending to watch the newscast. Seemingly satisfied, he took his post on the chair again.

Maya gently stroked Sara's back with her free hand as her younger sister stared at the television, or perhaps at nothing at all, her eyes half-closed. After the incident in the restroom at the rest stop, it took hours for Sara to stop crying, but now she simply lay there, her gaze empty and glazed. It seemed she had nothing left.

Maya ran her fingers up and down her sister's spine in an attempt to comfort her. There was no way for them to communicate between each other; Rais had made it clear that they were not allowed to speak unless asked a question. There was no way for Maya to relay a message, to create a plan.

Though... maybe it doesn't have to be verbal, she thought.

Maya stopped touching her sister's back for a moment. When she resumed, she took her index finger and surreptitiously drew the slow, lazy shape of a letter between Sara's shoulder blades—a large S.

Sara lifted her head curiously for just a moment, but she did not look up at Maya or say anything. Maya hoped desperately that she understood.

Q, she drew next.

Then U.

Rais sat in the chair in Maya's peripheral vision. She didn't dare glance over at him for fear of seeming suspicious. Instead she stared straight ahead, as she had been, and drew the letters.

E. E. Z. E.

She moved her finger slowly, deliberately, pausing for two seconds between each letter and five seconds between each word until she spelled out her message.

Squeeze my hand if you understand.

Maya did not even see Sara move. But their hands were close, on account of being cuffed together, and she felt cool, clammy fingers close tightly around her own for a moment.

She understood. Sara got the message.

Maya started anew, moving slowly as possible. There was no rush, and she needed to make sure that Sara got every word.

If you have a chance, she wrote, *you run.*

Do not look back.

Do not wait for me.

Find help. Get Dad.

Sara lay there, quietly and perfectly still, for the entire message. It was a quarter after three before Maya finished. Finally she felt the cool touch of a thin finger on the palm of her left hand, nestled partially under Sara's cheek. The finger traced a pattern on her palm, the letter N.

Not without you, Sara's message said.

Maya closed her eyes and sighed.

You have to, she wrote back. *Or there is no chance for either of us.*

She didn't give Sara an opportunity to respond. Once she had finished her message, she cleared her throat and said quietly, "I have to go to the bathroom."

Rais raised an eyebrow and gestured toward the open bathroom door on the far end of the room. "By all means."

"But…" Maya lifted her shackled wrist.

"So?" the assassin asked. "Take her with you. You have a free hand."

Maya bit her lip. She knew what he was doing; the sole window in the bathroom was small, barely large enough for Maya to fit through and wholly impossible while handcuffed to her sister.

She slid off the bed slowly, prodding her sister to come with her. Sara moved mechanically, as if she had forgotten how to properly use her limbs.

"You have one minute. Do not lock the door," Rais warned. "If you do I will kick it down."

Maya led the way and closed the door to the tiny bathroom, cramped with both of them standing in it. She flicked on the light—fairly certain she saw a roach skitter to safety beneath the sink—and then turned on the bath fan, which droned loudly overhead.

"I won't," Sara whispered almost immediately. "I won't go without—"

Maya quickly held a finger to her own lips to signal for quiet. For all she knew, Rais was standing right on the other side of the door with an ear to it. He did not take chances.

She quickly pulled the ballpoint pen from the hem of her pants. She needed something to write on, and the only thing available was toilet paper. Maya tore off a few squares and spread them on the small sink, but every time she pressed the pen to it, the paper tore easily. She tried again with a few fresh squares, but again the paper ripped.

This is no use, she thought bitterly. The shower curtain would do her no good; it was just a plastic sheet hanging over the tub. There were no curtains over the small window.

But there was something she could use.

"Stay still," she whispered in her sister's ear. Sara's pajama pants were white with a pineapple print on them—and they had pockets. Maya turned one of the pockets inside out and, as carefully as she could, tore it out until she had a rough-edged triangular scrap of fabric that had the fruity imprint on one side but was all-white on the other.

She quickly flattened it on the sink and wrote carefully as her sister watched. The pen snagged several times on the fabric, but Maya bit her tongue to avoid grunting in angry frustration as she wrote out a note.

Port Jersey.

Dubrovnik.

There was more that she wanted to write, but she was nearly out of time. Maya stowed the pen under the sink and tightly rolled the fabric note into a cylinder. Then she looked around desperately for a place to hide the note. She couldn't just stick it under the sink with the pen; that would be too conspicuous, and Rais was thorough. The shower was out of the question. Getting the note wet would run the ink.

An abrupt knock on the thin bathroom door startled them both.

"It's been a minute," Rais said clearly from the other side.

"I'm almost done," she said hastily. She held her breath as she lifted the lid from the toilet tank, hoping that the thrumming bathroom fan drowned out any scraping noise. She looped the rolled-up note through the chain on the flushing mechanism, high enough that it wouldn't touch the water.

"I said you have one minute. I am opening the door."

"Just give me a few seconds, please!" Maya pleaded as she quickly replaced the lid. Lastly, she tugged a few hairs from her head and dropped them atop the closed toilet tank. With any luck—with a lot of luck—anyone who was following their trail would recognize the clue.

She could only hope.

The knob to the bathroom door turned. Maya flushed the toilet and crouched in a gesture to suggest she was pulling up her pajama bottoms.

Rais stuck his head into the open door, his gaze directed at the floor. Slowly he panned up to the two girls, inspecting each in turn.

Maya held her breath. Sara reached for her sister's shackled hand and their fingers intertwined.

"Finished?" he asked slowly.

She nodded.

He looked left and right in distaste. "Wash your hands. This room is disgusting."

Maya did so, washing with gritty orange hand soap as Sara's wrist dangled limply next to her own. She dried her hands on the brown towel and the assassin nodded.

"Back on the bed. Go."

She led Sara back into the room and onto the bed. Rais lingered a moment, glancing around the small bathroom. Then he flicked off the fan and the light and returned to his chair.

Maya put her arm around Sara and held her close.

Dad will find it, she thought desperately. *He'll find it. I know he will.*

CHAPTER SIX

Reid headed south on the interstate, trying hard to ride the line between speeding and getting there quickly as he headed toward the rest stop where Thompson's truck had been ditched. Despite his anxiety to get a lead, find a clue, he was beginning to feel optimistic about being on the road. His grief was still present, sitting heavy in his gut as if he had swallowed a bowling ball, but now it was wrapped in a shell of resolution and tenacity.

Already he was feeling the familiar sensation of his Kent Steele persona taking the reins as he barreled down the highway in the black Trans Am, a trunk full of guns and gadgets at his disposal. There was a time and place to be Reid Lawson, but this wasn't it. Kent was their father too, whether the girls knew it or not. Kent had been Kate's husband. And Kent was a man of action. He didn't wait around for the police to find a lead, for some other agent to do his job.

He was *going* to find them. He just needed to know where they were going.

The interstate heading south through Virginia was mostly straight, two lanes, lined on both sides with thick trees, and thoroughly monotonous. Reid's frustration grew with every passing minute that he didn't get there fast enough.

Why south? he thought. *Where would Rais be taking them?*

What would I do if I was him? Where would I go?

"That's it," he said aloud to himself as a realization struck him like a blow to the head. Rais wanted to be found—but not by the police or the FBI or another CIA agent. He wanted to be found by Kent Steele, and Kent Steele alone.

I can't think in terms of what he would do. I have to think of what I would do.

What would I do?

The authorities would assume that since the truck was found south of Alexandria, that Rais was taking the girls further south. "Which means I would go..."

His musing was interrupted by the blaring tone of the burner phone in the center console.

"Go north," Watson said immediately.

"What did you find?"

"There's nothing to find at the rest stop. Turn it around first. Then we'll talk."

Reid didn't have to be told twice. He dropped the phone into the console, downshifted into third, and jerked the wheel to the left. There weren't many cars on the highway at this time of day on a Sunday; the Trans Am crossed the empty lane and skidded sideways into the grassy median. Its wheels did not screech against the pavement or lose purchase when the ground turned soft beneath them—Mitch must have installed high-performance radial tires. The Trans Am fishtailed across the median, the front end spinning only slightly as it kicked a cascade of dirt out behind it.

Reid straightened the car as he crossed the barren narrow strip between stretches of highway. As the car found asphalt again, he popped the clutch, shifted up, and slammed down on the pedal. The Trans Am shot forward like a bolt of lightning into the opposite lane.

Reid fought down the sudden exhilaration that spiked in his chest. His brain reacted strongly to anything adrenaline producing; it craved the thrill, the fleeting possibility of losing control and the galvanizing pleasure of gaining it back.

"Heading north," Reid said as he plucked up the phone again. "What did you find?"

"I've got a tech monitoring the police airwaves. Don't worry, I trust him. A blue sedan was reported abandoned at a used car lot this morning. In it they found a purse, with IDs and cards matching the woman that was killed at the rest stop."

Reid frowned. Rais had stolen the car and ditched it quickly. "Where?"

"That's the thing. It's about two hours north of your current location, in Maryland."

He scoffed in frustration. "Two hours? I don't have that kind of time to waste. He's already got a big lead on us."

"Working on it," Watson said cryptically. "There's more. The dealership says there's a car missing from their lot—a white SUV, eight years old. We have nothing to track it with other than waiting for it to get spotted. Satellite imaging would be like a needle in a haystack…"

"No," Reid said. "No, don't bother. The SUV will mostly likely be another dead end. He's toying with us. Changing direction, trying to throw us off from wherever he's really taking them."

"How do you know that?"

"Because that's what I would do." He thought for a moment. Rais already had a lead on them; they needed to get ahead of his game, or at least on par with it. "Have your tech look into any cars reported stolen in the last twelve hours or so, between here and New York."

"That's a pretty wide net to throw," Watson noted.

He was right; Reid knew that a car was stolen about every forty-five seconds in the US, amounting to hundreds of thousands each year. "All right, exclude the top ten most frequently stolen models," he said. As much as he didn't want to admit it, Rais was smart. He would likely know which cars to avoid and which to aim for. "Scratch off anything expensive or flashy, bright colors, distinguishing features, anything the cops would find easily. And, of course, anything new enough to be equipped with GPS. Focus on locations that wouldn't have many people around—vacant lots, closed businesses, industrial parks, that sort of thing."

"Got it," Watson said. "I'll call you back when I have info."

"Thanks." He stashed the phone in the center console again. He didn't have two hours to burn driving the highways. He needed something faster, or a better lead on where his girls might be. He wondered if Rais had once again changed direction; perhaps headed north just to turn west, heading inland, or even going south again.

He glanced over at the lanes of southbound traffic. *I wonder if I could be passing them right now, right next to me. I'd never know it.*

His thoughts were suddenly drowned out by a piercing yet familiar sound—the steady rising and falling of a wailing police siren. Reid swore under his breath as he glanced in the rearview mirror to see a police cruiser tailing him, its red and blue lights flashing.

Not what I need right now. The cop must have spotted him cross the median. He looked again; the cruiser was a Caprice. *5.7-liter engine. Top speed of a hundred and fifty. I doubt the Trans Am can maintain that.* Even so, he wasn't about to pull over and waste precious time.

Instead he slammed the pedal down anew, jumping from the previous eighty-five he was doing up to an even hundred miles an hour. The cruiser kept pace, leaping up in speed effortlessly. Still Reid kept both hands on the wheel, his hands steady, the familiarity and excitement of a high-speed chase returning to him.

Except this time he was the one being chased.

The phone rang again. "You were right," Watson said. "I got a...wait, is that a siren?"

"Sure is," Reid muttered. "Anything you can do about this?"

"Me? Not on an unofficial op."

"I can't outrun him..."

"But you can outdrive him," Watson replied. "Call Mitch."

"Call Mitch?" Reid repeated blankly. "And say what exactly...? Hello?"

Watson had already hung up. Reid swore under his breath and skirted around a minivan, swerving back into the left lane with one hand as he thumbed the flip phone. Watson told him that he'd programmed a number for the mechanic into the phone.

He found a number labeled with only the letter "M" and called as the siren continued to blare behind him.

Someone answered, but didn't speak.

"Mitch?" he asked.

The mechanic grunted in response.

Behind him, the cop moved into the right lane and accelerated, trying to get up next to him. Reid jerked the wheel quickly and the Trans Am slid flawlessly into the lane, blocking the cop car. Behind the closed windows and the roar of the engine he could faintly hear the echo of a PA system, the trooper ordering him to pull over.

"Mitch, I'm, uh..." *What am I supposed to say?* "I'm doing about one-ten down I-95 with a cop on my tail." He glanced in the rearview mirror and groaned as a second cruiser pulled onto the highway from a speed-trap vantage point. "Make that two."

"All right," Mitch said gruffly. "Give it a minute." He sounded tired, as if the notion of a high-speed police chase was as blasé as a trip to the grocery store.

"Give *what* a minute?"

"Distraction," Mitch grunted.

"I'm not sure I have a minute," Reid protested. "They've probably already got the license plate."

"Don't worry about that. It's a fake. Unregistered."

That's not going to inspire them to call off the pursuit, Reid thought glumly. "What sort of a distraction...hello? Mitch?" He threw the phone onto the passenger seat irritably.

With both hands back on the wheel, Reid veered around a pickup truck, back into the fast lane, and put the pedal fully down. The Trans Am responded with zeal, roaring forward as the needle leapt to one-thirty. He darted around much slower traffic, weaving in and out of both lanes, using the shoulder, but still the pair of cruisers kept up.

I can't outrun them. But I can outdrive them. Come on, Kent. Give me something. It had happened several times over the last month, ever since the memory suppressor had been removed, that a particular skill set from his former life as a CIA operative would come rushing back in times of need. He didn't know he spoke Arabic until he was faced with terrorists torturing him for information. He didn't know he could fend off three killers hand-to-hand until he had to fight for his life.

That's it. I just have to put myself in a desperate situation.

Reid grabbed the emergency brake just behind the gearshift and yanked it upward. There immediately came an awful screech from inside the Trans Am and the smell of something burning. At the same time, his hands spun the wheel to the right and the Trans Am fishtailed tightly, its back end once again crossing into the median as if he were trying to spin in the opposite direction.

The two cop cars followed suit, slamming on their brakes and trying to make the tight turnaround. But as they hit their brakes, facing south, Reid continued into the spin, doing a complete three-sixty. He pushed down the emergency brake, shifted, and slammed the gas again. The sports car jolted forward and left the confused cops quite literally in the dust.

Reid let out a whoop of victory as his heart thrummed in his chest. His excitement, however, was short-lived; he had his foot firmly on the gas, trying to maintain his speed, but the Trans Am was losing power. The speedometer needle dropped to ninety-five, then ninety, falling fast. He was in fifth gear, but his e-brake maneuver must have blown a cylinder, or else kicked dirt up into the engine.

The earsplitting wail of sirens made the bad news worse. The two cruisers were behind him and catching up fast, now joined by a third. The highway traffic moved aside to clear a path as Reid had to weave in and out of lanes, desperately trying to keep the needle up to little avail.

He groaned. It was going to be impossible to shake the cops at this rate. They were no more than sixty yards behind him and gaining. The cruisers formed a triangle, one in each lane with the third splitting the line behind them.

They're going to try the PIT maneuver—box me in and force the car sideways.

Come on, Mitch. Where's my distraction? He had no idea what the mechanic had planned, but he could really use it at the moment as the cruisers closed the gap on the failing sports car.

He got his answer an instant later as something huge leapt into his peripheral vision.

From the southbound side of the highway, a tractor trailer jumped the median doing at least seventy, its huge tires bouncing violently over the ruts in the grass. As it reached the pavement again—going the wrong direction—it teetered dangerously and the silver tank it was hauling tipped sideways, bearing down upon him.

CHAPTER SEVEN

For an instant, time slowed down as Reid found himself, and the entire car, engulfed in the shadow of an eighteen-wheeled machine that had all but left the ground.

In that oddly still moment, he could clearly see the tall blue letters stenciled down the side of the tanker—"POTABLE," they read—as the truck bore down, poised to crush him, the Trans Am, and any hope of finding his girls.

His higher brain, the cerebrum, seemed to have shut itself off in the shadow of the enormous truck, yet his limbs moved as if of their own minds. Instinct took over as his right grabbed the e-brake again and pulled. His left hand spun the wheel clockwise, and his foot mashed the gas pedal against the rubber floor mat. The Trans Am turned sideways and darted out, parallel to the truck, back into the sunlight and out from beneath it.

Reid felt the impact of the truck crunching against the road more than he heard it. The silver tank struck the pavement between the Trans Am and the cop cars, closing in at less than thirty yards. Brakes squealed and the cruisers skidded sideways as the huge silver tank split open at the bolted seams and released its cargo.

Nine thousand gallons of clean water cascaded out and flowed over the police cars, shoving them back like an aggressive riptide.

Reid didn't pause to see the fallout. The Trans Am was barely pushing seventy with the pedal to the floor, so he straightened out and headed further up the highway as best he could. The water-logged troopers undoubtedly called in the conspicuous car with the unregistered plates; there would be more trouble ahead if he didn't get off the road soon.

The burner rang, the screen displaying only the letter M.

"Thanks, Mitch," Reid answered.

The mechanic grunted, as seemed to be his primary method of communication.

"You knew where I was. You know where I am now." Reid shook his head. "You're tracking the car, aren't you?"

"John's idea," Mitch said simply. "Thought you might get yourself into some trouble. He was right." Reid started to protest, but Mitch interrupted. "Get off at the next exit. Turn right on River Drive. There's a park with a baseball field. Wait there."

"Wait there for what?"

"Transportation." Mitch hung up. Reid scoffed. The whole point of the Trans Am was supposed to be clandestine, staying off the agency's grid—not to exchange the CIA for someone else that might track him.

But without it, you'd have been caught by now.

He swallowed his anger and did as he was told, guiding the car off the exit another half a mile up the interstate and toward the park. He hoped that whatever Mitch had in store for him was fast; he had a lot of ground to cover quickly.

The park was sparsely populated for a Sunday. In the baseball field a group of neighborhood kids were playing a pick-up game, so Reid parked the Trans Am in the gravel lot outside the chain-link fence behind first base and waited. He didn't know what he was looking for, but he knew he had to move fast, so he popped the trunk, retrieved his bag, and waited beside the car for whatever Mitch had planned.

He had a suspicion that the grizzled mechanic was more than just a CIA asset. He was "an expert in vehicle procurement," Watson had said. Reid wondered if Mitch was a resource, someone like Bixby, the eccentric CIA engineer who specialized in weapons and handheld gear. And if that was the case, why was he helping Reid? No memories sparked in his head when he thought of Mitch's gruff appearance, his grunting demeanor. Was there a forgotten history there?

The phone rang in his pocket. It was Watson.

"You good?" the agent asked.

"Good as I can be, all things considered. Though Mitch's idea of a 'distraction' might be a little overambitious."

"He gets the job done. Anyway, your hunch was right. My guy found a report of a twelve-year-old Caddy stolen from an industrial park in New Jersey this morning. He snapped a satellite image of the place. Guess what he saw?"

"The missing white SUV," Reid ventured.

"Right," Watson confirmed. "Sitting in the parking lot of some junk heap called the Starlight Motel."

New Jersey? His hope fell. Rais had taken his girls even further north—his two-hour drive just became at least three and a half to have any hope of catching up. *He might be taking them into New York. A major metro area, easy to get lost in.* Reid had to get a better lead on him before that happened.

"The agency doesn't know what we know yet," Watson continued. "They have no reason to link the stolen Caddy to your girls. Cartwright confirmed that they're following the leads they've got and sending Strickland north to Maryland. But it's just a matter of time. Get there first and you'll have a head start on him."

Reid deliberated for a moment. He didn't trust Riker; that much was clear. In fact, the jury was still out even on his own boss, Deputy Director Cartwright. But... "Watson, what do you know about this Agent Strickland?"

"I only met him once or twice. He's young, a bit eager to please, but seems decent. Maybe even trustworthy. Why, what are you thinking?"

"I'm thinking..." Reid couldn't believe he was about to suggest it, but it was for his daughters. Their safety was the most important thing, no matter what the perceived cost. "I'm thinking that we shouldn't be the only ones with this intel. We need all the help we can get, and while I don't trust Riker to do the right thing, maybe Strickland will. Could you get information to him anonymously?"

"I think I could, yeah. I'd have to filter it through some of my asset connections, but it's doable."

"Good. I want to get him our intel—but *after* I've been there to see for myself. I don't want him gaining a lead on me. I just want someone to know what we know." More specifically, he wanted someone who wasn't Cartwright to know what they knew. *Because if I fail, I need someone to succeed.*

"If you say so, sure." Watson was silent for a moment. "Kent, there's one more thing. Back at that rest stop, Strickland found something…"

"What? What did he find?"

"Hair," Watson told him. "Brown hair, with the follicle still attached. Pulled out by the root."

Reid's throat ran dry. He didn't believe that Rais wanted to kill the girls—he couldn't allow himself to believe that. The assassin needed them alive if he wanted Kent Steele to find them.

But the thought was of little comfort as unwelcome images invaded Reid's thoughts, scenes of Rais grabbing his daughter by a fistful of hair, forcing her to go where he wanted. Hurting her. And if he was hurting them in any way at all, Reid was going to hurt him in every way.

"Strickland didn't think much of it," Watson continued, "but the police found more of it in the back seat of the dead woman's car. Like someone left them there on purpose. Like a…"

"Like a clue," Reid murmured. *It was Maya.* He just knew it. She was smart, smart enough to leave something behind. Smart enough to know that the scene would be swept over carefully and her hairs would be found. She was alive—or at least she had been when they were there. He was simultaneously proud that his daughter was so keen while rueful that she would ever have to think to do such a thing in the first place.

Oh god. A new realization took its place immediately: If Maya had purposely left her hair in the rest stop bathroom, then she was there when it happened. She had watched that monster murder an innocent woman. And if Maya was there... Sara might have been too. They had both been affected, mentally and emotionally, by the events of February, on the boardwalk; he didn't want to think of the trauma going through their minds now.

"Watson, I have to get to New Jersey fast."

"Working on it," the agent replied. "Just stay put, it'll be there any minute."

"What will be here?"

Watson answered, but his response was drowned out by the sudden, startling chirp of a siren directly behind him. He spun as a police cruiser crunched over the gravel lot toward him.

I don't have time for this. He snapped the phone shut and slipped it into his pocket. The passenger's side window was down; he could see that there were two officers inside. The car pulled right up alongside his and the door swung open.

"Sir, put the bag on the ground and your hands on your head." The officer was young, with a military-style high and tight fade and aviator shades over his eyes. Reid took notice that one hand was on the holster of his service pistol, the button clasp undone.

The driver got out as well, older, around Reid's age with a shaved head. He stood behind his open door, his hand also hovering near his belt.

Reid hesitated, unsure of what to do. *Local police must have heard the APB from the troopers.* It couldn't have been difficult to spot the Trans Am with the fake plates parked so openly next to the baseball field. He scolded himself for being so careless.

"Sir, put the bag down and hands on your head!" the young officer shouted forcefully.

Reid had nothing to threaten them with; his guns were in the bag, and even if he had one he wasn't about to shoot anyone. As far as these cops were aware, they were just doing their job, detaining a fugitive from a high-speed chase that had incapacitated three cars and, in all likelihood, still had the northbound lanes of I-95 shut down.

"This isn't what you think." Even as he said it, he lowered the bag to the gravel slowly. "I'm just trying to find my daughters." Both arms came up, his fingertips touching just behind his ears.

"Turn around," the young officer ordered. Reid did so. He heard the familiar clinking of handcuffs as the cop pulled a pair loose from the pouch on his belt. He waited for the cold bite of steel on his wrist.

"You have the right to remain silent…"

As soon as he felt contact, Reid sprang into action. He spun, grabbed the officer's right wrist with his own, and twisted it upward at an angle. The cop cried out in both surprise and pain, though Reid was careful not to twist far enough to break it. He wasn't going to injure the officers if he could help it.

In the same motion he grabbed the loose cuff with his left hand and snapped it around the officer's wrist. The driver had his gun out in an instant, shouting angrily.

"Back away! On the ground, now!"

Reid shoved forward with both arms and sent the young officer stumbling into the open door. It swung shut—or tried to, pushing the older cop backward. Reid tucked into a roll, coming up on his knees right beside the man. He snapped the Glock out of the cop's grip and tossed it over his shoulder.

The younger cop straightened and tried to yank his pistol loose. Reid grabbed the empty, swinging half of the handcuffs dangling from the officer's wrist and pulled, throwing the man off balance again. He looped the cuffs through the open window, yanking the cop into the door, and snapped the open loop of steel around the older officer's wrist.

As the pair struggled against each other and the door of the cruiser, Reid tugged the younger cop's pistol free and aimed it at them. They fell still immediately.

"I'm not going to shoot you," he told them as he retrieved his bag. "I just want you to stay quiet and don't move for a minute or so." He leveled the gun at the older officer. "Put your hand down, please."

The cop's free hand fell away from his shoulder-mounted radio.

"Just put down the gun," the younger officer said, his uncuffed hand out in a pacifying gesture. "Another unit is on its way. They will shoot you on sight. I don't think you want that."

Is he bluffing? No; Reid could hear sirens wailing in the distance. *About a minute out. Ninety seconds at best.* Whatever Mitch and Watson had planned, it needed to arrive *now*.

The boys on the baseball field had paused their game, now clustered behind the nearest concrete dugout and peering out in awe at the scene mere yards from them. Reid noticed in his periphery that one of the boys was on a cell phone, likely reporting the incident.

At least they're not filming it, he thought glumly, keeping the gun trained on the two cops. *Come on, Mitch...*

Then—the younger cop frowned at his partner. They glanced at each other and then skyward as a new sound joined the distant screaming sirens—a whining hum, like a high-pitched motor.

What is that? Definitely not a car. Not loud enough to be a chopper or a plane...

Reid looked up as well, but he couldn't tell what direction the sound was coming from. He didn't have to wonder long. From over left field came a tiny object, soaring quickly through the air like a buzzing bee. Its shape was indistinguishable; it appeared to be white, but it was difficult to look directly at it.

The underbelly is painted in reflective coating, Reid's mind told him. *Keeps the eyes from being able to focus on it.*

The object dropped in altitude as if it were falling from the sky. As it crossed over the pitcher's mound, something else dropped down from it—a steel cable with a narrow crossbar at the bottom, like a single rung of a ladder. *A rappelling line.*

"That must be my ride," he murmured. While the cops stared in disbelief at the literal UFO soaring toward them, Reid dropped the gun on the gravel. He made sure he had a tight grip on his bag, and as the crossbar swung toward him, he reached up and grabbed onto it.

He sucked in a breath as he was instantly swept into the sky, up twenty feet in seconds, then thirty, then fifty. The boys on the baseball field shouted and pointed as the flying object above Reid's head retracted the rappelling line rapidly, gaining altitude again at the same time.

He glanced down and saw two more police cars screeching into the park's lot, the drivers exiting their vehicles and looking upward. He was a hundred feet in the air before he reached the cockpit and settled into the single seat that waited there.

Reid shook his head in astonishment. The vehicle that had picked him up was little more than a small egg-shaped pod with four parallel arms in an X shape, each of which had a spinning rotor at the end. He knew what this was—a quadcopter, a single-person manned drone, fully automated and highly experimental.

A memory flashed in his mind: *A rooftop in Kandahar. Two snipers have you pinned at your location. You have no idea where they are. Make a move and you die. Then, a sound—a high-pitched whine, barely more than a hum. It reminds you of your string trimmer back home. A shape appears in the sky. It's hard to look at. You can barely see it, but you know help has arrived…*

The CIA had experimented with machines like this one to extract agents from hot zones. *He* had been part of the experiment.

There were no controls before him; just an LED screen that told him their air speed of two hundred sixteen miles an hour and an ETA of fifty-four minutes. Beside the screen was a headset. He plucked it up and fit it over his ears.

"Zero."

"Watson. Jesus. How did you get this?"

"I didn't."

"So Mitch," Reid said, confirming his suspicions. "He's not just an 'asset,' is he?"

"He's whatever you need him to be for you to trust that he wants to help."

The quadcopter's air speed increased steadily, leveling out at just under three hundred miles per hour. Several minutes fell off the ETA.

"What about the agency?" Reid asked. "Can they…?"

"Track it? No. Too small, flies at low altitudes. Besides, it's decommissioned. They thought the motor was too loud for it to be stealthy."

He breathed a small sigh of relief. He had a trajectory now, this Starlight Motel in New Jersey, and at last it wasn't a taunt from Rais that led him. If they were still there, he could put an end to this—or try to. He couldn't ignore the fact that this would only end in a confrontation with the assassin, and keeping his girls out of the crossfire.

"I want you to wait forty-five minutes and then send the motel lead to Strickland and local PD," he told Watson. "If he's there, I want everyone else there too."

Besides, by the time the CIA and police arrived, either his girls would be safe or Reid Lawson would be dead.

CHAPTER EIGHT

Maya hugged her sister closer to her. The handcuff chain rattled between their wrists; Sara's hand was drawn up over her own chest, her hand gripping Maya's on her shoulder as they huddled together in the backseat of the car.

The assassin drove, easing the car down the length of Port Jersey. The cargo terminal was long, several hundred yards by Maya's best guess. Tall stacks of containers loomed high on either side of them, forming a narrow lane with no more than a foot of room on either side of the car's mirrors.

The headlights were off, and it was dangerously dark, but it did not seem to bother Rais. Every now and then there would be a brief break between the cargo stacks and Maya could see bright lights in the distance, closer to the water's edge. She could even hear the drone of machinery. Crews were working. People were around. Yet that gave her little hope; Rais had so far shown a propensity for planning, and she doubted they would come into view of any prying eyes.

She would have to do something herself to keep them from leaving.

The clock in the car's center console told her it was four in the morning. It had been less than an hour since she had left the note in the toilet tank of the motel. Shortly thereafter, Rais had stood suddenly and announced that it was time to go. Without a word of explanation, he led them out of the motel room, but not to the white station wagon in which they'd arrived. Instead he led them to an older car a few doors down from their room. He seemed to have no problem as he jimmied open the door and put them in the backseat. Rais had tugged off the cover of the ignition column and hotwired the vehicle in a matter of seconds.

And now they were at the port, under the cover of darkness and drawing near to the northern tip of land, where the concrete ended and Newark Bay began. Rais slowed and put the car in park.

Maya peered beyond the windshield. There was a boat there, a fairly small one by commercial standards. It couldn't have been more than sixty feet long end to end, and was laden with cube-shaped steel containers that looked to be about five feet by five feet. The only light on that end of the dock, other than the moon and stars, came from two sickly yellow bulbs on the boat, one on the bow and another at the stern.

Rais turned off the engine and sat there in silence for a long moment. Then he flicked the headlights on and off, just once. Two men emerged from the boat's cabin. They glanced his way, and then disembarked down the narrow ramp between the ship and the dock.

The assassin twisted in his seat, staring directly at Maya. He said only one word, drawing it out slowly. "Stay." Then he got out of the car and closed the door again, standing only a few feet from it as the men approached.

Maya clenched her jaw and tried to slow her rapidly pulsing heartbeat. If they got on this boat and left shore, their chances of ever being found again would be diminished significantly. She could not hear what the men were saying; she heard only low tones as Rais spoke to them.

"Sara," she whispered. "You remember what I said?"

"I can't." Sara's voice broke. "I won't..."

"You have to." They were still handcuffed together, but the ramp to board the boat was narrow, barely more than two feet wide. They would have to remove the cuffs, she told herself. And when they did... "As soon as I move, you go. Find people. Hide if you have to. You need to—"

She didn't get to finish her statement. The rear door was yanked open and Rais peered in at them. "Get out."

Maya's knees felt weak as she slid out of the backseat, followed by Sara. She forced herself to look at the two men who had come from the boat. They were both light-skinned, with dark hair and dark features. One of the pair had a thin beard and short hair, and wore a black leather jacket with his arms folded across his chest. The other wore a brown coat, and his hair was longer, around his ears. He had a paunch that protruded over his belt and a smirk on his lips.

It was this man, the chubby one, that circled around the two girls, walking slowly. He said something in a foreign language—the same language, Maya realized, that Rais had spoken over the phone in the motel room.

Then he said a single word in English.

"Pretty." He laughed. His cohort in the leather jacket grinned. Rais stood there stoically.

With that one word, a comprehension crept into Maya's mind and tightened like icy fingers gripping a throat. There was something far more insidious happening here than simply being taken out of the country. She did not even want to think about it, let alone fathom it. It couldn't be real. Not this. Not to them.

Her gaze found Rais's chin. She couldn't stand to look at his green eyes.

"You." Her voice was quiet, quavering, struggling to find the words. "You're a monster."

He sighed gently. "Perhaps. That's all a matter of perspective. I need passage across the sea; you are my bartering chip. My ticket, as it were."

Maya's mouth ran dry. She did not cry or tremble. She just felt cold.

Rais was *selling* them.

"Ahem." Someone cleared their throat. Five pairs of eyes snapped to attention as a newcomer stepped into the dim glow of the boat's lights.

Maya's heart surged with sudden hope. The man was older, perhaps in his fifties, wearing khakis and a pressed white shirt—he looked official. Under one arm he held a white hard hat.

Rais had the Glock out and leveled in an instant. But he did not shoot. *Others would hear it,* Maya realized.

"Whoa!" The man dropped his hard hat and put both hands up.

"Hey." The foreigner in the black leather jacket stepped forward, between the gun and the newcomer. "Hey, is okay," he said in accented English. "Is okay."

Maya's mouth fell agape in confusion. *Okay?*

As Rais slowly lowered the gun, the thin man reached into his leather jacket and produced a crumpled manila envelope, folded on itself in thirds and taped shut. Something rectangular and thick was inside it, like a brick.

He handed it off as the official-looking man scooped up his hard hat.

My god. She knew damn well what was in the envelope. This man was being paid off to keep his crews away, to keep that area of the dock clear.

Anger and helplessness rose in equal measure. She wanted to shout at him—*please, wait, help*—but then his gaze met hers, for just a second, and she knew it was no use.

There was no remorse behind his eyes. No kindness. No sympathy. No sound escaped her throat.

Just as quickly as he had appeared, the man retreated back into the shadows. "Pleasure doing business," he muttered as he vanished.

This can't be happening. She felt numb. Never in her entire life had she ever met someone who would stand idly by while children were clearly in harm's way—and accept money to do nothing.

The chubby man barked something in his foreign tongue and made a vague gesture toward their hands. Rais said something in response that sounded like a succinct argument, but the other man insisted.

The assassin looked annoyed as he fished in his pocket and pulled out a small silver key. He grabbed at the chain of the handcuffs, forcing both their wrists aloft. "I'm going to take these off of you," he told them. "Then we're going to get on the boat. If you wish to make it back to dry land alive, you'll stay silent. You'll do as you're told." He pushed the key into the cuff around Maya's wrist and opened it. "And don't even think about jumping into the water. None of us will go after you. We will watch you freeze to death and drown. It would take only a couple of minutes." He unlocked Sara's cuff, and she instinctively rubbed her sore, reddened wrist.

Now. Do it now. You have to do something now. Maya's brain screamed at her, but she couldn't seem to move.

The foreigner in the black leather jacket stepped forward and grabbed her upper arm roughly. The sudden physical contact broke her paralysis, jarring her into action. She didn't even think about it.

One foot swung upward, as hard as she could muster, and connected with Rais's groin.

As it did, a memory flashed across her vision. It took only an instant, though it felt much longer, as if everything had slowed around her.

Shortly after the Amun terrorists had tried to kidnap her in New Jersey, her father had pulled her aside one day. He had to stick to his cover story—they were gang members abducting young girls in the area as part of an initiation—but still he told her: *I won't always be around. There won't always be someone there to help.*

Maya had played soccer for years; she had a powerful and well-placed kick. A hiss of breath escaped Rais as he doubled over, both hands flying impulsively to his crotch.

If someone attacks you, especially a man, it's because he's bigger. Stronger. He'll outweigh you. And because of all that, he'll think he can do what he wants. That you don't have a chance.

She jerked her left arm downward, quickly and violently, and pulled free of the leather-jacketed man. Then she launched herself forward, into him, and knocked him off balance.

You don't fight fair. You do whatever you need to do. Crotch. Nose. Eyes. You bite. You flail. You scream. They're already not fighting fair. You don't either.

Maya twisted her body back around and, at the same time, swung one thin arm in a wide arc. Rais was bent at the waist; his face was about eye level with her. Her fist smashed into the side of his nose.

Pain immediately splintered through her hand, starting at the knuckles and radiating up the length, all the way to her elbow. She cried out and grabbed at it. Even so, Rais took the blow hard, nearly falling to the dock.

An arm snaked around her waist and pulled her backward. Her feet left the ground, kicking at nothing as she thrashed both arms. She hadn't even realized she was screaming until a thick hand clamped over her nose and mouth, cutting off both the sound and her breath.

But then she saw her—a small figure getting smaller. Sara ran, back the way they had come, disappearing into the darkness of the cargo stacks.

I did it. She's gone. She's away. Whatever fate would befall Maya now didn't matter. *Don't stop running, Sara. Keep going, find people, find help.*

Another figure shot forward like an arrow—Rais. He sprinted after Sara, also vanishing into the shadows. He was fast, much faster than Sara, and had seemed to recover quickly from Maya's blows.

He won't find her. Not in the dark.

She couldn't breathe with the hand gripping her face. She clawed at it until the fingers slid down, only slightly, but enough for her to suck air in through her nose. The chubby man held her fast, one arm around her waist and her feet still off the ground. But she didn't fight him; she fell still and waited.

For several long moments the dock was quiet. The droning of machinery at the other end of the port echoed in the night, likely drowning out any chance of Maya's screams having been heard. She and the two men waited for Rais to return—the former praying desperately he came back empty-handed.

A short shriek shattered the silence, and Maya's limbs went limp.

Rais emerged from the darkness again. He had Sara under one arm, the way one might carry a surfboard, with his other hand clasped over her mouth to quiet her. Her face was bright red and she was sobbing, though her cries were muffled.

No. Maya had failed. Her attack had done nothing, least of all get Sara to safety.

Rais stopped a few feet short of Maya, staring her down with pure fury in his bright green eyes. A thin rivulet of blood ran from one nostril where she had struck him.

"I told you," he hissed. "I told you what would happen if you tried to do something. Now, you're going to watch."

Maya flailed again, trying to scream, but the man held her tight.

Rais said something harshly in the foreign tongue to the one in the leather jacket. He hurried over and took Sara, holding her still and keeping her silent.

The assassin unsheathed the large knife, the one he had used to murder Mr. Thompson and the woman in the rest stop bathroom. He forced Sara's arm out to one side and held it firmly.

No! Please don't hurt her. Don't. Don't... She tried to form words, to scream them out, but they came out only as shrill, muffled cries.

Sara tried to pull away as she wept, but Rais held her arm in a white-knuckled grip. He forced her fingers apart and wedged the knife in the space between her ring and pinky fingers.

"You're going to watch," he said again, staring directly at Maya, "as I cut off one of your sister's fingers." He pressed the knife to skin.

Don't. Don't. Please, god, don't...

The man holding her, the chubby one, muttered something.

Rais paused and looked up at him irritably.

The two had a quick exchange, not a word of which Maya understood. It wouldn't have mattered anyway; her gaze was locked on her little sister, whose eyes were clenched shut, tears running down both cheeks and over the hand that held her mouth tightly.

Rais growled in frustration. At long last he released his grip on Sara's hand. The chubby man released his grip on Maya, and at the same time the one in the leather jacket shoved Sara forward. Maya caught her sister in her arms and hugged her close.

The assassin stepped forward, speaking quietly. "This time, you're lucky. These gentlemen suggested that I not damage any merchandise before it gets to where it's going."

Maya trembled from head to toe, but she didn't dare move.

"Besides," he told her, "where you're going will be far worse than anything I might do to you. Now we're all going to get on the boat. Remember, you're only good to them alive."

The chubby man led the way up the ramp, Sara behind him and Maya right behind her as they stepped shakily onto the boat. There was no use in fighting back now. Her hand throbbed with pain where she'd struck Rais. There were three men and only two of them, and he was faster. He had found Sara in the dark. They had little chance of making it out on their own.

Maya glanced over the side of the boat at the black water below. For just a split second, she thought about jumping; freezing in its depth might be preferable to the fate that awaited them. But she couldn't do that. She couldn't leave Sara. She couldn't lose her last ounce of hope.

They were directed to the stern of the ship, where the man in the leather jacket took out a ring of keys and unlocked the padlock on the door of a boxy steel crate, painted a rusty orange.

He swung the door open, and Maya gasped in horror.

Inside the crate, squinting in the dim yellow light, were several other young girls, at least four or five that Maya could see.

Then she was shoved from behind, forced inside. Sara was too, and she fell to her knees on the floor of the small container. As the door swung behind them, Maya scrambled to her and wrapped Sara in her arms.

Then the door slammed shut, and they were plunged into darkness.

CHAPTER NINE

The sun set quickly in the overcast sky as the quadcopter raced north to deliver its cargo, one determined CIA operative and father, to the Starlight Motel in New Jersey.

His ETA was five minutes. A message on the screen blinked a warning: *Prepare to deploy.* He glanced out the side of the cockpit and saw, far below, that they were soaring over a wide industrial park of boxy warehouses and manufacturing facilities, sitting silent and dark, illuminated only by the dots of orange streetlights.

He unzipped the black duffel bag sitting in his lap. Inside he found two holsters and two guns. Reid struggled out of his jacket in the tiny cockpit and put on the shoulder rig that held a Glock 22, standard-issue—none of Bixby's high-tech biometric trigger locks like he had with the Glock 19. He pulled his jacket back on and tugged up the leg of his jeans to attach the ankle holster that held his backup weapon of choice, the Ruger LC9. It was a compact pistol with a stubby barrel, nine-millimeter caliber in a nine-round expanded box magazine that stuck out just an inch and a half further than the grip.

He had one hand on the rappelling crossbar, ready to disembark from the manned drone as soon as they reached a safe altitude and speed. He was just about to tug the headset from his ears when Watson's voice came through it.

"Zero."

"Nearly there. Just under two minutes—"

"We just got another photo, Kent," Watson cut him off. "Sent to your daughter's phone."

Icy fingers of panic gripped Reid's heart. "Of them?"

"Sitting on a bed," Watson confirmed. "Looks like it could be the motel."

"The number it came from, can it be traced?" Reid asked hopefully.

"Sorry. He already ditched it."

His hope deflated. Rais was smart; so far he had sent photos of only where he had been, not where he was. If there was any chance of Agent Zero catching up to him, the assassin wanted it to be on his terms. For the entire ride in the quadcopter, Reid had been nervously optimistic about the motel lead, anxious that they had might have caught up to Rais's game.

But if there was a photo...then there was a good chance they had already moved on.

No. You can't think like that. He wants you to find him. He chose a motel in the middle of nowhere specifically for that reason. He's baiting you. They're here. They have to be.

"Were they okay? Did they look...are they hurt...?"

"They looked okay," Watson told him. "Upset. Scared. But okay."

The message on the screen changed, blinking in red: *Deploy. Deploy.*

Regardless of the photo or his thoughts, he'd arrived. He had to see for himself. "I have to go."

"Make it quick," Watson told him. "One of my guys is calling in a false lead at the motel matching Rais's and your daughters' description."

"Thanks, John." Reid pulled off the headset, made sure he had a tight grip on the rappel bar, and stepped out of the quadcopter.

The controlled descent of fifty feet to the ground was faster than he anticipated and took his breath away. The familiar thrill, the rush of adrenaline, coursed through his veins as wind roared in his ears. He bent his knees slightly on approach and touched down onto asphalt in a crouch.

As soon as he released the rappel bar the line zipped back up to the quadcopter, and the drone buzzed away into the night, returning to wherever it had come from.

Reid glanced around quickly. He was in the parking lot of a warehouse across the street from the dingy motel, dimly lit by only a few yellow bulbs outside. A hand-painted sign facing the street told him that he was in the right place.

He scanned left and right as he hurried across the empty street. It was quiet here, eerily quiet. There were three cars in the lot, each spaced out along the row of rooms facing him—and one of them was clearly the white SUV that had been stolen from the used car lot in Maryland.

It was parked right outside of a room with a brass number 9 on the door.

There were no lights on inside; it didn't seem like anyone was staying there at the moment. Even so, he dropped his bag just outside the door and listened carefully for about three seconds.

He didn't hear anything, so he pulled the Glock from his shoulder holster and kicked the door in.

The jamb splintered easily as the door flew open and Reid stepped inside, the gun level at the darkness. Yet nothing moved in the shadows. There were still no sounds, no one crying out in surprise or scrambling for a weapon.

His left hand felt along the wall for a light switch and flicked it on. Room 9 had an orange carpet and yellow wallpaper that was curling at the corners. The room had recently been cleaned, insofar as "cleaned" seemed to go at the Starlight Motel. The bed had been hastily made and it reeked of cheap aerosol disinfectant.

But it was empty. His heart sank. There was no one here—no Sara or Maya or the assassin that had taken them.

Reid stepped carefully, looking over the room. Near the door was a green armchair. The fabric of the seat cushion and back was slightly discolored with the imprint of someone who had sat there recently. He knelt beside it, outlining the shape of the person with his gloved fingertips.

Someone sat here for hours. About six-foot, a hundred and eighty pounds. It was him. He sat here, next to the only point of entry, near the window.

Reid tucked his gun back into its holster and carefully peeled back the bedspread. The sheets were stained; they hadn't been changed. He inspected them cautiously, lifting each pillow in turn, careful not to disrupt any potential evidence.

He found two blonde hairs, long strands without the roots. They had fallen out naturally. He found a single brunette strand in the same fashion. *They were here, together, on this bed, while he sat there and watched them. But why?* Why had Rais brought them here? Why had they stopped? Was it another ploy in the assassin's cat-and-mouse game, or was he waiting for something?

Maybe he was waiting for me. I took too long to follow the clues. Now they're gone again.

If Watson had called in the fake report, the police would be at the motel in minutes, and Strickland was likely already on a chopper. But Reid refused to leave without something to go on, or else all of it would have been for nothing, just another dead end.

He hurried to the motel office.

The carpet was green and coarse beneath his boots, reminiscent of Astroturf. The place stank of cigarette smoke. Beyond the counter was a dark doorway, and behind it Reid could hear something playing at low volume, a radio or television.

He rang the service bell on the counter, a dissonant chime ringing out in the quiet office.

"Hmm." He heard a soft grunt from the back room, but no one came.

Reid rang the bell again three times in quick succession.

"All right, man! Jesus." A male voice. "I'm coming." A young man stepped out from the rear. He looked to be in his mid-twenties or early thirties; it was hard for Reid to tell on account of his bad skin and red-rimmed eyes, which he rubbed as if he'd just awoken from a nap. There was a small silver hoop in his left nostril and his dirty-blond hair was trussed up in mangy-looking dreadlocks.

He stared at Reid for a long moment, as if annoyed by the very concept of someone walking through the office door. "Yeah? What?"

"I'm looking for information," Reid said flatly. "There was a man here recently, Caucasian, early thirties or so, with two teenage girls. One brunette, and a younger one, blonde. He drove that white SUV here. They stayed in room nine—"

"You a cop?" the clerk interrupted.

Reid was quickly growing irritated. "No. I'm not a cop." He wanted to add that he was the father of those two girls, but he stopped himself; he didn't want this clerk to be able to identify him by any more than he already could.

"Look, bro, I don't know nothin' about teenage girls," the clerk insisted. "What people do here is their business—"

"I just want to know when he was here. If you saw the two girls. I want the name that the man gave you. I want to know if he paid in cash or with a card. If it was a card, I want the last four digits of the number. And I want to know if he said anything at all, or if you overheard anything, that might tell me where he went from here."

The clerk stared at him for a long moment, and then he let out a hoarse, raspy snicker. "My man, look around you. This ain't the kind of place that takes names or credit cards or anything like that. This is the kind of place people rent rooms by the hour, if you know what I mean."

Reid's nostrils flared. He'd had just about enough of this nitwit. "There must be something, anything, you can tell me. When did they check in? When did they check out? What did he say to you?"

The clerk shot him a pointed stare. "What's it worth to you? For fifty bucks I'll tell you whatever you want to know."

Reid's fury ignited like a fireball as he reached across the counter, grabbed the young clerk by the front of his T-shirt, and yanked him forward, almost off his feet. "You have *no* idea what you're keeping me from," he growled in the kid's face, "or how far I'll go to get it. You're going to tell me what I want to know or you'll be eating through a straw for the foreseeable future."

The clerk put his hands up, his eyes wide as Reid shook him. "All right, man! All right! There's a, uh, registry under the counter…let me grab it and I'll look it up. I'll tell you when they were here. Okay?"

Reid hissed a breath and released the young guy. He stumbled back, smoothed his T-shirt, and then reached for something unseen beneath the counter.

"Place like this," the clerk said slowly, "the kind of people we get here … they value their privacy, if you know what I mean. They don't care much for people snooping." He took two slow steps back, withdrawing his right arm from underneath the counter … as it gripped the dark brown slide of a sawed-off twelve-gauge shotgun.

Reid sighed ruefully and shook his head. "You're going to wish you hadn't done that." The clerk was wasting his time for the sake of protecting scumbags like Rais—not that he knew what Rais was involved in, but other sordid types, pimps and traffickers and the like.

"Go on back to the suburbs, man." The barrel of the shotgun was pointed at center mass, but it was shaky. Reid got the impression that the kid had used it to threaten, but never actually fired it before.

He had no doubt that he had the faster draw on the clerk; he wouldn't even hesitate to shoot him, in the shoulder or in the leg, if it meant getting what he needed. But he didn't want to fire a shot. The report would be heard for a half mile in the industrial park. It might spook whatever guests were staying in the motel—might even prompt someone to call the police, and he didn't need that attention.

Instead he took a different approach. "You sure that thing's loaded?" he asked.

The clerk glanced down at the shotgun for a dubious second. In that moment, with his gaze averted, Reid planted a hand firmly on the counter and vaulted over it easily. At the same time he swung out his right leg and kicked the shotgun out of the clerk's hands. As soon as his feet were on the ground he leaned forward and swung his elbow into the kid's nose. A sharp gasp erupted from the clerk's throat as blood flowed from both nostrils.

Then, just for good measure, Reid grabbed a fistful of filthy dreadlocks and slammed the guy's face into the counter.

The clerk collapsed to the rough green carpet, moaning as he spat blood onto the floor from his nose and two cracked lips. He groaned and tried to get to his hands and knees. "You...oh, god...you broke my fuckin' nose, man!"

Reid snapped up the shotgun. "That's the least of your concerns right now." He pressed the barrel into the dirty-blond dreadlocks.

The clerk immediately dropped to his stomach and whimpered. "Don't...don't kill me...please don't...please...don't kill me..."

"Give me your phone."

"I don't...I don't have one..."

Reid bent at the waist and quickly patted the guy down. He was being honest; he didn't have a phone, but he did have a wallet. Reid flipped it open and checked the driver's license.

"George." Reid scoffed. The clerk didn't look much like a George. "You got a car here, George?"

"I got, I got a dirt bike, p-parked out back..."

"Good enough. Here's what's going to happen, George. I'm taking your bike. You, you're going to walk out of here. Or run, if you prefer. You're going to go to the hospital and get your nose checked out. You're going to tell them that you were sucker-punched in a bar. You're not going to say a word about this place, or a word about me." He leaned over and lowered his voice. "Because I've got a police scanner, George. And if I hear one mention, even one *word* of a man fitting my description, I'm going to come to..." He checked the ID again. "Apartment 121B on Cedar Road, and I'm going to bring your shotgun with me. You got all that?"

"I got it, I got it." The clerk blubbered, blood and spittle hanging from his lips. "I got it, I promise I got it."

"Now, the man with the girls. When were they here?"

"There was...was a guy, like you said, but I didn't see no girls..."

"But you saw a man that fit that description?"

"Yes, yes. He was real serious. Barely said a word. Came last night, after dark, and paid for the night in cash..."

"When did he leave?"

"I don't know! Sometime in the night. Left the door open, or else I wouldn't have known he was gone..."

During the night? Reid's heart sank. He had hoped, but hadn't truly expected to find the girls at the motel—but he thought he was catching up. If they had a full day's lead on him... they could be anywhere.

Reid dropped the wallet and stepped back, taking the shotgun barrel from the kid's head. "Go."

The clerk scooped up the wallet and ran through the dark doorway, tripping once and falling onto his hands before hurrying out into the night.

Reid ejected the cartridges from the shotgun, four of them in all, and stuffed them into a jacket pocket. He wasn't actually going to take the gun with him; it was an illegal weapon by virtue of having its barrel and stock cut off, and likely unregistered even before its modifications. He wiped the shotgun clean of his prints before replacing it beneath the counter.

He didn't need to invite trouble. He had enough as it was.

The police would arrive at any moment, but he couldn't leave without something more to go on. He hurried back to the broken door of room 9 and searched again, this time not caring to replace anything or handle with care. He tore the pillows and sheets from the bed. He searched under the bed and chair. He pulled out the drawers of each shoddy nightstand and the bureau, but found nothing but an old Bible with a cracked spine. He fanned its pages and shook it out, just in case.

At every opportunity so far, Maya had left something behind on purpose. According to the clerk, the girls had spent most of a night here.

Reid hurried into the bathroom. It stank strongly of bleach as he checked the shower stall, the sink, the vanity with the cracked mirror. He opened the single small cabinet beneath the sink and found two spare rolls of toilet paper, a spray can of air freshener, and, curiously, a blue ballpoint pen.

Reid turned on the hot water in both the sink and the shower and closed the door to the tiny bathroom, letting it fill with steam. He inspected the mirror in the hopes that Maya had perhaps written an invisible message that would only show with condensation—but there was no message. Still nothing.

I'm missing something. She left a clue. I know she did.

Sirens wailed in the distance, floating to him through the open motel room door. The police were en route. He grunted in frustration and kicked at the toilet bowl with his boot, hard enough to chip the porcelain.

He looked down and blinked.

I should have seen that. Should have known.

Atop the toilet tank was a single hair, brown, long, with a white root still attached. He dropped to his hands and knees and found a few more scattered on the floor. They were Maya's hair, tugged loose from her head on purpose—to give him a clue.

He lifted the lid from the back of the toilet.

Reid reached in and tugged loose the furled scrap of fabric that was looped into the flush lever's chain. He unrolled it in his fingers, which began to tremble as soon as he recognized the familiar pattern of pineapples.

Sara.

The scrap was triangular; a pocket, he realized, torn loose from her favorite pajamas.

He held the scrap to his face. It could have been his imagination, but it still smelled like her, like his baby girl.

He turned the fabric over to the other side, the all-white side, where three words were written in blue ink.

"No," he whispered hoarsely.

Port Jersey. Dubrovnik.

Reid sprinted from the bathroom as fast as he could.

Rais was trying to take his girls out of the country…if he hadn't already.

CHAPTER TEN

No, no, no… As Reid leapt across the orange carpet of room 9, it felt as if his legs couldn't move fast enough, as if every muscle was straining to react at an impossible speed. He had to get to the port.

He understood now. The cars, the change of directions, even the murder of the woman in the rest stop bathroom—all of it would confuse the authorities, make Rais look desperate and meandering, as if he didn't know what he was doing.

He knew damn well what he was doing. He was taking Reid's girls to Europe—and from there, god only knew where. With a twelve-hour lead, they could be anywhere in the world. Away from the jurisdiction of the police and feds. Away from him…

He scooped up his bag without pausing and kept running, parallel to the row of motel rooms toward the office at the end. He barely heard the sirens, wasn't even cognizant of their blaring wail until he was suddenly awash in headlights.

Three police cruisers screeched into the narrow lot of the Starlight Motel. Reid blinked in their glare as officers poured from them, unseen behind the bright headlights, shouting so many warnings at him at once that not any one of them was intelligible.

He didn't stop. He couldn't stop, not now. Reid sprinted onward, around the corner of the motel and behind it. As George had said, there was a dirt bike waiting, faded with age and looking worse for the wear.

Reid leapt onto it, slinging his back securely over one shoulder. He squeezed the clutch and kick-started the engine. It sputtered once and then came to life in a high-pitched whine, strong and robust beneath him. Despite its appearance it seemed that the clerk had taken decent care of the parts that mattered.

The pursuing officers came around the corner, their rapid footfalls drowned out by the roar of the bike's engine. They held their hands out in front of them in warning. Two went for their guns.

Reid released the clutch and twisted the left handlebar, fully opening the throttle. The bike bucked so hard he nearly fell off, but he leaned into it at the last moment and the dirt bike sprang forward toward the officers like a shot, forcing them to scatter and leap out of the way.

He barely slowed as he reached the street, swinging the back end of the bike out and stabilizing with his right foot. Over the siren cry of the engine he heard another sound, faint but recognizable—the steady approach of a helicopter. A quick glance over his shoulder showed him a black Huey alighting in the parking lot across the street from the Starlight, the same lot that the quadcopter had delivered him to.

Agent Strickland had arrived, but Reid was not wasting time waiting around. He shifted and tore at the throttle again, this time hanging on securely as the bike streaked forward. He was certain that at least one of the cruisers would try to give chase, but he wasn't concerned about that—he had a lead on them and the bike was at least 250cc, and despite the lack of speedometer he knew it was capable of up to a hundred, maybe a hundred and ten miles an hour.

It also had no headlight, and he had no helmet, but he couldn't let that stop him. He hurtled through the industrial park as fast as he was able, the only vehicle on the road at that time of night.

He knew the way to Port Jersey. In the daytime, with traffic, it might have taken fifteen minutes to get there. At night, with no one around, ten minutes. On the dirt bike, doing an impetuous triple-digit speed, Reid got there in five.

Even so, it was the longest five minutes of his entire life. Every horrible thought that could invade his mind did so—his daughters smuggled out of the country. Never seeing them again. Never finding them. Fates worse than death, for both him and them.

It doesn't make sense. Rais wants me to find him. Doesn't he?

The burner phone sat heavy and obvious in his pocket. He wanted desperately to call Watson, to alert the police and the CIA and the FBI and whoever else possible about Port Jersey, to have a veritable army crash down upon the port and sweep every corner for any sign of his daughters.

The marine terminal of Port Jersey was a long, U-shaped cargo-handling harbor on the southern edge of Newark Bay, with a view of the Bayonne Bridge. To its north were Jersey City and the Hudson River; northwest was the island of Manhattan. But to the port's southeast was Lower Bay and, from there, the open Atlantic.

They're not out there, he told himself as he entered the port. *They'll be here. I'll find them.*

The dirt bike screamed past the dockworkers' parking lot and kept right on going, down the long rows of bright rectangular containers until the congestion of cargo would no longer allow him access. He slowed enough to lay the bike down, leapt off, and sprinted on foot as the bike continued to skid right into the side of a steel container.

The seaport was still alive despite the hour; powerful fluorescent lights on poles lit the docks while crews continued to work loading and unloading ships by crane and forklift. A huge freight ship sat in the comparably small harbor, a dry-bulk cargo barge nearly as large as the cruise ship Reid had been on just two days earlier. The cargo ship was laden with a seemingly impossible number of containers, stacked so high and deep to the point that it was hard to tell whether the crews were working to load it or offload it.

As he ran toward the ship, the bright lights, and the dockworkers, he yanked out the burner phone and called Watson. It rang four times before a recorded message told him that a voicemail box had not yet been set up for the number.

He gritted his teeth and briefly considered throwing the phone in anger before he jammed it back into his pocket. He hurried toward the first two men he saw. Both were wearing hard hats and bright yellow vests, one leaning against a dormant forklift while the other climbed up into the seat. Reid reached into his jacket as he ran over to them and pulled out the photo of his daughters, the one of them on vacation with him in Florida.

"Have either of you seen these girls?" he asked, waving the photo in their face.

The two confused men glanced at each other and then back at him. "Here?" one of them asked. "Sorry, pal, we haven't seen any girls."

Reid moved along, walking quickly among the crews as they worked. Anyone who wasn't actively doing something had the photo shoved into their bewildered noses. "Have you seen these girls? Around here, at the port? Any girls at all?"

"No."

"Nope."

"Can't say I have, buddy."

Reid nearly shouted in frustration as he spotted a trio of men standing outside a white trailer, sipping coffee from Styrofoam cups. He strode over to them. "I'm looking for two teenage girls," he said, showing them the photo. "There's reason to believe they might have been here. Have any of you seen them?"

The largest of the trio, a black man with a shaved head, scratched idly at his chin and said, "Look around, guy. This ain't exactly a place for kids."

Reid took a breath, trying to calm himself. "They weren't... they didn't come here by accident or choice. They were kidnapped. They're missing."

The large man sighed and shook his head. "Damn. I'm really sorry about that. But... we ain't seen any kids around here. If we did, we'd tell you. Hell, we'd probably call the cops."

Reid stalked off wordlessly, half angry and all desperate. His breath quickened; he felt slightly dizzy. The cargo port seemed impossibly huge, with hundreds—likely even thousands—of containers, drums, steel boxes, and crates piled high around him.

Suddenly those stacks looked like skyscrapers, lording over him from above.

Mild nausea washed over him as he thought, *What if they're in one, right now? What if they're here, locked away somewhere?* Could that have been Rais's game—to hide the girls, force him to look one way while Rais took a different tack? It didn't make sense to him, but he had to acknowledge that he wasn't thinking straight.

If they were here somewhere, he wouldn't have a prayer of finding them. He was one man. There was a lot that Kent Steele could do, but searching the entire industrial port alone was not among them.

I could call the police. I could even call Riker. He had already defied the CIA, tampered with evidence, and broken laws. Not to mention that he was definitely on Riker's bad side—if she knew he was meddling, he'd land in a jail cell in the best-case scenario. But the police had already caught him in their headlights back at the Starlight Motel. His image had undoubtedly been captured by dashboard cameras, which meant that Strickland and the CIA would know in minutes that Kent Steele was doing precisely what the agency didn't want him to do.

Doesn't matter now, he determined. Whatever fate would become of him, blacklisted or arrested or even sent to some godforsaken hole like H-6, it would be more than worth it if it meant his girls were safe.

He pulled out the burner and flipped it open, ready to call someone, anyone—but the phone rang in his hand. He answered it immediately.

"I need help," he said desperately. "I'm at Port Jersey, and I can't find them, not alone…"

"Kent." The voice on the other end of the line was not Watson, as he had expected. It was soft, feminine, and familiar. "It's me."

"Oh god. Maria." He said her name like a sigh. In that moment, despite everything, hearing her voice was a relief—maybe an infinitesimal one, but no less welcome. He felt a lump rising anew in his throat. "Maria, the girls, they're gone…"

"I know. Watson sent me a message. Kent, I'm so sorry."

He breathed into his free hand. "Where are you?"

"Ukraine," she told him. "I'm sorry it took so long for me to contact you. It's not easy finding a secure line around here."

"Maria, it was him. I *know* it was him."

"I believe you," she said. "But the agency doesn't. They still have me chasing false leads out here..."

"Because of Riker," he said scornfully.

"That doesn't matter right now. What matters is getting those girls back to you. What are you doing at Port Jersey?"

"I found a message," he told her. "It was from Maya, in her handwriting. It said to come here. It also said 'Dubrovnik.'"

"Croatia," Maria said quietly. She was silent for a moment. "All right. Kent, I'm going to do whatever I can to help you. Finding Rais is my op, and there's nothing more important to me right now than the safety of those girls. But this is going to be the hard part. Are you listening to me?"

"Yes. I'm listening."

"Kent... your girls are already gone."

Reid put a fist to his mouth as a sob bubbled up through his throat. "No." His voice cracked behind his closed fist. "They're not. They're not gone. You don't know that."

"How long has it been since they were taken? Kent, how long?"

"Um." He thought hard, but the numbers seemed muddied and confusing. "I don't... I don't..." He took a deep breath. "Thirty-two hours, maybe. Thirty-two to thirty-six."

"Right." Maria paused a moment before continuing. "Rais is a psychopath, but he's not an idiot. We know that. If he wanted the girls out of the country, they're already out of the country."

Reid leaned against a cargo container and sank slowly against it, coming to a seat on the concrete. "How am I supposed to find them?" he asked quietly.

"It's not just you. It's us—all of us. *We'll* find them. But I need you thinking clearly. If his plan was Port Jersey, he would have put them on a boat, right? How long would it take for them to get to Dubrovnik?"

He didn't answer. Instead he pressed his fingers against his closed eyes. *Maybe when I open them again none of this will be happening.*

"Kent?" Maria said sternly. "How long?"

Reid thought for a moment. "Um…six. Six to seven days. No, eight. They would have to travel across the Mediterranean. Eight days."

"Right. Up to eight days to get there, and they've been on a boat for one, at most. So we alert the agency. Have them find the manifests for any ship heading to Dubrovnik that left in the last twelve hours. We get the Coast Guard involved. We get you on a chopper, if we need to. We can stop that boat long before it ever reaches Europe."

"Yes. Okay. We can stop it." Reid wiped his eyes and took a long, calming breath. He knew Maria was right; his girls were already gone. If Rais's plan was to get them out of the US, he wasn't going to let Reid learn that if there was anything he could have done to prevent it.

"I'm going to help you find them as best I can from here," Maria told him, her voice strong and even and comforting. "First we need to get a message to Watson—"

"I tried to call him. He didn't answer."

"All right, I'll get a message to him," she assured him. "Let him contact the agency; he has resources that can keep you out of this. You don't spend a decade in the CIA without making some friends."

And some enemies, Reid thought bitterly.

"I'll keep in touch as best I'm able," she continued. "For now, don't go too far."

"I have nowhere else to go," he told her sardonically, looking out over the dark water of Lower Bay. Somewhere out there, perhaps hundreds of miles away by now, were his little girls…

"Just stay dark and keep out of trouble for a little while. We'll be in touch soon, I promise."

"Okay. Thank you, Maria. Really." Reid ended the call and rubbed his face. He wanted to say more—*I don't know what I would do without you*—and he immediately regretted not saying it. Talking with her didn't make the actual situation better, nor did it make him feel much better about it, but he knew that she would come through in whatever ways she could. And as usual, she was right. He had to control himself, get a grip, think clearly, stay focused.

But first, he had to get himself somewhere that he could stay out of the public eye, even if for only a short time… *No*, he thought. He was in this deep, and now his girls were offshore. The time for subterfuge had past. He had Cartwright's office number in Langley; it wasn't a secure line, but it was more than likely the CIA was already well aware that he was on the trail. He couldn't keep relying on people like Watson, Mitch, and Maria to stick their necks out for him and his daughters, no matter how much they wanted to help.

He flipped open the phone and dialed Cartwright's number.

"Hey, excuse me." A male voice startled Reid before he could press send. He glanced up to see an older man coming his way, mid-fifties or so. He looked official, wearing khaki pants and a white button-down shirt. He took off his white hard hat as he approached and tucked it under one arm.

Reid snapped the phone shut and stood up from the asphalt.

"I'm the site supervisor here," the man told him. "You need some help?"

"No. No, I'm… I'm fine." He was, of course, very far removed from "fine," but he said it nonetheless in an effort to avoid further attention.

"All right. Listen, I can't have you around here freaking out my guys when they're running heavy machinery. But if there's something you need, you can talk to me."

Reid nodded. He tried to keep his voice even as he spoke. "I'm looking for a couple of kids. They were abducted yesterday, and I have reason to believe they were here… that they might have been taken out of the country from this port."

The supervisor put a hand on his hip as he shook his head sadly. "I feel for you. I do. But nobody has seen any children around here. If they did they would've reported it to me. Now I can check with the daytime crew, if you want. Come on back to the office. I got a pot of coffee going, and I can make a call or two."

"No, it's fine." Reid had a feeling that no one would have seen the girls coming or going—and if they had, they were unlikely to offer it up. There was, however, another way the supervisor might be of help. "You know the schedules, right? Arrivals and departures? Can you tell me the last boat that left port bound for Croatia?"

The supervisor frowned. "We don't service that route here," he told Reid. "We get boats from up and down the east coast, plenty to the UK, even as far as Genoa, Palermo, Malta. But none of our ships are on routes to Dubrovnik."

"I understand," Reid said. His heart rate quickened. "You know...on second thought, a cup of coffee sounds really good. Do you mind? Might calm the nerves a bit."

"Sure. Come on." The supervisor waved for him to follow, back toward the docks and the unloading ship.

Reid wasn't interested in coffee. But he was very interested in the supervisor's choice of words, because Reid hadn't once mentioned Dubrovnik.

CHAPTER ELEVEN

It was pitch-black inside the cargo container. Even with her fingers only inches from her face, Maya could not see anything. She sat with her back to a steel wall, knees drawn up on either side of her sister, who sat leaning against her. Maya's other arm was curled protectively over Sara's chest.

For her to even think that this was a bad situation was a profound understatement. The container rocked slightly with the ebb of the boat on the ocean; they were out of the country, still in Rais's hands but now in potentially worse company. She had failed at her attempt to get Sara away safely.

Despite all of that, they were still alive and able-bodied. She refused to give up on the notion that there was a way out of this.

Sara had stopped sobbing some time ago and had settled into a rhythmic pattern of a sniffled inhalation and a jagged breath out, over and over. Maya squeezed her gently but her little sister did not respond.

Maya was aware that there were other girls in the container with them; she had caught just a single, quick glimpse of them when the doors were opened and the two of them had been shoved inside. They were like ghosts haunting the small space. In the utter darkness and the hours that followed, Maya was cognizant of their presence in strange ways—the hissing sounds of breath, the occasional slight shift in movement, the hairs on Maya's arms prickling at the sensation of another body being close to hers. But the others in the container said nothing and hardly budged.

Then, at some point during their voyage—Maya had completely lost track of time in the darkness—someone stirred, and though she didn't feel anything herself, one of the ghosts in the dark must have brushed against Sara. Her younger sister recoiled suddenly, gasping and drawing herself tighter against Maya.

"It's okay," she whispered in Sara's ear. She scolded herself again for saying that. It was the only thing that came to mind in the moment, like a reflex, to continue making the obviously false promise that anything about this was okay. "I've got you." She hugged her sister closer. "We have to be strong right now, all right? We can't give up. We won't."

"Please." A soft voice to Maya's right spoke quietly, in nearly a whisper. "Please don't talk. They don't like it when we talk."

The voice was feminine and young, with a slight drawl that suggested a Midwestern background. Maya's instinctual reaction to the voice was a flash of anger; now was not the time for complacency. It was the time for planning. Yet the girl sounded like she had already given up and given in.

Instead Maya swallowed her anger and said, "They can't hear us." She was certain that the sound of the boat's engines, the water lapping over the bow, and the steel walls of the container would make it impossible to hear their hushed voices, as long as they kept them low.

"But if they did…" The frightened Midwestern voice did not finish her thought—and Maya was glad for it. She didn't want to know what this poor girl might have seen, what might have been done to her, and she definitely didn't want Sara to have to hear it.

"They won't," she insisted. Then she asked, "How… how did you get here?"

Deafening silence reigned in the darkness for several long moments. It didn't seem like anyone was breathing, let alone speaking.

Then the tremulous Midwestern voice said, "A job. I was promised a job."

Maya didn't reply. She bit her lip, waiting for the girl to choose whether or not she would continue. Just when it seemed like she would remain silent, she said, "I'm from Oklahoma. That's where my...my family is." Her voice broke at the mention of her family.

"How long ago? When did you last see them?" Maya asked.

The girl sniffled. "I-I'm not sure. Maybe...about nine months, I think."

A surge of empathetic despair caught in Maya's throat. She wasn't sure she wanted to know where the girl had been kept for nine months, or what sort of things she had to do. She certainly wasn't going to ask; she could hear the girl quietly crying only a couple of feet to her right.

"They choose you." A new voice spoke, definitely young and female but clearer than the Midwestern girl, and deeper. *New Jersey*, Maya thought. The new girl's voice was level; not calm, but firm. She did not sound as upset as she did angry. "I don't know how...social media, I think. They pick girls who don't have great home lives. Young women who want to get away, or want something better. They get your contact information—for me it was an email, promising a modeling job. They offer good money, life in a big city. At first it seems too good to be true. If you're smart, you look deeper. But they're smart too. They ask for headshots and applications and references. They set up fake websites that look legit. They have phone numbers, and when you call, friendly people answer. Americans."

She paused for a long moment. "By then you're hooked. Everything that seemed too good to be true starts to make you feel special. You were chosen. Sometimes it's modeling, or acting...For me it was being an in-home nanny for some rich family. They hide all the red flags. You feel like you can't pass it up. But then, once you arrive and they have you...by the time you realize what's actually happening..." She lowered her voice to a whisper. "They already have you. There's nothing you can do."

"No," Maya said suddenly. The word slipped from her mouth as reflexively as scratching an itch, louder than she intended. "I don't believe that." Everything the girl was saying was truly terrible, and Maya was no stranger to the notion—she had seen such things on the news, had read articles about it online. Most people tended to think that it couldn't happen to them, to their children, not in the United States. Yet it did, and with harrowing frequency.

But that's not what she didn't believe. She refused to believe that there wasn't anything they could do about it.

"There are at least six of us," she said. "Maybe seven? And only three of them." *The two foreign men and Rais.*

"They have guns," the girl from Oklahoma whispered.

"I know. And they're careful. But if it's a choice between letting them do what they want with us and fighting back—I would rather fight, even if it means I might die."

She was hoping to inspire something in the other girls, to gather their courage and form a plan. If they all worked together and struck at the most opportune time, using some sort of signal or secret tell, then maybe, just maybe they could…

"There aren't seven of us." It was the Jersey girl again.

"I saw you," Maya said. "When they opened the container, for just a second, I saw at least four faces, maybe five—"

"You saw faces," the girl said, "and they're here, physically, but there's a reason only two of us are talking at all. They've been drugged. They're alive, maybe awake, but they have no idea what's going on. What's happening to them."

Panic ran up and down Maya's spine like a tingle of electricity. "Drugged?" she said in a whisper. "Why?"

The girl sighed. "To make them complacent. Ones that cry too loud, scream or shout, make trouble for them… they shoot them up with a needle and it all feels like a bad dream. Other times they'll get them hooked on something. It's a way to keep us in line."

Maya hugged Sara closer to her. She had already made some trouble for them; if they recognized her as a potential threat, they might try to drug her. She needed to be able to fight back, to keep a clear head. And Sara… if that happened to Sara, how would she ever get away?

"Okay," Maya said, thinking aloud. "Okay, even if there are only four of us that can do anything, we could still do something. We could cause a distraction and make a run for it—all of us in different directions. There are only three of them; they can't chase us all, and only one of us has to get away and alert the authorities."

Once again silence overtook the container. Maya felt herself grow angry again at their hesitation. For her there shouldn't have been any; it was a simple and clear-cut matter. They needed to get away however possible, or at least try.

"We've seen what happens," the Jersey girl said, "when you try to escape."

The girl from Oklahoma sniffled and whispered one word. "Anita."

Maya wasn't sure she wanted to know—and was even less sure she wanted Sara to hear it—but she couldn't help herself. "Who is Anita?"

"Who *was* Anita," said Jersey solemnly. "She was a girl, a young woman, where they were holding us. It was some kind of warehouse. I don't know where; they brought us in blind, bags over our heads." The girl swallowed and then said, "Anita was strong, stronger than us. She had ideas, like you. Everyone else was too afraid to try. Not her. She waited until there was only one man guarding us, and when she had a chance, Anita took it. She punched him. Broke his nose. Then she ran. But… they caught up."

"What did they do?" Maya's voice was barely a whisper. She wrapped one arm gently around Sara's head in an attempt to cover her ears.

"They… they took things from her."

"What do you mean?" Maya couldn't keep the tremble from her voice, because she was already pretty sure she knew what they meant before they said it. "What did they take?"

Oklahoma was crying softly again. "Everything. They took everything."

"And afterwards," the Jersey girl said, "they showed us pictures. They had taken photos of it. They took her kidneys. Her liver. Her heart. Anything that might be worth something to someone else. They showed us photos and they said, 'This is what will happen to you if you run.'"

The girl from Oklahoma was sobbing now. Maya wanted to reach out, to console her, but she held herself back and clung to Sara.

"They want us alive," said Jersey. "But dead is still more valuable than nothing at all."

Maya's own breath came shallow and slow. She stared at nothing in particular—not that she could see anything anyhow, but her gaze blurred as her mind worked. All this while she had been thinking that Rais was the threat; he had proven that he was willing to kill to get what he wanted, and even that he was willing to hurt them. She was entirely certain that he would have cut off Sara's finger back at the dock had the foreigner not intervened. But he needed them if he wanted to get to their father. If they were left in the hands of these monstrous men, these traffickers, they would no longer be important. She and Sara would just become another face, another body, and anyone who gave them trouble was drugged or worse.

It seemed to her like an impossible situation, especially since anything she might do or try could be reflected back upon Sara.

Hard as she tried to consider a way out, only one thought stuck in her mind. It was the only thing that came to her, the only possible positive outcome.

Dad will come for us.

"I thought that too, for a while," said Jersey. Maya hadn't even realized she'd spoken the words aloud. "I thought someone would come. They had to. They would find me, find us. But…no one came. No one knows. And the farther we get, the farther they'll ever be from finding us again."

"He's different," said Maya quietly. She knew how that must sound to them, like some sort of false hope, but she couldn't accurately explain why her father was different or how he would find them. "He can do things. Find people. He's good at it. He'll come."

"Believe that for as long as you can," Jersey said in a whisper. "It's the only thing that ever helped me sleep."

Maya sighed and leaned back against the wall of the container. The steel was cold; it had been growing colder for some time now, though it was still warm and humid inside their small box. Sara sat still and silent in her arms. She hadn't said a word since they'd been put in there, and Maya was growing worried that she'd gone catatonic.

Suddenly Maya sat up straight, frowning in the darkness. It was quiet; too quiet. "Do you hear that?" she asked in a whisper.

"I don't hear anything," Jersey said.

"Exactly." The engines had ceased. The boat was still rocking slightly, but there was no sensation of forward momentum. "We've stopped." She listened as intently as she could. Outside the container she could hear the muffled shouts of men, but had no idea what they were saying or if they were even speaking English.

It should have taken us days to reach Dubrovnik by boat, she thought. Though she was uncertain of how long they had been in the container, it couldn't have been more than a matter of hours. *Where are we?*

Suddenly a chain rattled heavily on the steel ceiling. Maya jumped slightly, startled by the sound, but Sara didn't move at all. Then there was a groan of creaking metal, and the large steel crate bucked and swayed. They were in the air, being lifted, likely hoisted by a crane, she realized. They were being unloaded from the boat. *Putting us on a different boat?* she wondered, thinking about the way Rais had switched vehicles to elude the authorities.

Then they were coming down, being lowered again, and set upon the ground with a heavy, jarring jolt. Maya waited, staying stock-still in the silent darkness. It didn't feel like another boat; there was no swaying. It felt like solid ground.

More clinking of metal as someone on the other side removed the padlock. Over the time in the container, Maya had become disoriented; she didn't realize that she and Sara were sitting mere inches from the door until one entire side of the container swung outward, pulled open by someone outside.

The sudden flood of daylight blinded her temporarily. She put up a hand, shielding her eyes and squinting until the spots dissolved from her vision. When she lowered her hand again, she sucked in a breath.

The first thing she saw was the chubby man from the dock standing there, scowling down at her. The second thing she noticed was the barrel of the black submachine gun that he carried in one hand, a strap securing the weapon over his shoulder.

"Plane," he said gruffly in accented English. "No talking. Walk. Do not run. Make trouble for me, I make more trouble for you." He stepped to the side. Behind him, at a distance of no more than fifty feet, was an airplane, its rear hatch opened with a ramp lowered.

Maya slowly got to her feet, pulling Sara up with her. She peered into her younger sister's eyes. Sara looked back at her, but her gaze was empty and glassy. It was all too much for her. She appeared to have shut down mentally.

Maya prodded her to walk as they stepped out of the container. They were immediately met by a blast of cold air as a frigid breeze blew over them. She looked left and right; they were at another cargo terminal, it seemed, but this one was a ghost town in some flat, frozen place. The sky overhead was gray and there was an inch of snow on the ground. She hugged one arm around her sister and the other around herself as they walked, in sandals and thin pajamas, from the container to the waiting plane.

There were other men, more of them now. Whether they too were on the boat or came from the plane she wasn't sure, but there were at least five of them that she could see, all dark-featured and dangerous looking. They were spanned every ten to fifteen feet between the container and airplane. There was no way to run. Nowhere to go. To the right was the ocean, the dock, and the boat they had come in on; to the left was practically nothing, a mostly bare cargo terminal with a single concrete building and open, empty space.

Maya thought about the man at Port Jersey, the one with the white hard hat who had accepted money and looked the other way when they were put on the boat. There were likely people here too that would take bribes to ignore what was happening right in front of them. The thought brought tears to her eyes, but she refused to let them fall in front of these men.

They reached the airplane and walked up the ramp, into the cargo hold. The plane looked old, barely more than a thick cylinder with a tail and a propeller under each wing. The rear was hollow, with thick canvas harnesses hung from the ceiling and walls, but no cargo.

There was someone waiting for them, however; a despicably familiar face. Rais sat at the far end of the cargo hold, on the floor, leaning back casually against the curved interior wall. He regarded them with a slight nod as they entered and gestured for them to sit across from him.

Maya directed Sara into place and then sat beside her. Sara stared at the floor, her mouth open slightly and her breaths shallow. Maya stared at Rais with an undisguised scowl. He stared back passively.

The other girls were loaded quickly. Those who could walk did so; those who could not, the girls who had been drugged, were half-carried and half-dragged to the waiting plane. Maya couldn't bring herself to look at them. Instead she kept her gaze forward.

Someone sat beside her, on the opposite side from Sara, and Maya hazarded a quick glance. The girl was dark-haired, Latina, and at least a few years older than her—she assumed it was the girl she had been referring to in her mind as Jersey. She noticed the girl's swollen, black-and-blue eye and cheek. Opposite Jersey was a girl with straight blonde hair, her sharp, angular cheeks puffy and red from sobbing. Oklahoma.

More important than just their physical appearance was their demeanor—their heads hung low, avoiding eye contact with any of the rough-looking traffickers among them, who stood over the cowering girls while holding onto the canvas straps hanging from the ceiling. The young women had seen and experienced awful things, that much was clear. Things beyond Maya's comprehension despite what she herself had experienced in the last twenty-four hours.

In that moment, she made two realizations. The first was that they had traveled north by boat, likely beyond the US border; the cold weather told her that much. It was hot inside the cargo plane and stank of fuel, but at least she wouldn't freeze to death in her tank top and pajama bottoms.

The second thing she came to realize, hesitant as she was to admit it even to herself, was that she was helpless in this situation. Any attempt to flee or get Sara to safety would result in atrocities the likes of which she hadn't even imagined only hours earlier. They had only one hope now, the hope that Jersey had told her to cling to for as long as she could.

Her father had to come for them. Or else they were already dead.

Chapter Twelve

The shift supervisor's office at Port Jersey was a white trailer on cinder blocks—likely so it could be easily moved by crane if need be, Reid thought. The man with the white hard hat led the way up three wooden stairs and pushed the door open, closing it again behind them. It was not at all lost on him that the supervisor twisted the locking mechanism in the knob.

Reid had agreed to come with him under the pretense of coffee and a few phone calls, but those were far from his mind at the moment. This man knew something, and Reid was going to find out what it was.

"How do you take it?" the supervisor asked. He crossed the short span to a narrow table set up with a coffee machine, paper cups, and powdered creamer.

"Black is fine. Thanks." Reid quickly surveyed the office from end to end. There were two desks, one on each side, and four chairs. The whole trailer was about forty feet long, twelve feet wide. There was a small bathroom and another point of egress at the rear—undoubtedly locked as well—and the primary entrance was to Reid's back.

Not ideal, he thought, *but private enough for questioning.*

"Here you go." The supervisor set two paper cups on the steel desk nearer to them and then took a seat in a gray swivel chair behind it. "I'm very sorry you have to go through this. Hell of a thing, I imagine. How long did you say since your girls have gone missing, Mr....?"

"Townsend," Reid told him. "But you can call me Frank." He took a seat in the metal chair across the desk and sipped the coffee. It was lukewarm and tasted awful.

"Well, Frank, I'm Bill," the supervisor replied warmly. "You wanna...talk about it at all?"

"They were taken yesterday from their home in New York," Reid lied.

"And what makes you think they ended up here?" Bill asked.

Reid shrugged one shoulder. "Just a hunch."

"A hunch," Bill repeated, folding his hands on the desk. "There wasn't like a, uh, tip? Or some kind of evidence?"

He's fishing, Reid thought. He was asking questions to see just how much Reid knew, trying hard to sound blasé.

"No tips," he told Bill. "No evidence. I just thought that this would be a likely place to take them out of the country."

Bill raised an eyebrow. It didn't look like he was quite buying it. "Did you, uh, tell the police about this hunch of yours?"

"No. I didn't think they'd believe me."

"I see." Bill took a cell phone out of his pocket and typed out a message. "Sorry, just replying to a text from the wife. So, Mr. Townsend, nobody knows you're here?"

"Besides the guys I talked to outside? No." *A text from the wife. Sure.*

Bill stuffed the phone back into his pocket. "Well. Like I said, I'm sorry this happened, but I'm afraid we just can't help you. Now, if you felt inclined to get the police involved, we'd be happy to show them whatever they want to see. They could open every container, search every boat. But you have my word, they're not going to find any girls."

Reid nodded. At least that answered one question—Maria had been right. The girls were already gone from this place. He kept his voice as calm and even as he could as he said, "I understand. I don't think police intervention will be necessary." He reached into his jacket and took out the folded photo of them. "But just in case, this is them here." He turned the picture.

Bill tried. He tried very hard not to show a reaction, and very nearly succeeded. But Kent Steele was a trained CIA agent with years of field and interrogation experience. He saw the tiny twitch of Bill's eyebrows as his eyes impulsively widened slightly. He saw the irrepressible dilation of his pupils—a sure sign of deception.

"I'll certainly keep an eye out," Bill promised.

"Thank you." Reid folded the photo again. "Do you have kids, Bill?"

The supervisor shook his head. "Nope. Just never happened for us."

"But you know them."

Bill blinked at Reid, a confused but polite smile on his lips. "Sorry?"

Reid tucked the photo back into his jacket, and at the same time his hand found the grip of his Glock 22. He pulled it out, not aiming, but showing it. "You know them," he said again.

"Whoa, whoa..." Bill said uneasily as he started to rise.

"Stay seated," Reid commanded as he pointed the Glock. Bill sank again into his chair, eyes wide and afraid. "You've seen them, these two girls. I can tell."

"No, never, I swear it..."

"Outside, you said none of your boats go to Dubrovnik. I didn't mention Dubrovnik."

"What?" Bill's face contorted into a frown. "Well, s-sure you did..."

"I didn't." He racked the slide on the Glock to put a round in the chamber. "Tell me what you know, Bill."

The supervisor gulped and placed his hands flat on the desk in front of him. "Listen, Frank, pal, we can talk. Okay? But not with a gun in my face."

"I find it helps people be honest."

"Yeah, okay, but think about this," Bill implored. "You fire that thing in here and there are thirty guys out there that are going to hear it. They'll all come running. Most of them are good guys, innocent guys, family men. You going to shoot them? You got enough bullets for that? Because if not, you're still the one holding the gun, and they will kick your damn skull in."

Reid nodded slowly. "You've got a good point, Bill." He holstered the Glock. "That's not the way to go about this."

"Right," Bill agreed with a sigh of relief. "Let's just talk, and—"

Reid lurched forward suddenly, reaching across the desk and grabbing Bill by two handfuls of collar. He hefted the man up, out of his chair, and yanked him clear over the desk. Coffee spilled to the floor and paperwork flew as he brought the hapless supervisor crashing to the floor.

Before Bill could recover, let alone shout for help, Reid pressed his knee into the man's throat, cutting off not only his ability to speak but his air supply as well.

He leaned over, close to the supervisor's face. "Listen to me, Bill, and listen well." He spoke quickly, his voice edged with a growl. "Those two girls in that picture are my children. My daughters. My family. My life. They mean everything to me. You mean *nothing* to me. I would just as soon leave you bleeding out on this floor if it means getting even one step closer to them. If you think help is coming, you're wrong. I've got two guns, twenty-seven rounds, and two hands, and I'm pretty confident that I can get through you and anyone else that wants to try to stand in my way."

Bill's face turned dark red, his circulation cut off, as a wet choking sound escaped his lips. But Reid did not relent. Not yet.

"There is *nothing* I won't do to get to them. And trust me, I've done some pretty horrible things. You know something. I think you saw them. When I let my knee off your throat, you're going to tell me everything. You're not going to shout for help or try to draw attention, because then it will be even worse for you. Case in point."

Reid grabbed Bill's right hand and, without hesitation, without thinking twice, turned the man's index finger sideways. It broke easily with a dull *thock*, like snapping a chicken bone, sticking out at a ninety-degree angle from the rest of his hand.

Bill tried to scream, but with Reid's knee firmly on his neck all he could do was gag as his face turned purple.

Reid relieved the pressure, only a bit, just enough so that Bill could suck in some air. The man's mouth gasped open like a fish, and when he exhaled it came out as a moan of pain. "You ... you son of a bitch ..." he wheezed.

They never learn the first time. "Let me tell you something, Bill," Reid hissed, leaning down close to Bill's face. "In every interrogation, bar none, it always seems that the subject thinks they're going to be the nut that doesn't crack. But they all crack eventually." Reid pressed his knee down again, and then he broke Bill's pinky finger.

The supervisor clenched his eyes shut tightly as his mouth yawned in a silent scream.

"You've got eight more, Bill. I'm a patient man, but I don't have much time."

He let up slightly and Bill whimpered, spittle dripping from his puffy, purple lips. "They were here," he said hoarsely. He retched and then said, "They were here, this morning. Around four. On a boat..."

"The man who was with them," Reid said, "he was American, right? Green eyes? Dark hair?" He had to confirm that it was Rais. At least then maybe he and Maria could convince the agency of the truth. "Answer me, Bill."

"One of them was..."

"One of them?" Reid frowned. "What are you talking about?"

"The others were...the Slavs..." Bill panted.

"The Slavs? Who are the Slavs?"

"I don't know...who they are. Slovak, or m-maybe Czech. They have a b-boat, a small one, with con...containers. They're empty. All except one or, or two."

Panic seized Reid's chest like a heart attack. In nearly a whisper he asked, "What's in the containers, Bill?"

A sob escaped the supervisor's throat. "God help me..."

"He's not here, Bill. I am." Reid grabbed an unbroken finger and gripped it tightly. "What's in the containers?!"

"...P-people."

"Children?"

Bill sniffled. "Girls. Always girls."

Reid's face slackened like a stroke. Eastern European men had taken his little girls away, across the ocean, and this man—this *monster*—helped them. The ball of rage in his chest exploded and he forgot himself again. He pressed on Bill's throat with a knee almost hard enough to crush the man's windpipe and grabbed his middle finger.

"You let *traffickers...*"

He snapped the finger.

"...take my children?"

He broke another.

"For what? For money, Bill?"

He gripped the supervisor's thumb and jerked it back until it touched his forearm. The bone popped and muscle tore. Already the mangled hand was swollen to nearly double its normal size. Blue-black contusions stained the skin at the break points.

Bill's eyes were wide enough to fall out of his head, bloodshot and unblinking. But he could not make a sound, not with Reid's knee on his throat.

Just kill him. It would be easy. Just don't move for another thirty seconds and he'll be dead. He deserves nothing less.

No. I can't. Not yet.

He eased off of Bill's throat and the man sucked in a rattling breath. Every exhalation came with a hoarse moan. "*Hnngh... hnngh... hnngh...*"

"Where did they go?" Reid positioned himself so that Bill was forced to look in his eyes. "You knew about Dubrovnik, but you said none of your ships go there. So where did they go? Bill, where did they take my daughters?"

"They..." His words were little more than croaking whimpers. "They'll kill me."

"Maybe so. But I won't. I'll leave you alive. I'm going to break the rest of your fingers, Bill. And if I still don't have the information I want, I'll break your arms and legs. But I'll leave you alive to live with what you've done. To look down at your own mangled, disfigured limbs and be reminded of what you really are." He grabbed Bill's other hand to demonstrate that he was not bluffing—and he wasn't. "Where did they go?"

"N-north." The supervisor sobbed again, which caught in his throat as a cough. "There's a, an island, just off the—*ack*—coast of Nova Scotia. Th-there's a depot there ..."

"A cargo depot?" Reid asked impatiently. "And they do the same thing you do? They look the other way for these men? Take money while they abduct girls? Young women?"

Bill squeezed his eyes shut, tears streaming down his face as he nodded.

Nova Scotia. It wouldn't make sense, going north just to go east; that would take much longer than eight days. Unless...

"At this cargo depot, they get put on a plane." Reid worked the thought out aloud. "Is that it? They leave here on a boat, get on a plane, and go to Dubrovnik?"

Bill nodded again, his breaths coming jagged and rasping.

Reid let himself fall backward and sat on the floor, rubbing his face. *It's no more than nine to ten hours from here to Nova Scotia by boat. They left at four in the morning. It's past nine at night.*

His girls were on a plane, right at that moment, headed to Croatia. Maria's plans of using the Coast Guard, the CIA, flying out by chopper...none of that would work. Not now.

"One more question, Bill, and then we're done here. The American man with the green eyes—did he go with them? Or did he stay here?"

"He..." Bill choked and retched once. "He left. G-got on the boat. *Hnnggh*...left his car here."

Reid sighed in dismay. Rais had taken his girls to Croatia with the intention that Reid would follow—leave the safety of the United States, leave what he knew, leave behind the police and jurisdiction.

Because he knows I will. He knows I'll follow.

He wanted very much to kill the man laid out on the floor before him, his face purple, capillaries burst in his eyes. It would be easy; there was a letter opener on the desk. A slip of its tip into the femoral artery of his thigh and Bill the supervisor would bleed out on the trailer floor in less than a minute. It would be *too* easy.

He wanted this man to suffer, to live with what he had done. He took Bill's wallet from his pocket and pulled out his driver's license. "I'm keeping this," Reid told him. "You can try to run, try to hide, but you're going to be caught. You're going to be arrested for what you've done here. You'll spend the rest of your life in prison—and guys like you, they tend not to fare so well."

Bill could only whimper.

Suddenly the locked doorknob of the trailer jiggled. Reid looked up sharply as someone banged a heavy fist on the other side.

"Bill!" A deep male voice. "Bill, you okay in there?"

Reid rose and parted the blinds over one of the small windows, only slightly—but still enough to see that no fewer than a dozen dockworkers were gathered directly outside the office.

The text. The message Bill sent, allegedly to his wife; he must have warned his guys.

"Open up or we'll knock this door down!" threatened another voice.

Bill weakly lifted his head and tried to call out for help, but his voice was little more than a hoarse croak. Reid examined his options; he could try the rear door, but he had no doubt there were people there too. Instead he drew his gun.

A moment later the door burst inward, the lock breaking easily with a dozen large, angry men waiting on the other side.

Chapter Thirteen

The man immediately outside the door, the one who had kicked it in, was the large bald man that Reid had spoken to earlier. He filled the narrow doorway, shoulders heaving, gaze angry—and was met with the barrel of a pistol three feet from his face.

Reid had the Glock aloft, gripped in both hands. He didn't want to shoot anyone, but he wasn't lying when he told Bill that nothing, no one, would get between him and his girls.

For a moment neither man spoke; they simply stared.

At long last the large dock worker put his hands up slowly. "Hey," he said. "Nobody needs to get hurt here, all right?"

"Back up," Reid ordered. "Get back."

The man took a step back, down the three wooden steps that led up to the trailer, all without taking his eyes off of Reid or the gun. The workers behind him backed up as well, slowly. Reid noted with some dismay that some of them wielded pipes, wrenches, lengths of chain—Bill had been right. They took care of their own.

They just don't know that their own aids and abets human trafficking.

Reid stood in the trailer's doorway, his gun up but not pointed directly at any one of them. He mustered a clear, strong voice as he said, "Most of you are likely innocent in this—maybe all of you. But if you make a move, I will shoot you."

The large man at the head of the dock-working mob frowned deeply. "Innocent? What are you talking about?"

"Your boss, Bill, is part of a trafficking ring," Reid told them. "He was helping a group of foreigners move abducted girls out of the country."

"Nah. No way." The big man shook his head. "I've known that man for sixteen years. I don't believe that."

You'd be surprised what people are capable of. He couldn't help but think of his late wife, Kate, and his children, unknowing for his entire CIA career.

Reid knew he was not going to be able to convince these men of the truth—and there was no point in doing so anyway. He didn't have to prove it to them; he had to prove it to the authorities. But he did have to make it off the docks alive.

He took the first wooden step down, tracking the barrel left to right as the dock workers spread, taking small steps backward and fanning out into a semicircle. They were looking for an opening, an opportunity to disarm him. And then . . .

"Jesus!" someone shouted. Without Reid blocking the doorway, the inside of the trailer was visible—as was Bill, lying on the floor, his face purple and one hand mangled and breath labored.

"Somebody call the cops!" another crew member said.

Reid moved off the last stair and kept the trailer to his back, sidestepping parallel to it. He needed to get back to the car, to get the hell out of there. The big man at the front of the crowd reached behind him; someone handed off a pipe wrench, nearly three feet long and at least twenty-five pounds.

That would crush my skull in one blow.

"Nobody needs to die tonight," he reminded the crew. "Just back off, and I'll leave—"

There was sudden movement in his periphery. A man with a handlebar mustache swung a length of chain, overhand, about six feet from him. Reid bladed his body, making himself a narrower target, as the chain whistled past his nose and smacked the ground angrily.

His reaction was all instinct. Someone had made a bid for him, and he returned it in kind. In a half second the Glock was up, under his elbow, and he fired a single shot.

The man yelped and fell as he took the bullet in the thigh.

The shot seemed impossibly loud in the open night air of the cargo port. The big man hefted the pipe wrench, bringing it up over his shoulder like a baseball bat.

Reid swung to his left and had the gun pointed at the man's forehead before he could fully wind up. "Don't," he said hoarsely.

The large man froze, but kept the wrench back, over his shoulder, ready to swing. Two others hurried to their downed friend, who hissed breaths through his teeth as he gripped his thigh and groaned in pain.

I need to get out of here, now. He could make a run for it, sprint for the dirt bike he'd left behind, but his knee still wasn't completely healed since he'd torn a tendon the month earlier. Some of these men looked like they were in good shape; he wasn't confident he could outrun them. And if they caught up to him...

"You have kids of your own?" Reid asked the large man at the head of the dock mob. "I bet a lot of you do. Put yourselves in my shoes. My little girls went missing yesterday. And whether you believe it or not, your boss, he saw them. He watched them get put on a boat against their will. What would you do?"

"Not this," the big man said somberly. "Not like this."

"But you'd do something. You'd look for them. And if you knew that someone had seen them, and done nothing—"

"Let's just rush him, Leon!" A man behind the larger one stared at Reid as he spoke to the mob leader. "He can't shoot us all!"

"I can try," Reid promised. "But I don't want to do that. I just want to leave."

The tension in the air crackled like electricity between them. Reid recognized this moment; the fuse had been lit and it was mere seconds before detonation, before these men got antsy, anxious, and did something brash. They wouldn't stay at bay forever, and he would have to make some very difficult choices.

The lead man, Leon, tensed. The muscles in his thick forearms stood out in sharp relief as he tightened his grip around the pipe wrench, ready to swing.

But then—he frowned. Leon pulled his gaze away from the gun for just a second, cocking his head slightly like a dog hearing a strange noise.

Then Reid heard it too. The sound of an engine, getting louder by the second. It was coming fast.

Tires squealed behind him, and an instant later the high beams came on, bright and blinding. The crowded dock workers squinted and shielded their eyes from the sudden blaze of light as a black sports car screeched to an abrupt stop just behind Reid, so close its right bumper nearly touched his thigh.

For the briefest of moments Reid thought it was the Trans Am that he had left behind in Virginia; he did a quick double-take and saw that it was a newer car, a recent model. Then a gruff voice called out to him through the open window.

"Get in."

He didn't wait around to wonder what was going on. With the gun still leveled at Leon, Reid took two quick steps backward and jumped into the passenger side of the car. His feet were barely off the ground before the driver slammed it into reverse.

Leon surged forward, swinging his pipe wrench down overhead. He caught the very front of the car's hood, the wrench glancing off of it and leaving a sizeable dent as the car jolted backward.

The grizzled driver spun the wheel expertly. The back end of the sleek sports car swung out, fishtailing slightly, and then he threw it into drive while still moving. The driver mashed the gas pedal down and the car took off like a shot, doing sixty down the narrow cargo lane.

Reid breathed a heavy sigh. "Thanks again, Mitch."

"Mm." The bearded mechanic grunted in response.

Of course Reid had questions, but there were more pressing matters at the moment. He holstered his Glock and flipped the burner open as he did some mental math—the girls had a little more than a seventeen-hour lead on him. That was just barely enough time for the cargo ship to reach the southern tip of Nova Scotia, and for a plane from there to reach Dubrovnik, assuming that it was a direct flight path. With any luck, the plane they were on hadn't landed yet.

He dialed Watson's number. *Pick up this time. Pick up...*

The call was answered mid-ring, but Watson said nothing.

"It's me," Reid said quickly. "The girls were put on a boat to Nova Scotia, possibly one of the offshore islands, and from there a plane to Croatia. We need to contact all cargo depots in the province and have all planes grounded. Call the Dubrovnik authorities, have them send police to the airport to..." Reid trailed off. He heard nothing on the other line, not even the sound of breathing. "Hello? Watson, are you there?"

There was a long moment of silence before the woman on the other end of the line said, "Agent Watson is not available at the moment. But you can speak to me, Agent Steele."

CHAPTER FOURTEEN

Reid froze at the stern sound of the deputy director's voice. "Riker," he said softly.

Ashleigh Riker sighed irritably. "We told you, Zero. We warned you not to, and somehow you got Watson involved…"

"You've got it wrong. He had nothing to do with this," Reid lied.

"He tipped his hand too far when he sent Agent Strickland leads through his own assets." She scoffed through the phone. "I should have suspected something like this would happen."

Reid pinched the bridge of his nose. If Watson had been discovered, then he no longer had an ally inside the agency; no tech to obtain satellite photos, no method of tracking leads. Worse still, the agency had the burner number—which meant they were undoubtedly tracking him at that very moment.

Then there's no point in hiding anything from them.

"All right, listen to me," Reid said quickly. "Rais has taken my girls out of the country. He made some kind of deal with a group of Slavic traffickers—"

"The assassin again," Riker interrupted. "Do you have evidence? Did you see him?"

Reid grunted in frustration. "No. But I know it's him—"

"And what were you going to do? Take on everyone by yourself? You tried that once before and it didn't work out so well for you … or for us. Now you've already gone and made another mess—"

"I didn't kill anyone," Reid said forcefully.

"No, you only injured and crippled them," the deputy director shot back sardonically. "We connected the dots here. Two cops accosted in Maryland, the hotel clerk with the broken face, the shift supervisor at Port Jersey, a dockworker shot in the leg…You are out of control, again—"

Reid felt heat rising in his face despite the chilly air from the open passenger window. "We're talking about my children here…"

"Yes, and we told *you*. This isn't coming from me, or Cartwright, or even from Director Mullen. This is coming from the Director of National Intelligence. I would say you're disavowed, but you were never really fully reinstated, so I don't even know if I *can* disavow you." Riker paused for a moment, her voice growing calm as she said, "Face facts, Agent Steele. You defied orders. You went rogue. You broke laws and interfered with an open investigation. Right now you are a criminal. You're a vigilante that is considered armed and very dangerous. The FBI has been notified, as well as police departments across six states. If I have to alert Interpol, I will."

"You don't have to make this harder than it already is," Reid implored. "We can work together. I've already gotten farther than Strickland on my own."

"You made it harder on yourself." Her voice was cold. There was no remorse in it. "Here's what you're going to do. You're going to stop, right now, and you're going to wait where you are with this phone number active until agents arrive. They will bring you back to Langley. If you do that, maybe, just *maybe* you'll avoid prison."

Reid gritted his teeth and glanced over at Mitch, stoically driving beside him. "I have another deal," he said.

Riker scoffed. "You're not in a position to make deals, Agent—"

"Shut up and listen," he snapped. "I'm in a car headed north for Nova Scotia. I will turn it around and drive back to Langley, but only if you listen to what I have to say."

The deputy director was silent for a moment. "How can I trust you'll come in?"

"Because having my girls safe is the most important thing in the world to me right now. I can't do anything alone with the information I have. You can. The agency can. If you do what I ask and find them, I'll come in."

"Tell me."

"My daughters were put on a cargo ship that headed north at four o'clock this morning," Reid explained quickly. "Its destination was a Nova Scotia depot, possibly one of the outlying islands. It would have arrived there hours ago; there'd be no way to catch up to it now, but I have it on authority that from there they would have been put on a plane and sent to Dubrovnik, in Croatia. Depending on the type of plane, they may not have arrived yet. We can search manifests, flight patterns, find out where they are and when they'll get there. We can alert the Croatian authorities and get the police to the airport. If we have any agents in the area, we can get them there. Whatever we can do, do it, and I'll come in. But we need to move *now*."

"Fine. Consider it done." Riker snapped her fingers to someone in the background. "But I'm sending a chopper to your location to pick you up. If I don't see your face in the next hour, there won't be a judge or a jury. Do you understand? There's no due process for this. There's only a hole."

"Understood." Reid snapped the phone shut, ending the call, and tossed the burner out the open window.

"You really think she's going to do all that?" Mitch asked. "To find a couple of kids?"

"I don't know." *I can only hope so.* Reid stared out the window. Early on, Watson had told him that Cartwright was the one who put him up to it, had him help and supply Reid. *Where was he in all this? What is he doing to help me—to help my girls?*

"Where are we going?" Reid asked.

"Taking you to an airstrip in Hatfield," Mitch grunted. "There's a plane there. Assuming you still need one."

He nodded. "I'm not stopping until I see their faces." No matter what he told Riker, he wasn't about to trust the fate of his daughters in the deputy director's hands—or anyone else's, for that matter. He had already come too far for that. "Where did you hide the tracking unit?"

He could surmise, just by Mitch's sudden presence back at Port Jersey, that it wasn't just the Trans Am that had been bugged. Mitch had followed him here, and while Reid had no idea how he'd gotten here so fast—by helicopter, or maybe even by the same type of drone that had delivered him to the motel—the mechanic was definitely still tracking him.

"It's in the bag," Mitch grunted. "Silicon transponder sewed into the fabric."

Reid scoffed. Maria was right again; he really couldn't trust anyone in this line of work. "Let me guess, John told you I'd do something stupid..."

"You did." Mitch kept his eyes on the road, not looking over, barely blinking. "Those men might have killed you back there on the dock."

And I might have killed some of them, Reid thought. He scrutinized the man behind the wheel—the thick, unruly beard; small, squinting eyes; baseball cap pulled over his hair and brow. "Can the agency track me with it?"

"Not unless they have the frequency and know it's you."

Reid thought for a moment. He had tossed the burner because the CIA now had the number and could use it to find his location, but it had also been his only line of communication to Maria. "Can you get that info to Johansson?"

Mitch nodded once.

So he knows her too. "Who are you really?" he asked.

"Mechanic," Mitch said simply. "Friend of John's."

Sure, Reid thought. *And I'm just a history professor.* "You knew me. Before the memory suppressor, you knew me, didn't you?"

"You knew me too."

"But..." Reid turned the thought over in his mind like kneading dough. It seemed clear that Mitch wasn't just an asset; he was CIA, and Reid was fairly certain that everything about his current identity, from his beard and hat to the gruff, grunting demeanor and even his name, was all just intrigue to hide his real identity.

Because a memory might spark in my mind. Because I might remember.

"But you don't want me to remember," he said.

"Some things are better left in the past," Mitch said softly.

Reid wanted to press the issue. He wanted to remember as much as he could, but he knew better. After all, would he be honest about his identity to a relative stranger? Especially if he just wanted to help them?

They drove southwest for another ten minutes, doing ten over the speed limit and traveling in silence. Finally they pulled off the highway and eased down a long, tree-lined thoroughfare until they reached an access road and a sign for a place called Crosswind Airfield. It was comprised of little more than a squat office building, two narrow runways, and an open-air hangar that housed about a dozen or so small aircraft.

The lights were on, but Reid didn't see any people. Instead of stopping the car at the office, Mitch circled it, around to the second runway behind the building.

Reid gaped in surprise. There was a plane waiting there, just as Mitch had said, obscured from the road by the office building—but it wasn't just any plane.

"That's a Cessna Citation." Sitting before them was a nine-million-dollar business-class jet. *Fifty-four-foot wingspan, top speed of five hundred sixty miles an hour.*

"Mm-hmm." Mitch seemed unimpressed.

"And the pilot?"

"Friend of mine," Mitch said simply.

"A friend," Reid murmured. This didn't feel right at all, blindly trusting someone he didn't know who refused to give up his identity. The Cessna, the drone, the Trans Am; Mitch watching his back, saving him three times now from bad situations—none of it felt right. Every instinct as an agent told him not to get on the plane.

"You know this is dangerous," Reid said. "You know the kind of trouble this could bring you. I need to know why you're doing all this for me."

"Like John told you," Mitch said gruffly. "Not doing it for you. Doing it for those girls."

"You're stepping way out of line for this." Reid shook his head. "You feel that you owe me something, don't you? Is this some sort of atonement?"

Mitch said nothing in response.

"All right. Then I'll find my own way." He didn't trust it enough to put his faith in someone who couldn't give him a straight answer. He reached for the door handle.

"Hold up, Zero."

Reid paused, his hand on the door.

The mechanic took off his baseball cap and ran a hand over his matted brown hair. "Back then... not just two years ago, but even before that... I wasn't exactly a good person. I did something stupid. Got in deep. Not only did you save my life, but you covered for me. You made it so I stayed out of H-6."

Reid tried to evoke a memory, but nothing came to him out of Mitch's vague explanation. No new memories sparked in his brain.

"I never got the chance to repay the favor, until now. But when John told me about the suppressor, I didn't want you to remember." Mitch pulled his hat back on and cleared his throat. "Because if you remembered who I was, our history, you might not trust me. Might not accept my help."

Reid bit his lip. He didn't know what to say, or even think. Mitch was admitting that he was some untrustworthy aspect of Kent Steele's past, but at the same time he had proven himself beneficial and supportive. As an agent, his instinct was to mistrust, to avoid, to lie and to deceive.

As a father, he was grateful beyond words.

He reached into his pocket for the ID card that was stowed there. "Here. This is the driver's license of William Johnson. He's the crew supervisor at Port Jersey who's been accepting bribes and allowing a group of men he calls 'the Slavs' to take girls out of the country by cargo ship. I don't trust Riker as far as I can throw her. You personally make sure he gets what's coming to him and we'll call this favor even."

Mitch took the ID and looked it over. "I will."

"And whatever you can do to follow up in Nova Scotia, in Croatia…"

"We will."

Reid nodded. "Thank you, Mitch." He shook the mechanic's hand. "And be careful. If the CIA knows I'm in on this then they might know about the drone, or find out about the plane."

"I'll be fine," he grunted.

Reid reached again for the door handle and pushed it open. As he climbed out, a thought occurred to him. Mitch's words ran through his head. *Not only did you save my life, but you covered for me. I never got the chance to repay the favor, until now.*

He bent at the waist and peered into the cab of the car. "And Watson? What was his angle on this? Why did he help me?" He couldn't believe that it was merely Cartwright's suggestion that spurred Watson into action.

Mitch didn't look up. "That's not for me to say. I hope you get the chance to ask him yourself."

"Yeah," he murmured. "Me too. Thanks again, Mitch." He hitched his bag onto his shoulder and strode toward the waiting Cessna. As he approached, the entry ramp came down and a man stood in the open oval-shaped doorway—the pilot, Reid presumed. He was white, tall, with a square jaw, but that was about all Reid could tell. Despite the darkness outside he wore aviator sunglasses and a black baseball cap.

Reid ascended the stairs and held out his hand. "Thanks for your help," he said. "I'm Reid—"

The pilot gave him a tight smile. "Nothing personal, but the less I know about you, the better."

Reid nodded. "Understood." He took a seat as the entry ramp closed again and the pilot retreated to the cockpit. In minutes they were in the air, the barely illuminated sports car below getting smaller by the second.

He was on his way, and he had a long flight ahead of him to figure out how he was going to bait and kill the man who took his girls.

CHAPTER FIFTEEN

The plane ride to Dubrovnik was excruciating, more than seven hours of anxiety and fretting and tortuous thoughts. Reid had tossed the burner so that the agency couldn't track him, and now he had no method of outside communication. There was Wi-Fi on the Cessna, and a built-in console that could access the internet, but he didn't dare try to contact anyone—least of all Maria, who was still considered to be in the field, or his other supposed ally within the CIA, Deputy Director Cartwright.

For a brief period, he had thought of Cartwright as someone in the agency that he could trust. But where was he now? What was he doing to help Reid's girls? He had sent Watson, that much was true, but only because he feared what Kent Steele might do if left to his own devices.

Cartwright had the opportunity to show his true colors, but now that the CIA knew that Agent Zero was on the move, the deputy director had done nothing. He was a bureaucrat, nothing more. He was a middleman playing both sides while keeping himself safe, Reid was certain.

He was no better than Riker in Reid's eyes. He had his chance to show a moral backbone and he folded.

Reid tried to doze, to steal what little sleep he could on the plane, but he couldn't get comfortable and every time he closed his eyes horrible images swam in his vision. Instead he spent the time thinking, overthinking, pacing the aisle, splashing cold water on his face in the tiny bathroom, and thinking some more.

He desperately wished he knew what was happening out there. If Riker had sent a chopper, then she knew that Reid was no longer at the position they'd traced him to. Would she still keep her end of their deal?

You really think she's going to do all that? That had been Mitch's question. *To find a couple of kids?*

The more Reid thought about those words, the more harrowing they became. Children went missing every day. Women, men, people of all ages were kidnapped, abducted, worse. *How far would the CIA go to see two girls saved, regardless of who they belonged to?*

He didn't know the answer. But he felt very much alone, more than he ever had before.

There was one thing of which he was certain. Rais had not taken the girls to Croatia to elude Reid; he was baiting him, taunting him, forcing him onto unfamiliar terrain so that the assassin could have the upper hand.

Reid would have to bait him first. Send him an invitation that he wouldn't be able to turn down. He had a few ideas about how to do it, but each of them required him to make Agent Zero's presence known—and doing so could alert the CIA to his whereabouts.

That barely mattered now, he decided. He had come this far. He wasn't about to back down or shirk away. *Let them know where I am. I'll lead them there myself.*

At long last he couldn't stand being so alone with his thoughts. Besides, he reasoned, they should nearly be there. He knocked twice on the cockpit door and it unlocked from the other side.

The pilot pulled off his headset. "ETA is about thirty minutes."

Reid nodded and gestured to the empty copilot seat. "May I ...?"

"Sure. Just no personal stuff. I'd prefer plausible deniability wherever possible."

"Not a problem." Reid settled into the chair, wondering who this pilot was that he would fly someone a third of the way around the world as a favor—or, perhaps more appropriately, who Mitch was that he might be owed such a favor.

For a moment they were both silent, the pilot handling the yoke and Reid watching. He scanned over the console, the dials, the levers...and despite his position, he nearly chuckled.

I know how to fly this plane. He'd never done it, or at least no memories sparked of him ever flying before, but he had the sensation of controls in his hands, bumping over turbulence, adjusting for altitude.

A simulator. I learned how to fly in a simulator. He made a mental note to file that information away for later use. It could come in handy.

"Any idea what's going on down there?" Reid asked. "In Dubrovnik?"

The pilot shook his head without looking over. "Nope."

Reid frowned. "Air traffic control should have said something if planes are being searched." If there was a police presence, as he had asked of Riker, the pilot would be aware.

"I suppose now's as good a time as any," the pilot murmured. Then louder he said, "I'm not landing in Dubrovnik."

"What?" A tense ball of panic formed in Reid's throat. "But that's where I need to be. That's where we're supposed to go..."

"That's where *you're* supposed to go," the pilot corrected. "And you are. My flight path is to Montenegro, under the pretense of a private courier delivery. Landing in Dubrovnik would be too suspicious to anyone that might be paying attention. You're going to have to jump."

"Jump," Reid repeated, stunned. "As in...?"

"Parachute," the pilot finished. "Is that a problem? I was told you're experienced."

I'm going to have to jump out of a plane. The lump in Reid's throat felt as if it swelled to the size of a tangerine. *I've never done that before...*

Yes, you have. Plenty of times. Feelings, images, flashed through his mind. Again, just like the realization that he could pilot a plane, no specific memory came back associated with it—only the knowledge that he could do it if he needed to.

And he needed to. It was for the girls. He reminded himself— *whatever it takes.*

"No," Reid said. "Not a problem."

"Good," said the pilot. "I can get you within a mile of the airport, but not directly into their airspace. Our trajectory will take us just north of there, over the mountains. I'm told you need to find the cargo depot. It's at the northern end of the airport."

Reid nodded along, only half hearing the pilot's words. He was going to have to jump out of an airplane.

"What about you?" he asked. "You won't get far with your door open."

"Not my first rodeo." The pilot grinned. "I'll decrease altitude, reduce airspeed, and get another sixty or seventy miles before I have to call it in. I'll tell them a faulty latch forced the door open and I'll make an emergency landing in Tivat." He shrugged. "No big deal."

"Sure." *No big deal to risk life and limb so I can get into Croatia without being spotted.* "Um...thanks. For your help."

"Don't mention it, Zero," the pilot said casually, both hands on the yoke.

Reid narrowed his eyes. He had the sneaking suspicion that this pilot might be another remnant of his past, someone he couldn't remember—and perhaps, like Mitch, someone who didn't want to be remembered.

You've made a lot of enemies, Cartwright had told him over the phone, shortly after he found his girls missing.

Apparently he had made a few friends, or at least allies, as well.

"ETA is twenty-five," the pilot said, fitting the headset back over his ears. "You should get ready."

"Right." He rose from the seat to get ready to leap out of an airplane.

He secured the straps over his shoulders and tightened the nylon around each thigh before clipping the parachute over his chest in the front. He secured his duffel bag to his waist by yanking one of the handles free of the fabric, looping it through three belt loops, and tying it tight.

He was as ready as he could be—at least in the preparatory sense. His legs felt weak and his mind was reeling with the prospect of making the jump.

The pilot glanced over his shoulder from the open cockpit door. "Two minutes," he announced. "After you do what you came here to do, you'll be able to make it back all right?"

"I'll find a way," Reid told him. "Assuming I'm not dead or in prison."

The pilot nodded solemnly, understanding that Reid wasn't joking. "After my stop in Tivat, I'll be in Montenegro for the next thirty-six hours, give or take. If you finish up here and can get there…" He handed Reid a white card with a handwritten phone number on it, but no name. "Give a call."

"Thank you." Reid tucked the card into his pocket.

"I have to secure the cockpit now," the pilot told him. "Count to sixty, and then do it." He pushed the cockpit door closed. Reid heard it lock from the opposite side.

This is insane, he told himself.

You can do this. You've done it before.

That doesn't make it any easier.

He started counting aloud. "One, two, three…"

The altimeter in the cockpit had told him that they were at a cruising altitude of about twelve thousand feet.

"Eleven, twelve, thirteen…"

Most parachutes require about eight hundred to twelve hundred feet of free fall to open, his mind told him.

"Twenty-three, twenty-four, twenty-five…"

At this height, your fall rate will be about a hundred and fifteen miles an hour.

"Thirty-seven, thirty-eight, thirty-nine…"

Minimum safe opening height is about two thousand feet.

"Forty-four, forty-five…"

Which means you'll have just under a full minute of free fall.

Free fall.

This is insane.

"Sixty!" Reid grabbed the edge of the rounded door frame with one hand and the red lever with the other. Yet he hesitated.

Do it now.

You have to go now.

He forced himself to wrench the lever upward with a grunt and pushed outward. The door gave way and jerked violently, sliding open parallel to the body of the plane.

Reid quickly grabbed onto the door frame with his other hand, steadying himself as a torrent of intense wind tore at his clothes, threatening to yank him out into nothing.

He looked out over the edge. Down below, far below, was the darkness of the ocean, the mountains, and a vague mass of lights. The city.

Terror gripped him. He couldn't do this, couldn't leap out of a plane moving at this speed, at this height…

It's for them, the voice in his head reminded him. *It's for the girls.*

"The girls. Sara. Maya." He said it aloud but he couldn't hear his own voice. He pictured their faces—smiling, happy, home. But then another thought intruded, the photo that Rais had sent him as a taunt—fraught, terrified, distressed.

He let go of the door frame and shoved off hard with the heels of his feet, tumbling out of the plane twelve thousand feet over Croatia.

Chapter Sixteen

The wind whipped around Reid's ears with such intensity that it felt as if there was no sound at all, no sound in the entire world. There was no falling sensation, like he'd felt before jumping from a high-dive or down the first hill of a roller coaster; he felt weightless, as if he were unmoving, simply floating in place.

His body responded instinctively, knowing just what to do. His legs were bent slightly, muscles relaxed; his arms were out, elbows crooked, palms flat in front of his face.

It did not feel as if he were hurtling toward the ground, but rather that the ground was rushing up to meet him. Reid glanced downward and saw the lights of Dubrovnik, the yellow-lit runways of the airport, the dark shadows of the mountains...

The mountains. Account for the mountains.

He panicked slightly as he realized that he hadn't been counting and had no idea how long he'd been falling. *Relax. You'll know when.* His body angled, aiming for a trajectory closer to Dubrovnik Airport.

For several seconds, he forgot himself, forgot all of his problems as he was suspended in a bizarre limbo. This was something that Reid Lawson would never, ever have done. Kent Steele had done it dozens of times. Yet here they both were, one and the same, simultaneously at ease and anxious.

Then, before his mind even registered the thought, his hand found the ripcord and tore at it. The parachute billowed out above him, slowing his descent so quickly it felt as if he had been jerked back upward into the air.

He glanced up; the parachute was, thankfully, black. With any luck, no one would notice his descent onto the dark sloping hillside closest to the airport. He bent his legs as he landed in the dirt, jogging into the impact. He immediately unclipped the parachute from his chest and slipped it off, and then crouched in the darkness overlooking the airport.

It would be just after nine o'clock local time, by his best estimate. The weather was mild; it might have been cold if the air wasn't so still. Dubrovnik Airport was quite small by international standards. A horseshoe-shaped tract of runway sat beside a long, industrial-modern building, all nestled in the base of low-lying mountains. The city center was closer to the coast, about twelve miles away.

But that's not where Reid was going, at least not yet.

Instead of heading toward the airport, he slung his bag over a shoulder and strode quickly down the hillside in the other direction, toward a rectangular gray building on the opposite side of the runway. A yellow-and-red airplane, emblazoned with the logo of an international freight carrier, sat on an off-ramp of runway as a crew worked to unload it under bright yellow pole lights.

As he drew nearer, he scanned the runway and frowned in dismay. Two police cars were on the tarmac, their lights off, with four officers watching the crew unloading the cargo plane. He had expected more of a presence from his arrangement with Riker. He'd expected barricades, police, perhaps canines, even Interpol. There was none of that.

There were only two possible answers that he could conceive—either Riker had not allocated the promised time and resources to Dubrovnik and had merely tipped off the Croatian authorities, or the police had not found anything. If his math was right, and the girls had been ferried immediately from a boat onto a plane in Nova Scotia, then they would have arrived hours ago—perhaps even before he was in the air, before he even spoke to Riker.

And if that was the case, then Rais had a seven-hour lead on him. *They could be anywhere by now.* He had to find out for himself what was going on, and he couldn't very well walk up to the police on the tarmac and ask them if they'd found any girls in the cargo planes. Instead, he clung to the shadows of the blocky building and slipped quietly inside.

The freight terminal was a wide, warehouse-like building with a high ceiling and concrete floors. The place was more than half-empty; the city wasn't exactly a huge freight hub, and there were only a few employees milling about.

He strode up to the first man he saw and asked, "English?"

The Croatian man frowned and scratched his chin. "Yes," he said uncertainly.

"Manager?" To the man's deeper frown he said, "Supervisor? Boss."

"Ah, boss. Yes." The man pointed toward a back corner of the depot. "There."

"Thank you." Reid hurried past him toward the rear office.

Despite how frustrating and exasperating the long flight had been, there was a strange benefit to it—all that nervous energy that had been balled up inside him for so long had to go somewhere, had to be exerted. He was ready to get answers. After so many hours of doing nothing, Reid was ready to do anything.

He pushed open the steel, white-painted door and into the small office. The man seated behind the desk glanced up suddenly from his computer screen. He was heavyset, with a scraggly beard dotted in gray covering his bulbous chin. He wore a wrinkled blue uniform and managed to look both surprised and irritated at Reid's intrusion.

He asked something in Croatian that Reid didn't understand.

"English?" He lowered his black bag to the floor as he gave the office a quick once-over. Behind the desk was a file cabinet and a single small window with the blinds closed. Otherwise the room was remarkably sparse.

"Who are you?" the man asked. "What do you want?"

Reid closed the door. "The police out there. Were there more? Were they here, asking questions?"

The man's eyes narrowed. "They found nothing. Who are you ...?"

They found nothing. "Was it because there was nothing to find, or because it was already gone?" Reid asked. To the supervisor's silence, he said, "A plane arrived here from Nova Scotia sometime today. Was that before the police came?"

"I have answered their questions already," the man said indignantly. "So unless you can tell me who you are, I am going to ask you to leave."

Reid shook his head. "I'm going to need to see your flight manifests."

"Those are confidential documents," he argued. "Are you American?"

"Yes." Reid didn't have time to argue. He needed answers. He grabbed the guest chair opposite the man's desk, four-legged and metal, and jammed it under the doorknob so that no one could push it open from the other side.

That got the supervisor's attention. He stood suddenly, knocking papers from his desktop. "What do you think you're doing?"

"I'm looking for something." Reid pulled the Glock from its holster.

The man's eyes widened in fright. "There is no money here," he said quickly. "Nothing of value ..."

"I disagree. The cargo that was on that plane is very valuable. Now I need to know if that plane arrived here, when it did, and where that cargo went."

The supervisor did not answer, but the corner of his mouth twitched. His hands trembled visibly. "I don't ... I don't know what you're talking about ..."

He knows.

Reid sighed. "I don't have time to waste. Put your hands flat on the desk." He unzipped his bag and rifled through it, certain that Watson would have included what he needed.

"Wh-what?" the man stammered.

"Put. Your hands. Flat." Reid tapped the metal surface twice. "Right there. Or I will shoot you."

Shaking, the man put his thick hands down on the desk. As he did, Reid found what he was looking for—a black tactical lockback knife. He flicked it open. The blade was stubby and wide, spade-shaped, but wickedly sharp. It would suit his needs just fine.

"One more time," he said quietly. "Did that plane land here? When did it land here? Where did the cargo go?"

The supervisor gulped. His hands shook so badly that his wedding ring clacked against the metal desktop. The man was terrified—but he was not protesting any knowledge. *He's afraid to say.* He thought of Bill, back at Port Jersey. *They'll kill me*, he said. They were afraid of what the traffickers would do to them.

Now they'll be afraid of me.

In one swift motion Reid slammed the blade down, slicing easily through the meaty palm of the supervisor's hand until the tip grated against the metal on the other side.

The man threw back his head and screamed as he tried to pull his hand away, but Reid held it fast. After several seconds he yanked the bloody knife out and the supervisor crumpled to the floor, whimpering and cradling his skewered hand.

"Now," said Reid. "Where did they take the girls?"

"I don't... I don't know..."

Someone banged heavily on the office door from the other side, trying in vain to push it open. The wedged chair held it shut. "Marko!" a voice shouted, followed by a frantic line in Croatian.

"Marko?" Reid asked. "Is that your name?"

"Y-yes..." the supervisor stammered.

"Do you have kids, Marko?" Reid had to speak up over the shouts coming from the other side of the door.

Marko whimpered again and nodded.

"So do I." Reid knelt and wiped the blood from the blade on Marko's shirt. "Two girls. They were on that plane. Do you want your children to grow up fatherless?"

"No," he sobbed. "No, no."

"Then tell me something, Marko. Or else you're useless to me."

Marko sucked in a jagged breath. "Th-they landed here. Hours ago, before the police came. They... they have a van waiting. The girls go in it. No one sees anything. No one talks."

"Where does the van go?" Reid was running out of time. The men outside would undoubtedly alert the police out on the runway.

"I don't know..."

Reid pressed the Glock against the man's temple, hard enough to leave a red ring in his skin.

"I don't know!" he shouted.

Something heavy slammed against the door. A husky voice shouted in Croatian. Someone was trying to break it down, and it wouldn't hold forever.

Reid grunted. "You must have a way to contact them."

"No, they always come to me..."

"Something, Marko! Give me something, or I will kill you—"

The men on the other side of the door slammed it again. The chair jarred slightly. *I need more time.* Reid pointed the gun straight up at the ceiling and fired twice. Marko cried out in shock at the deafening report. The men outside shouted frantically, their voices growing distant as they scattered. *At least for now,* Reid thought.

"My patience has worn out, Marko. Goodbye..."

"Wait!" the supervisor shrieked. "Wait, please wait. The... the manifests..."

"What about them?" Reid growled.

"The cargo manifests for their, their flights. The documents claim they are bringing in textiles." Marko's eyes were squeezed shut tightly, waiting for a bullet to enter his skull.

"Textiles? As in, fabric? Materials?"

"Yes. Yes. Under a company name. Tkanina."

"Tkanina," Reid repeated. "Is that Croatian?"

"Yes," Marko gasped. "It just means 'cloth.' It... it is probably fake. I never checked. I didn't ask questions."

Tkanina. That's a start. "Anything else, Marko?"

"No, no. I swear I do not know any more than that."

Reid believed him. The front of the man's shirt was slick with the blood from his hand; the front of his pants was soaked with urine.

There was shouting again from the other side of the door. Reid stood, holstered his Glock, and snatched up his bag.

"*Policija!*" someone barked. Then a command in Croatian.

"One more thing," Reid said quickly as he yanked open the blinds over the small window. "The names and ages of your children. Say them."

Marko sniffled. "Miroslav. Thirteen." He whimpered. "Lana. Fifteen."

"A girl." Reid scoffed. "You have a little girl. You're disgusting." He shoved the window open and hazarded a glance out into the darkness. The office was facing the rear of the building; there was nothing out there but the gentle slope of the low mountains beyond.

He tossed his bag out first. Before he climbed out after it, he said, "You're going to tell the police all this, Marko. You're going to admit what you've done. You're going to have them here, ready to bust the next plane and the Slavs. And you're going to go to jail for what you've done. Because I won't be far. I'll be watching. If you try to run, or tip anyone off, I'll find you. I will kill you, Marko. Understand?"

"Yes. Yes. I understand. Yes." The man sniffled and wiped his leaking nose with his good hand.

Reid grabbed onto the windowsill with both hands. It was going to be a challenge, squeezing himself through this tiny portal.

But before he could, something heavy slammed against the door. The chair fell aside and the jamb sprang open, three angry Croatian police officers on the other side.

CHAPTER SEVENTEEN

Reid's hand was already inside his jacket as the door swung inward. He yanked out the Glock and fired two shots toward the door.

He had no intention of shooting anyone that didn't deserve it. Reid tracked his aim slightly to the left just before pulling the trigger and both bullets buried in the wall. Yet it had the desired effect; the cops and cargo workers crowded outside the small office took cover, vanishing from the frame.

The distraction gave him the precious few seconds he needed. He forced the doubt of the earlier moment out of his mind as he crouched and pounced, pushing off his toes and shoving his hands straight in front of him in a swan dive. His body careened through the narrow window, but he felt his toes snag the sill as he landed painfully onto the pavement outside, tucking into a sloppy roll. His shoulder throbbed; he'd have a substantial bruise there later.

He snatched up his bag as he scrambled to his feet and broke into a sprint, running parallel between the freight terminal and the low mountains behind it. He immediately regretted firing the shots; though it gave him the necessary time to escape, he had just authorized the police to use deadly force against him. And he had only seen three officers, when he knew there were at least four…

As soon as the thought crossed his mind someone came into view just ahead of him, another cop rounding the corner of the building with his service pistol drawn and pointed downward. Reid did not pause or even slow down; he lowered his shoulder and slammed into the cop at full speed like a defensive tackle.

"*Oomph!*" The officer took a hundred seventy-six pounds of Agent Zero to the midsection. For a moment the man's entire body was off the ground, weightless, and then he crashed to the asphalt hard on his back.

Reid vaulted over him without slowing and sprinted onward. He stuck to the shadows, clinging close to the base of the mountains. Sirens screamed behind him as the police took to their cars. He needed to buy some time, at least enough to find a place to hide. He scrambled up the gentle slope of the mountain for about ten yards, tore off his jacket, and threw it into the dirt. Then he doubled back and continued parallel to the runway. With any luck the police would find the jacket and assume he made a run for the hills.

Reid ran until the tarmac ended in flat, dark fields, occasionally stealing a glance over his shoulder to see headlights and flashers in the distance. But they weren't far; they would come this way soon enough. After nearly a half mile of running he paused, catching his breath, and crouched low in the shadows of the grassy field. He unzipped his bag and pulled out a change of clothes. He replaced his white T-shirt with an olive-green one, secured his shoulder holster, and then pulled on a brown blazer to replace the jacket he'd tossed. Deeper in the bag he found a blue baseball cap—*thanks Watson*, he thought—and pulled it on.

Still in the grass and shadows, he circled wide around the airport, approaching it from the east. Even under the cover of darkness he wasn't terribly keen on staying on foot, not while the police were searching. He couldn't be sure they had gotten a decent look at him, but he didn't want to take the chance. Besides, it was a twelve-mile hike to walk to Dubrovnik proper.

When he reached the road he walked just beyond the shoulder toward the front of the airport. He just had to get to the bus terminal, and from there he could take a shuttle into the city. He was hoping the police would assume that the perpetrator with the gun wouldn't be stupid enough to just get on a bus.

He was less than twenty yards from the bus terminal when two police officers exited the airport right next to the waiting shuttle.

Reid cursed and quickly leaned against a metal signpost, trying to look casual.

He checked his periphery. One of the uniformed officers boarded the bus. The other mulled about near its doors, chatting with tourists. Likely asking them if they'd seen anyone fitting Reid's description.

If he stayed and waited for his chance to board a shuttle, they might find him. The airport wasn't large and despite Dubrovnik's popularity as a tourist spot, there weren't nearly as many visitors in the colder months. *But what choice do I have? I can't rent a car. I can't walk it without risking being seen…*

"Hey!" A gray sedan pulled to a halt directly in front of him. The passenger window was down, and the driver leaned over to address Reid. "Hello, my friend! Yes, you. Are you American?"

Reid realized he was leaning against a sign for a taxi stand. The gray car had two words stenciled on the door in faded letters, in both English and (presumably) Croatian: Taxi Service.

"You need ride?" The driver's English wasn't great, but at least he spoke it.

"Yes. I do." Reid tossed his bag in and slid after it into the backseat. "Drive into Dubrovnik. City center."

"You got it." The taxi pulled away from the curb. Reid turned his head away as they cruised past the bus and the police officers. In less than a minute they were out of the airport and on their way to the city. "You alone, my friend? Where is your family?"

"I'm meeting them," Reid said succinctly. The driver was about his age, maybe a year or two younger, with a heavy five o'clock shadow and tired eyes. But he smiled pleasantly—he had an American tourist in the backseat, which Reid understood to probably mean he expected a nice tip. "I only have US dollars. Is that a problem?"

"No, no problem. Happens a lot with tourists. Forget to change money. Lacking of… of, uh …" He snapped his fingers as if it would conjure the word.

"Foresight?" Reid offered.

"Sense," said the driver.

Reid scoffed lightly. He noticed a thick sheaf of travel brochures in the pocket of the seat back, advertising things to do and places to stay in the city.

One of them in particular caught his eye.

"Where are you staying, friend?"

"I'm staying here." Reid passed the bright brochure up to the driver. It looked like a beautiful place; the cover advertised crystal-clear pools and modern villas overlooking the Adriatic coast.

"Oh," said the driver, impressed. "Villa Maya, huh? I had a feeling you were wealthy man." He winked in the rearview mirror.

Reid took the hint. In his pocket he still had the wad of emergency cash he had taken from his closet before leaving Virginia. He peeled off a hundred-dollar bill and passed it to the driver. "This is for you," he said. "And keep the change. But we have to make a stop first."

"Stop where?"

"I'm looking for a place that I believe operates somewhere in the city. It's a company by the name of Tkanina."

The driver chuckled. "You know that means 'fabric,' yes? You are looking for a place called 'Fabric'?"

"Yes."

The driver laughed lightly again, but he typed it into the GPS on the cell phone mounted on his dashboard. The taxi swerved slightly on the road, reminding Reid to buckle his seatbelt.

"Huh," the driver said softly after a moment. "How about it. There is a Tkanina in Dubrovnik. Other side of the city from your place, but not far from here. You still want to go?"

"I do," Reid told him.

"You are the boss."

It only took another four minutes to reach the destination, located in a small commercial area outside of Dubrovnik proper. The address they had been led to was pretty much exactly as Reid had expected; beige brick, nondescript, with no signs or indication of what might be inside.

"Turn off your headlights. Park over there, in the next lot over," Reid instructed. The taxi rolled past the dark, silent building and stopped in the lot of an adjacent facility. The sign suggested the place manufactured bicycle parts, but it was deserted at this time of night. "Pop your trunk, please."

Reid got out of the car and stowed his black bag. Then he came around and knelt beside the driver's side window. "I'm leaving my bag with you," he said. "I want you to wait for me. I don't know how long this will take; it might be only a few minutes. It might be an hour. But if you wait, there's another hundred in it for you."

The driver's eyes lit up. "Sure thing, my friend. I wait here."

"Thank you." Reid straightened, but then another thought occurred to him. "And, uh, you might hear noises."

"Noises?" The driver raised an eyebrow.

"Loud noises. But please. Stay and wait for me."

The taxi driver grinned as he reclined his seat back and wove his fingers behind his head, as if sitting in a lounge chair. "My friend, I am chill. See? I stay. I wait."

"Thanks." Reid left the car and trotted across the dark parking lot towards the cube-like Tkanina building. The only light outside was mounted on the front, a few yards over the steel double-door entrance, casting a pale glow over the front several parking spaces. Reid edged around the halo of it and inspected the building's façade; there didn't appear to be any cameras, and the windows were too high up in the walls for him to get a look inside.

He tried the front doors. They were locked, naturally, but after a quick inspection he determined he could dismantle the lock from the outside. He snapped open the spade-shaped lockback knife, still stained with some of Marko's blood, and set to work.

It took him under a minute to take the left door handle off and pull the locking bolt out, but it felt like much longer. His mind was racing. He wasn't expecting to find his girls here; the traffickers and Rais alike would be stupendously foolish to trust that sort of information with a soft touch like Marko at the freight terminal. Even so, he hoped to find something—or more aptly, some*one*—inside.

He slipped into the building as quietly as he could and immediately drew his Glock 22. It took several seconds for his eyes to adjust to the darkness of the shop floor … and when they did, his face fell in abject disappointment.

The shadows fell long over rows and rows of workstations. Many of them were equipped with industrial-grade sewing machines. Along the far wall were wide devices with rollers wrapped in wide swaths of fabric in various colors.

This is actually a textile mill. He had expected a mostly empty building, or perhaps even a thinly veiled front, but this appeared to be a bona fide business. It could have been owned by the traffickers as a way to launder their money, he reasoned, or perhaps a pass-through entity like the men at the ports had been, paid off to falsify incoming cargo in order to get the girls into the country.

Regardless, he had come this far, and he was definitely going to have a look around. He crossed the shop floor carefully and quietly, his path illuminated only by the wan moonlight from the windows recessed high in the walls overhead. At the far end of the floor he found entrances to a couple of office, unlocked and empty.

Beyond them were two sets of stairs. One was made of steel and led up to another partial level of the plant. The second was concrete and led down into the darkness of a basement.

Reid stood at the base of the steel stairs for a full minute, listening intently. He heard nothing but the blood rushing in his own ears; no footfalls, no voices, nothing.

He took the stairs down, wishing he had brought a flashlight.

At the bottom he squeezed his eyes shut for several seconds to allow them to adjust to the darkness quicker. When he opened them again he could make out the faint silhouettes of more machines, lots of them—he was standing at the edge of a subterranean level of the plant, a floor just as vast and wide as the one above. But it was incredibly dark, too dark to navigate. He held the Glock in one hand as the other fumbled along the wall in the hopes of a light switch.

Something caught his eye and he glanced upward. In the corner of the ceiling was a small, single red dot of light.

Reid squinted at it. The light was attached to a rectangular black box. A camera, he realized, directed at a downward angle.

Toward the entrance.

Directly at him.

The hairs on the back of his neck stood on end as he heard shuffling footsteps in the darkness.

And then the shooting began.

CHAPTER EIGHTEEN

Reid saw the muzzle flash a quarter of a heartbeat before he heard the torrent of automatic gunfire split the stillness of the wide basement. He threw himself to the concrete floor, landing hard on his side and scrambling to a seated position.

The burst was short and punctuated by silence. Reid felt his surroundings and put his back to a machine for cover, gripping the Glock tightly. His breath was shallow and quiet as he listened intently.

Then a voice came, harsh, male, and guttural. "You, go that way! You, over there!" The man wasn't speaking English, but Reid understood him all the same. *Slovak*, he thought. *I know Slovak—and these men must be with the Slavs.*

Footfalls followed, breaking off into separate directions. Reid closed his eyes—they were doing him little good in the Stygian darkness anyway—and listened to the steps, their distance, their pace.

"He told us you might come." The man spoke again but in English this time, and loudly, both for Reid's benefit. "Your American friend."

Rais. He knew I might find this place.

"He said that if you did, you would come alone." The man was walking steadily, moving across the floor, getting closer to Reid's position. "This is true, yes? You are alone."

To the left, twenty yards and closing. He craned his neck slightly. *To the right, further away. They can't see either. They don't know where I am.*

"He said that if you found us, we should not kill you," the man continued. "Only to scare you away. But now that you are here, I think we will kill you anyway. We cannot risk you telling anyone what you might have found."

What I might have found? There was something here, something the traffickers were afraid of getting out. *First things first.* Reid tensed as the Slav to his left closed in, inching closer.

Suddenly there was a dull sound, a heavy click, and Reid was blinded by light. Several rows of powerful fluorescent lights blazed on overhead, all at once, turning the sheer darkness into veritable daylight. Reid shielded his eyes at the sudden harshness, grimacing as white enveloped his vision.

The Slav was drawing near. Any second he would be upon him. Reid lifted the Glock blindly in the direction of the footfalls. *Wait. Wait…* He opened his eyes slightly, barely a millimeter, in time to see a silhouette step around the machine he was hiding behind.

Reid instantly fired off two shots. There was a yelp. The silhouette vanished from sight as it fell. A gun clattered to the floor.

He skirted around the other side of the machine and dared to open his eyes. His vision was adjusting; he quickly checked his six, but there was no one there. He held his breath, listening. There were no footfalls. The other men were holding their positions.

The man on the other side of the machine groaned in pain. Reid wasn't sure where he'd hit him, but it sounded like it was enough to take him out of the fight, at least for now.

He checked his surroundings. He was standing in a straight corridor of machinery, about six feet wide, lined on both sides by the same type of device arranged side-by-side the whole way down the row. It was taller than he was and about as narrow, with a large round cylinder attached to the front, reminiscent of the chamber on a revolver. But instead of bullets, each deep divot held a thick spool of colored thread.

Spinning machines. They make fabric here, in the basement. Suddenly Reid realized what that meant; they were not importing fabric at all, but falsifying the incoming cargo documents for the traffickers.

"Jakub?" the Slav who had taunted him called out. "Jakub," he asked in Slovak, "are you alive?"

The wounded man groaned and said, "*Ano.*" Yes.

The footfalls resumed, slower this time, and only one pair, though Reid knew there were at least two other men in the basement with him. He knelt and quickly untied his boots, tugged them off, and crept down the corridor of machinery in his socks.

"Jakub," the first man called out again. "You have your gun?"

"Yes," the wounded man hissed.

"You stay there. Watch the door. He does not leave."

They were assuming that Reid did not speak Slovak, that they could formulate a plan in their foreign tongue. He reached the end of the row and paused.

"I'm coming around," the man said. "If you see him—"

Reid took a breath, and then whipped around the corner with the Glock level. Jakub was lying on the floor at the far end of the row, blood standing out bright against the dark concrete as he shimmied toward his gun, oblivious to Reid's appearance behind him.

The other Slav stepped into view, and Reid fired twice.

His first shot missed, but the second struck the man in the shoulder and spun his body ninety degrees. As he twisted, the Slav brought a black SMG up with one hand and squeezed the trigger.

A hail of bullets flew wildly. Reid leapt forward, taking cover behind the next row of machines, but not fast enough. A sharp pain stung at his right bicep; a bullet had torn into his blazer and grazed his arm.

He inspected it quickly and saw it was bleeding badly, but was a fairly superficial wound.

Rapid footfalls echoed as the shoulder-shot Slav scurried away. "Michal," the man cried out in Slovak, "he removed his shoes. Be cautious!"

Reid could hear the steps of the Slav getting farther away, heading toward the farthest row of machines, but he could not hear anything from the third, this Michal. Either he was savvy or anxious, perhaps both.

He glanced over his shoulder to make sure no one was behind him and noticed a few drops of bright red blood on the floor. The gash on his arm had left a trail; it would be easy to follow him, to know where he was, but he had no idea where the third man might be.

He decided to take a chance. Reid lifted the Glock and fired two shots into the wall.

There was a scuffle of boots, a flurry of movement from the next row over, followed immediately by a short burst of automatic fire. He was right; the third man, Michal, was nervous and had an itchy trigger finger.

Reid took a running start and slid forward on his heel and knee, like a batter sliding into home plate, across the open aisle of machinery. The Slav was facing him and had a submachine gun pointed in his direction—but upward, directed at center mass, while Reid had gone low. Before the man could reposition his shot, even before the surprise registered on his face, Reid took aim and fired again, just once.

Michal's head jerked as the bullet struck his forehead. He fell flat onto his back, limbs splayed.

"Michal?" the talkative Slav shouted.

Reid hurried over to check the body. "Michal is dead," he called out in Slovak.

A long moment of silence followed.

"You son of a bitch!" the man suddenly screamed in his native tongue. "I'll kill you!" His footfalls became angry stomps, seemingly several rows away from Reid's position. A burst of gunfire rang out; then more stomps, and another burst.

The Slav was stalking aisle by aisle, spraying bullets down the rows of machines. Another burst tore at the air. He was only three or four rows away.

Reid quickly knelt and pulled loose his Ruger LC9.

More stomps. Another burst, closer.

He wedged himself in the narrow space between two of the machines as best he could.

Stomps. Shots. A shout: "Where are you?!"

Reid held the LC9 out to his left. The Glock to his right. His arm burned, his other shoulder throbbed, but he kept each as steady as he could.

The gun came around the corner first, black with a stubby barrel. It was followed by an arm, which pointed it down the lane of spinning machines as a hail of bullets cascaded past him. A stray shot struck the cylinder to Reid's left and he forgot to breathe.

Then the man showed himself, stalking across the aisle, glancing down its length…

Reid fired the LC9. The bullet hit the Slav's ribcage and he doubled over with the impact. As he glanced up, fury and pain in his eyes, Reid fired a second shot into the man's neck. A thin fountain of blood jetted from the wound. For a moment the Slav tried weakly to raise his gun again, his hand shaking, but it fell limply to his side before he could level it. The man collapsed to the floor.

Reid climbed out from between the two machines and remained still for a moment, just listening. He heard no more footfalls; only the slight groans of the first man he'd shot. *Two down. One to go.*

"Jakub," he called out in Slovak. "Your friends are dead. Put your gun down and slide it away." Reid tucked the Ruger back into his ankle holster but held onto the Glock, clearing the other aisles as he approached the last Slav's position.

"How do I know you won't kill me?" Jakub called back. His voice was weak. He had likely lost a lot of blood.

"I don't know where I hit you," Reid called back. "You might already be dead. How fast or slow that happens is up to you." He paused; Jakub would be in the next aisle over, the closest to the entrance. The Slav seemed to be deliberating. But after a moment, he heard the clatter of a dropped gun, and then the sound of it sliding away.

Reid swung into view with his gun directed downward. He blinked in surprise; Jakub was young, with long hair pulled into a ponytail. *He can't be more than twenty.* Reid had to remind himself that young or not, this man had aligned himself with traffickers.

He had done horrible things to innocent people—including Reid's own children.

Jakub's face was white as a sheet. The kid had managed to pull himself into a seated position with his back to a machine and his legs splayed out in front of him, sitting in a growing puddle of his own blood. One red-stained hand was pressed over his abdomen; Reid had shot him just above the navel.

"Do you have a phone, Jakub?" Reid asked. "A way to contact the others?"

"Who?" Jakub asked, his voice faltering. "Which ones?"

Reid knelt. "The ones with the green-eyed American. The ones that have my daughters."

Jakub's eyes widened in shock. He let out a slight whimper.

"Yes," Reid said. "Two of those girls are my children. Everyone you ever harmed or helped to bring harm to was someone's child. This is your atonement. Make the call."

With some difficulty and several groans of pain, Jakub managed to liberate a cell phone from his pocket. He smeared blood across the screen as he pressed a button.

Reid took the phone from him, not taking his eyes from the young Slav. After two rings, a harsh voice answered.

"*Čo?*" the voice snapped. What?

"I want you to listen to this," Reid said calmly in Slovak. He pulled the trigger on the Glock. Jakub's body jerked once and fell still. "That was the sound of Jakub's death. The other two are dead as well. Put the American on the phone."

The line was silent, a slight static hissing in Reid's ear.

Then a voice came on the line, an eerily calm tone that made his skin crawl and his stomach flip with rage.

"Kent. Steele." Rais enunciated each syllable as if he had tasted something delicious. "I knew you would come. I knew you would persevere—"

"Shut up," Reid snapped. He couldn't tolerate the sound of the assassin's voice. "I know what you want, and it has nothing to do with them. So let's finish it. You and I. Tonight."

"What do you have in mind?" Rais sounded amused.

"I came alone. You do the same—leave your new 'friends' behind. But you bring the girls. I want to see them, to know they're safe. Then we'll finish this."

"I will bring one girl," the assassin said simply.

Reid's entire body shook in a fresh wave of fury, his fingers gripping the phone so hard it felt it might snap in his hand. "This is not a negotiation, you psychopath, these are my *children*."

"And despite that I am holding all the cards, so to speak," Rais interjected calmly, "I am allowing you to set some terms. But I have terms of my own. Therefore, it is very much a negotiation. I will bring one girl. You will see her. You will know she is safe. She will know the location of the other girl. If you are still alive afterwards, she can tell you. If you're not, I will release them. Their only use to me is to get to you. You have my word."

Reid shook his head. He didn't like it. He didn't trust Rais at his word, not for a second. But as the assassin had keenly pointed out, he held the power here. He had the girls. Reid had nothing but his anger and his determination—and his life, which was what Rais wanted most of all.

"Fine," Reid hissed, his teeth gritted. "Villa Maya. That's where we'll meet. One hour. I'll be waiting." He hung up and quickly checked to see if there was any other useful information on the phone—GPS history, contacts, anything. But it was a burner, nothing of use on it. He grunted and dropped it to the floor next to Jakub's body.

Then he left, back the way he had come, up the concrete stairs to the shop floor of the facility. He had to get ready. He was going to kill Rais—and this time, he was going to make sure the man was not coming back.

CHAPTER NINETEEN

As much as Reid wanted to search the rest of the Tkanina building, he hurried out into the night. He reasoned that there must have been some evidence there that the traffickers did not want found, or else they wouldn't have defended it so vehemently. But his girls were more important right now. That was a job for the police.

He jogged to the parking lot and was dismayed, though not altogether shocked, that the gray taxi was gone. His bag, all his gear that Watson had gathered for him, had been in the trunk. He groaned in frustration and kicked at a rock, sending it skittering across the parking lot.

Headlights blared suddenly from around the corner as an engine roared. The gray sedan screeched to a halt right beside him.

The driver peered out at him. The man was obviously shaken. "You were right, my friend," he said. "Loud noises." He'd heard the gunshots, Reid realized, and probably hid the car until he saw Reid emerge.

He slid into the back as the man quickly pulled away. "Thanks for staying." He passed a hundred-dollar bill over the seat as promised.

"You in trouble?" the driver asked.

"No. Not yet, anyway. But someone else is." He slid the magazine from the Glock and checked the clip; he'd fired eleven shots so far. Two from the Ruger. Fourteen rounds left between them. *More than enough to kill one man.* "I need to go to Villa Maya now. As fast as you're able."

"You got it." The driver left the parking lot and the commercial zone, heading quickly for Dubrovnik proper.

Reid buckled his seatbelt and examined his options. The CIA undoubtedly had their eye on Dubrovnik Airport; he was certain they had heard the report of an American man firing at police. Strickland was likely on his way to Croatia, but Reid doubted he had arrived yet. Even if he had, his orders would be to detain Agent Zero on sight.

He had no way of contacting Maria, and he couldn't very well contact the Croatian police without possibly getting himself arrested. He briefly considered getting in touch with his friend in Interpol, the Italian agent Vicente Baraf, to notify him of Rais's presence in Croatia. But Baraf was a protocol-abiding agent and his office would want to clear the claim with the CIA, which would only alert Interpol to the now-rogue Agent Zero being in Europe—and that was assuming that Riker hadn't done that already.

Simply put, he had no allies—he was alone, which was exactly how Rais wanted it.

Although, he thought, *maybe there is one person.* He didn't like it, but he needed some sort of security for his girls... in case he failed against the Amun assassin.

"Can I use your phone for a moment?" he asked the driver. "I've lost mine."

"Sure, my friend." He passed a smartphone over his shoulder to Reid. "Local call, yes?"

"Yeah," Reid murmured. "Of course." He dialed the number to an office at Langley, the only contact number he knew by heart.

"Cartwright," answered the familiar yet harried voice.

"It's me."

"Zero!" the deputy director exclaimed. "Jesus, where are you calling from? Are you in Croatia...?"

"Yes. Cartwright, it's Rais. I spoke with him on the phone. He's here."

Cartwright was silent for a long moment. "You know what this means, don't you?"

Reid closed his eyes. "Yes." He understood that Cartwright wasn't talking about Rais; he was referring to Reid calling on an unsecure line at Langley. In just the last five seconds, Reid had essentially gone on the record to admit that he had defied Riker, defied CIA orders, left the country, and pursued the lead on his own. "But there's good reason. I've confirmed that it's him. You need to pull Maria from Ukraine. It's her op. I assume Strickland is en route; he needs to know this too. There's a company here in Dubrovnik called Tkanina." He spelled it out for Cartwright. "They're a front for human trafficking. And the supervisor at the cargo terminal, Marko, he's involved as well."

"Stop this," Cartwright said. It wasn't an order; it was a plea. "Stop now and it might not be too late for you. Strickland is eighty minutes out. I can have Johansson there in two hours, max. Wait for them. Let them handle this. Get your girls back safely, come home, and I'll help you in whatever way I can."

"But you can't make any promises." Reid was unsure if Cartwright was being genuine in his appeal or just saying what he knew was likely being recorded.

"No," Cartwright admitted, "I can't. You've already crossed the line."

Then what's a little further? Reid thought. He couldn't wait for Strickland or Johansson to appear. He couldn't stand idly by and let someone else save the day. Besides, if he gave Rais even an iota of reason to believe that he hadn't come alone, hadn't given the assassin what he wanted, he might never see his daughters again.

"I'm on my way to meet him now," Reid said.

"Kent, that is a monumentally bad idea—"

"I can't wait for them. Can't risk it."

"At least tell us where you're going," Cartwright asked.

"You'll know soon enough." He had to end the call soon; if anyone was listening in they would be able to track the taxi driver's phone. But before he did, he had one more question. "What's happened to Watson?"

"He's being detained currently," Cartwright said with a sigh. "Here at Langley. It's not up to me what happens from here, but it doesn't look good for him."

Reid shook his head. John knew what he was doing, what he was getting himself into, but it didn't make it right. And the fact that Cartwright could have done more, could be helping him at that very moment, was downright vexing.

"I'll do what I can for him," the deputy director promised. "He's my agent. The same goes for you—"

"Not anymore." Reid ended the call.

He knew what would come next. With the confirmation that he had left the country, he would be officially disavowed by the CIA. Interpol and the Croatian authorities would be notified. Anyone who might have been an ally would now be an enemy.

Doesn't matter, he thought. The girls were what mattered. Putting an end to Rais was what mattered. Whatever came after would have to wait until there was an after.

He turned the cell phone off, pulled the battery, and handed them both back to the driver. "You're going to want to leave that off for a while."

The driver furrowed his brow in concern as he glanced at Reid in the rearview mirror. "My friend ... I am beginning to think you are not here for vacation."

Reid said nothing in response. He looked out the window as the taxi wound through the streets toward the coast, into downtown Dubrovnik. It was a beautiful city rife with history, established more than a thousand years prior as the capital of the Republic of Ragusa. It was one of the most popular tourist destinations on the Adriatic Sea, not only for its charming coastline dotted with orange-roofed villas, but for its famous stone walls that ran for more than a mile around the city on both the landward and seaward sides. The barriers were more than twenty feet thick in some places, a complex system of towers and turrets designed to protect the people from marauders. These days they attracted more than a million tourists a year. Reid had only ever seen them in photos; even now, in the taxi, he couldn't get a clear view under the night sky.

A seemingly innocent city, Reid thought. *A perfect place for the traffickers to use as a hub.* People often felt safe visiting big cities, being in public, in a crowd; they didn't seem to consider how easy it was to get lost in one. How simple it is for a kidnapper to snatch a child or abduct a woman, even in broad daylight, even right in front of other people.

"We are here," the driver announced as the car came to an abrupt stop outside a low stone wall lit with orange sconces that surrounded the seaside resort of Villa Maya.

Reid peeled one more bill from his supply of cash. "You picked up an American man at the airport," he told the driver. "This man did not speak, other than to ask you to bring him here. You did not get a good look at him. You assumed he was a tourist, and nothing more. Do you understand?"

"Yes, I understand." The driver reached for the outstretched bill, but Reid held it fast in his grip.

"I need one more favor," he said. "Do you have pay phones here? Can you get to one?"

The driver frowned, but he nodded slowly. "At the airport, yes."

"Good. I want you to wait forty-five minutes, and then call in a bomb threat to Villa Maya. Do you understand what I mean?"

The driver hesitated before asking, "Will there be a...bomb?"

Reid shook his head. "No. I just don't want anyone around for what's going to happen here. If you do what I ask, no one will get hurt."

The driver bit his lip before nodding slowly. "Yes. I will do what you ask." He tugged on the bill again, but still Reid did not release it.

"It's important. Very important." Finally he let go of the bill. "Thank you for your help." He hefted his bag and got out of the car. The taxi pulled away almost immediately, heading—Reid hoped— back toward the airport and a pay phone.

He entered Villa Maya through the open iron gates. It was a high-end resort, wide swaths of manicured grass dotted with trees and private stone-walled villas. Near the center of the property was a larger structure, housing the front desk, concierge, and house-keeping services. Reid meandered casually, scoping the property while trying his best to look like a tourist.

He noticed that the resort was sparsely populated; guests roaming the grounds were few, and those that did were primarily older, almost exclusively a fifty-plus crowd. *The sort of people who might not move very quickly in an emergency situation.*

Reid took note of the latticework and vines sprawling up one side of the guest services building. The vantage point atop the two-story structure. Behind the building were two large, irregularly shaped pools, each aglow in blue light. No one was swimming at this time of night.

He realized that the assassin might arrive early and attempt to scope the grounds as well. It was unfamiliar terrain to both of them and there weren't many places to hide. And, Reid couldn't help but realize, it was a thoroughly bizarre place for their showdown.

Someone is going to die here tonight.

He quickly walked the perimeter, parallel to the stone wall that surrounded the resort. There were three other points of egress besides the front entrance; two were service entrances for staff, both of which were gated and locked. The third was a walkway with a red wooden gate.

If I was Rais… If he was Rais, and he stayed true to his word and brought one daughter as proof of life, he would send her in through the front entrance. She would be conspicuous—but also a distraction. He, on the other hand, would slip in another way to gain the element of surprise.

Reid needed a vantage point from which he could see both the main entrance and this secondary one—which meant he needed to be as high up as he was able. He grabbed up his bag and hurried back to the guest services building, slinging it over one shoulder and making sure the coast was clear before climbing hand over hand up the latticework. With no small effort and some amount of pain, thanks to his aching shoulder and the gash on his left bicep where a bullet had grazed him, he managed to pull himself up onto the flat roof of the building.

From the top of the twenty-five-foot structure he could see nearly the entire grounds of the resort, save for areas bathed in shadow or obscured by trees and villas. He had a clear line of sight to the front entrance and the dimly lit path to the guest services building. He could see anyone making an approach toward the resort center from any direction. He noted with some dismay that he did not have a perfectly clear visual on the red gate at the rear of the property; there was a tree in the way. But he could see directly to the left and right of the gate, and he wasn't going to find a better vantage point than the flat rooftop.

Then he waited, watching.

Reid's plan was exceedingly simple. He knew that if Rais was true to his word, he would send one daughter in first, while he entered the resort elsewhere. He would try to elicit an emotional response in Reid—flush him out of hiding by using either Sara or Maya. But Reid would stand his ground, stay in his lofty position. He would be able to see his daughter from up there…and would also see Rais coming.

His failsafe was the bomb threat that he asked the cab driver to call in. As soon as the resort got the threat, they would evacuate their guests and call the police. He was hoping that with the evacuation, none of the guests would get caught in any potential crossfire. He knew that he was risking being arrested himself, but if it meant that at least one daughter was safe and knew the location of the other, it would be worth it.

His other failsafe, most uncomplicated of all, was the Glock in his hand. He wasn't taking any chances. Rais wanted a fight; he wanted to best Agent Zero in hand-to-hand combat. He had something to prove. Reid had nothing to prove to this psychopath. The only thing that mattered was his daughters' safety with as little collateral damage as possible.

If everything went according to plan, one of his daughters would appear. The bomb threat would be delivered. The grounds would be evacuated. Rais would attempt to enter the resort. As soon as he had eyes on Rais, Reid was going to shoot him—nonlethally, if he could exercise any measure of self-control—and then obtain the other daughter's location. The police would arrive, but the truth could be sorted later. The authorities could get to his other girl, and when Maria arrived in Croatia, she would help him.

It was certainly not flawless, but it was simple.

Reid waited. Every minute that ticked by felt like an hour. Every shift of the shadows gained his attention as trees swayed in the gentle breeze or guests roamed the walking paths. They had no idea what was about to happen.

What he wouldn't have given for a pair of binoculars. Or night vision goggles. Or both.

He checked his watch. If the cab driver came through, he would be calling the resort with the bomb threat in just a few minutes. Yet there was no sign of…

A silhouette appeared at the far end of the dimly lit walkway. Reid squinted hard, unsure of whether or not his eyes were playing tricks on him.

The figure was small, slight framed. She shuffled down the path, barely illuminated by the low-voltage lighting that lined the way to the building and his vantage point.

She had blonde hair. A tie-dyed shirt. White pants, with some sort of pattern on them…

Pineapples. He was sure of it.

Sara stepped listlessly down the path, her feet dragging slowly, her head bowed low so that her chin nearly touched her chest. Reid's heart surged with the desire to clamber down, to run to her, to hug her close to him and tell her that everything was going to be okay.

He tightened his grip on the Glock. He couldn't go to her. Not yet.

But it was her, clearly her, his little girl stepping cautiously forward. She looked terrified. Reid bit his lip to keep his eyes from welling. He had to stay focused, to keep his eyes open. This was what Rais wanted—for him to get distracted so that the assassin could get the drop on him.

That's not going to happen. I'm going to kill him.

He couldn't go to her, couldn't even call out to her without giving away his position. He had to stay put, to wait until there was another sign.

He didn't have to wait long, because a moment later, all hell broke loose.

Chapter Twenty

A sharp, blaring tone rang out over the entire resort, shrill and undulating. Reid winced with the tone; it was emitting from a loudspeaker not far from where he was lying in wait.

He knew immediately what it meant. The bomb threat had been called.

The resort staff hurried out from the building beneath him as guests crept out of their villas, confused and afraid. Shouts of warning in several languages filled the air, including English—he picked out a few phrases among the din as staff ushered guests toward the front entrance, assuring them that this was not a drill; they were evacuating, and everyone should proceed in an orderly fashion.

He glanced out over the front of the awning again…but Sara had seemingly vanished. *Where did she go?* Reid crawled frantically over the rooftop, looking over each edge for any sign of her, and saw none; only concerned hotel guests rushing for the exit.

Perhaps a well-meaning member of the hotel staff had spotted her and pulled her away, he thought. Regardless, he had seen her, he was certain of it, and now she was gone. He saw no other choice; he was not going to lose her again.

Reid scrambled over the edge of the building and down the latticework, dropping the last ten feet and tucking into a roll. He kept the pistol at his side as he looked around for Sara. There was still no sign of her. He sprinted around the building, toward the rear of the guest services and the too-blue pools.

His fingers gripped the Glock tightly. He was well aware that he was out in the open now. If the assassin was lurking about, he'd have an opportunity to get the drop on Reid.

Where is she?

The blaring alarm continued as Reid tracked his pistol forward. But he saw no one; the guests and employees had evacuated.

I've scared him away, Reid realized. Rais must have known that Reid would have a plan, but he must not have anticipated the noise and the pending police presence. The assassin wanted a fight, just the two of them. He didn't want an audience and he certainly didn't want the authorities. *He must have run away when he heard the alarm.*

As disappointed as he was that he wouldn't get the chance to kill the assassin, there were more pressing matters to deal with. The police would be there in moments. He had to get to Sara and find out where Maya was being held. Rais might try to double back, to meet him there instead. If Sara could help him convince the police, then an entire force could be there to save his other daughter.

Reid rounded the guest services building, trying to find Sara. The grounds were empty, but he kept his eyes open in case Rais was still present. He did not see any movement, anyone else, until he reached the building again.

As he approached from the rear, he saw a small figure standing at the edge of one of the pools. Her blonde hair was bathed in dim blue light as she stared into the water.

"Sara!" he called to her. "Sara, my god, you're okay…"

She flinched as he touched her shoulder. He knelt, his arms open, ready to engulf her in a hug, sweep her up, get her to safety…

She looked up at him. Her eyes were red-rimmed and puffy from crying, her cheeks sharp and her features entirely foreign.

Reid's arms fell limply to his sides. His mouth fell open but words failed.

"I'm sorry," the girl said in a whisper.

"You're not…" Reid's mind felt as if it had short-circuited. This girl was not Sara at all. She was older, at least eighteen, but short and thin-framed like his daughter. And wearing her clothes.

"I'm sorry," the girl said again. "He … he made me …"

"Where is she?" Reid gripped the girl's shoulder, harder than he intended. She shrank away from him; he had forgotten for a moment that he was still holding the Glock in his other hand. He quickly holstered it. "Where?"

The girl shook her head. "I don't know. I'm sorry. He made us switch clothes. He told me to come here, and keep my face hidden … and to give you this." She held something out to him. A folded slip of paper.

His fingers trembled as he opened it. There were only three words written on it, in tight, neat handwriting. *Wall,* the note said. *Minceta Tower.*

Reid crumpled the note as he clenched a fist. Rais had never intended to show up at the resort. He wasn't going to let Reid choose the location or set any terms. He still had both his daughters, and now he was baiting Reid into coming where he wanted him.

Sirens wailed from beyond the stone walls of the resort. "Go," Reid told the girl. "Get to the police. Tell them to call the American embassy. Tell them everything you know. Understand? Everything you know. They'll take care of you, okay?"

The girl nodded, tears welling anew in her eyes. "I'm sorry …" she said again.

"Go." He pushed her gently in the direction of the resort entrance. Her feet shuffled against the pavement—her feet in Sara's sandals. In his daughter's clothes. "Wait …" He cleared his throat and forced potential tears away. "Are they … when you last saw them, were they okay?"

The girl nodded. "But they won't be for long. They still believe … they think you'll find them."

I will find them. He nodded to her. "Go, hurry." He let the crumpled note fall from his hand and into the pool as the girl scurried away toward safety. The sirens were louder now, just beyond the stone wall, blending with the still-blaring tone of the resort's alarm.

Reid sprinted for the red gate, the rear entrance of the resort, and shoved through it as fast as his legs would carry him, toward the walls of Dubrovnik.

Villa Maya overlooked the coast and the Adriatic Sea to the south, so Reid ran parallel to the coastline for several blocks. The great stone walls that rose up from the sea protected the peninsular section of the city that jutted outward where the natural rocky cliffs could not. Minceta Tower, as the note had specified, was the highest point of the sea-facing wall, built in the fifteenth century at the behest of Pope Pius II to defend against the Turkish threat.

Try as he might to distract his mind with the facts, Reid's fury only grew as he sprinted in long strides toward the stone fortifications. Rais had given his word, and then betrayed it.

What did I expect? Reid scolded himself for being so naïve. He should have seen this coming, should have known that the assassin would double-cross him.

The entrance to the walls and the tower beyond was gated, closed off to tourists after dark. There was a small guard house, but no one inside. He checked the perimeter; there were cameras, but that was of little concern to him now. He shrugged out of his blazer and threw it over a shoulder as he climbed the gate. At the top, he laid the blazer over the sharp wire and scrambled over the fence, dropping safely on the other side, pulling the blazer down with him and putting it back on.

The walls were like a corridor, partitions on either side of him reaching just past his waist. He pulled out the Glock as he took a stone staircase up, two steps at a time, clearing the corner before continuing onward. The lighting was dim, the walls illuminated only from spotlights recessed into the sea cliffs and on the land side, shining upward and casting long shadows along his narrow route. He had roughly a six-foot span from each short parapet on either side—not much room to maneuver, but equally unfit for a surprise attack from the assassin. Still he could not help but feel like a rat in a maze.

His eyes adjusted to the moonlight and shadows as he followed the serpentine trail upward, up the slope of the hillside. Reid hazarded a glance over the edge. Sixty feet below the sheer cliff was a sharp, rocky outcropping, and beyond it the black water of the Adriatic.

The jagged battlements of Minceta Tower were just ahead, fully illuminated in white spotlights. A stone staircase led up to the darkened entrance of the castle-like tower. Reid's jaw clenched tightly as he drew near.

He's here. Rais had chosen a place that he could defend if needed, a place where he had the high ground, where Kent Steele would have to come find him. He was fully aware that he could be walking into a trap.

The narrow causeway widened into a semicircular balcony as he approached the tower, the walls on either side rising higher, nearly ten feet. No one would see them from the ground; they would be completely obscured by the parapets and tower. *This was what he wanted. Just me and him.*

His throat ran dry as he examined the stairs, the dark and open entrance, squinting to try to see some sign of life on or inside the tower. He could see nothing—at least not above him. But before him, on the wide balcony and between the high walls, was the vague lump of a shadow.

As he crept closer, he saw that the shape was a body.

The man was lying fetal on his side, facing the opposite direction. Reid knelt beside the body and gently rolled him over onto his back. The once-blue shirt of a security guard was stained and slick with blood. A gruesome smile had been sliced clear across his neck, the whites of his still-wide eyes shining in the moonlight.

A patrolman, Reid reasoned. Someone to make sure the tourists stayed off the walls at night. Unsuspecting and entirely innocent in all of this.

There was another object, small and silver and oblong, lying near the dead man's head. As Reid reached for it, it vibrated violently against the stone floor, startling him.

He flipped the phone open and slowly put it to his ear.

"Hello, Agent Steele."

A shiver ran down Reid's spine as he rose to his feet. He checked the tower in his periphery but still saw no movement.

"You lied to me," Reid said softly. "You gave your word and you broke it—"

"Yes," Rais interrupted. "A man who built a life on lies and murder broke his word to another man who built a life on lies and murder."

"No. I have a life. A real life. And at its center are two girls who have nothing to do with this. They are just children. Let them go. Come deal with me. That's what you want, right?"

"Throw your gun into the sea," the assassin ordered.

Reid hissed a scoff through his nose. Rais was most definitely in the tower; he was watching Reid at that very moment.

"Or what? You'll shoot me?" He knew that wasn't what Rais wanted.

"I was not entirely untrue to my word," the assassin said. "I did bring one girl. She is in the tower with me."

Reid's heartbeat doubled its pace. His first instinct was to sprint, run into the tower, find his daughter and shoot the assassin dead.

"She has a knife to her throat," Rais continued. "If you want her back alive, throw your gun into the sea. If you would like her blood to run down these stone stairs, then do what you're thinking. Keep your gun. Rush the tower. But I will kill her."

"Don't," Reid said quickly. "This is between you and me. It has nothing to do with her—"

"She is an instrument," Rais responded calmly. "Her purpose was to get you to this point. Her life now means nothing to me. You have a choice, Agent Steele. Keep your gun, rush the tower, and kill me—but she will be dead by then. You could save one daughter.

Trade one life for the assurance of the other. Or throw your gun, and perhaps you'll save both."

"Proof of life," Reid demanded. His voice sounded weaker than he intended. Rais had the upper hand in every way. "I want to hear her voice."

Rais chuckled. "You have no leverage to make demands. I will give you three seconds to make your decision."

Reid didn't hesitate. Contrary to the assassin's words, there was no choice. He would never risk sacrificing either of his girls. He heaved the Glock over the wall and into the Adriatic.

"Let me see her," he insisted. "At least hear her..." "The other gun," Rais said. "The one on your ankle. I believe you favor the Ruger."

Reid gritted his teeth so hard he felt they might crack, but he complied, tugging the LC9 loose and sending it into the sea after the Glock.

"And now the bag."

Reid had nearly forgotten about the small black duffel lying next to the guard's body. Angry, seething, he reared back and hurled the bag by its strap, up over the wall and into oblivion.

"I've done what you asked," he growled into the phone. "Now you have to give me something, anything... hello? Hello?!" Rais had ended the call. Reid threw the phone in fury, sending it skittering over the stones, and turned to rush into the tower.

But before he could take even two steps, a silhouette appeared in the dark doorway to Minceta Tower. The figure slowly descended the stairs, bathed in the white glow of the spotlights. He looked different than he had last time they had met, but the only thing Reid could focus on was his wild green eyes, shining like bright emeralds. His face was impassive, but his eyes were keenly grinning.

"No." Reid shook his head. "No, you bring her out. You bring her out here so I can see..." He trailed off as the realization struck him.

Stupid. His blood ran cold. *I've been so stupid. They're not here at all.* Rais had bluffed. Neither of his girls was on the walls. The assassin had come alone. His hands trembled with rage and remorse in equal measure.

Rais paused on the stairs, looking down on Reid with something that nearly approached pity. "Agent Steele. Your daughters were *never* here."

CHAPTER TWENTY ONE

Panic seized Reid's chest so tightly he staggered back a step, steadying himself against the wave of nausea that threatened to overtake him.

"What?" he heard himself whisper.

"Your daughters were never here in Croatia," the assassin repeated. "Your eldest is very smart. I thought that she might find a way to leave you something. So I made sure that she heard 'Dubrovnik.' I found her message to you in the motel." A smirk played on Rais's lips. He was enjoying this, enjoying Reid's shock and utter disbelief. "She led you here for me. I thought you might discover that before we landed, so there was a second plane in Nova Scotia. It departed ten minutes before your daughters arrived there, and it was bound for Dubrovnik. But the plane your daughters were on never came here. And so the authorities found nothing."

Reid shook his head slowly, refusing to believe it. "But the cargo depot... the textile mill..."

"Oh, the traffickers do use this place," Rais said casually. "But at my request they landed elsewhere. They are an unscrupulous group that had hoped to be Amun in the past. It was not difficult for me to convince them that Amun was still functioning underground, and that they could be welcomed into the fold." He chuckled. "From what I hear, you took care of several of their members. Two birds with one stone, as they say. Perhaps if you survive—if you win this night—you can still find them."

Reid's lower lip trembled as a fresh wave of horror crashed down upon him. "You..." He struggled to form the words. "You gave my daughters...to them?"

Rais frowned. "Of course I did. Don't you see? Not only will I not tell you where they are, but I don't *know* where they are. What matters is that you are here, with me. I have destroyed your family. Now I will destroy you."

Bile rose up in Reid's throat. His legs felt weak. He knew this man was a psychopath, a murderer, even a monster—but he had underestimated the full lengths to which one person was willing to go for such a seemingly insane belief. Reid had believed that Maya's message gave him an upper hand; that he was gaining on them. But he was merely being baited.

His girls could be anywhere. Finding them now would be an insurmountable task alone. He would have to contact the agency and turn himself in. Whatever it took.

But first, he had to deal with this animal, or else the specter of Amun would continue to haunt him to the ends of the earth.

Just let go, prodded the voice in his head. *Let go of the wrath. Be the man you know you are.* His life was not built on lies and murder, but that was all that Rais could understand. And because of that, Reid could always have the upper hand. He would not let his rage blindly control him.

He cleared his throat and kept the waver out of his voice as he said, "There's one problem with your plan." In his periphery he glanced down at the security guard's body. "You haven't destroyed anything. Not yet. My family is still out there, and I'm still breathing."

The assassin's smirk slackened, dragging his mouth into a frown.

"You have no love for anything or anyone," Reid continued. "Your vendetta and your beliefs fuel your actions. They motivate and guide you to a meaningless end. But here's the truth, Rais. You mean nothing to me. You're just another insurgent, a part of the job. My daughters might have been instruments to your ends, but to me, they are the ends. They're all that matters. I'm not going to waste my time on you. I'm going to go find my girls now."

His heart racing in his chest, Reid turned around and walked away, noting and relishing the look of absolute astonishment on Rais's usually passive face.

"No," the assassin muttered.

Reid counted his paces.

"No!" Rais snarled. "I have come too far! You will *not* turn your back on me!"

He heard footfalls pounding the stone stairs. Coming up behind him, fast. He counted. Of course he knew he could not just walk away from Rais—but making the assassin believe he would, taunting him and diminishing his belief, was his bluff. He knew from experience how blind rage breeds carelessness.

All he needed was a moment of carelessness. A split-second of negligence, the slightest window of opportunity.

Reid took one more step and crouched on his right knee. He swung his hips and cantilevered his body, bringing his left leg up and around in a vicious roundhouse kick.

As Rais rushed up to angrily attack from behind, Reid's heel connected with the side of the assassin's face. He felt the sharp impact up his calf, resonating through to his hip. Rais's head twisted first, his shoulders jerking wildly and his body following. He fell silently to the stone in a heap.

Reid did not wait around to inspect the damage or even to see if Rais was still conscious. He tucked into a roll and came up on his knees next to the guard's body. He did not expect a gun, but on the man's belt was another weapon—a thin leather blackjack, about ten inches long, one end curving into a beaver-tail shape and weighed heavily with a disc of lead. A well-placed blow with the blackjack could crack a skull like a melon.

Reid rose quickly and spun, rearing back with the leather-wrapped weapon—but an arm shot forward and stopped his forearm. Reid blinked in bewilderment. He had put nearly his entire body weight into that kick, yet Rais was standing, his lips snarling in the moonlight. The left half of the assassin's face was purple and slightly misshapen; he certainly had an orbital fracture, yet he had recovered as if nothing had happened.

He savagely twisted Reid's arm to one side. The familiar sensation of Kent Steele reflexes kicked in and he jumped, both feet leaving the air as he somersaulted with his twisted arm to avoid it snapping. Then he lurched forward, bending his arm as his elbow connected with the broken side of Rais's face.

The assassin staggered back two steps, but otherwise showed no reaction of pain or injury.

How? Reid wondered in frustration. *How can he take hits like that and keep coming like nothing happened?*

"Curious, isn't it." Rais grinned and wiped blood from his cheek. "Damaged nerves, courtesy of many previous encounters—including ours. It is not without its drawbacks, but is occasionally quite useful."

Damaged nerves. Reid's knowledge of the nervous system was admittedly limited, but if Rais could continue taking blows like that without feeling them, Reid would have to change his strategy. During their last encounter in Sion, he had stabbed the assassin half a dozen times in the back and chest—he could only hope the dead nerves did not extend to other parts of his body.

Rais reached into his jacket and produced a wickedly curved hunting knife, its blade razor sharp and glinting in the moonlight. Reid took an instinctive step back and tightened his grip on the blackjack.

"This knife killed the old man," Rais told him. "And it was at your daughter's throat. Yet I had the feeling it was not the first time she had a blade to her naked neck. It is no small wonder how you've come all this way and still cannot keep those close to you safe from—"

Reid leapt forward, his scorching anger rising up, getting the better of him. He swung the blackjack upward, but too wide; Rais skirted to one side and avoided it easily. But Reid did not let up. He swung the lead-laden weapon rapidly back and forth, arcing and coming close but missing by fractions of an inch each time.

A small voice at the back of his mind shouted a warning, told him that the assassin was getting inside his head, but he ignored it. The image of the glinting blade on either of his children's throats was too much to keep him thinking straight. He did not even realize that he was shouting unintelligibly, grunting louder in frustration with each near miss. Rais danced left and right, waiting for an opening, an opportunity.

Wait. Watch him. He's keeping his head turned. Reid feigned a swing and instead jumped backward two steps, breathing hard. The assassin seemed slightly winded as well, but he still wore his malicious grin—turned slightly to his left.

He's keeping his right eye on me. Reid understood immediately. The roundhouse kick to the face must have detached his retina or otherwise caused some amount of damage to Rais's left eye. He had to keep his head turned to see Reid attack from that side.

He circled slowly, like a shark, sidestepping to the left. As he did, Rais stepped in time to his right, keeping his head tilted further than he should have needed. For several seconds they circled, each waiting for the other to make a move.

Stay on his left. Reid moved steadily, refusing to make the move. His anger was still palpable, throbbing in his chest, every limb aching to take a shot, but his brain sent signals forcing them to hold. Wait. Watch. And then...

A shadow of agitation flickered across the assassin's face. Rais swiped across from the right and Reid leaned away from it—but it was a false lead. Instead of swiping outward, Rais tossed the knife to his left hand and jabbed forward. Reid tried to counter his weight to the other side quickly enough to avoid it, but the thrust came faster.

The knife pierced his abdomen just a finger's span to the right of his belly button. He twisted away before the curved tip penetrated more than an inch or two, but it was still plenty enough to send scorching pain throughout his torso.

He backpedaled several feet, taking small quick steps as he examined the wound with his fingertips. He refused to take his eyes off the assassin, but Rais held his ground, apparently relishing drawing blood.

It's shallow. His fingers came back slick and sticky. *Bleeding badly, but shallow. The abdominal wall and subcutaneous layers are more than an inch thick. He didn't puncture anything.* Reid didn't know if that was true or if it was something his mind was trained to tell himself to keep going—but it hardly mattered in the moment. This was a fight to the death.

Rais approached slowly, the knife loose in his grip. The bloody tip was pointed at Reid's heart.

He's going to fight dirty. You have to fight dirty too. Words he had once said to Maya flashed through his mind: *Don't fight fair. Do whatever you need to do.* He had to do that now if he was ever going to see or speak to his daughters again.

Maneuver around him. Force him to turn his head.

Reid dropped the blackjack. It landed on the stone with a heavy thud. The pain in his abdomen was making his limbs weak, which would make his blows sluggish. Besides, he didn't need it for what he was planning.

Rais paused, raising an eyebrow at the move. He kept the hunting knife in his loose grip, holding it with just his fingertips. Reid read the body language; the assassin was going to attempt a flick of a slash at a soft part of his body. Likely his throat. If he was successful, it would be the end of their duel. There would be no coming back from that.

He gritted his teeth and let Rais get a bit closer. Then he lurched forward and feigned to the right. Rais turned his head, tracking the movement with the knife tip—and Reid crouched low, bounced off his foot, back to the left and into the assassin's blind spot. He stuck out his elbow as he crossed in front and jammed it into Rais's solar plexus. The younger man let out a surprised whoosh of breath as he doubled over, giving Reid the precious two seconds he needed to slump his shoulders and shrug out of his brown blazer.

As it slipped down the length of his forearms he grabbed the ends of both sleeves and spun around behind Rais, wrapping the blazer around the assassin's body and yanking upward. Years-old training flooded flawlessly back into his muscle memory—he was using it as a *kusari-fundo*, a Japanese technique that utilized a length of chain, rope, or, in this case, a blazer.

He forced both of Rais's arms up into the air at an awkward angle and twisted the sleeves around his throat, and then brought them together at the nape of his neck. Reid turned his body and dropped to one knee, at the same time pulling the gathered sleeves over his shoulder with his full weight behind the throw.

Rais's entire body left the ground with a sharp gasp of shock. For a moment he was weightless, his head on Reid's shoulder and his legs straight up in the air.

Then he came crashing down, flat on his stomach and face. The dull slap of flesh against stone was accompanied by a sharp crack of bone as something in his body gave to the unyielding surface.

Breathing hard, Reid reached to snatch up the hunting knife—or tried to. A hand grabbed at his wrist and yanked, sending him stumbling to regain his balance. Rais twisted and kicked at Reid in a blow that ordinarily would have merely glanced off of him, if not for its trajectory. His foot landed squarely on the abdominal stab wound.

He staggered again and cried out in pain as Rais scrambled to his feet and shrugged out of the tangled blazer. The assassin swung low, scooping the air with two fingers extended, as if he were swinging a bowling ball.

Both fingers found purchase in Reid's open wound.

Reid's mouth fell open in a wide, silent scream. No sound came; his breath caught in his throat with the inexorable pain. Rais's index and middle finger dug deeper into him, holding firm like steel. Reid wrapped both hands around the assassin's arm, trying in vain to pull free, but his limbs quickly drained of all strength.

Rais leaned into it, pushing forward, his bloody, pulpy mess of a face only inches from Reid's. His wild green eyes were unyielding, his teeth gritted and lips pulled back in a snarl.

Reid reached for Rais's throat, his face, anything to stop him, but he had no power left in his grip. All that was left was the pain, radiating from his core to every part of him.

In response, Rais swung his skull forward in a powerful head-butt. Reid couldn't pull away, so instead he turned his head and the blow landed solidly across his cheek and jaw, sending his head lolling backward and reeling. He barely felt the fist that connected a moment later with the side of his face.

This is it. The last thing he would ever see was this maniacal fanatic's bloody, snarling visage. Not his girls. There would be no saving them now. He had failed.

CHAPTER TWENTY TWO

Rais grunted and pushed forward again, sending a fresh shockwave through Reid's body. He gasped as he stepped backward in a vain attempt to alleviate the pressure.

His right heel touched something on the ground behind him.

He did not dare look back, but he knew what it was. The security guard's body. His foot was against it, and Rais was unaware, his bared teeth and wild eyes unblinking.

Reid carefully lifted his foot and stepped backward, hoping he would step far enough to clear the body. As he moved, Rais moved with him, forward, maintaining his iron-like grip on the stab wound.

Reid cleared the body.

Rais did not.

The assassin's snarl melted as his foot pushed against the downed guard. He stumbled forward. His grip on Reid came loose as his hands shot out to catch himself. Reid jumped to the side as Rais fell forward, tripping over the body he had left there.

Everything hurt, and he had barely an ounce of strength left in him, but he was free. He had little chance of running from Rais now. Instead he hurried painfully toward the only sanctuary he could see: he clambered on his hands and feet up the stone stairs of Minceta Tower.

As he reached the dark entranceway he glanced over his shoulder to see Rais pulling himself to his feet. The assassin was slow to get up. He was injured as well; the shoulder throw must have at least hurt him and, with any luck, broken something that would impede him.

Only a few feet beyond the door inside the tower was inky darkness, strangely welcoming, the stone cool to the touch beneath his hands. Reid felt along the floor and rounded wall, creeping forward inches at a time, half-dragging his nearly useless body behind him. He wheezed in pain with every breath and mentally cursed himself for it; he would be easy to locate in the darkness if he couldn't stay silent.

Behind him came a panting heave of a sigh as Rais reached the top of the stairs. A glimpse at the doorway showed him the assassin's silhouette, heavily favoring his right leg and holding one hand over his ribs.

Even so, Rais hissed a quiet laugh. "You've spent so much time ... coming for me." His phrases were punctuated with an inward, pained rasp through his gritted teeth. "But now, you run *from* me."

Reid bit the inside of his cheek and gasped shallow breaths to keep quiet, continuing to feel his way around Minceta Tower. The medieval fortress was empty inside, merely stone walls and stairs, weathered by time and tourism. He reached a rounded corner and felt his way around it, putting out both arms at nearly full span to find himself in a short corridor.

"A train station in Denmark ... the ice rink in Sion ... twice now you have failed to kill me ... and I, you ... there won't be a third." His voice was getting closer now; Rais was moving faster than Reid.

As he pulled himself along the corridor the relief of stone began to take shape before his eyes. They were adjusting to the darkness—no, there was a light source somewhere nearby, dim but present. He rose to his feet and shuffled forward, trying to quicken his pace.

"Look at what it took to get you to me." Closer still. Rais had reached the corridor. "What I had to do. To take what is most precious to you in this world."

The corridor opened; to Reid's left he could see the faint outline of a narrow stone staircase leading upward, the aperture at the top illuminated in bluish moonlight. *The top of the tower.*

Rais's shambling footfalls ceased. Reid paused as well, holding his breath in the absolute silence of the tower. "Do you want to know how I found them?" His voice lowered to a whisper. "Do you know how I knew you, Reid Lawson?"

An involuntary shudder crept up Reid's spine at the mention of his name, his real name. Ever since discovering the girls missing, he hadn't stopped long enough to consider how the Amun assassin had found his home in Alexandria. He had assumed it was a CIA mole, like the former director Steve Bolton, who had provided Rais with the information.

Every instinct told him to keep moving, to climb the stairs. Reach the top of the tower. Hold the high ground. The narrow stairs would make for a defensible position, even in his state. Yet he could not move, and not for lack of strength. He was uncontrollably compelled to hear it.

"It was your wife."

Crouched in the shadow of the staircase, Reid froze, certain that he misheard the words.

"Kate Lawson."

No. There was no way. *Kate didn't know about me. About my past.*

"You don't believe me," said Rais quietly. "She worked at the museum. Restorations department."

Reid shivered, suddenly feeling very, very cold.

"At the time ... I didn't know who she was."

No. A vision of Kate danced across his conscious. Smiling, happy. Alive. *Make him stop.*

"I didn't know the ... catalyst that it might be."

Reid's legs suddenly felt weak. He dropped to his knees on the stone.

"I didn't even know her name. All I had was a photo, and a location."

"Stop," Reid hissed to the darkness. "You're lying."

Rais chuckled. "No, Kent Steele. Agent Zero. Reid Lawson. Whoever you really are." He paused for a long moment. "Amun sent me to kill your wife."

"It's not true," he moaned. "It's not." But even as he said it, a headache spun into the front of his skull, and a new memory flashed into his mind—no matter how much he hopelessly wished it wouldn't.

You're at the black site, designation H-6. The Special Forces troop stationed there calls it Hell Six. You believe Sheikh Mustafar knows more than he's telling, but interrogation tactics are proving fruitless.

Then—there's a call for you. It's Deputy Director Cartwright. Your boss. He doesn't mince words.

Your wife, Kate, had died.

"You..." Reid stammered.

Local PD responded. The official report was that she had suffered a sudden, devastating stroke. But you know better.

It happened as she was leaving work, walking to her car.

Sudden paralysis of the diaphragm that led to respiratory failure.

She simply stopped breathing.

"God, no..."

They had gotten to her. Your target, the organization you knew only as the Fraternity back then... they had sent someone to the US, just for her.

To send you a message. You were getting too close.

Suddenly a deluge of fragmented memories flooded back to him concurrently: Kate's autopsy revealed that she had ingested a high level of TTX—tetrodotoxin, a powerful poison that causes respiratory paralysis. His wife had died alone on the sidewalk, appearing to have choked on nothing at all.

Almost immediately, the CIA hacked the database and altered the records to reflect an embolism that caused a sudden ischemic stroke. The lie that he, Reid Lawson, had genuinely believed for the last two years.

The same lie he had told his children. His wife's parents. Her sister.

And yet Kent Steele knew the truth, and had kept it buried, repressed, shoved down deep.

Your mind fills in the gaps, Maria had once told him about the memory suppressor. *Your brain makes up the details for you.*

He had convinced himself of the lie, because the heartache of losing her was already too much. But her murder was his fault.

Agent Kent Steele knew that then. Mad with grief, he had gone on his murderous spree across Europe and the Middle East, leaving a trail of bodies in his wake. He tortured anyone who might have had information. He promised them amnesty for intel, and then he killed them anyway.

The agency had tried to call him back in. He ignored them.

On his knees on the cold stone floor of Minceta Tower, Reid heaved a single, racking sob that boiled up from deep inside him and escaped his cracked lips.

He heard shuffling footsteps in the darkness. *This is what that murderer wants,* he realized vaguely. Rais really had destroyed his family; not when he took the girls, but two years earlier. *He's been waiting, biding his time to remind me of the truth. Waiting for me to be at my weakest.*

He would get no such satisfaction.

A savage fury rose up in him. He wanted to tear this man apart, to rend him limb from limb. To watch the light die in his eyes. This killer—this *monster*—had taken the most precious gift he had ever received in his life, the one that he never felt he fully deserved. The mother of his children. The greatest love of his life.

He understood now. The rumors of his rampage that he couldn't comprehend, the allegations of ferocity that he previously could not fathom... he understood it all now.

With a primal shout he lurched forward in the direction of the shuffling footfalls, keeping his head low and his arms outstretched in front of him. There was still pain, pain in his abdomen and face and limbs, but it paled in comparison to the fresh anguish in his heart.

Reid struck the assassin in his broken midsection with a shoulder and Rais yelped, but Reid didn't stop there. He drove the vicious tackle onward until both men slammed agonizingly into a stone wall of the corridor. Colors swam in Reid's vision as they both fell to the floor in a heap, but again he pushed physical boundaries aside as he groped at the air until his hands found purchase around Rais's throat.

He squeezed with all the strength he could muster. Beneath him Rais belched choking gasps as his fingers clawed at Reid's arms, his face, his neck. He leaned forward, pushing his body weight into the stranglehold, animalistic grunts from Reid's own throat mingling with the dying rasps of his wife's killer.

He was going to crush this man's windpipe, and then he was going to listen to the mellifluous sounds of him choking to death.

Reid was barely aware that the hands had fallen away from his face before a solid object struck the side of his head with such force that blinding white flashed before his eyes like lightning. Dazed, he loosened his grip and fell slightly aside—enough for Rais to push out from beneath him and scramble away on his hands and knees.

Reid's head throbbed. His vision blurred and his fingers came away wet from his temple. *A loose stone*, he reasoned. *Too hard to have been a fist.* The fuzziness subsided enough for him to see Rais pulling himself up the stone stairs, bathed in blue moonlight, toward the top of the tower with wheezing, labored breaths.

"No," he growled. "You're not getting away from me." Reid pulled himself to his feet with a painful moan and staggered after him. He leaned most of his body weight against the black iron railing as he forced himself up, step by step.

Rais had reached the top of the tower, but was nowhere to be seen. *Lying in wait*, Reid thought, reminding himself that the assassin was armed with a stone. He didn't care. He was going to see this through, one way or another. At the top of the stairs he stepped through the open doorway and into the moonlight—and then immediately staggered backward again as a fist came sailing down, a sizeable chunk of stone within it.

The rock missed his skull by fractions of an inch and glanced off his shoulder instead. Reid responded in kind, twisting his body to the left and landing a solid jab to Rais's nose. It flattened beneath his fist and the assassin fell backward.

The top of Minceta Tower was a wide, circular stone rooftop surrounded by slotted parapets. Typically it served as one of the most popular vantage points in Dubrovnik, if not all of Croatia, but on this night, it would serve only as the site of death for one of the two men who fought with their last ounces of strength atop the seaside fortress.

Reid knelt beside Rais before he could recover and planted one knee firmly on the assassin's throat, as he had before with the supervisor at Port Jersey. He leaned on the leg, watching Rais's face turn red and then purple, his green eyes wide and staring up at the night sky. In under a minute it would be over.

Not just for him. Not just for me. For Kate. For my daughters…
My daughters.

It wasn't over. It wouldn't be over. The girls were still out there, and even when this was finished he would still have to find them. He couldn't simply trust that the CIA or Interpol would locate them. He needed something to go on.

As much as he wanted to end Rais's life right then and there, the man still had at least one piece of information to give him. He removed his knee from the murderer's throat and leaned close to his purple, bruised, and broken face.

"Tell me where they landed," he said quietly. "My girls. Where were they taken?"

Rais replied with a wet gasp. Bloody spittle erupted from his lips.

Reid lifted the assassin's head with both hands and slammed it down onto the stones. Rais grimaced in agony, his eyes squeezed shut.

"Where?" He slammed the killer's head down again, harder this time. "Where?!"

Rais's split lips moved as he wheezed, trying form words. "Slo … vah …"

"Slovakia? What city?" Reid demanded. "Kosice? Bratislava?"

Rais gasped as he tried to suck in another breath.

In sheer exasperation, Reid slammed his head down once more, leaving a round, red spatter against the stones. "Give me something," he snarled through gritted teeth. "How do you contact them? Where are they headquartered? Your death can be slow and horrible. Or I can split your skull quickly." He leaned closer, hissing into the assassin's ear. "You took my daughters. You killed my wife, you son of a bitch. You owe me something."

"I…I did…"

"Did what? What did you do?" Reid's hands shook with rage. "What did you do with them?!"

"Didn't," Rais rasped. He reached up with one shaky hand and gripped Reid's shoulder, using it to slowly pull himself to a seated position.

The assassin's face was a bloody mess, his nose lying crooked and broken, one eye swollen to little more than a crescent. The back and side of his head was slick in the moonlight; his skull was cracked. He was no longer a threat. He was already a dead man. As Reid had threatened, it was only a matter of time.

"Didn't…" His voice was croaking and hoarse, and every breath came with a crackling hiss from his damaged throat. "Didn't…kill her."

Reid scoffed and shoved his hand away violently. "You did. You told me you did."

"I was…sent." He coughed and spat a mouthful of blood onto the stone. "But some…someone else…got there first."

"No." Reid got to his feet, standing over the assassin, his fists balled at his sides. "You did it. I remember it now. Tetrodotoxin. You poisoned her."

Rais shook his head slowly. "Wish…I did. Would have…cut her throat. But…I don't…poison."

He looked up at Reid and met his gaze with his one good eye. There was no discernible deceit behind it. Reid turned away from that eye, refusing to believe it. *He's lying. After everything he's said and done…after all the lives he's taken and the attempts on mine, I know he would say anything.*

But then… Rais had to know, had to feel that he was already dead. Kent Steele had won. The assassin was useless and broken.

Reid pressed his fingers to his temples and forced himself to think, to try to conjure a memory of Rais, or anyone from Amun, ever using a poison like TTX.

None came.

It's not his style. He kills with guns, knives, and his bare hands.

Reid hissed another scoff before turning back to Rais. He grabbed two handfuls of the man's black jacket and hefted him to his feet. Rais moaned torturously with the sudden movement, but Reid didn't care. He was incensed, confused, and thoroughly maddened by his fallible memory. The lies. The deceit. The death.

"Then who?" He shook Rais like a limp doll in his hands. "If it wasn't you, then who?"

Rais groaned again. His legs trembled beneath him, threatening to give out. One bloody hand reached up and clasped around Reid's left fist. The assassin leaned forward, his head nearly coming to rest on Reid's shoulder.

"Don't you know?!" Reid nearly screamed.

"Yes." He coughed blood onto the front of Reid's shirt. "It was … CIA."

Before Reid could react, before he could even suck in another breath, Rais pushed both feet hard against the stones beneath them, his full weight leaning against Reid. They fell backward together, hitting the partition between parapets at waist level.

Still clutching each other, the two men tumbled end over end off of Minceta Tower, falling forty feet through silent darkness to the unforgiving stone below.

CHAPTER TWENTY THREE

Maya held Sara close to her, one arm hugged around her younger sister's shoulders as the white cargo van rumbled down a highway. To her right was the brown-skinned girl with the swollen eye from the plane, the one she had been calling Jersey. Across from her, seated on the floor, were three other girls. One of them stared at nothing in particular on the floor, never once lifting her gaze or attempting to communicate.

The other two were clearly drugged, their eyes barely open or not at all, their heads lolling listlessly with every bump in the road.

Once the plane from Nova Scotia had landed and the rear hatch opened, the girls had been immediately ushered out and into the back of two waiting vans. There were six men in all, reeking of cigarette smoke and carrying some form of weapon, pistols and submachine guns, and they split the girls into two groups.

Mercifully, they had kept Sara and Maya together. How long that would last, she didn't know.

As soon as she was out of the plane's hold, Maya stole glances to the left and right. Wherever they were, it was night, and there was no one else on the tarmac. A lonely freight terminal stood at a distance to the plane's left; to the right, only darkness dotted with runway lights.

Then the most bewildering thing had happened: Rais, who had accompanied them on the plane, split off from the group and simply walked away. He did not say a word—did not even look at them, not once, as he strode off across the dark tarmac.

He simply left, and the girls were put into the van.

Maya's heart raced with panic as her mind raced with possibilities. It took her a few minutes to work it out, but she was able to make some suppositions from Rais's abandonment of them. The first, and most crushing, was that they had likely not landed in Dubrovnik at all. Though she had no way of being certain, she was fairly sure that Croatia had been a red herring designed to throw the authorities, and their father, off the trail.

The second thing she surmised, with no small amount of alarm, was that they had fulfilled their usefulness to the assassin, and he was now handing them over to these Slavic traffickers. They were no longer special; their names and relations meant nothing to these men. They were merely two more faces to do with whatever they had planned for the girls in the van.

The final thing she had realized was that their father was heading into a trap, one set by Rais. This was based on not only her first two realizations, but also by what she witnessed when she reached the van. The traffickers forced Sara to exchange clothes with the blonde girl from the plane, the one Maya had been thinking of as Oklahoma. They did so, Oklahoma trembling in fear of the unknown and Sara moving slowly, mechanically, and listlessly.

Sara was still in a stupor, in some state of catatonia that Maya could not break.

The blonde girl was taken away in the same direction that Rais had stalked off in. Maya knew full well what that meant; though a few years older, she was the same height and relative build as Sara. In her clothes, under the cover of darkness, Oklahoma could pass as her little sister.

Then the doors to the van had closed and the two vehicles rumbled away.

The only light in the rear cabin came through the windshield; there were no windows in the back of the van. The seats had been removed, so the six girls sat on the floor, huddled three to a side. Maya noted as her eyes adjusted to the dimness that the interior latches had been removed; there was no way to open the doors from her position. A grate of steel had been welded between the rear and the front seats, where one man drove and another sat shotgun.

They had been driving for hours; Maya wasn't sure exactly how long, but her legs were cramping from being seated in the same position for such a length of time. Still, she hoped against hope that they never reached their destination, because she could only partially imagine what might await them.

Suddenly the van bounced over a jarring rut in the road. The girl sitting across from Maya, one of the pair who had obviously been drugged, slumped forward. She didn't even try to stop herself as her head smacked against the metal floor of the van.

Maya instinctively reached out to help her, touching her shoulder—and then immediately yanked her hand back.

The girl's skin was ice cold. As the van passed under the orange glow of a streetlight, Maya caught a glimpse of her face. Both lips were blue.

Maya drew her knees to her chest and pulled Sara tighter, shuddering from head to toe. She couldn't tear her gaze from the lifeless girl; it was only a small mercy that her eyes were closed.

Warm fingers touched her forearm and she jumped again. "Hey." Jersey, the girl beside her, spoke in a whisper. "It's okay."

Maya shook her head as fresh tears welled in her eyes. Hadn't she scolded herself more than once for saying the same thing to Sara? "It's not," she whispered back. "It's not. Nothing about this is okay."

Jersey bit her lip for a moment, glancing down at the girl on the floor. "At least this way," she said, "they can't hurt her anymore."

Maya wiped her eyes, finally forcing herself to look elsewhere. It was a horrifically grim outlook to have—though not untrue.

"Where are they taking us?" she asked.

Jersey shook her head. "I don't know. But... there's something you should know." She looked past Maya, at the younger girl nestled against her. "They never put us in groups like this unless they're moving us. When we get to wherever we're going... there's a good chance that they'll—"

The man in the passenger seat rapped angrily against the steel grate with two knuckles and barked harshly at them in his foreign tongue. Maya didn't need to know his language to know that he was threatening them into silence.

Jersey fell quiet, but Maya already knew what she was going to say. *They'll separate us. They'll take Sara from me.* She told herself that she couldn't let that happen, but she already knew there was little she could do about it.

She leaned her head against her sister so her cheek was touching Sara's forehead. In as low a voice as she could muster, she said, "I know you're in there. I know you can see and hear everything that's going on. I don't think your mind wants to admit or process what's happening, but... but you have to, Sara."

It was time to face hard facts. Rais was going after their father, and was going to use another girl as a decoy while they were taken elsewhere, possibly to another country. These traffickers were operating on an international level; they were careful professionals who had done this before, had not yet been apprehended, and would do it again.

For them, her and her sister, there would be only one thing waiting for them on the other side of this journey—and it was lying at her feet, cold-skinned and blue-lipped. That was the end of their road if they didn't do something about it, even if that something might mean the same end.

"You have to be strong," Maya urged her sister quietly. "You have to snap out of this. The second you see anything that looks like an opportunity, you need to take it. Fight back with everything you have. If you can run, run like your life depends on it. Because... because it does, Sara. Your life depends on it."

She looked down into her sister's face, hoping for any sign of life behind her eyes. And there was one—a single tear rolled down her cheek and spilled onto the pink T-shirt she had exchanged with Oklahoma.

Sara's lips moved, only slightly, with no sound, or so little sound that Maya couldn't hear it. She craned neck so her ear was right next to Sara's mouth.

And she heard it: "I want to go home."

Maya squeezed her eyes shut and forced herself not to cry. Not while she was telling her sister she needed to be strong. "Me too, peanut. Please listen to me. Be strong. Think of Dad. Think of Mom. Think of whatever you need to, to remind yourself that this isn't the end—"

The brakes of the van squealed in protest as it rolled to a stop. Both men got out, and a moment later Maya could hear them chattering with others outside the vehicle. Then the rear doors creaked open and an intensely bright flashlight beam fell across them. Maya shielded her eyes until it was swept away, leaving only the silhouettes of four men.

One of the men lifted an arm, pointing and speaking brusquely in a Slavic language. Suddenly arms were reaching inside the van, trying to tear Sara away from her.

CHAPTER TWENTY FOUR

Reid waded through darkness, impossibly slow. Maybe not moving at all—he had no limbs. He was disjointed from his body, somewhere in a black abyss. Or nowhere. There was no sound, no color. No feeling.

"Kent?"

A voice. Not far. He looked around—if there even was an around to see. It was a woman. It sounded almost like...

Kate? He tried to call out to her, but had no voice.

"Jesus, Kent..."

The voice again. *Kate!* He was sure of it.

A brilliant white light exploded above him. He couldn't look directly at it, but he knew what it was.

"Stay with me, Kent!"

Kate. The light was a beacon. She was calling him home.

No, he realized—it couldn't be. Kate didn't know Kent. She knew Reid. Her husband, father of her children. Accessory to her murder.

The light went out. Then: warm lips on his. A scent. Flowery. Lavender.

Next: the pain. Pain everywhere, rushing back into his core, radiating out to his limbs, through his skull. As suddenly as a stroke, as easily as telling a lie, he had a body again. And he knew it because of the pain.

Reid turned his head, coughed, tasted blood. It was dark out. Bright stubborn spots in his vision impeded his view, but as they slowly dissipated he began to remember. Minceta Tower loomed over him—and another form. A woman. Blonde hair. Gray, worried eyes.

Maria. He tried to say it, but only coughed violently again.

"You scared me to death," she said in a deep sigh. "Don't try to move until I can figure out what you've done to yourself."

He didn't do this to himself. He was lying at the base of the medieval fortress. He had fallen off—no, been pushed off, along with…

Reid ignored Maria's warning and rolled to his right, off of the soft object beneath him and onto the cool stone. He turned his head; Rais's one open green eye returned his gaze. The back of his head was split open, its contents spilled in a gory halo.

If Reid could have laughed, he might have. *He broke my fall.* The man who believed it was his destiny to kill Kent Steele had unintentionally saved his life.

He sat up slowly with a long groan. Everything hurt. He wiggled each finger, flexed his arms and legs. Nothing seemed broken. He wiped his bleary eyes and regarded Maria. She was really there, kneeling beside him, looking terrified and relieved at the same time. In one hand was a small white wand—a penlight. The white light he had seen. It wasn't a beacon at all; she had checked his pupils for a sign of life.

He had a thousand questions, but they would have to wait. "Help me up," he murmured, offering her a hand.

She frowned. "Kent…I think you fell off the tower. Can you even stand?"

"One way to find out."

She scoffed and helped pull him to his feet. He groaned again. *I'm not going to get far in this state,* he thought irritably. But his legs held, shaky as they were.

"Listen, if you can move, then we should go," Maria said quickly. "That dead security guard's radio was just squawking. It won't be long until someone comes looking for him."

Reid nodded. "Yeah. We should go." He reached down and grabbed hold of Rais's left leg.

"What the hell are you doing?" she insisted.

He pulled, but he didn't have enough strength to get anywhere.

"Kent!" Maria barked. "What do you think you're doing?"

"Throwing his body into the Adriatic Sea," he muttered. He didn't have the faculty at the moment to fully explain it to her, but he knew it was what he needed to do before he could leave. This monster wearing a human face had come for his wife, had come for his daughters, and had come for him. Twice he had been left for dead and returned. Even now, with his skull open and his brains spilled on the walls of Dubrovnik, Reid was not going to take any chance at all.

You're not thinking straight. You're concussed.

I don't care. I'm doing this.

He squeezed his eyes shut. Had those words been said aloud, or in his head? He wasn't sure. He turned to Maria. "You can either help me and we do this quickly, or you can watch me struggle."

"My god," she murmured. But then she grabbed onto the other leg and together they dragged the corpse of Rais roughly twenty feet along the wall, where the barrier between stone and sea rose only a few feet high. They heaved his remains onto the ramparts, and then sent him tumbling over the wall.

Reid leaned over to watch as Rais fell past the recessed spotlights and bounced once off of the slick rocky outcropping below. He watched as the black sea swallowed the body, pulling it out with the tide.

"All right now," Maria said softly. "Let's go." She supported him under one arm and together they moved as quickly as they could away from the tower, off of the walls. They were nearly at the gate when they spotted a bouncing flashlight beam and ducked into the shadows as a Croatian patrolman passed them by, chattering into his radio. Once he was past they moved again, out of the unlocked gate and to a white coupe that Maria had waiting nearby.

She helped him into the passenger's seat first and then drove rapidly away from the coast, toward the city center.

"Where are we going?" he asked, his voice weak and wavering.

"Someplace safe," Maria said simply.

Reid shook his head. "They're still out there somewhere. I need to...need to find them."

"I know," Maria said quietly. "But you're in terrible shape. You need to at least get patched up. You can't keep going like this. Get some rest, even if just for a short while."

"They might not have a short while." Reid stared out the window.

After a few silent minutes, Maria asked, "Do you want to tell me what happened?"

"He baited me," Reid admitted. "He knew I would come." Though the pain in his body was still present and reaching, his head was clearing, no longer swimming in the fog of near-unconsciousness. "Did you know about her?"

Maria shook her head. "Who?"

"Kate."

She sighed ruefully. "Oh, Kent. You remember?"

"I do now. But not thanks to you. Did you know?"

Her expression was empathetically woeful. "Yes," she admitted in a whisper. "I'm sorry. It just didn't...it didn't feel like something you needed to deal with right now. You said it yourself before: sometimes ignorance really can be bliss."

"Bliss." He scoffed loudly. "That wasn't your call to make. I deserved to know. More importantly, I deserved to hear it from someone I trust. Not... *him*."

"You're right. And I'm so sorry for keeping it from you. It's not much of a defense, but it's the only one I have...her murder was what spurred your rampage before. You became obsessed. You didn't listen to anyone, not even me. You became violent and cold. When I saw you again, back at that fountain in Rome, and you mentioned an embolism, I decided not to tell you the truth out of fear that you would go back to that version of Kent." She paused for a long moment. "Maybe ignorance isn't bliss. Sometimes it's just...impartial."

He stared out the window again. He didn't want to look at her—not because of his anger, but because if he saw her face he would have to admit that she might have been right.

"Do you know who did it?" he asked candidly.

Maria frowned. "Well…yes. Kent, it was Rais. He poisoned Kate—"

"He didn't. He told me so himself, right before we fell off the tower. He was sent to kill her, but someone else got to her first."

"You don't honestly believe that, do you?"

Reid nodded. "I do. He wanted to be the one to do it. He would have wanted to take the credit for hurting me like that. But in the end, despite how completely backwards his sense of belief and morals might be, he couldn't accept responsibility for it. He had nothing to gain from admitting it."

"I hate to say it, but that makes strange sense." Maria turned the car toward the orange and white villas of Old Town Dubrovnik, maintaining the speed limit and keeping a watchful eye on the rearview mirror. "So…did he know who it was?"

"He claimed he did." *CIA.* Those had been Rais's last words. Reid believed that the assassin had not actually been his wife's killer—but he couldn't be sure if pinning it on the agency was genuine, or one final taunt. *I'll sure as hell find out, though.*

"Are you going to tell me …?" Maria prodded.

Reid turned to her. "My girls never landed in Dubrovnik; Rais handed them off to traffickers in Slovakia. By now they could be anywhere. I can't find them alone. I need help, and I'm not sure it can be the agency. I really want to trust you. I think maybe I *need* to trust you, or else I might go insane. So I need to know if you'll make that choice."

"The choice between you or the agency?"

"Between me," Reid said, "and everyone else. Anyone else."

"It's you," she said without hesitating. "It always will be."

"Thank you," he murmured. Regardless of what had happened with Kate and who might have known about it, he needed Maria's help if he was going to have any chance of finding the girls. She had been there for him before, and she was there for him now.

Maria pulled the white coupe off the road and into the lot of a gas station. She eased to a stop alongside the building, just outside the door to the men's restroom, and put the car in park.

"What's this?" Reid asked. "What are we doing here?"

"You're not going anywhere until you get yourself cleaned up," Maria explained. "Give me one sec." She got out of the car, pushed open the restroom door, and checked it to make sure it was clear before coming around to Reid's side.

"Wait," he protested as she opened the car door. "Did you not hear what I just said about the girls? We need to go. We have to follow the lead..."

Maria shook her head. "Kent, you're covered in blood. You're stabbed. You fell off a damn tower! I know you well enough to know that a hospital is out of the question, but there's a field kit in the trunk. At least let me clean you up as best I can. Then, I promise we'll go. Together."

He had to admit that she was right. He was in no condition to go running off again. Besides, they would have to secure better transport than a white coupe to get to Slovakia. Still, now that the Rais ordeal was over and his focus was back on the girls, his heart broke anew at the thought of them out there alone in the hands of traffickers.

"Hey. Come on," Maria coaxed gently. She helped him out of the car and retrieved a black bag from the trunk. Then, while she supported him under one shoulder, they entered the restroom and Maria locked the door behind them. The bathroom was small, two stalls and a urinal, tiled in white and surprisingly clean. "Sit," she ordered as she lowered the lid on the first toilet.

He did as he was told, easing himself down with a groan. Maria knelt before him on the tile, opened the bag, and pulled out various first-aid implements. "You should have waited for me," she noted. "I was en route."

"Couldn't. Rais lied, told me he had the girls. God, he..." Reid scoffed. "He even sent another girl that looked like Sara, probably a trafficking victim, to throw me off. Maybe I wasn't using my head. But I couldn't risk it. How did you find me?"

"There was a transponder in your bag." She took up a pair of medical shears and carefully cut off his bloodied T-shirt. "Mitch gave me the frequency to trace it. The signal went dead, but I had the last-known coordinates. And you were still there. Lean back a little. This is going to sting."

Reid winced through his teeth as she cleaned the blood from around the minor stab wound in his abdomen. He gripped the steel handicap bar bolted to the wall of the stall and held his breath as she pinched the edges of his wound and applied a liquid adhesive to the skin to hold it shut. Then she pressed a bandage over the wound site, and he let out a relieved breath.

"There's something else you should know." She tore open an alcohol swab and dabbed at the dried blood on his face. "Strickland is here, in Croatia."

Reid had nearly forgotten about Agent Strickland, the CIA's alleged answer to his kidnapped girls. "Good. Maybe he can help, if we can get him intel. Work on two fronts—"

"No, Kent. He's here for you. His orders are to find and apprehend you … by whatever means necessary."

Reid stared back in bewilderment. "To find me? But … what about my girls?"

Maria looked away. "Since the Dubrovnik lead, the agency has passed the case on to Interpol."

"No." Reid shook his head. "No, they have no personal investment, no skin in the game. They're probably dealing with a thousand missing persons cases a day…"

"Kent, you shot at cops. They know about the shooting at the textile mill too. They're assuming the bomb at the resort was you—"

"It wasn't a bomb," he argued, "it was a bomb *threat*—"

"And now they're going to find a dead security guard and Rais's brains spilled all over the walls," she continued unabated. "You are considered an armed and highly dangerous vigilante. Not only are you disavowed, but you are highest priority at the moment. Techs are scanning airwaves, police frequencies, messaging apps, and social media for any possible sign of you."

"What about Cartwright?" he asked. He knew it was a long shot, but there had to be someone else on his side, someone else out there looking for his girls. "If I could talk to him on a secure line, explain what happened, he could do something…"

"And how far do you think he's going to stick his neck out for you if it might mean his career on the line?"

He sighed. She was right. Cartwright would be of little help; even if he wanted to, he would have to convince the higher-ups that Kent Steele wasn't a threat.

And some of those higher-ups might already want me dead for what I know.

"What about you?" he asked. "Rais was your op. You could tell them you came here, heard a disturbance at the walls. You found Rais dead—"

"Kent…"

"Then your op is over, you can take on the search for my girls—"

"Kent!" Maria practically shouted. He fell silent as she put a hand on his knee. "I'm sorry. That won't work."

He stared down at her, his eyes meeting her vibrant gray ones. Then he chuckled bitterly, because he realized what she meant. The CIA had changed her op as well. "Because you've been sent here to apprehend me too."

She nodded. "Obviously I'm not doing that. But…yes. You're my op now." She rummaged around in the black duffel again and pulled out a fresh T-shirt for him. "I came prepared. Figured you might need a change of clothes. There's a jacket in here too."

Reid took the shirt, but did not put it on. Instead he leaned back on the toilet seat and buried his face in both hands. It was all he could do not to scoff scornfully at the situation. He couldn't contact the CIA. He couldn't reach out to any friends at Interpol for fear of them reporting him. He had two field agents assigned to go after him—one of whom was treating his wounds.

He had come all this way, and even killed Rais, and the only reward he got was that he could barely move on his own.

He felt Maria's hands on his arms, sliding up around him, hugging him to her. He felt her warm fingers on the back of his neck, on his shoulder, and he breathed in her scent.

"I've come so far," he whispered. "If anything, I'm further now than I was before. I have no idea how to get to them, Maria. The only lead I had was Tkanina, and I can't go back there if the agency knows about it."

"Kent," she said softly in his ear. "We'll find a way."

"And every moment that we spend finding a way is another moment they could be ..." He trailed off, not wanting to say it. "You know what those traffickers do. They drug girls. They rape. They sell them to people who will do even worse than that." He wiped his eyes on the back of his hand. "They're children. They're *my* children. And I ... I can't get to them."

He glanced up at her, but she stared away pensively. After a long moment he asked, "What? What is it?"

Maria closed her eyes and sighed. "I'm going to make a call. I think ... I think I might know someone who can help."

Reid frowned. Whoever Maria would be calling did not seem like someone she was interested in speaking with. She rose from the floor and took a cell phone from her black bag.

"*Dobryy vechir,*" she said into the phone. "*Tse ye Calendula. Meni potribna informatsiya.*" Good evening. It's Calendula. I need information.

Reid blinked in shock and confusion. He understood every word she said ... because he also spoke fluent Russian. And "Calendula" sounded an awful lot like a codename, like her CIA handle of Marigold.

A horrible feeling sunk in as he stared at her. Whoever was on the other end of the line was not CIA, nor Interpol. In no unclear terms, she mentioned the Slavic traffickers. She told the stranger on the line about Tkanina, about the cargo depot in Nova Scotia, and about Slovakia.

Reid drank in every word. *No,* he realized, *not Russian. It's Ukrainian. The words are similar, but the grammar is different. Simpler.* Maria was speaking Ukrainian. *Why Ukrainian?*

"For the asset," she said quietly as she avoided his gaze. She listened to the speaker on the other end for a moment. She glanced at him, and in that instant he knew. Her split-second rueful gaze told him everything.

Reid rose slowly from the toilet lid, shaky on his legs as Maria ended the call.

"Who was that?" he demanded immediately.

"It's not what you think..."

"Who was it, Maria?" he asked again louder.

"That was an asset."

"No. Assets don't collect unreported intel on human traffickers..."

"I have a lead," she told him.

"I don't believe it." He felt his face growing hot as he pointed at her. "Maria... are you a double agent?"

CHAPTER TWENTY FIVE

"No," Maria insisted. "That was a friend in the Foreign Intelligence Service—"

"So now it wasn't an asset?" Reid scoffed. "You told them it was 'for the asset.' I got every word. That wasn't an asset; *I'm* the asset. For what?"

Maria sighed shortly. "Kent, there's a lot more going on here than you understand."

Reid tried to look her in the eye, but she didn't meet his gaze. He was frustrated and desperate, not to mention physically exhausted and aching all over.

Your girls are the priority, he reminded himself. *You need to get going—even if it means going alone.*

"I'm taking the car," he told her. "Give me the lead." He pulled on the T-shirt and brown jacket that she had brought for him, and then held his hand out for the keys.

"I'm coming with you—"

"You're not," he said abruptly. "If you want me to believe I can trust you, you won't follow me. If you do, I'll know where you stand."

"It's by you," she insisted. "No matter what."

"Please give me the keys."

Maria stared for a moment, as if she could will him to change his mind, but he shook his head. She passed him the key ring wordlessly. Then she reached again into her black bag, this time retrieving a small notepad and pen. She scribbled down a name and a number, tore off the sheet, and handed it to him.

"What is this?" he asked, scanning it.

"It's the name of a hotel in Bratislava," she told him. "It's a known spot for their ... clientele."

Reid scoffed lightly, feeling the heat rise in his face anew. "You have a 'contact' with this sort of intel on traffickers and they did nothing with it?"

"Slovakia is part of the EU. My ... contact can't move against them. It's outside of their jurisdiction—"

"No, but they can spy on them," Reid countered.

"Isn't that exactly what you and I do?"

"That's different. We act."

"We try," said Maria. "But you can't save everyone."

"I don't have time to stand here and split hairs with you. I'm going." He took two pained steps toward the restroom door before she called out to him again.

"Wait. At least take the field bag." She scooped up the small bag and handed it to him. "It's got medicine. Painkillers ..."

"Epinephrine?" he asked.

Maria blinked at him. "You can't be serious." At his stare, she nodded. "Yeah. Three doses."

He took the bag. "Transponder? Any way to track me?"

"Of course not," she said. "It was my kit. I wouldn't allow that."

He unlocked the door.

"There's a phone in there too," she called after him. "A burner. Mitch's number is in there. It would take you ten hours to drive to Bratislava. Call him. He could arrange something faster."

He hesitated for a moment; strange as it was, he realized suddenly that his anger with her was more due to her lying to him than possibly being a double agent.

But isn't lying part of the job?

"Thank you," he murmured. Then he left her there, standing in the open doorway of a Croatian bathroom as he climbed gingerly into the driver's seat of the white coupe and started the engine.

He let it idle for a moment, thinking. He hadn't paused long enough to process everything that had happened in just the last hour or so—the resort, the fight with Rais, and now whatever this was with Maria.

And you don't have time for that now.

He shifted the coupe into drive and screeched out of the gas station's lot. As soon as he was on the roads of Old Town again, he unzipped the field bag and dug around for the burner. A quick scroll through the contacts showed only two numbers in it: one under "M," and another under "C."

Cartwright? he thought. *Can't be. Maria was on an op. She wouldn't need to contact him this way.* Even if it was the deputy director, he wasn't about to risk calling and having his signal traced. Instead he called the number under "M."

"Did you find him?" the voice said immediately.

Reid frowned. It didn't sound anything like the gruff mechanic he'd met in Virginia. "Mitch?"

"Zero." He was silent for a moment. "It's me."

I was right. The mechanic had been disguising not only his appearance but also his voice, intentionally keeping Reid from remembering him. "I need a ride. I'm in Old Town Dubrovnik and need to get to Bratislava."

"And Maria…?" Mitch asked.

"Left her behind," he replied simply.

Mitch paused again. Then he said, "I've got a chopper nearby. But no pilot."

Reid thought back to just a few days prior, when a helicopter took him and four others over the Mediterranean Sea toward a cruise ship to stop the outbreak of mutated smallpox. He had watched the pilot, and realized that he knew how to fly.

"That shouldn't be a problem."

Seventy minutes later, Reid set a decommissioned medevac chopper down on the ninth-hole fairway of a Slovakian golf course. His hunch had been correct; his hands worked the controls seamlessly, working the cyclic and anti-torque pedals in near-perfect concert, the knowledge of flight returning to him entirely in the moment.

He powered down the helicopter and climbed out with a groan. He was still in a lot of pain from his fight with Rais, but he had also had plenty of time to think on his flight from Croatia to Bratislava. And though his thoughts were fairly jumbled and complex, layers of problems upon other problems that would, eventually, require resolution, he had come to two conclusions.

The first was one that he had already established: he was going to get his girls back safely, come hell or high water. The second was that he would break every skull that got between him and them, no matter who it was or which side they claimed to be on. There were no sides, not anymore; there was only right and wrong.

They think they've seen a rampage. I'll give them a rampage.

It was just after midnight local time when he set the chopper down and abandoned it there on the green of a golf course attached to a five-star hotel in the ritzy end of the Slovakian capital, known more for its shopping and tourism than for its rich history. Bratislava was one of Europe's smaller capitals, but Slovakia's largest city, with still-standing castles settled along the Danube River.

The hotel that he was looking for was called the District, a posh luxury accommodation only a few blocks from where he had set down. There was no one on the golf course at this time of night, but people had undoubtedly seen it flying low across the sky. Most might not think twice to see a medical helicopter overhead—but there would be more than a few questions when it was found on the fairway.

He took up the field kit and hurried in the direction of the District. As he walked, trying to ignore the pain in his aching limbs, he unzipped the bag and rooted around in it. As Maria had promised, there was an orange prescription bottle with no label but containing a handful of pills that he recognized as hydrocodone. He stuffed the bottle in his pocket; he wouldn't be taking any painkillers now, not when he needed to keep his head clear, but he felt better about having them.

Also in the bag he found the three shots of epinephrine, narrow tubes with stubby capped needles wrapped in plastic. Those he pushed into his back pocket. He also took the liquid adhesive in case his wound split open.

There didn't seem to be anything else that would be useful to him in the med kit, so he dropped the rest of the bag into a trash bin on a corner—along with the burner that Maria had given him. He did not want to be tracked, not by the agency or by her, and at the moment he didn't trust that she wouldn't try to follow.

Then he strode the remaining half block to the District.

The five-star hotel was twice as tall as it was wide, looming large and vain over its neighbors, the exterior alternating in silver and black stripes all the way to the top, sixteen floors up. He slowed his approach as he neared the revolving glass entrance. He could only imagine how he would look to the high-profile clientele and staff inside—his face bruised, lacking luggage, and wearing jeans with minor blood spatters on them.

He passed by the entrance and skirted around the building until he found a small loading bay for deliveries, down a side street off the main boulevard. Beside the rolling garage-bay door was another entrance, a steel door with a small button beside it. He pressed it, and from inside came a loud and angry buzz.

Reid pressed it a second time and waited. A few moments later the door pushed open, only a few inches, as a confused young bellboy peered out at him.

"*Môžem ti pomôcť?*" the bellboy asked in Slovak. May I help you?

"*Tak ľúto.*" Reid surged forward, elbowing open the door as the other arm snaked around the bellboy's neck, cutting off both his ability to cry out and the blood supply to his brain.

So sorry. Reid checked left and right as he applied the sleeper hold to the bellboy. There was no one else on the loading bay, not this late at night. In seconds, the young man in his arms was unconscious. Reid carefully lowered him to the ground and took his ID badge.

Then he went in search of the way up.

Sixteen. That was the number that Maria had written on the paper, beneath the name of the hotel. It wasn't a room number; it was a floor. The top floor, the penthouse suite, which—in a place like this—was generally only accessible by those with a key.

Or by the employees-only freight elevator. It wasn't difficult to find the double-wide steel box that would take him to his destination. He scanned the bellboy's keycard over a sensor and the doors whooshed aside for him.

He pressed the button for the penthouse and pulled one of the epinephrine shots from his back pocket. As the elevator rumbled upward, he peeled off the plastic and popped the cap from the tube, exposing the short needle.

Reid couldn't recall ever having done this before, but knowledge trickled into his mind like an open sieve. *An intramuscular injection in the lateral thigh results in a more rapid onset and faster rise of blood levels.* He took his jeans down enough to expose the upper portion of his outer thigh.

You can't be serious, Maria had said. But he was deadly serious. He was going to get some answers, and in order to do that, he had to be able to move.

An ordinary EpiPen, the kind people carried around in case of bee stings or food allergies, administered a zero-point-three-milligram dose of epinephrine. The CIA field kit shots yielded a maximum dose of ten times that, three milligrams of synthetic epinephrine, the chemical compound that most people knew simply as adrenaline.

He took a breath, and then he jammed the needle into his thigh.

CHAPTER TWENTY SIX

At first, nothing happened. The elevator continued its ascent toward the penthouse, climbing up past floor eight, floor nine, floor ten...Reid dropped the needle to the floor and buckled his pants, concerned that perhaps there was something wrong.

His heartbeat tripled its pace in a millisecond. He shot one hand out to steady himself against the wall of the freight elevator as every muscle in his body contracted, relaxed, and then spasmed again. His vision went blurry for a moment as his pupils dilated to twice their size, and then came back into focus, sharper than before.

He gasped. Sweat beaded on his forehead. His rushing heartbeat pounded in his ears like a kettledrum. Fingers twitched involuntarily. The pain was still there, but it was distant, like a memory or the physical manifestation of déjà vu.

Suddenly the elevator was moving too slow, far too slow. He could climb the shaft faster than this. He had to move, *now*, to get out of this steel box. The epinephrine high would only last for a few minutes.

At long last the elevator doors opened and he stepped out instantly, scanning left and right. He felt as if he saw everything in a single glance; he was in a kitchen, in the penthouse suite. The freight elevator was cleverly disguised as a wide oak cabinet, slightly recessed into the wall. But it didn't hold his interest, and neither did the kitchen. There was no one here.

Sounds—a man's voice, deep, coming from another room. Reid stalked quickly into a dining room, across the open floor plan to a parlor, adjacent to which was a bedroom.

Little could have prepared him for what he found there.

He took in everything at once, his gaze flitting around the expansive bedroom like a hummingbird and piecing together each individual sight like a heinous mosaic.

Three girls in various states of undress. One on the floor. Drugged or unconscious. At least one of them clearly... Jesus, she can't be any older than Maya. A teenager.

One man, on the bed in a pair of silk boxer shorts. Fat. Hairy. Mid- to late forties. Gold chain. Thick mustache with a ridge of black hair. Surprised to see me. Obviously affluent. Looks like the kind of guy that gets his way— no matter what his way might be.

He saw it all in an instant as he crossed the threshold to the room. Every muscle and sense was on overdrive; he could smell the man's cologne, mingled with his body odor. His breath... grapes. Red wine. There was another scent, one that he couldn't put a label to.

It was a pheromone. It was fear. *These girls are terrified. Afraid for their lives.*

The time it took Reid to gather all of the sensory information from the room was the same amount of time that it took the fat man in his boxer shorts to recover from his surprise long enough to shout at him in Slovak.

"Who are you?!" the man demanded indignantly. "What are you doing—"

In response, Reid strode to the bed in two quick steps. As the fat man desperately tried to clamber away, Reid grabbed the edge of the bed sheet—*Egyptian cotton, two-thousand-thread count*—and yanked it upward and outward. The man cried out as he tumbled off the farther end of the king-sized bed, landing in a heap of hirsute limbs.

Reid tossed the sheet to the two frightened girls who had scurried to the corner. "Cover yourselves," he said in Slovak, "and stay put. Don't move." Then, for good measure, he repeated it in English. He couldn't be sure they were Slovakian.

"Help!" the fat man shouted. Rather than try to stand, he screamed from the floor. "Help me!"

A door opened elsewhere in the penthouse. The fat man was not alone. Reid spun on a heel and strode out to meet whatever new threat was present. His hand grabbed at whatever weapon it could find within reach—the drawer of a bureau—and tugged it loose without breaking his stride to the parlor.

Two men. Black suits. Not traffickers—bodyguards.

The pair of men rushed into the suite from the front door. They were armed; each had a hand snaked inside their suit jacket, reaching for a shoulder holster. Reid flung the drawer overhand at the one closest to him and it struck the man square in the face before he could get a hand up to stop it.

The second bodyguard had his weapon free, aiming—*a silenced Walther PPK*, Reid noted. *But the safety is still on. Amateur.* He put one foot on an exquisite marble coffee table and leapt into the air toward the guard, swinging one foot out to deliver a crushing blow to the side of the man's head. He bounced off the wall and crumpled to the floor.

Click. Reid heard the snap of a safety and immediately dropped into a crouch as two silenced shots flew over his head. The first guard had his gun loose. Blood oozed from his nose and snarling lips as he tried to track the movement with his barrel.

Reid tucked into a roll diagonal to the guard and came up directly beside him, nearly shoulder to shoulder. As the man tried to bring his gun around, Reid struck at the forearm with a flat hand, forcing him to drop his weapon, and then delivered a flurry of short but powerful punches to his torso. The stunned guard stumbled backward. Reid grabbed the man's face with one palm and helped him the rest of the way down, bouncing his head off the edge of the marble table.

He quickly double-checked to ensure that neither man was moving—they weren't—before snatching up both pistols. One of them he tucked into the back of his pants.

The other he brought with him back to the bedroom.

"Answer!" the fat man shouted into a cell phone, crouched partially behind the bed. "Answer!"

Reid took careful aim and fired once. The silenced PPK barked and the cell phone flew away from the man's ear, along with the top half of his middle finger. He screamed and gripped his bleeding hand. One of the girls shrieked.

"Calm down," he told them in English. "Put your clothes on. I'm not going to hurt you." Turning back to the affluent man in his underwear, he added, "I *am* going to hurt you. Stand up."

The fat man stayed at his spot on the floor, one hand wrapped around his injured one. "You have no idea what you've done," he grunted in pain. "Do you know who I am?"

Reid leaned forward, dangerously close to the man's puffy face. "Do you know who *I* am?" he asked quietly.

"N-no," he stammered. "I have never seen you before in my life."

"That's right. You haven't." Reid glanced over his shoulder. One of the girls was getting dressed while the other was helping the third off the floor. He tossed them the bellboy's keycard. "This will get you down the freight elevator in the kitchen. Take it and go directly to the police. Don't stop for anything or anyone." He knew there might be some information to be gained from the girls, but he doubted it was much. Besides, to them, he was an assailant with a gun. The terrified trio had likely dealt with enough of those to last a lifetime.

The information that he really wanted was in front of him.

"Get on the bed," he ordered.

The fat man scoffed. "You will be a dead man if you touch me."

Reid sighed and shot off two of his toes.

The man wailed and rolled onto his side. Behind him, one of the girls stifled a scream and ran out of the room. The other girl scooped up their friend as best she could and half-dragged her toward the door.

The fat man whimpered, writhing on the floor. Reid leaned over again, now that they were alone in the room, and spoke softly. "You will be a dead man if you don't tell me what I want to know. If you do, you might get out of here with the rest of your fingers and toes."

"You fool," the man gasped. "I am—"

"I don't care who you are," Reid interrupted. "I don't care how much money you have, or what sort of power or influence you believe in. There is only one thing I care about, and that is my daughters."

The fat man's gaze met his, eyes wide and fearful.

"Yes. That's right. The men that supplied you with these girls have my daughters. Both of them. Teenagers." A noise reached his ears; Reid lifted the pistol and, without taking his eyes off of the naked man before him, fired twice at the open doorway. The bodyguard he had kicked in the head caught both bullets in center mass. He fell forward on the carpet. "I'm not sure what more I have to do to prove that I'm very serious. But I can get creative."

The man on the floor wheezed another breath, and then another—*no*, Reid realized. *He's laughing.* The fat man was chuckling between hissing, pained breaths.

"Was something funny about that?" Reid demanded.

"Yes," the man rasped. "You … you idiot. You have just murdered a member of *Slovenská Informa ná Služba.*"

What? Reid balked. *SIS?* If this man was telling the truth, then the bodyguard was not merely a bodyguard at all, but an agent of the Slovak Information Service—the country's version of the CIA.

"You're lying," he challenged.

"No," said the man. "I am Filip Varga, the Slovakian representative of the European Commission."

Reid sat heavily on the edge of the bed. The epinephrine was starting to wear off, the pain and exhaustion creeping back into his limbs twofold.

Worse, the man on the floor missing three digits was one of the twenty-eight members of the governing body of the entire European Union.

And worse still, Reid had told him that he was the father of two trafficked girls. If the CIA or Interpol caught wind of this—and they undoubtedly would—they would know that he assaulted one of the highest-ranking officials in Europe, short of a president or prime minister.

"Filip." Reid stood from the bed and crossed to the opposite wall, where a long mirror hung in an ornate black frame. "I don't have much time. And I need information. This doesn't stop with you; you're just a roadside attraction." He swung out an elbow, shattering the glass. "I'm into this pretty deep. There's no stopping now." Reid sifted through the broken glass on the floor and pinched a narrow shard between his fingers.

"What...what are you going to do?" Varga asked in alarm.

Reid rubbed his face as he approached the man on the floor. He was so tired, aching, run-down. He still had two shots of epinephrine, but he couldn't risk another so soon; he could give himself a heart attack.

"I'm going to ask you a question," Reid told him. "If you're telling the truth, I'll ask another, until I'm satisfied. If you're lying—and I will know if you're lying—I'm going to cut your face."

Varga blanched, the color draining from his cheeks. "You wouldn't dare," he said in a horrified whisper. "You know who I am, what this could mean for you..."

Reid flicked the shard of glass out in a halfhearted swipe, but still enough to scrape the skin off of Varga's forehead. The cut immediately pooled with blood as one chubby hand rushed up to feel it, smearing red across his face.

"I would dare," Reid said. "And I don't care who you are. You're a rapist, and a pedophile. Here's my first question: I want to know how you contact them."

Varga wiped at his forehead again. "There is a phone number..."

"What is it?"

"It...it was in my phone. You shot it."

Reid groaned. His exhaustion was making him irritable. "And if you lost your phone?"

"It is in my home, on the other side of Bratislava. Written on a scrap of paper in my safe."

He didn't have time for that. Besides, it could be a runaround, an attempt for Varga to get out of this. "Next question. How do they bring the girls to you? They bring them here for you, or do you meet elsewhere?"

"Here," said Varga breathlessly. "Always here. In the penthouse. They bring them up..."

"You expect me to believe that human traffickers just march underage girls across the lobby of a five-star hotel?" Reid was growing angry, irritable from his own pain and his lack of answers. The shard of glass trembled in his fingers, a half-inch from Varga's face.

"Yes!" he cried. "Think about it, think of any hotel in the world." He spoke quickly, as if pleading for his life. "A man walks in with a few girls. Well dressed. Well behaved. They are quiet. Compliant. Would you think twice? They, they do things to them. Give them drugs. Threaten. Sometimes... sometimes beat them. To keep them in line."

With every horrific description, an image flashed through Reid's mind of some atrocity happening to his own daughters. He grabbed Varga's face with one hand, holding him by the chin, and pressed the shard of glass to his cheek.

"Filip," he said dangerously, "to me it sounds like you know more than the average client should know about these men and what they do."

"P-please..."

Reid pressed on the glass, drawing a bead of blood. He had to steady his own hand from tearing a thick gash down Varga's face. "A man like you, in a position you're in, would be of great help to these traffickers. Wouldn't you?"

"I-I-I..." Varga's chest heaved as he hyperventilated.

"Are they Slovak?" Reid demanded. He pressed harder on the shard.

"Yes! Yes. M-mostly. Some are, are Bulgarian. Croatian..."

"And you help them? With what—faking flight manifests? Crossing borders? And in return, you get what you want when you want it?"

Varga cried out as the sharp glass punctured a hole through his cheek. "Yes," he whimpered. "I help them. Sometimes..."

"Give me something I can use or I will cut the flesh from your face." Despite the pain and exasperation, Reid's hand stopped trembling. He was fully prepared to make good on his threat. "Where do they operate?"

"Everywhere." Varga grimaced. "All over…"

"Where are they based?!" Reid shouted. "They must be head-quartered somewhere. They must keep the girls somewhere. Where, Varga?"

"Please, please…" Varga pleaded as a rivulet of blood ran down his face. "I don't know. I don't know. They operate all over, in several countries. No single place."

"That doesn't help me," Reid growled. The traffickers had to have a base of operations. They just had to, or else his girls still could be anywhere. "Give me something, or…"

He heard nothing over the sound of Varga's whimpers, and barely caught the glimpse of movement in his periphery before the other SIS agent leapt toward the bed, reaching for the pistol Reid had left there.

Reid's hand shot out and swept the pistol off the bed and onto the floor a half-second before the agent's hands slapped down on nothing but Egyptian cotton. He leapt again, this time to the floor to retrieve the PPK. Reid leapt as well, springing up from his crouched position over Varga and falling atop the SIS agent.

As the man's hand reached the gun, Reid drove the shard of glass down into the back of it. The agent screamed and rolled, throwing Reid to the side and off of him. He grabbed up the pistol with his other hand and turned to fire…

Reid had the second gun loose, the one tucked into the back of his jeans. He fired only once, a *thwip* of a silenced shot into the SIS agent's forehead. The man's head jerked back, a nine-millimeter-sized hole frothing blood between his eyes. His body fell forward onto the carpet.

"Help, I am being attacked!" he heard Varga say frantically. The fat man had reached the hotel phone on the nightstand. "Penthouse… please, come quickly…"

Reid had no choice. He raised the gun again and fired two shots.

CHAPTER TWENTY SEVEN

Both bullets found home, but not in Filip Varga. Reid fired both shots into the phone on the nightstand.

He had already killed two SIS agents—*agents that would have killed me*, he reasoned; *agents that knew damn well what was going on in here and allowed it*—but he was not about to kill a global official, even if he was a monster. Varga would face a court for what he had done.

But he had made the call, and Reid needed to get out of there. He pulled himself painfully up off the floor and stowed the gun in his jeans again.

"I know your name and your face," he warned the politician. "This is far from over." Then he fled from the bedroom, leaving Varga mutilated and bleeding on the floor.

He paused in the parlor. He had given the girls his keycard for the freight elevator, and he couldn't very well take the penthouse elevator back down. Someone would be on their way up, or waiting for him at the bottom.

I could make a stand here. Fight my way out. No, he told himself. That would be suicide...

"This way!" a feminine voice called out in Ukrainian.

Reid spun around. In the doorway to the kitchen was a young girl with auburn hair—one of the three he had freed from Varga. The seemingly youngest of them.

The one that had reminded him of Maya.

"What are you doing?" he hissed. "I told you to leave..."

She flashed the keycard and motioned for him to follow. He dashed into the kitchen after her as she opened the freight elevator doors.

As they descended to the main level, Reid leaned heavily against a wall with one arm.

"Are you all right?" the girl asked.

"I'll be fine. Why did you stay?"

"I sent the others away," she told him. "But I heard what you said. You are a father of two girls that were kidnapped?"

"Yes," he admitted quietly.

Then, curiously, the girl put both arms around his waist and hugged him. It was brief, but it was so powerfully reminiscent of holding one of his own girls that Reid held his breath and bit his lip to shove back the emotional wave that crashed down on him.

"Thank you," she said quietly.

"You are Ukrainian?" he asked.

She shook her head. "Moldovan. But I have been here since age thirteen. Then I was sold to the Slavs."

Sold? My god. She had been—still was—just a child. "Is there anything at all you can—"

The elevator doors opened and Reid found himself face to face with a very surprised, and very burly, man on the other side. He wore a red blazer and had the shoulders of a college linebacker. *Hotel security*, Reid realized grimly.

"Stop..." The man put up a hand in warning.

Reid half-surged and half-stumbled forward, driving an elbow into the guard's solar plexus. As the man grunted and doubled over, Reid sprang up, slamming one knee into his forehead with such force that the guard crashed to the tiled floor and slid, unconscious.

Reid staggered and fell to his hands and knees with the exertion. The girl grabbed his shoulder and helped him back up. Together they hurried to the loading bay, exiting the hotel through the same door that he had first entered.

Outside, the coast was clear, but he could hear sirens wailing and getting very close. He put his arm around the girl's shoulders as they stepped out onto the boulevard and strode quickly up the sidewalk.

"Laugh like I just told you a joke," Reid said quietly in Ukrainian. The girl threw her head back and laughed right on cue as two police cars approached, blue lights flashing.

He forced himself to grin. It felt odd and foreign on his face. He couldn't remember the last time he had genuinely smiled.

The police cars screamed past them and screeched to a halt outside the hotel as the two of them kept walking.

"Thank you," Reid said. "What's your name?"

"Maya."

"I'm sorry?" Reid blinked.

"I said Aiya."

"Oh." He shook his head. He knew the name; it was Hebrew for "bird," but for a moment he really thought she had said... "Aiya, I want you to go straight to the police. Find the other two girls. Ask for Interpol. They're working on finding the men that took you. But first, I need to know if there's anything you can tell me about these traffickers."

"There is not much," Aiya admitted regretfully. "They do not use their real names in front of us. They speak only in Slovak. When they take us places like this, it is in darkness or blind-folded, so we cannot know where we are or where we are going." She shuddered; likely not from the cold, Reid realized. "They are... careful."

He sighed. The ordeal with Varga had yielded little fruit, and now it seemed he had reached yet another dead end.

"There may be one thing," Aiya said. "A small city, northeast of here, called Staremesto. Do you know it?"

"No, but I could find it. What about Staremesto?"

"That is where I was before I was sold. Find a club called Macicka. Ask for Matej."

Macicka. Reid knew the term in Slovak; it meant "kitten" or, depending on whom he might ask, a far more vulgar word. "Who is Matej?"

"The one who sold me," Aiya told him. "He was my handler."

"Handler?" That was the word in Ukrainian that Aiya used, or at least the translation that he knew… *Oh.* He realized what she meant. *He was her pimp. Jesus… a prostitute at thirteen.* Reid could hardly fathom it.

"Pretend to be a wealthy American," she continued. "Tell him Veronika sent you. He will meet you."

"And Veronika is…?"

"No one," she said with a shrug. "It is a code word for the type of thing that will get you alone with him. Matej will know how to meet with them. Only… you may have to make sure that he cannot warn them."

He understood the implication, and he would damn well make sure that Matej could not warn the traffickers. Anyone who pimped teenage girls deserved what was coming to them.

He took his arm from around her shoulders. "Thank you, Aiya. Now go, and don't stop for anyone."

"May I know your name first?" she asked.

He shook his head. "I'm afraid not. It might make things harder for you."

"I understand. Goodbye… and I wish you luck finding your daughters." Aiya turned and hurried down the sidewalk.

He watched her go until she vanished around the corner. Then he asked a passing couple how he might get to Staremesto. They gave him directions and he thanked them as pleasantly as he could muster. Then he traveled three blocks further, just to put some distance between him and the District, and found a parking garage adjacent to another hotel.

He was certain that Filip Varga would report the American man who broke into his hotel room and assaulted him, but he doubted the politician would mention that he was looking for his daughters from human traffickers. The trio of girls would link him to enough problems as it was. Even so, Reid promised himself that he would put in a call to his friend in Interpol, Agent Vicente Baraf, and make sure that he was aware of Varga's transgressions.

But that would have to wait.

The young couple had told him it was a forty-five-minute drive to Staremesto. Reid bet himself he could make it there in half that.

I just need a vehicle. Something fast.

CHAPTER TWENTY EIGHT

"No!" Maya screamed from the back of the white window-less cargo van as the Slavic men reached for her sister. She pushed herself in front of Sara, her arms out, feet planted, trying anything to keep them from taking her away, from separating them.

Powerful arms grabbed onto hers and yanked her from the van. She tried to resist, but they were strong, much stronger than she was. They pulled her easily through the open rear doors and flung her to the ground. She landed hard on her hands and knees in gravel.

When Maya turned again, she saw another of the Slavic men grabbing Sara, wrapping her in a bear hug and pulling her out of the van. Sara did not scream or cry out, but there was some sign of life in her as she struggled against his grip, legs kicking, her face bright red and teeth gritted. But the man held her with her arms pinned to her sides, and her attempts to wriggle free were fruitless.

This is it, Maya told herself. *This is the only opportunity you'll get.* She leapt up from her hands and feet and rushed at the closest Slav, the one that had thrown her to the ground. She barreled into him hard with both hands and knocked him off balance, into the van. Then she turned and kicked out her foot, striking another traf-ficker in the crotch.

He grimaced, and then responded with a swinging backhand to her face.

Maya was again forced to the ground, her cheek stinging and stars in her vision. *Get up.* Her legs felt weak. *You can't fail now. Or you'll never see her again.*

She heard a primal scream behind her—not one of pain or anguish, but of anger. When she turned again, Jersey had leapt upon the Slav's back. The Latina girl had both arms around his neck, pulling with all her might as wet chokes escaped his lips.

Maya wanted to rise, to help her, to fight back, but something pressed against the back of her skull. Hard, unforgiving, unmistakable.

The Slav reached up behind him and grabbed Jersey by the shoulders. He twisted his body and threw the girl down to the gravel. She landed hard on her back beside Maya.

"Stupid girl," hissed the man behind her. Maya closed her eyes. She had failed. She waited for a bullet to end her life.

But then the pressure of the barrel subsided. She dared to glance over her shoulder. The Slav towered over her, seeming to be impossibly tall, with deep-set eyes and a chin bristled in coarse hair. He had a submachine gun in his hand, but it was not pointed at Maya.

"No!" she shrieked again, but her cry was drowned out by a short blast from the gun.

Jersey's body jerked once in the gravel and fell still.

Maya froze, breathing hard as her vision instantly blurred. This girl had spent her last moments alive trying to help her sister, a complete stranger to her. *I didn't even know her real name.*

Tears ran freely down both cheeks as she looked up at her sister, hanging limp in the grip of the Slav, her legs swinging uselessly. She had stopped struggling, merely staring down in shock at the body on the ground.

Then the man behind Maya grabbed her roughly by a handful of hair. She cried out in surprise and pain as he dragged her to her feet, barking at his comrades in their foreign language. The Slav holding Sara stalked off with her still in his arms.

The horrifying reality seemed to have finally set in with her then. Sara writhed anew, legs kicking at the man's thighs and shins, shrieking for her sister. "Maya!" she screamed. "Maya!"

Maya squirmed, trying desperately to pull free, but she was held tight.

What can I do? she thought in an agonizing panic. *What can I do? What would Dad do?*

No answers came to her as the man carried Sara toward the open compartment of a waiting boxcar.

It was only then that Maya noticed their surroundings. There was a train, but this was not a station. There was no platform; only gravel beneath her feet. *A freight train terminal,* she realized.

Get the details, her mind told her. *It's all you can do.*

Her gaze flitted left and right as the Slav held her head still. There were no signs, at least none that she could see. There were boxcars, several of them, most a solid color and a few with logos and words on them, but in a foreign language.

Wait. She spotted one word that she recognized. *Warszawa. Polish for Warsaw. Did the boxcar come from Warsaw, or is going there? Are we in Poland?* It didn't matter. It was something.

She could only watch as the Slav shoved her sister into the open compartment, followed by the two other girls who had been in the van with them. *Red boxcar. Two down from the Warszawa one. There—a number, twenty-three, stenciled on the side in yellow.*

Then the Slav slid the door to the boxcar closed, affording Maya one last glimpse of her sister's frantic, frightened face.

As she stood there in place, trembling, she felt a sharp pinch against her upper arm. She flinched and tried to pull away, but the Slav pushed the plunger at the back of the syringe.

She was being drugged.

He yanked the needle from her skin and tugged on her hair, pulling her backward. She took awkward steps to keep up, gasping as he half-dragged her across a set of tracks to another waiting train. A second trafficker followed, and together they lifted her up and forced her into the open door of a boxcar.

Then they slid the door shut after her.

Maya trembled from head to toe, nearly hyperventilating. She didn't know how much time she had before the drug took effect and rendered her as useless as the girls she had seen on the plane and in the van, but it couldn't be more than a couple of minutes.

And she needed to get a message written.

She pulled off one of her black flip-flops. The nylon straps met in the middle and were secured by a small metal clip. She could hardly see a thing inside the boxcar, but she felt for the clip and pulled as hard as she could. It yanked free of the shoe and slid off the nylon straps. She pried the small curled piece of metal with her fingers, feeling it sink into the flesh of her thumb as she did. It was sharp; sharp enough for what she needed.

A wave of dizziness washed over her, but Maya shook her head, forcing herself to stay alert for just a minute longer. She sat on the floor of the boxcar, pulled up one pant leg of her pajamas, and pressed the metal clip to the skin of her calf.

Carefully, and without being able to see what she was doing, she traced the letter "R" with the sharp corner of the metal clip. Teeth gritted against the pain and fighting off the drowsiness threatening to consume her, she carved an "E."

Slowly she wrote out her message: *R-E-D. 2-3. P-O-L-A*... The metal clip fell from her fingers as her muscles relaxed against her will and she slipped into unconsciousness.

CHAPTER TWENTY NINE

Reid slowed the motorcycle as he approached the Macicka Club, but he did not stop. He cruised on for another block and turned down an alley, stowing the red and black sports bike among a collection of metal trash cans. He separated the ignition wires and replaced the plastic plate, and then hiked quickly back toward the club.

After he hotwired the motorcycle he had found in the parking garage in Bratislava, it had taken him only twenty minutes to reach Staremesto. He stopped just long enough to ask for directions at a twenty-four-hour convenience store from a cashier behind a plate of thick glass, and then another five minutes to find the club.

While Bratislava was a city rich in history, culture, and architecture, Staremesto was like the runoff thereof. It seemed as if the worst neighborhoods of the capital had separated and drifted north; its buildings were dilapidated and crumbling, windows broken, not a blade of grass to be seen, and the few trees that managed to poke out of the cracked earth struggled to survive.

The Macicka Club was a cracked brick building, windowless; the only indication of what might be inside was a pink neon-lit sign shaped in a crude likeness of a cat's face. It looked as if a child had twisted the glass tubing. Reid pushed through the heavy front door and was immediately assaulted by loud electronic music, the beat pulsing in his ears.

He scanned the joint left to right as he entered. Every light bulb in the entire place was red, casting an eerie yet flattering glow over what Reid was certain was a sleazy establishment. The bar ran along the eastern wall. In the center of the single wide space was a circular platform, about three feet high, with a golden pole extending to the ceiling. Twirling slowly around it was a topless brunette woman, swinging in lazy circles by both arms and one leg.

Reid counted seventeen patrons in the club, not including the bartender and the dancer. But no one looked his way as he entered; it was nearly one o'clock in the morning, and the majority of them were too drunk to exist outside the microcosm of the bare-breasted woman.

He strode to the bar and rapped twice on the rough wooden top.

"What?" the bartender asked gruffly in Slovak.

"Matej," Reid replied.

The bartender narrowed his eyes. "Why?"

"Veronika sent me."

"Show me."

Reid wasn't sure what the man wanted to be shown, but he could guess. He reached into his pocket and pulled out the few bills he had left, all hundreds, and flashed them to the bartender.

The man nodded once and gestured for Reid to follow. He led the way to a black door at the rear of the bar, and then down a set of creaky wooden steps. At the bottom was a small basement with cinderblock walls, a small round table, and two men playing cards.

The bartender went back up the stairs again wordlessly, leaving Reid standing there with the two men. He looked them over; one was older, mid-forties, mostly bald and a bit chubby. He wore only a white tank top and jeans. The second man across from him was young, thirty at best, with a shaved head and dark circles under his eyes. He wore a blue tracksuit and a gold chain around his neck.

Neither of the men spoke to him, or even looked at him, as they finished out their hand of poker. Reid stood there quietly with his hands clasped in front of him. Beyond their card table was another doorway, dark, and from beyond it came sounds. Grunting. Gasping. Giggling.

No doubt johns enjoying Matej's "wares," Reid thought sullenly.

After a full minute or so, the younger man looked up at Reid. "I am Matej. What do you want?" he asked in Slovak.

Reid blinked. "Um…I'm sorry. English?" he asked, feigning ignorance.

The young man scoffed in annoyance. "What do you want?" he asked in accented English.

"Uh, Veronika sent me."

Matej shrugged. "So?"

"So…right. Of course." Reid again showed his folded bills.

Matej reached for them, but Reid quickly pulled them back. "I want to see first."

The young man sighed through his nose, his nostrils flaring. He turned to his chubby partner and said in Slovak, "Fucking Americans. Almost not worth the money."

"Almost," his partner chuckled.

Matej faked a wide smile. "Right this way, *sir*." He led the way through the darkened doorway. On the other side was a corridor, and to their right was a row of shoddily constructed partitions made of particle board and hung bed sheets. Behind them, Reid could hear noises that made his skin crawl.

The young Slovakian led him to the last of four booths in the row. He pulled back the curtain-like bed sheet with an exaggerated flourish as he said, "May I introduce you to Hanna."

The site beyond the bed sheet nearly made Reid physically ill. The booth was barely large enough to accommodate the twin-sized mattress that lay on the concrete floor. Atop it was a girl with dyed blonde hair, growing out brown at the roots. Her eyes were half-closed as she looked up at Reid; she looked either exhausted or high or both. Her midsection was covered in a dirty sheet, but her bare legs and shoulders suggested she was nude underneath it.

She couldn't have been more than eighteen, and that was being generous.

"Thirty minutes," Metaj said, "for one hundred American."

Reid cleared his throat. "How old is she?"

"Does it matter?" Metaj chuckled. "Don't worry. She is young enough."

"Young enough for what?"

"You said Veronika sent you. You know what this means, do you not?"

Reid resisted the urge to cave the man's skull in and replied, "Yes." *I do now.* "But I misspoke. I meant to say Aiya."

"What?" Matej frowned as he turned to look at Reid.

"Aiya sent me." He slammed his head forward, smashing the top of his cranium into Matej's face. The young man staggered back, blood exploding from his nose as he crashed into the flimsy particle board partition. It gave way easily, collapsing into the next, creating a domino effect of boards and sheets cascading down around surprised johns and girls. Shouts and cries filled the basement as Reid stepped out of the booth.

The chubby man in the white tank leapt up with such force he toppled his metal folding chair. "What the hell...?" he demanded in Slovak as he charged through the dark doorway.

Reid took out the silenced pistol and fired twice. His aim was shaky; one shot went wide and struck nothing but concrete. The other found home in the man's shoulder. He yelped and fell, grasping at his wound.

A john squirmed out from under the collapsed booths on his elbows and knees, trying to get away. Reid planted a boot on his back and forced him to the ground. As he did, a second man tried to make a run for it, pulling his pants up as he did.

Reid took aim again, more carefully this time, and fired a shot into the john's thigh. He spun and hit the ground before he even reached the doorway.

"You're staying," he told the man beneath his boot. "Help these girls out, and then sit on the floor, or I will shoot you." He lifted his boot and the compliant john scrambled to find a prostitute under the wrecked makeshift brothel.

Reid quickly checked his clip. Only four shots left. He craned his neck, listening for any signal from upstairs, but he couldn't hear anything over the gasps of pain and confused shouts in the basement. He doubted anyone up there had heard anything behind the black door and pulsing dance music.

In the farthest booth, Hanna drew up her knees in the corner as Matej rolled himself over onto his belly, blood dribbling down his chin. He spat out two teeth and groaned.

Reid grabbed the young man by a pant leg, dragged him out of the booth, and kicked him over onto his back. "Aiya," he said, his voice a low growl. "A girl you sold last year. A girl you pimped when she was only thirteen. You remember her?"

"Y-yes," Matej gurgled.

"I need to find the men you sold her to."

I don't... I don't know..."

Reid pressed the silenced Walther PPK to Matej's forearm and pulled the trigger. Matej screamed; two of the girls screamed with him. One of the johns attempted to scramble to the doorway on his hands and knees.

Reid shot him in the ass. The man howled and stopped moving.

"The next one to move gets one in the forehead," he warned them. He turned his attention back to Matej. "Tell me how to find them."

He had to wait several seconds while the young man took hissing, pained breaths. "I don't... know... I call... them..."

"Where's the number? On your phone?" Reid fished into the pocket of the blue tracksuit and came out with a smartphone. "What name?"

"M-Mirko."

He scrolled through the contacts to confirm there was a Mirko. "Is that a real name, or an alias?"

"Don't know..."

"Where do they operate? They must have a base, a central place..."

"I always meet them," Matej grunted. "Always a... different place."

Reid scoffed. He had figured out Matej's game. "You pimp underage girls here. And when they get too 'old' for your clientele, you sell them to these Slavs? Is that it?"

"Please..."

"Matej, if you have any other information about these men this would be a very good time to tell me. It's the only thing that's going to save your life."

"I don't... please..."

Reid put the pistol against Matej's forehead and shot him once. As he stood, he noticed that two of the girls, and one of the johns, were sobbing uncontrollably. Trembling. *They think I'm going to kill them.*

In the last booth of the row, the blonde girl Hanna still sat in the corner, her knees drawn up to her chest.

"Can you understand me?" he asked in English.

"Yes," she said quietly. She was not crying, but stared at the floor and didn't look directly at him.

"I'm leaving," he told her. "I want you to wait one minute, and then get the phone from the other man. Call the police. Do not let these men leave. Understand?"

"Yes," she said again.

He wanted to say more. He wanted to tell the girl that they were safe now, that it would be okay, and that they could go back to their countries and their homes and their families. But even though Hanna was not crying, he could tell she was terrified of him.

Instead he left the booth and walked back to the wooden staircase. Along the way he paused beside the chubby man lying on the floor, gasping in pain and holding his shot shoulder. Reid aimed the pistol at him and the man whimpered.

Only one round left. The police will be here soon, and he's not worth the bullet. Reid scoffed and climbed the stairs, exiting the basement again through the black door.

The bartender grinned as Reid passed by and called out to him. "Done so soon?" he taunted.

Without breaking his stride, Reid fired his last round into the bartender's stomach. The man yelped and collapsed against a rack of liquor bottles, several of which smashed to the floor. The pole dancer shrieked in horror. Several drunken patrons looked around dazedly, wondering what was happening.

Reid felt no remorse. It was a nonlethal shot; it would take the bartender hours to bleed out from the wound, and he deserved it for being complicit in Metaj's activities.

He pushed out of the club and into the night.

Three police cars and two more unmarked waited for him outside.

CHAPTER THIRTY

Reid did not wait around for any orders to freeze or halt or put his hands in the air. Instead he dropped his spent pistol and backpedaled, grunting in pain as he shouldered his way back into the Macicka club.

Several of the patrons stood now, confused, trying to make sense of what had happened through the alcohol-marinated brains. Reid ignored them, shoving past them toward the rear of the building. There had to be a back door. He found one, an entranceway into a small storeroom of cheap liquor that ended in a windowless security door that had to lead out of the building.

He pushed through it to find himself face to face with the barrel of a silver Colt Python.

Reid skidded to a halt and froze, hands slightly aloft. Then he looked past the barrel and sucked in a breath.

"Baraf?"

The man holding the gun was not as surprised to see him. Interpol Agent Vicente Baraf kept his revolver trained between Reid's eyes. "Please do not move, Agent Steele."

I have to. Reid sidestepped, circling the agent so that his back was to the alley and his escape route. "Or what, Vicente?" He called Baraf's bluff. They had been on not one, but two potentially world-saving ops together.

"You've gone too far, Kent. I need you to come with me."

"You know what's going on," Reid pleaded. "You know my daughters are out there. I have a lead. I have to follow it…"

"Give us the lead," Baraf insisted. "Give me the lead. You have my word I will take it to the ends of the earth, but you cannot go on like this—"

Reid shook his head. "I have to go."

"Do not move, Agent!"

"Are you going to shoot me?" Reid looked him in the eye and he knew the answer. He slowly turned around so that he was facing away from Baraf. "Then it's going to have to be in the back. Because I'm going." He took a step. "Five seconds," Reid said.

Behind him, Baraf sighed heavily. "Fine. Five seconds."

Reid didn't wait around. He broke into a sprint.

"*Merda!*" Baraf swore. The last thing Reid heard was the agent radioing in. "Suspect is on foot, behind the building. Use nonlethal force..."

Thanks, Baraf. He turned the corner and kept on running— or tried to. His legs did not want to keep the same pace his brain insisted they did. He glanced down to see a spot of red on his T-shirt; his stab wound had opened, at least slightly, and was bleeding again.

Reid had to pause, leaning against a brick wall. As much as he wanted to run, he simply couldn't. Not in his state.

He pulled a plastic-wrapped tube out of his back pocket. He knew it was a bad idea so soon after the last one, but he had little choice. He tore it open, popped off the cap, and slammed the stubby needle of epinephrine into his upper arm.

Shouts echoed from behind him, not far. He forced himself to keep jogging, to move until the adrenaline kicked in. He was nearly to the motorcycle's hiding place when his heartbeat jumped from first to fifth gear in an instant.

He gasped audibly and steadied himself against a trash can. Every muscle tensed; the pain in his limbs dissipated, but he felt as if his heart might explode. But he could hardly worry about that now. There were only a few minutes before the drug would wear off.

He sprinted full speed the rest of the way to the bike, tearing off the ignition plate and throwing it aside. The two wires sparked in his hand as he twisted them, but he barely felt it. The motorcycle roared to life, the engine robust and growling.

At almost the same time, blaring headlights appeared at the mouth of the alley, engulfing him in light and accompanied by blue flashers. Police cars. There was a voice over the PA in English—"Stop, or we will use force"—but Reid ignored it. He jumped on the bike, spun the back tire a hundred eighty degrees, and opened the throttle as he hurtled toward the waiting cars.

The two officers waiting at the end of the alley shouted in panic and leapt aside as Reid came roaring toward them. He slid the bike sideways, bashing the rear tire against one of the cop cars, and revved the accelerator again. The motorcycle shot forward like a bolt, firing up to sixty in seconds.

There were few pedestrians on the streets of Staremesto at this time of night, and even fewer cars; Reid had the road practically to himself as he opened the throttle fully and accelerated up to ninety. Over his shoulder he saw the blue flashers of the pursuing police cars, but they had little chance of catching up to him.

Suddenly there were headlights ahead as a car turned the corner, coming directly toward him. The cruiser flicked on its flashing lights and accelerated, as if playing a dangerous game of chicken. Reid leaned forward, his grip white-knuckled against the handlebars. The adrenaline coursed through his veins; he was in full control of every tiny movement, every fractional correction.

He was less than fifty feet from the oncoming cruiser when he twitched the bike to the right and skirted around it, coming within an inch of taking off the side mirror.

His heart drummed in his chest; blood pounded in his ears. *Who alerted Interpol?* he wondered. It couldn't have been anyone in the club; the police might have gotten there that fast, but not the agents. No, they must have been en route before he ever arrived in Staremesto.

Then he realized—the girl, Aiya. If she told the authorities the same thing she told Reid about Matej, it would have been easy to put two and two together and realize that it was his next destination. He couldn't be angry with her; she didn't know him, didn't know that he was CIA. Or used to be. To her he was just a man, a stranger, and he couldn't blame her for wanting to make sure that the perpetrators were brought to justice.

Even more curious, though, was the sudden appearance of Agent Baraf. It seemed odd that in an agency that operated in a hundred ninety-two countries, the entirety of the United Nations, the one Italian agent that he knew personally would show up in the slums of Eastern Europe.

Unless he came for me, Reid thought.

He slowed the bike to seventy and kicked out the rear tire, steadying with one boot dragging across the pavement as the motorcycle slid to the left, drifting into a turn. Then he twisted the throttle again and jetted forward—

Less than two blocks ahead, a pair of white cruisers suddenly leapt into the intersection, headlights and flashers off. They created a blockade, bumper to bumper, perpendicular in the road.

Merda! Reid didn't have the room to stop. He kicked out the rear tire again, but not to turn; instead he brought the bike into a sideways skid, slowly laying it down in the road until it was nearly on its side. He swung a leg over so that he was on one side of the bike. At the same time, sparks flew up behind him as the body of the bike hit pavement, skidding down the asphalt at sixty miles an hour.

The cops scrambled out of their cars, drew their guns—and then stared in astonishment at the bike flying toward them on its side, its rider standing atop it.

I'm definitely going to feel this later, he thought glumly. In the instant before the motorcycle slammed into the blockade of cop cars, Reid jumped. With the inertia of the skidding bike, he leapt clear over the cop cars, over the heads of the crouching police officers...

His forearms hit the road first, his head tucked as close to his chest as he could manage as he threw himself into a roll. He felt the impact against his arms, his shoulders, down his back as he rolled, coming up on his feet, and breaking into a sprint.

There was a dull ache down his entire back. When the epinephrine wore off, he was *definitely* going to feel that.

He expected to hear the screech of tires as the police cars pursued him. Instead, he winced with the sharp report of gunfire. *What happened to nonlethal?!* He ran serpentine as bullets flew past him. *Corner. Alley.* He turned, kept sprinting, hoping he could lose them on foot...

Headlights suddenly flickered on, powerful halogens so bright he had to put up a hand to shield his eyes as he skidded to a stop, his breath coming rapid and shallow. A car blocked his path. He had nowhere to go; he couldn't very well turn around and face the two officers that were shooting at him.

"Get in!"

Reid blinked. "Maria?"

"Come on!" she insisted. He couldn't see her behind the halogens, but it was definitely her. He thought briefly of the rock and the hard place, and then sprinted ahead and jumped into the passenger's side of the car.

She immediately shifted and slammed the accelerator. The black turbo-charged muscle car roared in agreement and took off toward the mouth of the alley.

"You followed me," he said, panting for breath. "I told you what that would mean to me if you did."

"That's a strange way of saying 'thanks, Maria, for saving my ass.'" She kept both hands on the wheel, staring straight ahead as they barreled out of the alley. They smashed aside the front end of one of the approaching police cruisers as it attempted to cut off their path and kept right on going as if nothing had happened.

"Do you know where you're going?"

"No," she admitted as she spun the wheel sharply, sending the car into a skid around the next corner. "I don't know this town. But if we can lose them and find our way back to the highway, we can...oh, dammit." She looked in the rearview mirror.

Reid twisted in his seat. The single police cruiser had given chase, and was joined by two other cars. *Interpol,* he thought. They had caught up while he attempted to flee on foot.

"Are you okay?" she asked.

Reid hadn't even realized he'd been drumming frantically on the center console with the fingers of his left hand. "For now. But in a minute or two I won't be." To her confused glance, he added, "I took a shot."

"Jesus," she murmured. "How many?"

"Two," he confessed. "In the span of about an hour."

"Kent!" she scolded. "You're going to give yourself a heart attack—"

"Watch it!" he shouted as a black sedan leapt in front of them, attempting to block their path. Maria spun the wheel. Reid gripped the handle over the window as the car slid sideways, and then backward, pulling a complete one-eighty. She shifted and slammed the gas again, heading straight for the pursuing vehicles.

As expected, they screeched to a halt, creating another blockade across the road. Maria slammed the brakes and the black car stopped two-thirds of the way to them. Reid quickly looked left and right; there were no alleys, no crossroads on which to escape between the two roadblocks.

They were trapped.

"Maria," he said. "Is this one of Mitch's cars?"

"Yes…" She realized what he was asking. "You think these windows are bulletproof?"

"I'm willing to take that chance if you are."

She put her hand on the gear shift. He put his over hers—not in a romantic gesture or one of solidarity, but to stop her.

"Wait. Why are you doing this?"

Maria looked him right in the eye. "I'm doing this for you. For your girls."

He could see no deceit behind her gaze. She was a trained CIA agent—among other things, apparently—but in the moment, he believed her. He took his hand off of hers and she shifted, popped the clutch, and the car lurched forward toward the barricade of vehicles.

Reid fastened his seatbelt a second before the front end of the muscle car plowed into the front end of an Interpol car and the rear of a police cruiser, pushing them both forward. But not enough to get through.

Maria swore, shifted up, and slammed the gas anew. The powerful engine roared and the tires spun, shoving the cars aside. The smell of burnt rubber filled the vehicle.

Pops of pistol fire joined the engine. Reid covered his head with his hands as bullets smacked against the windows and windshield. The glass spider-webbed, but held.

Thanks, Mitch, he thought once again.

Maria shifted into fifth, and the muscle car eked through the gap. The sound of scraping metal squealed up either side of them as they shot forward again.

Reid glanced behind him and noted with dismay that two of the cars were already in pursuit again. *They're not going to give up.* Pain was leaking back into his limbs as the epinephrine wore off. He was right; he definitely felt the fallout from his daredevil stunt.

"I need to know who you are," he said quickly.

"What, *now?*" Maria asked incredulously. She downshifted and spun into a tight turn.

"Yes, now. I said it before—I want to trust you. I might *need* to. But first I need to know what side you're on." A burning odor emanated from the air vents.

"There are no sides, Kent," Maria insisted. "This isn't about the CIA or FIS. If anything, I'm on my own side…" She fishtailed again and shot up a side street, narrowly avoiding a passing van.

"What does that even mean?" he asked. The two cars behind them spun into the turn, keeping pace. "You're playing two agencies for your own agenda? How do I know you're not playing me too?"

She scoffed. "My job right now is to either arrest you or recruit you. Obviously I'm not doing either. Think about it, Kent. We're not that different. What side are you on?"

"I'm on my own…" He trailed off. He'd almost given the same answer that she had.

"These last few ops, ever since you've been back, have you even once actually felt like you were CIA again?" she asked quickly. "Or have you been looking over your shoulder, wondering who you can trust, if you can trust anyone?"

He looked down at his hands. She was right. He didn't feel like CIA, and he recently found himself doubting everyone's words and intentions.

But Maria was different. She had more than words and intentions for him; she acted. She showed her true colors in ways that risked her own safety and well-being.

Maria shifted again, or tried to. The gears grinded horribly and the burning smell increased. "Shit," she muttered. "I think we blew our transmission. We can't keep going like this. We need to lose them long enough to get away on foot, find a place to hide."

She was right. They couldn't keep going like this, and he certainly couldn't get very far on foot. The pain in his abdomen returned with a vengeance; his wound had torn open again, judging by the widened blood spot on his shirt.

He emptied his pockets into the center console—the bottle of painkillers, the liquid adhesive, the last shot of epinephrine, his cash, and Metaj's phone.

"What are you doing?" she asked.

He popped the top of the pill bottle and swallowed two dry. "If there's any chance of fixing this, you'll keep this stuff safe for me."

"Kent, what are you—"

"This phone is from a pimp here in Staremesto named Metaj." Reid lifted his shirt and pinched the bloody edges of his wound together with a groan. "He sells girls to the traffickers. There's a…number in there for someone named Mirko. He's the contact." He applied a bead of the liquid adhesive. "If something happens to me, if I can't get out of this, promise you'll follow it. Promise you'll find them."

They both bounced in their seats as something beneath the hood blew. Smoke billowed from beneath it.

"Don't…" she warned.

"They want me. Get somewhere safe." He pushed open the door and leapt out of the moving car, hitting the pavement painfully hard and rolling several times.

CHAPTER THIRTY ONE

"**E**ight." The interrogator slapped down a manila folder on the table in front of Reid. "Eight dead. Several more wounded." He shrugged out of his black suit jacket and hung it on the back of a blue plastic chair, but he did not sit. Instead he paced the length of the steel table bolted to the floor between them.

The man was Interpol, around fifty, his dark hair shifting gray and deep crow's feet at the corners of his eyes. Judging by his accent, Reid could assume he was French, though he spoke in English.

"Eight bodies found in two countries, three cities, over the span of only a few hours. Every witness to these crimes claims that an American man fitting your description committed them." The interrogator leaned forward on the table, his fingers splayed, and stared into Reid's eyes.

Reid stared back passively and said nothing.

After leaping from the car, he had risen in the middle of the road and stood directly in the path of one of the oncoming cars. It had screeched to a halt only feet from hitting him; it was an unmarked car of Interpol's. The second car, a police cruiser, had screamed past him, pursuing Maria.

As the Interpol agents trained their guns on him and Reid put his hands in the air in surrender, the black muscle car skidded sideways. The police cruiser careened into the side of it, injuring the driver. The last he saw of Maria was a flash of blonde hair as she escaped from the passenger's side of the disabled muscle car, fleeing into the night.

He had no idea what might have happened to her since, but he hoped that she was able to make a getaway. She was the only chance he had now of finding his girls.

Unfortunately, Baraf was not among his captors, at least not that Reid could see. They put him in handcuffs and drove him the forty-five minutes back to Bratislava, to Interpol's regional office in Slovakia, where he was cuffed to a loop in the steel table. Hardly a word had been spoken to him until he arrived in the boxy interrogation room, being scrutinized by the French interrogator.

"You have no passport, no identification whatsoever—nothing on you at all," the interrogator continued. "We've contacted the US embassy and your government. We sent them your photo and the charges pending against you. They claim to know nothing about your identity. You understand what this means?"

Reid simply stared, keeping his mouth shut and his eyes on the man, but he did understand. It meant that the CIA had officially disavowed him, that the United States, his home country, would feign ignorance to any and all of his activities.

It meant that he would be tried in a Slovakian court. And then, either during his time or when it was up—if it was ever up—he would likely be tried in Croatia as well. It meant that if he could not find a way out of this, he could very well spend the rest of his days in European prisons.

"We will find the necessary evidence linking you to these crimes," the interrogator promised, resuming his pacing. "But you can make this easier on everyone, including yourself, by telling me who you are. Why you did the things you did."

Reid tracked the man's movement back and forth opposite the table. He was desperate, screaming internally; his girls were still out there, potentially getting farther by the minute. His own future was just as bleak. Yet he kept his composure, staring back at the interrogator and not uttering a single word. The two tablets of hydrocodone he had taken before jumping out of the car helped keep his hands from trembling and the sweat from rolling down his forehead. He was certain that Interpol could—and would—find evidence against him, in the form of his hair, his blood, and his fingerprints at the scenes.

Still he said nothing.

"Fine," the interrogator said finally. He was trained not to lose his cool, but Reid could tell that the man was growing frustrated by his silence. "You may have it your way. I am certain the Slovakian government would have little problem adding a charge of obstruction of justice to your already impressive list."

There was a knock at the door to the tiny room. The interrogator opened it and spoke silently for a moment with whoever was on the other side; Reid could not see them from his vantage point, nor could he hear their hushed words. The interrogator left, closing the door behind him and leaving Reid alone.

He shifted uncomfortably in his seat and sighed. *You can't let this be it.* Yet there was no way he could see out of this. He was handcuffed to a bolted table. Even if he wasn't, what could he do? Fight his way out of Interpol headquarters while unarmed, injured, and partially high on painkillers?

Reid glanced up at the camera in the corner of the room, staring into the lens. They already knew his face, and whether or not they ever discovered his real identity was moot. He had reached the end of his rope, but his daughters still needed help. If he couldn't provide it, someone had to.

He closed his eyes and sighed. "My name is Reid Lawson," he said into the empty room. He knew that every word was being recorded, that someone was listening. "Two days ago my daughters were taken from their home by a known terrorist and given to a human trafficking organization that operates here in Slovakia…"

Reid opened his eyes and paused, furrowing his brow in confusion. The small red light next to the lens of the mounted camera had flickered off.

A moment later the steel door swung open again and a familiar face entered the room—though it looked neither pleasant nor happy to see him.

Vicente Baraf slowly lowered himself into the chair opposite Reid. He wore a cream-colored suit and his dark hair was slicked straight back atop his head.

He opened the folder before he spoke; inside were crime scene photos, pictures of the dead men from the Tkanina facility. He flipped to the next; it was of one of the dead SIS agents from the penthouse.

"The camera is off," Baraf murmured. "As is the audio feed. I convinced them to give me five minutes with you. I have a notable history of building positive rapport with criminals."

Reid blinked in surprise. "You didn't tell them …?"

"Of our history? That I know you?" Baraf shook his head. "No."

Reid's gaze flitted around the room. The walls were solid; there was no two-way glass, and if the audio and visual equipment truly was off, then they could speak freely. Still, Reid kept his voice low.

"Please listen to me," he pleaded. "What you might have been told is not necessarily the whole truth—"

"Ten men," Baraf interrupted. "Your occupation is covert operations, yet you openly killed ten men. Regardless of what I've been told, how do you expect me, or anyone, to help you when you leave that many corpses behind?"

"Every one of them deserved what they got," Reid said adamantly. "Every single one was a trafficker, or a pimp, or an accomplice …"

"That is not your decision to make!" Baraf hissed. "You are not judge or jury! Just an indiscriminate executioner!" He took a breath, calming himself. "You killed two SIS agents, Kent. You maimed a member of the European Commission."

"Filip Varga is in on it!" Reid said in a harsh whisper. "He aids and abets the traffickers. He admitted it to me."

"And yet there is no evidence."

"The girls," Reid countered. "The three girls from the penthouse of the District. They went to the police, right?"

"Yes, three girls went to the police," Baraf confirmed. "They reported that they had been trafficked, forced into prostitution. But they said nothing about Varga or the hotel."

Reid couldn't believe what he was hearing. "Because they're scared!" he insisted. "They've been threatened, beaten, *raped* by people like him. People in positions of power. I bet you they wouldn't pick the traffickers out of a lineup for fear of repercussion." He leaned forward, the chain of his handcuffs rattling. "Please believe me. You know I have no reason to lie about this."

Baraf nodded slowly. "I know you don't. And I do believe you. But you have no evidence, and I need more than just your word. I could look into it, build a case, but that would take time. Someone like Varga would cover his tracks. He could create a lot of problems, tie up litigation for months, even years…"

"Where is he now?" Reid demanded.

"In the hospital, being treated for his wounds. But he has already released a statement to the press. He claims that an American man broke into the penthouse, shot his SIS agents, and threatened to kill him. He claims it was politically motivated. Once he is released, he will hold a press conference, and I am certain that people will rally behind him."

"And what about the European Commission?" Reid asked. "They could open an investigation on him. I can come forward, make my identity known, my affiliation…"

"Kent," Baraf said calmly, "right now you have no affiliation. You have been disavowed by not only your agency, but your government." He folded his hands upon the table between them. "We received word minutes ago that someone from the US embassy is coming to retrieve you. I think you know what that means."

Reid's heart sank. *Strickland*, he thought bitterly. Agent Zero was Strickland's new op, according to Maria; the CIA was sending him to return Kent Steele to the States. Whatever the Slovakians might have had planned for this unknown American criminal would likely be quite comfortable compared to the hole that the agency could throw him in.

"But they don't have jurisdiction here," Reid argued.

"No," Baraf agreed, "but under the United Nations' anti-terrorism laws, you can be repatriated until you are tried before the International Criminal Court."

Reid balked; the ICC was an intergovernmental tribunal based in the Netherlands that tried criminals charged with crimes against humanity, war crimes, and international terrorism.

But he also knew it would never get that far. Once he was in Strickland's hands he would vanish. It was likely he would never see the US again at all; only the inside of a dirt hole at a CIA black site.

He appreciated what Baraf had done—not only letting him run in Staremesto, but keeping quiet about his identity—but there was nothing more the Italian agent could do for him. He'd gone too far, and this was the last time they would see one another.

Reid closed his eyes and sighed. "If this is going to be it for me," he said quietly, "I want you to promise me two things. Not only as a friend, but as an agent. As someone who believes in justice."

Baraf said nothing, but he raised an eyebrow and nodded once.

"First, promise me you will look into Varga. Find…" His mind raced. "Find the dates of his penthouse stays at the District. Find the security footage from those dates. Talk to the girl named Aiya. Tell her that you spoke to me…"

"That will still not be enough for someone in his position."

"Try!" Reid slammed a hand down on the table. "My daughters were taken because people like him use their power to get what they want, when they want it, regardless of the repercussions. If I can't do anything about it, I would expect someone I call a friend to take me at my word."

"I will," Baraf promised quietly. "I will try. The second thing?"

"My girls," he said. "Their names are Sara and Maya Lawson, ages fourteen and sixteen. They were brought here by cargo plane to Bratislava. I don't know where they are, but they were taken by Slovakian traffickers."

"I will make sure my office has all of this information—"

"No, Baraf. I'm asking *you*. Personally. I want you to take this on. No one else."

The door to the interrogation room opened before Baraf could make his promise. They both looked up to see the French agent, the interrogator, standing in the doorway.

"The American official is here to take him to the embassy," the man said in French. Reid understood every word, but he did not let it show.

Baraf nodded. He stood and pulled a pair of handcuffs from his belt. He secured the second pair onto Reid's wrists before unlocking the first, and then he directed Reid by the shoulder toward the door to escort him into the waiting hands of the CIA. They walked down a corridor that ended in a second thick steel door. A guard behind reinforced glass buzzed them through.

"Thank you, Agent." On the other side of the door, Maria Johansson stood with her arms folded, looking stern. "I'll take him from here."

CHAPTER THIRTY TWO

Both Baraf and Reid glanced at her in bewilderment. None of the other three Interpol agents in the room with them, including the French interrogator, were the slightest bit aware that anything was amiss. Reid tried hard not to indicate any surprise, but she was not at all who he had been expecting to appear.

He shot a glance at Baraf. The Italian agent knew Maria well, having helped the two of them stop not only Amun from bombing the Economic Forum in Switzerland, but also securing the deadly smallpox virus in the Mediterranean Sea. There was little doubt that Baraf was very much aware of what her presence meant.

But will he say anything?

Baraf returned his gaze. His nostrils flared for a moment. Then he turned back to Maria and extended his hand. "Agent Vicente Baraf, Interpol."

"Maria Johansson, CIA." She flashed her credentials. "I'm here on behalf of the embassy to transfer the prisoner. My office should have already cleared it with you?" She raised an eyebrow at Baraf questioningly.

Reid understood what she was doing; forcing the Interpol agent to make a decision. Either break the law and help a friend, or have the both of them detained.

Baraf's throat flexed in a gulp. "Yes," he said after a moment. "Your director called."

Reid let out a small breath of relief as Maria took him by the shoulder. "Thank you, Agents. We will be in full cooperation with

234

your office regarding the investigation into this man's charges, and will be petitioning the ICC to review his case."

She turned Reid around. "Move," she ordered him. "Quickly," she added in a whisper. He started down the white corridor with Maria on his heels.

"Wait!" the French interrogator called out to them. Reid froze. *They know something is wrong with this.* "You are going to escort this man alone? Standard protocol is for us to send a car with you."

Maria paused. Her gaze flitted from the Frenchman to Baraf. The Italian agent could do little but shrug slightly and murmur, "It is … protocol."

She wheeled on the French agent and narrowed her eyes. "What is your name?"

"It is Bisset," he answered, startled by her sudden intensity. "Agent Bisset."

"Do you not think me capable of escorting a man in handcuffs ten minutes downtown?" she asked accusingly.

"Well, I … of course … it is just …" the interrogator stammered.

"Is it because I'm a woman?" Maria said with undue hostility. "Are you a chauvinist, Agent Bisset?"

"Do not be ridiculous!" Bisset said defensively, blinking quickly between her and Baraf.

"Now I'm ridiculous?" Maria scoffed. "I am bringing this man to the embassy. You follow if you feel you must. Just know that I'll be having a talk with your supervisor about your attitude towards the opposite sex."

"I … I didn't mean …" Bisset gave up with a sigh of incredulity as Maria took Reid again by the shoulder and marched him down the corridor. Reid could have laughed at the situation—could have, if he didn't realize what it meant for Maria to show up at an Interpol office and intercept a murder suspect.

As soon as they were clear of the building and in the parking deck, he spun on her and hissed, "What are you doing here? Why did you do that?"

"What do you mean, why?" she asked, astonished. "So you don't spend the rest of your life in Hell Six, that's why..."

He shook his head. "I mean, you gave them your real name. You showed your CIA credentials. The agency is going to know in minutes, and then you'll be in just as much hot water as I am..."

"Kent," she cut him off. "Who do you think sent me here?"

He blinked. He hadn't thought about it, but there was no way that Maria could have waltzed into an Interpol regional office, flashed a badge, and been allowed to take a prisoner away. "Someone authorized this," he murmured.

"I told you before; you're my op right now. I'm supposed to apprehend you." She gestured at the handcuffs. "Looks like I did that."

"Who?" he insisted. "Who put you on this?"

She didn't need to say. He knew by her pointed glance who made the call. *Cartwright.*

"He knows our history," Reid said. "He can't possibly believe you're going to turn me in."

"Maybe he does, maybe he doesn't," Maria said quickly. "Maybe he doesn't want to see you in a place like H-6. Maybe he doesn't trust that an Eastern European prison can hold Agent Zero. But none of that matters right now, because I'm not the only one who was told to come here. We need to go, now." She turned and marched down a row of the concrete parking deck.

Reid hurried after her, the handcuffs still rattling around his wrists. "And where are we going?"

"Well," she said breathlessly, not breaking her stride, "in a few minutes I'm going to call it in that Kent Steele very cleverly managed to elude me. They'll send Strickland after you, so we'll have to change cars. Then we're going after your girls—all three of us." She paused by a blue four-door sedan and pressed a button on the fob to unlock the doors.

"Three?" he asked, an eyebrow raised. Reid pulled open the car door and peered into the cab. Seated in the backseat was a familiar young face framed in auburn hair.

"Aiya," he said in utter surprise.

The trafficked Moldovan girl nodded to him from the rear of the blue car. "Hello again," she said quietly in Ukrainian.

He turned to Maria. "What is she—"

"Get in!" Maria hissed. "And get down."

Reid slid into the passenger's seat and ducked low. A moment later a black SUV rumbled slowly past them, heading toward the entrance to the Interpol office from which they had just emerged. He sat up slightly, just enough to peer above the frame of the window. The SUV parked only four spaces away from them, and a man got out of the car.

He looked young, late twenties at best, with a military-style fade cut and a thick neck. His muscular arms tested the limits of a black rayon T-shirt, and he made no attempt to hide the Glock holstered on his hip.

The young agent paused in the parking deck and looked around. Reid ducked down again as his gaze swept over the blue sedan. He didn't need to ask; he already knew who he was.

"All clear," Maria said. Reid sat up again as she shifted into drive and screeched out of the parking deck. "That was him," she confirmed to his unasked question. "Strickland."

"He looks young," Reid noted.

"He is young. You've got almost a decade on him." Maria smirked, but it faded quickly. "From what I hear, he's a former Ranger. Tough as nails and loyal to a fault. A total Boy Scout. Not like some of us." She tossed something into his lap; the keys to the handcuffs.

"Thanks," he muttered as he unlocked the cuffs. "Do you want to tell me what she's doing here?" He jerked a thumb toward the backseat and the Moldovan girl seated there.

"When you were arrested, I called in a favor," Maria told him. "My, uh, 'contact' put in a call to the trafficker from the phone you grabbed, Mirko." She glanced his way and noted his obvious disapproval. "I had to," she explained. "The call had to come from a man or they would have known something was wrong."

She had a point, he admitted to himself, but it still didn't explain Aiya's presence ... then the realization struck him and he groaned. "Maria. Are you planning on using her as *bait*?"

"We set up a meeting," she said quickly as she navigated the downtown streets. "They're expecting your dead pimp, Metaj. We can't very well show up without a girl. Aiya here is a foreign prostitute with no identification and no known family. All I had to do was flash a fake Interpol badge and the Bratislava police gladly handed her over."

Reid shook his head. "This feels wrong." He twisted in his seat and said in Ukrainian, "Did she tell you who we are? What we're doing?"

"Of course I did," Maria muttered.

Aiya nodded. "Yes," she confirmed. "And I want to help."

"You don't owe me anything," Reid told her. And he meant it.

"I believe I do," the girl said simply, staring out the window.

Reid turned back around, facing forward again. In English he asked, "Where and when?"

"About thirty minutes north of here, and in about one hour," said Maria.

"Location?"

"They set it up. Gave us coordinates. The best I can tell is that it's a bridge in the middle of nowhere."

"Okay." Reid thought for a moment. "Then we're going to need to change cars, and we're going to need to cut my hair."

"Why?"

"Because they're expecting Metaj," he replied. "Their location is likely remote and dark. I need to at least resemble him enough for us to get the drop on them."

She nodded. "Anything else?"

"Gun?"

"Glove box. Along with the rest of your stuff."

He twisted the latch and found the items he'd asked her to hold into—the painkillers, the epinephrine shot, his money. There was also a small pistol waiting for him there, a Ruger LC9. He turned it in his hands, its weight familiar and comfortable.

Not unlike him and Maria, working together, just like on an op.

Reid had to remind himself yet again that he was unsure where they stood, how he felt. On the one hand he wanted desperately to trust her. On the other, she had betrayed him, and more than once. She had failed to tell him the truth about Kate. She was, in some form, a double agent—perhaps a bizarre sort of triple agent.

The simple and unassailable truth was that he didn't know her, not fully, not enough to put his and his daughters' lives in her hands. Yet the other, far more vulnerable position in his mind was that the situation felt better when she was by his side. Not just better; it felt *right*.

Maria pulled the car into the parking lot of an all-night drug store and parked before pointing out a Jeep the color of rust. "Two birds, one stone," she said. "I'll get the car if you get the clippers."

He nodded and got out of the car, tucking the snub-nosed LC9 into the back of his jeans as he made his way inside to prepare for his meeting with the human traffickers who had his daughters.

CHAPTER THIRTY THREE

Reid sat in the backseat of the Jeep as Aiya slowly ran the electric clippers over his scalp, plugged into the auxiliary port in the center console, while Maria drove. He hadn't had it cut in several weeks; thick clumps of dark hair fell liberally to the car's floor as they headed for the rendezvous point the traffickers had given them.

Strange, he thought as he watched the loose hair fall past his shoulders. He couldn't help but think of it as potential evidence—not unlike the strands his own daughter had tugged from her head and left behind for forensics to find.

I'm coming, Maya. Nothing and no one is going to stop me now.

"Okay," Aiya murmured as she brushed hair from the back of his neck. "I think that is good."

Reid ran a hand over his shorn scalp, cut down to about a quarter-inch. He knew he didn't actually look like Metaj, but he had a similar height and build, close-cropped hair, and a few days' growth on his chin. If it was dark enough, he could at least resemble the dead pimp enough to keep any alarm bells from ringing with the traffickers.

"Do we need to go over the plan again?" he asked in Ukrainian, for Aiya's benefit.

"No," the girl said quietly. "I understand."

"I'm clear," Maria confirmed. "Besides, we're almost to the drop point." She drove on for another mile or so, winding through the Slovakian countryside on a narrow two-lane road surrounded by trees. Then she cut the headlights and pulled to the shoulder.

"All right," she said, "I think this is as good a place as any."

Reid passed her a black triangular case, about the length of his forearm. He didn't know where Maria had gotten it, but it was one of the items they'd transferred from her blue sedan to the Jeep. The case was hard plastic and molded in the shape of a butt stock; inside the hollow stock were the pieces of a collapsible sniper rifle, twenty-two gauge and semiautomatic with a six-round clip, the type that black ops personnel carried.

"You'll be okay?" Maria asked as he handed her the case.

He nodded. "Six minutes," he reminded her.

She pushed out of the Jeep and left the driver's side door open as Reid got out and came around. He watched as her silhouette vanished into the dark tree line, and then he climbed behind the wheel.

Their plan was simple enough. The meeting with the traffickers would take place in six minutes' time, and according to GPS it was to be held on a small bridge about a quarter mile from their current location. Six minutes was long enough for Maria to trek north on foot through the woods and find a good vantage point. Reid and Aiya would meet with the traffickers just long enough for Reid to ascertain the identity of the one called Mirko. They had worked out a subtle hand gesture for Reid to identify him to Maria; once she saw the signal, she would take out any comrades Mirko had brought along. In the confusion of an active shooter, Reid would incapacitate Mirko, and they would force him, in all the worst ways, to divulge whatever information he had about where they took the trafficked girls.

He glanced in the rearview mirror at the Moldovan girl in the backseat. Her only task in the plan was to keep her head down while they met with the traffickers; with a little luck, they would not recognize her as one of the girls who had escaped Varga's penthouse. Reid had a hunch that the traffickers would not remember faces so well. The girls they trafficked were stock to them, little more than chattel.

"There's still time," Reid said quietly in Ukrainian. "You don't have to do this." As much as he appreciated her help, he did not at all feel right about using the girl as bait.

"I want to do this." Her voice wavered slightly. "Most of my life, I have done little that could be called noble or … or even good. This is my chance."

"You have nothing to prove—" Reid began.

"I have to prove it to myself," she said simply.

He nodded and shifted the Jeep into drive, pulling back onto the road and easing it in the direction of the rendezvous point. Maria's intel had told them that he needed only to follow the country road a short distance further and he would end up on the bridge.

After a couple hundred yards the trees waned on either side of the road and gave way to a wide swath of what might have been farmland. The fields grew tall and wild with yellow grass; the place had not been cultivated in some time, abandoned and lost to neglect. Reid squinted in the glow of the headlights as he saw a dilapidated farmhouse ahead, a gray-planked structure with a peaked roof.

Then the road curved slightly, and suddenly the farmhouse was directly in their path, as if built right in the center of the pavement. Reid bit his lip and his heartbeat sped up as he realized what he was looking at.

The rendezvous point was a covered bridge.

It spanned no more than forty feet over a thin tributary that likely emptied into the Danube. The bridge's entire length was housed in a simple wooden structure that, from a distance, had looked as if it could be a farmhouse. But no; the traffickers had chosen cover for their meeting.

Maria won't have a vantage point.

From inside the covered bridge, Reid could see a pair of head-lights, but they were not approaching; the vehicle was still. *They're already here.*

"What do we do?" Aiya whispered behind him. In the rearview mirror he could see the wide, fearful whites of her eyes.

"We can't stop now," he told her. "And we can't turn around. They'll already have seen us coming." He slowed their approach, creeping toward the bridge as his mind raced for an alternate plan. "Aiya, I want you to stay in the car. I'll handle this."

"No," she said adamantly. "They will know something is wrong if they do not see me."

"I'll tell them I want the money first—" "It will not work," Aiya argued. "These men do not bargain. You must remember, they are monsters; girls like me are not people to them. We are a resource, a currency to be traded. The trade must be made or there will be no deal." She paused for a moment before adding, "Metaj was not one of them. He was merely a seller. They would not have hesitated to kill him if a deal did not go their way, and he knew that. Acting any differently would risk your own life."

Reid held his breath as the front tires of the Jeep rolled onto the bridge and into the darkness of the timber trusses overhead. He eased the car to a stop. Not twenty feet before them were the blaring headlights of the other car. He could hardly see any details, other than the two bright lights; judging by their height, the vehicle was a truck or an SUV.

The headlights flashed once. Reid did the same, flicking them off and then on again. There was movement in the darkness behind the opposing headlights, and then silhouettes as the traffickers got out and stood in front of their car, waiting.

Three of them. At least that I can see. Possibly a fourth still in the car. His heart thumped in his chest, blood rushing in his ears. Ordinarily he would have little doubt about taking on a trio of criminals, even all at once, but his body was beyond sore. Pain had made a seemingly permanent home in his aching limbs. There was still one shot of epinephrine in his jacket pocket, but he did not want to use it. He might need it later, to get the girls out of wherever they were being held.

Though it'll do you little good if you're dead.

He turned his head slightly and said to Aiya, "As soon as any shooting starts, I want you to take cover behind the car, okay?"

"Yes," she said in a whisper. He could tell she was petrified—she had been already, and their rapidly collapsing plan only made matters worse.

"I promise you, Aiya. I will *not* let them take you again." He pushed open the door and climbed out of the Jeep, circling around to her side. He yanked open the door and whispered, "I'm sorry." Then he grabbed her roughly by the upper arm and half-dragged her out of the car.

Aiya cried out. Whether she was acting her part or genuinely surprised, Reid couldn't tell, but it was hardly the time to wonder. He gripped her firmly as they took a position in front of their car, mere shapes in the headlights.

For a moment, neither side spoke. Reid scrutinized the three silhouettes; the two on either side of the car had dark, oddly shaped protrusions just above their hips. *Submachine guns*, he realized, *hanging from a shoulder strap*. The man in the center was tall and broad-shouldered, and had both arms folded across his expansive chest.

"Mirko," Reid said at last. He did his best to affect a Slovakian accent and the gruff demeanor he'd heard from Metaj.

The large man standing between the headlights unfolded his arms and stepped forward slowly, until Reid could see his dark, deep-set eyes, the angular shadow of a beard on his face.

Mirko flicked something into the air and it landed at Reid's feet. He stooped to pick it up; it was a silver money clip, and folded within it was eight hundred euros. He nearly scoffed aloud. *A young woman's life is worth less than a thousand dollars to them.* He had no remorse about killing the pimp, but he suddenly wished he could have killed him twice.

Still gripping Aiya's arm with his left hand, Reid took a step toward the Slovakian trafficker. His gaze flitted left and right; neither of the flanking men had their hands on their weapons. If he was fast enough, he could draw the Ruger and gun them each down, and then turn it on Mirko. He would only have to hope that there was no one else waiting inside their vehicle, no ace in the hole ...

"That's far enough," Mirko announced in a Slovak basso, raising one hand. "Just the girl. I want to see her face."

Reid glanced over at Aiya, who kept her head ducked low as instructed. Her auburn bangs hung over her eyes, obscuring her features. If she had any reaction to Mirko's demand, she didn't show it.

"Why?" Reid demanded. "What does it matter?"

Mirko chuckled mirthlessly. "Because, friend, you are not Metaj. Metaj is dead."

CHAPTER THIRTY FOUR

Reid froze, though his heart doubled its pace. Aiya did not look up or even move; then he remembered that she did not speak the traffickers' language. She had no idea what had been said.

"Do you think us stupid?" Mirko asked. The two Slovakian men behind him hefted their weapons in a casual, hip-height grip, the barrels aimed at Reid. "How would an operation like ours survive if we did not keep our eyes and ears open? We know about the murders at Macicka. We know that three of our girls escaped from the District."

As much as he wanted to reach for his weapon, Reid did not dare move. A single blast from either of the machine guns trained on them would cut both him and Aiya down instantly.

"At first we thought you might have been police," Mirko continued. "We were not going to come. But then a mutual 'friend' called."

Varga, Reid realized bitterly. The corrupt politician must have tipped off the traffickers about the lone American who attacked him in the penthouse.

"You are the one who killed our men at Tkanina?" Mirko asked.

"Yes." Reid held his head high and admitted it loudly. "I did."

"And the other American? The one from Amun? Does he live?"

Reid narrowed his eyes. He recalled what Rais had told him about the traffickers; they had helped the assassin get across the ocean with the girls because they hoped to become Amun themselves.

Mirko must have been among those who helped Rais...which meant the Slovakian had aided in the kidnapping of his daughters.

"No," Reid told him. "I killed him and threw his body into the sea."

Mirko nodded slowly. "That is unfortunate news for us." He sighed. "We are going to kill you both. This can be quickly or this can be slowly. We can kill you first, or we can kill the girl in front of your eyes. This all depends on you." The large Slovakian took a step closer and said, "I want to know who you are, and I need to know who else knows what you know."

Reid stepped instinctively in front of Aiya. "No one else knows. It's only me."

Mirko scoffed. "I don't believe you. You have come too far to have done all of this on your own." He turned to his two compatriots. "Take them both. We'll get our answers somewhere a little more private."

The two armed Slovakians advanced, the submachine guns raised.

Reid felt a pressure at the small of his back. Aiya was reaching for the LC9 he had stowed there.

"Don't," he hissed. She did not respond, other than to tug the small pistol loose from his pants. He couldn't blame her for wanting to protect herself; he had promised to protect her, to keep her out of the hands of these men, and he appeared to be failing. Even so, he had to think fast, or the brash actions of the girl could mean the end for both of them.

"Wait!" he called to Mirko. "I'll tell you what you want to know."

Mirko put up a hand and the two men paused.

"My name is Agent Kent Steele," Reid said quickly in Slovak, "of the American Central Intelligence Agency. Everything that has happened has been part of a sting operation between Interpol and the CIA to bring your organization down. I didn't come here alone; you are surrounded. And if you make a move against us, my people will open fire."

Mirko narrowed his eyes at Reid. Then the large Slovakian's face twisted into a wide grin. "That is a good story," he said. "But it is not true. They would not have waited this long to move against us."

"Are you sure about that?" Reid pointed at Mirko with two fingers, his index and middle, his thumb straight up in the air like the shape of a gun.

The signal.

"I am quite sure—"

A sharp crack echoed in the covered bridge as the Slovakian on the left jerked once and fell forward, a neat hole in the back of his head. The other Slovak spun, cursing, and sprayed a fusillade of bullets past their vehicle and out into the night.

Reid spun to the right as Aiya raised the Ruger and fired off several deafening rounds from the tiny weapon, shooting the second gunman dead.

Mirko crouched in front of the truck, bewildered as he yanked a heavy pistol loose from his jacket. Reid charged forward, closing the small gap in seconds—but not before the Slovakian fired off a single thunderous shot. Reid skirted to the right and it missed him by a few feet. He led with a knee aimed for Mirko's face and it hit home. The trafficker's head snapped back and struck the grille of the SUV.

Reid grabbed at the pistol in an attempt to twist it from Mirko's grip, but the bigger man held tight, pushing against the resistance. Reid grabbed it with his second hand, intent on getting the gun away from him. Mirko's large fist swung up and slammed into the side of his head. Reid grunted and fell to the side. As he did, he kicked one foot upward and into the Slovakian's wrist. The gun flew from his grip.

Mirko growled and rolled over onto him, wrapping both meaty hands around Reid's throat.

Why isn't anyone shooting?! he thought desperately. The large Slovakian was strong—stronger than he was, especially with his injuries—and had a significant weight advantage too. Reid would have to rely on tactics if he was going to survive.

Instead of trying to pry Mirko's hands away from his throat, he curled his middle fingers inward, pressing hard on the soft fleshy patch between the Slovakian's thumb and index finger of each hand. There was a pressure point there, an intensely painful one that forced open the hands.

Mirko gritted his teeth as his grip weakened, trying in vain to strangle the American to death. Reid pulled the feeble fingers from his neck and released them. One hand shot up and hooked a finger into the suprasternal notch, the shallow depression where the collarbones meet. He pressed hard, inward and downward; the skin there was pliant, flexible, and his finger hooked around cartilage as he pulled.

Mirko yelped in pain; Reid knew firsthand that it was an extremely unpleasant sensation, sending nerve endings firing throughout the ribs and back. As the Slovakian's body came forward, Reid's elbow came up and landed a solid blow across the bridge of his nose and between the eyes. He rolled his body over, sending Mirko onto his back as Reid staggered to his feet, searching around for the lost pistol.

Mirko reeled, clawing at the air and finding purchase on the grille of the SUV. Reid spotted the gun and surged for it, but Mirko leapt up and snaked a heavy arm around his neck, capturing Reid in a chokehold. He tried to tuck his chin, to get an arm up in time, but he couldn't seem to move fast enough. Mirko hissed in his ear as he clenched, cutting off his air supply. Reid went limp, hoping to drag the Slovakian to the ground with him, but Mirko had no problem holding him aloft as he slowly squeezed the life out of him.

Another single shot erupted; high-pitched and cracking. *A twenty-two*, Reid knew. Mirko's grip tightened for a moment as he groaned, and then slackened. They both fell to the bridge—Mirko on his side, gasping, and Reid on his hands and knees, panting for breath.

"You okay?" Maria knelt in a firing position beside the traffickers' SUV, the black tactical rifle still to her shoulder.

"Yeah…" Reid said breathlessly. "Did you clear the car?"

She nodded and stood. "There's no one else…" Her gaze lifted and her face fell. "Oh, no. Kent."

He followed her gaze and a deflating breath escaped his lungs. Aiya was on her back, awash in the headlights of the Jeep, legs writhing as if trying to kick away an invisible assailant.

Reid got to his feet and staggered to her, sliding to his knees at her side. Her heart was still beating, but every pulse pumped blood from the hole in her chest. Mirko's single shot had missed him, or so he had thought. But it hadn't been intended for him at all. The Slovakian was aiming for the bigger threat, the girl with the gun.

"Aiya? Aiya!" Reid pressed both hands over the wound to stanch the blood flow. "Just hang on, okay? We're going to get you to a hospital. You'll be fine..." Blood pooled around his hands as he said it. He didn't even realize he was speaking English; the girl had no idea what he was saying.

Her fingers found the sleeves of his jacket, clinging to him as if it might save her life. "Find them," Aiya said in Ukrainian, her voice quavering. "Keep them safe."

"I will, I promise I will, just hang on..." The blood wasn't stopping. Part of him knew it wouldn't. "Maria!" he called out. "I need help! Maria..."

Aiya's hands fell away from his jacket. A final breath hissed from her throat. Reid's head fell forward, his chin nearly touching his chest. He hadn't protected her from them at all. He had failed, just like he had failed to find his own girls. All he saw was the blood— blood on his hands, blood staining her shirt. Blood on the bridge, the pool of it slowly inching toward the silver and black Lorcin nine-mil pistol he had taken from Mirko.

He snatched it up and stood.

"Kent..." Maria warned as he stalked over to the Slovakian.

Reid flipped the gun around. Shooting him was too good for him; he was going to bash Mirko's skull in.

Mirko lay on his side, eyes closed and teeth gritted, grimacing from the bullet Maria had lodged in his back.

"Kent!" Maria barked. She dropped the sniper rifle and jumped to her feet as he brought the Lorcin up overhead, ready to smash it down into Mirko's forehead. She stopped his arm and stepped between him and the downed Slovakian. "No!" she told him harshly. "We need information! That was the whole point of this!"

He tried to pull out of her grip, but she was strong. "Let me go!"

"Think of your girls," Maria said, one hand holding his arm back and the other on his chest. "Sara and Maya. They are still out there. This man might know where they're going. Let me handle this." She touched his chin and forced him to look into her gray eyes. "I'll talk to him. Go take care of Aiya and the Jeep."

Reid slowly lowered his hand and the pistol. "Fine," he murmured. "But when you're done, I'm going to kill him."

"Go," Maria ordered again. She lowered her hand from his chest and pulled out a silver butterfly knife.

Reid tucked the Lorcin into the back of his jeans and turned away, walking slowly back over to Aiya's body and the Jeep. Behind him, Maria made demands in Slovak. Mirko screamed. But it barely registered with him.

What had transpired over the last two days had certainly been a horrific ordeal for his daughters—one that was ongoing at that very moment. He couldn't imagine what might be happening to them. The very thought of it made his blood boil and sent shivers down his spine at the same time. But for a girl like Aiya, the horror had been most of her life. It happened every day, in every corner of the world, even in the sort of places that no one ever believed such things could happen.

It wasn't right and it wasn't fair. She deserved the chance she would now never get.

Mirko's screams rose an octave as Reid bent and gingerly lifted her body. He slid her gently into the backseat of the Jeep. In the trunk was an orange nylon bag, a roadside kit, and inside were three flares. He popped one, the potassium perchlorate and magnesium igniting in a hissing red flame. He watched it for a moment, the intense light dancing in his eyes and the scent filling his nostrils.

Then he dropped it into the backseat of the Jeep. The clumps of hair that Aiya had cut from his head lit first, and then the carpet. The vinyl of the seats melted and the foam beneath it caught fire.

He closed the door to the Jeep before the fire reached Aiya's body. His makeshift funeral pyre was far less than she deserved, but he wasn't about to leave her body lying on the bridge for the authorities to find.

Mirko's pained, primal shrieks had become little more than background noise by then, as Reid stooped to retrieve the LC9 from where Aiya had dropped it. He checked the clip; four shots left in the nine-round magazine. She had fired five of them at the Slovakians.

For good measure, he retrieved the two submachine guns from the fallen Slavs. They were both Agram 2000 models, a Croatian-made gun based on the Beretta M12. *One-point-eight kilograms. Twenty-two-round feed system with nine-millimeter Parabellum rounds.*

Maria stood, her chest heaving and hands matching his—stained red. Mirko writhed on the ground, whimpering like a wounded animal. Reid didn't even look at him, much less feel any kind of remorse or sense of regret.

"Done?" he asked.

She nodded. "Got it."

He fired two shots from the Lorcin into Mirko. The Slovakian's whimpers immediately fell silent. "You drive." He climbed into the passenger seat of the traffickers' SUV as Maria stowed the black sniper rifle and got behind the wheel. He was exhausted, aching, bloody, angry—but his resolve had not changed one iota. If anything, Aiya's death gave him a renewed sense of duty.

Baraf's words spun through his mind. *You are not judge or jury,* the Interpol agent had said. *Just an indiscriminate executioner.*

But Baraf was wrong. He was discriminate, relentlessly so. He would not only find his girls. He would find every perpetrator of their capture, and he would kill every single one of them if he had to.

The SUV was a newer model, with GPS in the dashboard. Maria jabbed at the touchscreen for a moment as she told him, "The girls are alive. They landed in Slovakia and were taken north, across the border."

"North?" Reid frowned. "Into Poland?"

Maria shook her head as she backed the SUV out from under the covered bridge. The Jeep beyond them was fully ablaze, the flames licking the windows. "Czechia," she corrected. She straightened the vehicle and accelerated, the powerful engine roaring under the hood. "Do you trust me yet?"

"No," Reid said candidly. Then he added, "But whatever we have to work out can wait. I don't trust you, but... I believe you want to help." Whatever her motivations were for coming this far with him, for defying the CIA and Interpol and joining him in his hunt, would become clear eventually. What mattered was rescuing his girls, regardless of the incentive behind it.

If Maria had anything to say about it, she held her tongue. "I ditched my phone so the agency can't track it," she told him instead. "But that also means I can't contact Mitch."

"So we're going to need to find something faster than this," Reid posited.

Maria nodded. "So we're going to need to steal a helicopter."

CHAPTER THIRTY FIVE

The light burned her eyes as Maya regained consciousness slowly, squinting through the slushy haze that was her brain as the drugs she'd been shot with began to wear off. Sensory perceptions came to her slowly, as if in a single-file line, waiting their turn to be recognized.

She was aware that she was rocking slightly. A steady sound resonated beneath her—*cha-chunk, cha-chunk, cha-chunk…* The train. She was still on the train. But there were lights. It had been dark in the freight car when she had been closed within it.

She was lying on something soft. A bed? She dared to open her eyes, slowly, as she sat up and groaned. A headache pounded in her skull as she examined her surroundings in astonishment.

She had been moved, that much was clear; she was in a tiny room, lying on a cot with a low ceiling. A bunk bed. Beside her was a window, the shade pulled down. On the other side was a sliding door, a second shade over the glass.

A sleeper car, Maya realized. She had never been in one before, but she had seen them in movies. This one was modern and plain, white-walled, clean, with bright white bulbs in the sockets. Somehow she had gone from the freight train to a passenger car. *But what does that mean?*

She flexed the numbness from her fingers and toes before trying to stand. Her legs were shaky, her knees like jelly. Maya steadied herself on the railing of the top bunk for a moment as she regained her composure.

Pain prickled in her left calf as normal blood flow returned, rising to a burning sensation. A small amount of dark blood stained the leg of her flannel pajama pants.

Sara, she remembered urgently. *She was put on a different train.* Maya yanked the drawstring for the shade over the window. It was still dark outside, impossibly so; she could not see more than a few feet beyond the glass, only the silhouettes of trees flying by as the train wound its way through what appeared to be countryside.

She tried the latch, but the window wouldn't budge.

Maya pushed as hard as she could, groaning in frustration at the stubborn frame. She looked around desperately for something to break the glass. She had to get off this train, to find help, to get to Sara—

The door to the compartment slid open behind her.

Maya spun, flattening her back against the far wall and window as a man entered the cabin. He pulled the door closed again behind him before he turned to her.

The man smiled. He was short, no taller than five-six, with a bald head and silver-rimmed glasses. He wore a tweed jacket and a tie, and in his hand he held a Styrofoam cup.

He smiled with his thin lips as he said, "Ah, good. You are awake."

Maya said nothing in return, breathing rapidly through her nose. The man spoke English, but he had an acute accent—German, she thought. Maybe Austrian.

"I wanted to wait for you," he continued. His smile never waned, but to her it was not the least bit friendly. "How is your head?"

"Who are you?" Maya asked. Her tongue felt thick and dry, the words malformed.

"I think it is better if you do not know my name. I certainly do not want to know yours." The man chuckled as if he had told a joke. "I suppose if you must call me something, you may call me ... Klaus." He held out the white Styrofoam cup. "Here. For you."

Maya shook her head quickly. She was not drinking anything from any stranger, no matter how nonthreatening he attempted to be.

"It is just water," he promised. Still she did not move. This man, the alleged Klaus, set the cup down on a small table near the door. "I will put it here, whenever you are ready." He loosened the tie knotted at his throat. "Before we begin, I want to ask you a few questions."

Begin? Maya's pulse raced. *Begin what?* She already knew the answer, but her mind refused to acknowledge it.

"I must insist that you are honest with me," Klaus said. He slowly moved to the bunk bed and sat on the cot. Maya shrank away into the far corner of the compartment. "You are quite timid. Like a little mouse." He smiled again at that. "What was I saying? Oh, yes. This is quite an expensive train ride for me, and I must ensure that what I am paying for is accurate. First question: You are American?"

Maya bit her lower lip, saying nothing.

Klaus sighed disappointedly. "My dear, just outside this compartment is a man with pockets. And in one of those pockets is another syringe, waiting there just for you. Personally, I would very much prefer that it not come to that. Do you agree?"

She gulped, feeling as if she might choke. She certainly did not want to be drugged again—especially not now, trapped in this compartment with this horrible man.

"Yes," she said quietly. Her voice cracked as she said, "I am American."

"Good." He smiled wide at that. "Second question: What is your age?"

A sob threatened to bubble up in her throat, but she held it back. "Six...sixteen," she told him.

The man's eyes gleamed. His seemingly disarming demeanor, his casual attitude, and worst of all, his intentions were downright horrifying—perhaps more so than the murderous Slovakians.

"Very good. My final question: You are a virgin, yes?"

Maya gasped instinctively. She had no idea how the traffickers would even know that—unless they were making an assumption, or otherwise just telling this man, clearly their client, that she was.

Tears formed in her eyes. If she refused to tell him, she would get drugged again, and she did not want to think about what might happen to her if she was unconscious. If she told him, this monster would likely be getting what he wanted.

But, she realized, there was a third option—one that just might get her out of this situation.

Maya mustered as clear a voice as she could. "No," she lied. "I'm not."

Klaus clucked his tongue as he shook his head. "Well," he said, "then I will have to ask you to excuse me for a moment." He rose from the cot and slid the door to the compartment aside.

Maya stayed in her corner, pressed hard against the white wall, wishing she could disappear into it. She heard the man speaking to someone out in the corridor in the harsh Eastern European tongue of the traffickers. A gruff voice responded.

He won't want me now, she told herself. *He'll leave me alone. I'm not what he wants.*

The voices outside crescendoed into an argument.

He'll leave me alone.

Then they calmed, and the man in the spectacles returned to the compartment. He slid the door closed behind him. Every muscle in Maya's body went taut.

"I apologize," he said as he shrugged out of his tweed jacket. "I needed to renegotiate my price." Klaus tugged off the tie around his neck.

Maya's breath came in ragged gulps. *No*, she thought. *I'm not going to let this happen.*

"I'll fight," she promised. Her voice cracked as she said it. "I'll scream. I won't let you."

Klaus grinned wide as he took off his silver-rimmed glasses and set them beside the cup of water. "My dear ... I am counting on it."

He lurched forward, his hands outstretched. Maya shrieked and put both arms up defensively. The man grabbed onto her forearms and yanked her from the corner, spinning her and throwing her onto her back on the small cot.

She flailed her arms and legs, her eyes closed tightly, as Klaus clambered atop her. Some of her blows connected, but her limbs were still weak from the drugs and they bounced off harmlessly. Klaus pressed his body weight upon her, forcing her legs still. His hands scrambled to keep hers steady.

"Yes," he hissed. "Struggle. Fight…"

Maya opened her eyes to see the man leering down at her, a maniacal glint in his eyes. A pit of horror solidified in her stomach; he was *enjoying* this. He wanted her to fight him off. He wanted her to try, and he wanted to dominate.

She pulled a hand loose from his grip and swung it up again, slapping him solidly across the face. He grunted with the blow. His lips peeled back in a malicious grin as he licked a bead of blood from the corner of his mouth.

Then he struck back, slapping Maya's cheek hard enough to force her head to the side. She winced. Despite his relatively small stature, he was stronger than she was. He forced her arms above her head, crossed at the wrists, and held them with one hand.

Maya struggled against his grip, trying hard to pull a hand free, to get a leg out from beneath him.

Klaus's other hand forced her shirt up, exposing her stomach. "I think you were lying," he rasped. "I think you are *exactly* what I am looking for. We will find out, won't we?" He hooked a thumb into the waistline of her pajama pants.

Stop! Maya shouted internally. But it was not an order directed at the rapist. Every instinct was driving her to fight, to struggle, to pry herself loose from him—but her mind was telling her body to stop.

Don't fight. That's what he wants. That's why he waited for you to wake up. That's why he didn't want you drugged.

Klaus adjusted his body weight, struggling to keep her still and push her pants down past her waist. The terror and panic of the moment demanded that she be combative, but she forced herself to slacken her muscles. She let the tension run from her shoulders, her arms, her wrists. She stopped trying to kick her legs out. Her head lolled to one side on the pillow, staring at the white wall.

The man held her wrists roughly, but he paused, glaring down at her. "What is this?" he growled. "What are you doing?"

"My name is Maya Lawson," she said, rapidly and quietly. "I was born in Fairfax, Virginia—"

"Shut up!" Klaus hissed. "You are ruining everything!"

"My parents are Reid and Katherine Lawson. I have a younger sister, Sara, fourteen years old—"

Her assailant slapped her across the face, hard, but Maya bit her tongue to keep from crying out. She would give him no satisfaction.

"Fight back!" he screamed in her face. He struck her again with an open palm. The side of her face stung. She felt warm blood on her lips. But she refused to struggle, refused to give in to anything this savage wanted.

Maya turned her head to look up at him. "I am someone's daughter," she told him, unblinking. "Someone's sister. A child…"

Klaus grunted in fury as he drove a closed fist across her cheek. She gasped in pain, but did not yelp or cry out. He rolled off of her angrily and threw open the compartment door, stomping indignantly into the hallway.

Maya quickly sat up and drew her knees to her chest. She touched the side of her face; it was tender and sore, but nothing seemed broken.

She wiped the blood from her lips as a dark-featured Slav suddenly filled the doorway. Like the others he had a submachine gun on a strap over one shoulder. Maya froze; she could not help but remember the story of Anita from the cargo ship container. The girl who had tried to fight back and failed. She remembered Jersey, killed in the gravel of a foreign country thousands of miles from home.

If that was to be her fate, so be it, she decided. She would not succumb to someone like her attempted rapist.

The Slav shouted at her, his words foreign, as he advanced into the compartment. He grabbed her by an arm and yanked her to her feet, bellowing all the while.

Maya saw a chance and took it. She surged forward and got both hands on the submachine gun, wrenching it away from the Slav. The strap went taut around his shoulder.

The man put out both hands and shoved her violently. Maya reeled backward. Her head struck the window hard and she fell to the floor of the compartment. Stars swam in her vision.

She felt the distinct prick of a needle sinking into her arm. She was being drugged again.

Then the compartment door slid closed. She was alone. She had eluded Klaus, at least for now, but she had no idea what might happen while she was unconscious. She might be moved again. Or perhaps something far worse, something more sinister—someone else, someone who did not care if she was awake or not.

Maya scrambled to her feet before the drugs took hold. Her head throbbed painfully and she nearly stumbled as she pulled the shade up again over the window. The glass had cracked where her head had struck it. She pounded on the pane with a fist, hoping that it would give, that she could break it open and escape. Broken glass and a leap from a moving train was preferable to the relative unknown of what might await her in the sleeper car.

The glass would not give, and the strength drained from her arms. She fell to her knees.

Before losing consciousness, she thought she heard shouting from outside her compartment. Then a strange sound, muffled, as if from a distance... *A drum roll?* she thought. *No, of course not.* It sounded like gunfire. But before she could discern it, Maya fell to her side and slipped back into the darkness.

CHAPTER THIRTY SIX

R eid scrambled up the chain-link fence and slung his jacket over the barbed wire at the top. Maria followed suit, tossing the jacket back down to him before dropping to her feet in the Bratislava impound lot.

There were cameras, he knew, and likely alarms. But he was far beyond worrying about his face being seen.

They sprinted across the lot, past cars and trucks and motor-cycles, toward the red and white medevac chopper, the same one Reid had landed on the fairway near the District hotel.

"You can fly this, right?" he asked.

"Of course," Maria said. She pulled open the door and climbed up into the cockpit. Reid remained on the ground, the Lorcin pistol in one hand and an Agram SMG in the other.

There was a shout from nearby and the sweep of a flashlight beam as a Bratislava police officer spoke quickly into his radio. Reid fired off two shots from the pistol, deliberately missing, and the officer leapt for cover.

The impound lot was just across the street from the precinct. He knew others would be coming soon.

The rotors of the chopper whirred to life, spinning slowly and gaining speed as several officers poured from the precinct doors, running toward the lot. Reid sprayed several rounds from the Agram through the fence, over their heads. They ducked and cov-ered or clambered behind cars.

He slid open the side door of the AW109 helicopter and climbed up, securing the Lorcin in his jeans and hanging onto a white looped strap in the ceiling. As the skids rose from the asphalt, he fired again, intentionally pulling his aim. Then he yanked the door closed as rounds from service pistols smacked the side of the chopper.

Maria maneuvered the stick and banked to the right, gaining altitude as she directed the helicopter behind a building and away from the line of fire of the police. Reid climbed over the seat and joined her in the cockpit with a painful groan. He pulled a headset over his ears.

"You okay?" Maria asked.

He nodded. "Are we? Any damage?"

"Doesn't appear to be." She pulled back on the stick and the chopper rose above the Bratislava skyline. She kept the nav lights and strobes off, flying dark as they headed northwest.

"You know…" He paused, not sure how to articulate what he was feeling. "Those cameras at the impound lot would have likely caught your face."

"I know."

Reid didn't say anything more about it. Maria had already shown him, more than once, that she was not necessarily on the side of the CIA, but by blatantly breaking into the lot and stealing the chopper, she was tipping her hand to them as well.

"How long?" he asked.

"At max airspeed, less than an hour to get to Snêžka," she replied. The trafficker Mirko, under extreme duress from Maria's butterfly knife, had told her that the American girls in question had been put on a nine-car freight train heading into the Czech Republic, on a remote set of tracks that wound through the Krkonoše mountain range and passed by the tallest peak, Snêžka. But Reid knew that even with that intel…

"We'll need a way to find a more precise location," Maria said. "Otherwise, we'll just be flying over a mountain, looking for trains."

"I know." Reid nodded. He didn't like it, but there was a way. "I have an idea about that."

❧   ❧   ❧

"You sure you want to do this?" Maria asked.

"Do you have a better way?" he asked. They were over the north-west border, out of Slovakia and headed for the mountain region of the Czech Republic. Shortly after crossing into new airspace a voice had come over the radio, first asking them to identify themselves and then threatening to force them to land. Maria had turned the radio off; they knew that shooting down the chopper would be a last resort, and by the time it was seriously considered they'd have reached their destination.

But first, they needed a destination.

Maria shook her head. She did not have any better ideas for locating the train that had Reid's girls on it. She switched the radio back on and said in Slovak, "My name is Agent Maria Johansson of the American Central Intelligence Agency. Over."

There was a pregnant pause before the radio controller on the other side said anything. The man spoke in Czech, but the two lan-guages were mutually intelligible enough for each to understand the other. "Agent Johansson, you will land the helicopter at the next available site. I will relay the coordinates—"

"Negative," Maria interrupted. "This flight is part of an opera-tion sanctioned by Interpol and the CIA. If you want me to put down this chopper, you will first put me through to my deputy director in Langley, Virginia." She gave the number, the one she and Reid both knew by heart, to the controller. "This is an emergency situation. He'll give you the clearance you need. Over."

The controller scoffed audibly in the headset. "A moment," he said curtly, and then there was only silence. Reid and Maria exchanged a glance and waited.

A full minute went by, and then most of another before anyone spoke in the headset again. When they did, they spoke English and did not sound the least bit pleased.

"This is Deputy Director Shawn Cartwright of the CIA. Identify yourself."

"It's Johansson, sir."

"Johansson," Cartwright growled, "just what the hell are you—"

"She's not alone," Reid added.

Cartwright pitched a heavy sigh. "The two of you are in an insurmountable amount of trouble," he told them, his voice low. The number Maria had given the controller was Cartwright's main line; regardless of where he actually stood, they knew he was undoubtedly being monitored. "Land the helo, and give me your location..."

"Can't do that," Reid said. "We know where the girls are. We're en route. But we need help..."

"I'm in no position to help you," Cartwright insisted. "You're disavowed. You broke laws. You've killed...I've lost track of how many. You land the chopper, and you wait for Agent Strickland and Interpol to arrive."

"We both know we're not going to do that," Reid countered. "You can help us now. You can be the one to end this." With Cartwright's CIA resources he could have the information they needed within minutes—but only if he was willing to do so. "We're looking for a freight train owned by Czech Railways, nine cars long, currently somewhere on or near the Snêžka mountain pass in Czechia."

"Zero, I won't—"

"Like you said," Reid persisted, "I'm disavowed, which means you're not my boss right now. I'm asking as a friend."

"We can alert the Czech authorities," Cartwright said. "Have them stop the train and search it, find your kids..."

"That won't work. As soon as they get word that the police are onto them, they might do something to the girls," Reid said quickly. "Move them again, or...or get rid of them."

Cartwright groaned through the headset. "I could lose my job, Kent. Ruin my entire career. Maybe worse..."

"And my two teenage daughters could be raped," Reid snapped. He surprised even himself with his words; it was the first time he had acknowledged, aloud, the atrocities that his girls could be facing at that very moment. "Or beaten. Or killed. They're just kids,

Cartwright. And I'm not just talking about my own here, but any of them that these traffickers have taken. None of them deserve this. And these men, they deserve everything that's coming to them."

The deputy director was quiet for a moment. Reid had taken the moral high ground, appealed to his emotions; there was no way Cartwright could turn them down.

At least he thought.

"I'm sorry, Zero." For just a moment, Cartwright sounded genuinely remorseful. "You went rogue. I can't help you now." The line fell silent.

"Cartwright? Hello?" There was no answer. Reid yanked off the headset and furiously threw it to the floor of the chopper.

He now saw the undeniable truth—the deputy director was a bureaucrat, nothing more. He believed in image and protocol, not the welfare of people. Not the security of a nation or even the world. And certainly not the safety of two kids lost somewhere in Eastern Europe. Cartwright was a middleman playing both sides, telling his agents that it was those above his pay grade making the wrong moves while kowtowing to the higher-ups to advance his career.

He was no better than Riker in Reid's eyes. He had his chance to show a moral backbone and he folded.

Reid slipped the headset back on as Maria flew north, heading toward the Krkonoŝe mountains. "We'll find them," she promised. "Together. Even if we have to fly all over this mountain. We'll find them."

"And what if they're not here?" Reid argued. "What if they're past the mountain? What if they're in Poland? What if Mirko lied to us?"

Maria said nothing while Reid stared out the windshield, scanning the darkness below for any lights that might be a train.

The Czech controller came back through the headset. "Your agency has denied clearance of your flight. Land the chopper," he warned, "or you will be fired upon. This is your final—"

The line crackled with static, like a lost signal—and then another voice came through. "Agent Marigold?"

Reid and Maria exchanged a confused glance. The voice sounded young, male, and decidedly American.

"Affirmative," she said. "Identify?"

"My name is…well, never mind what my name is," the young man said quickly. "I have the coordinates to your missing train." He quickly rattled off a series of numbers, and then repeated them. "Got that?"

"Yeah," said Maria, astonished. "Got it."

"Good." Before either of them could say anything else, the line crackled again and the angry-sounding Czech controller returned.

Maria flicked off the radio. "Do you think…?"

She didn't have to finish her statement. It was obvious; Cartwright had a CIA tech track the train and hack the Czech radio frequency long enough to deliver their heading. Whether it meant that the deputy director had a change of heart or was just putting on a show for any eavesdroppers didn't matter.

They had a location, and although the train would continue to move steadily forward, they would be there in minutes.

Reid held on as Maria banked left, dropping in altitude and approaching the looming mountain of Snêžka from the northeast. He did a quick weapons check; there were four rounds in the Ruger. Six in the Lorcin. Each of the Agram SMGs was at least half capacity. He slung the strap of one submachine gun across his chest and left the other for Maria.

The nose dipped as they dropped lower. Reid craned his neck and felt a surge of hope. In the darkness of the mountain below, he saw a string of lights. From their height, it looked like a brightly speckled inchworm, barely moving as the helicopter raced toward it. But there was no doubt; it was a train.

"There! I see it!" he shouted into the headset.

Maria nodded and adjusted the tail rotor to align with the train's direction. "I'll get ahead of it and set down on the tracks. We'll force it to stop, and then do a sweep—"

"No," Reid said. "We need the full element of surprise." He was too close to risk letting anything further happen to his girls now.

"Get as low as you can." He climbed over the seat to the rear cabin, grabbed onto the loop in the ceiling, and slid the door open.

"Kent!" Maria shouted into the headset. "You're not exactly in the best state to be jumping onto moving trains."

He resisted the urge to tell her that he had, earlier that same night, leapt out of an airplane. Instead he leaned out over the darkness as they descended, cold wind whipping around his face, and counted the cars of the train. There were nine, just as Mirko had said—the engine, five freight cars, and curiously, at the center of the train, three passenger cars.

He frowned. The only time passenger cars would be attached to a freight train was if they were new or being transported to another train. Whichever was the case, they wouldn't actively be carrying passengers… *Unless the traffickers are using them*, he thought.

"There's a flashlight in the stock of the rifle," Maria told him. "You might need it."

"Thanks." He took the black flashlight and secured it, with the two pistols, in his jeans as best he could. The helo dipped again; they were no more than a hundred feet above the train. Close, but not close enough.

Reid reached into his jacket and took out the plastic-wrapped parcel there. He tore open the epinephrine shot and popped the cap from the needle. It was his last one—but with a few minutes of adrenaline, enough rounds, and a little luck, he wouldn't need another.

"I'll secure from the rear," Reid said into the headset. "Give me a few minutes to make some leeway before you stop the train. Once you do, start at the front and we'll meet somewhere in the middle."

"Ten-four."

"And Maria?" He still wasn't sure how he felt about her, but he knew that something needed to be said. "Just in case this is it for me, I just want to say—"

"Save it," she interrupted. "You and I don't say goodbyes. Not now, not ever. Whatever you want to say can wait until after."

He nodded. "All right. Then how about just a 'thank you'?"

"That I'll take," she said simply. "Fifty feet."

Reid looked out over the edge of the chopper's skid as the train came into sharper relief. *Almost there.* He took off the headset and tossed it into the cabin behind him.

Then he gripped the epinephrine shot and jammed the stubby needle into his upper thigh.

The helicopter dipped lower, rocking slightly, as Reid gauged their height. It was hard to tell in the dark, but it looked like the skids were about twenty-five to thirty feet over the top of the freight train.

He sucked in a breath as the familiar sensation of surging adrenaline coursed through him. His pulse tripled; his muscles contracted. The pain seeped from his limbs.

Reid exhaled, and leapt out of the helicopter.

CHAPTER THIRTY SEVEN

R eid watched his own feet as he fell. It was a strange sensation, falling onto something that was moving below him. The train chugged forward even as he dropped toward it; for a brief moment, it looked like he would miss it entirely, as if the last freight car would rush out from under him before he landed.

Then his feet found purchase on the solid but unsteady surface.

He reeled, misjudging the momentum of a literal speeding freight train, and his feet flew out from under him. He tumbled onto his back and into a roll, but he didn't have the runway to land it. His hands shot out, grabbing onto anything they could find—the top rung of a rusty ladder at the rear of the car. The bottom half of his body swung out over nothing, but he held fast.

Something silver and black skittered past his head and soared off the train car, into the night. The Lorcin had come loose from his pants when he landed. He groaned and quickly pulled himself back to the roof of the freight car.

Atop the car was a square hatch about two feet wide. He strained to open the locking arm, teeth gritted, but finally it gave way with a heavy clunk. Reid readied his flashlight and the Ruger, and then he pulled open the steel hatch. There was no movement below him that he could discern; no sounds. He shined the light down into the dark hole. There was something in there ... He lowered himself to his stomach and dared to stick his head in.

The last freight car in the train was an actual freight car, filled with crates of an unknown something. He shined the flashlight around the inside but saw no people, no faces.

Panic gripped him. *What if we have the wrong train?* Despite Cartwright's help, it was still entirely possibly that Mirko had lied to them.

He scrambled to his feet. The epinephrine wouldn't last forever and he needed to clear as much as he could before Maria stopped the train. Reid took a running start and leapt over the coupling to the next car, landing shaky on his feet. Both arms shot out to steady himself, and then he rushed to the next hatch. After a similar struggle to open it, he readied the flashlight and the Ruger and dropped through the opening, his arms crossed over his chest.

He landed with a thud inside the freight car and immediately heard a surprised cry. He crouched, bringing both the light and the pistol up, sweeping the beam over three faces.

Two young women were huddled in the far corner, holding each other and squinting into his light. Their faces were chalk white, save for the purple bruises apparent on their skin. A third girl sat with her back to the car's wall, legs splayed in front of her. Her eyes were closed and her head lolled gently with the rhythm of the moving train.

Reid couldn't tell if she was alive or dead.

Besides the three girls, the freight car was empty. After sweeping every corner with the flashlight, he turned back to the two in the corner. "English?" he asked urgently. "Speak English?"

"*N-nyet*," stammered a blonde one of the pair.

Russian. He knew Russian. "I am…American police," he said quickly in her native tongue. "The train will soon stop. You will be safe. But you must keep still and be quiet."

Tears welled in their eyes at the notion of being safe, being freed from the hellish train.

"But I need to know," he asked. "Are there other girls on this train?"

"Yes," the blonde girl confirmed. "I have seen others. Sometimes the train stops for just a minute or two. Men come aboard. Men leave. Sometimes we are taken to the…the…" She seemed to have trouble finding the right term. "The cars with the beds."

"The passenger cars? Girls are taken to the passenger cars?" He shoved the LC9 back into his jeans. "Remember what I said. Be still and silent, no matter what happens." He leapt up, gripping the edge of the hatch overhead and pulling himself back onto the top of the train and into the cold wind.

Why do they take girls there? he wondered, although deep inside his brain he knew the answer. There was still one more freight car between him and the three passenger cars, and then three more freight cars beyond them before the engine. Once Maria stopped the train, she would clear from the front. He had to keep going.

Reid glanced skyward. *But where is Maria?* He had lost sight of the helicopter; in fact, he couldn't even hear it.

But he could see the hulking shadow of the mountain, looming impossibly large directly in front of the speeding train. *The tracks don't go around Sněžka,* he realized grimly. *They go through it. The mountain pass is underground.*

The train barreled toward the yawning black mouth of a subterranean tunnel. Reid bolted forward, leaping the next coupling and continuing down the length of the third freight car. He had no time to try to wrench open the top hatch, no time to clear it. A wall of stone rushed towards him as the first few cars of the train entered the tunnel.

He held his breath and leaped, tucking his head down and his arms in as he fell between cars. The stone whooshed over his head, so close he felt a breeze on his freshly shorn scalp. Then he landed, catching himself by the waist on the railing of the passenger car's small balcony.

He grunted as the air was forced from his lungs, but he held himself. A half second later or a slightly miscalculated jump and the stone top of the tunnel would have taken his head off his shoulders.

Reid pulled himself onto the small steel balcony behind the passenger car, hanging over the car coupling, and took a few breaths. He had no idea how long it had been since he had taken the epinephrine shot; two minutes? Possibly less? Either way it would wear off soon.

He hefted the Agram, finger on the trigger, and put his other hand on the sliding door to the passenger car. He did not know what might be waiting for him on the other side; the small window had been covered.

He yanked the door open and stepped into the corridor of the bright car.

Not five feet from him, a man spun in surprise. He had an unlit cigarette pinched in his lips, a plastic lighter halfway to his mouth, and an SMG hanging from a strap. The cigarette fell as the man fumbled for his gun.

Reid fired a short burst and cut the Slav down. From the sleeper cabins to his left came shouts and shrieks of fear and shock—and not just female. His stomach tied itself in a knot as he forced himself to realize what the traffickers were doing with the passenger cars.

But he didn't believe it, didn't want to believe it, until he saw it for himself.

He tore open the door to the first sleeper cabin and gaped in disgust. On the bottom bunk of two cots was a girl, her face red, tears streaking her cheeks. Atop her was a small man, bald, wearing round, silver eyeglasses, his pants pushed down past his hips.

The both of them were frozen in alarm at the report of the gunfire—yet the man's hand was still firmly around the girl's throat.

Fresh anger washed over Reid as he grabbed the small man by the nape of the neck and hauled him backward. The bespectacled rapist yelped as he was tossed out of the cabin and into a heap in the corridor.

"Wait, wait!" he shouted. "Please … do not hurt me." His English was heavily accented—Austrian, Reid guessed. "I-I have money. Lots of it …"

Reid pulled out the Ruger and shot him once in the forehead.

The girl in the room was not Sara. But she couldn't have been much older.

"English?" Reid asked her.

She nodded fervently, her eyes wide in terror.

"Get under the bed and stay there." She did not have to be told twice; she scrambled off the bunk and slid beneath it.

As Reid stepped back into the corridor, he saw a flash of movement and heard another cabin door slide shut. He strode to it and threw it open, the LC9 pointed at the nose of a fat man trembling from head to toe, wearing only a white tank top and briefs.

"Out." Reid gestured with the gun. The man put up his hands and whimpered slightly as he stepped out of the cabin. Reid glanced beyond him; the young woman on the bed was not one of his daughters. But she was unconscious, lying on her back with her limbs splayed.

"Please don't shoot me," the fat man whined.

Reid raised an eyebrow. "You're American?"

"Yes ... a-and I have children, two of them ..."

"So do I." He raised the Ruger. "And I'd like to keep them safe from people like you—"

Before he could fire, the far door of the passenger car was flung open, men beyond it shouting in Slovak. Reid ducked and tucked in his arms as a hail of automatic gunfire tore down the corridor and into the fat man. Reid spun and threw himself into the sleeper car, falling to the floor on his back. He raised the Agram, breathing hard, waiting for the Slovakians to come find him.

The unconscious woman's arm dangled near his face. A pool of blood spread to the doorway of the cabin as steady footfalls sounded in the corridor beyond. There were three of them, he surmised from the sound of their boots. And he was a sitting duck.

"Come out," one of them called gruffly in Slovak. "And we will not kill you."

He had no way out; the only point of egress was the narrow window of the cabin, and he wouldn't be able to get it open and safely climb out before they reached him. Reid stayed on the floor, on his back, the gun aimed at the doorway. If he was lucky, they would aim high, for center mass, and he could get the drop on them—but likely only one, maybe two, before they realized his position.

The footsteps treaded closer as Reid struggled to control his breathing. The epinephrine was wearing off. The pain was returning to his body, accompanied by fresh aches in his ribs where he had leaped down onto the passenger car.

He saw the black muzzle of a machine gun as it twisted around the corner, pointing into the room—upward, as he had suspected—and as the body followed, Reid pulled the trigger and fired four rounds through the Slovakian. The man squeezed his own trigger as he fell, sending bullets uselessly into the ceiling.

The other two shouted angrily and kept their distance. Reid had given away his position. He scrambled to his feet, looking around wildly, but there was nowhere to go that wouldn't put the unconscious young woman in harm's way.

His mind raced for an answer when suddenly the entire train jolted, the brakes beneath them shrieking. Reid swayed and grabbed onto the top cot for support; out in the corridor he heard the two men yell, their bodies thumping against the floor as they fell over.

He had his opening. He snatched up the Agram and slid on his knees into the hallway, firing low, at hip level, until the clip was empty. The barrel smoked as the train rolled to a complete stop. The two Slavs were dead.

Maria, he thought. She must have had to fly over the mountain when the train went into the tunnel and blocked its route from the other side.

The Agram was out of ammunition and his Ruger had only a few shots left. He grabbed up one of the dead men's guns—an Uzi, a gun notorious for poor accuracy at anything other than close range. It was less than ideal for much more than spraying bullets, but it would serve his purposes.

He cleared the other two sleeper cabins in the car. They were both empty. He told the girl hiding under the cot to stay still and quiet, just as he had told the others, and then he hurried to the front of the passenger car. The door was still open, but the entrance to the next car was closed.

Since the passenger cars on this train were intended merely for transport, they were not properly coupled; Reid had to climb over a short railing to reach the next car. He winced as he did, pain shooting in his legs and abdomen. The epinephrine had worn off, veritably wasted, while he still had yet to find his daughters.

But this was not the time to show weakness. He paused yet again with his hand on the door, took a few calming breaths, and threw it open.

Reid pushed into the car with the Uzi leading the way to find the corridor empty. There were no Slavic traffickers, no shouts of surprise, no hail of gunfire. He paused, listening intently. He had killed four Slovakians in the last passenger car; was it possible there were only four on the train?

There was a sound, barely audible in the relative silence of the car. At first he thought it was someone breathing, but it could have been the hissing of some train apparatus, like the cooling brakes beneath him.

His throat was dry but his hands were steady as he reached for the door to the nearest sleeper cabin and threw it open, immediately barging in and clearing the tiny room with the Uzi.

There was no one inside. *But if there's anyone in the other three, they'll be ready for me.*

Nevertheless, he pressed on, his fingers on the latch of the next cabin. He sucked in a breath and wrenched it open.

It too was empty.

Reid just barely heard the quiet click of a latch as a door slid open elsewhere in the passenger car.

He was on his feet in an instant, the Uzi in hand. But he couldn't tell which direction the sound had come from, if it was an entrance door to the passenger car or if it was a sleeper cabin opening.

He paused at the threshold, listening, trying to determine which way to aim. The wrong choice could mean someone getting a clear shot at him—or several. He could throw himself into the corridor, against the far wall, hopefully diverting their attention and aim enough to get a few shots in himself. It was risky, but it was preferable to sticking his head out or waiting for someone to reach to his position.

He let out a silent breath and then launched his body into the corridor, raising the Uzi at the same time toward the figure standing in the aisle of the passenger car. His shoulder hit the opposite wall painfully. His index finger was heavy on the trigger—

Reid's breath caught in his throat as he got visual on his assailant. The Slovak trafficker was armed with an Agram, but it was not pointed at Reid. It was pressed to the temple of his hostage.

Her eyes were half-closed. Her skin was chalk-white and she could barely stand on her own, held up mostly by the thick Slavic arm around her neck.

He had found her. He had finally found her—looking barely conscious and with a gun pressed to her skull.

"Maya," he said in a whisper.

CHAPTER THIRTY EIGHT

"**P**ut down the gun," the trafficker said in Slovakian, "or I kill this girl."

Reid dropped the Uzi as if it were on fire. "Okay," he said quickly. "Just let her go. It's me you want, right?" *He doesn't know who she is. He doesn't know she's why I've come*, he thought desperately.

"On your knees," the Slovak demanded.

Reid held up one hand, palm out. *Don't hurt her. Please don't hurt her.* "First, let the girl go. Then I'll do whatever you ask."

The trafficker's grip tightened around Maya's neck. Reid gasped as she let out a weak choking sound.

"Please..." he implored as he lowered himself to one knee. The Uzi was within arm's reach. But it might as well have been a mile away for all the good it would do him.

Maya's eyelids fluttered slightly. Her lips parted and she murmured a single word: "Dad?"

Tears stung at Reid's eyes. "Yes," he said in English. "I'm here."

The trafficker furrowed his brow; it was doubtful that he understood their words, but he recognized the emotion behind the exchange. "You know her?" he asked in Slovak. His mouth curled into a wicked grin. "You came here for this one?"

Reid said nothing. If he admitted the truth, the man might pull the trigger. *But if I don't, he'll hurt her anyway. If he kills me, he'll hurt her anyway.* There wasn't an angle on the situation that Reid could see ending with anything other than him failing to have saved his daughter.

"I came for her," he said quietly in Slovak. "I'm her father."

For a moment the trafficker looked quite surprised. Then his malicious grin returned. "Then for what you have done to my friends, you will watch her die."

"No—"

The trafficker let go of his grip on Maya. She tried to stand on her own, but her legs gave out from beneath her and she collapsed to the floor of the passenger car. The Slovak aimed his Agram downward...

Reid scrambled forward, reaching for the Uzi, desperate to grab it up in time.

It was barely in his grip as a blast of gunfire tore the air. He winced at the deafening report; his eyes squeezed shut and refused to ever open again as his heart seized.

No.

Beyond his eyelids, someone grunted and fell.

What?

Reid opened his eyes. The Slovakian was splayed out on the floor of the train car, a pool of blood widening around him. Beside him was Maya, lying still—too still. Beyond them both was the open door at the front of the passenger car.

Maria stood in it, her submachine gun barrel smoking.

"Maya." Reid dropped the Uzi and scrambled on his hands and knees to her side. She was on her back, her eyes barely open, like two crescent moons on her too-white skin.

He quickly checked her over; she wasn't hit. Tears flooded his eyes when he saw the purple and blue bruises across the side of her face. "Maya, baby, say something." His trembling fingers touched her neck. She had a pulse; weak, but steady. "Maya. I found you. Talk to me...please...I came for you. I'm here. I found you." The words spilled from his lips as if they would wake her, but she did not move, did not respond in any way.

He hugged her to his chest and rocked gently, his tears spilling down his cheeks and onto her forehead.

Maria knelt beside them and checked Maya's pupils. "It looks like she's been drugged." Maria set about checking the girl's body for any other wounds. "I don't think anything is broken..."

Maya moaned softly. Reid released his grip on her, holding her up by her shoulders. "Maya?"

"Dad," she murmured softly.

"Yes, it's me. I'm here ..."

"Sara," she said in a whisper.

"Sara? What about Sara?" Reid turned desperately to Maria. "You cleared the first half of the train, right?"

Maria turned toward him, but she didn't look him in the eye. "I did. But Kent ... there were no other American girls aboard."

"No." Reid shook his head. He didn't believe it—he couldn't believe it. "No, no. She's here. She has to be here. Sara is *here*." He sniffed once and wiped his eyes. "There's a ... there's one car I didn't clear, a freight car. But I can't get to it if we're in the tunnel. We need to move the helicopter off the tracks, get the train out, and then I can check it. She's in there ..." He was rambling, speaking a mile a minute. His other daughter *had* to be on the train. All of the traffickers aboard were dead; there was no one left to give them a lead, to tell them where she was.

"Kent. Look at this." Maria, still kneeling beside Maya, pointed out the thin, dark blood stain on Maya's pant leg. Maria gently peeled back the fabric, small threads sticking to the still-healing wound.

Reid's hand flew over his mouth when he saw the source of the blood.

There on Maya's calf were thin letters, a message carved into her skin. The very sight of it made bile rise in his throat, but he forced himself to lean in and see what it said.

RED

23

POLA

Those were the three lines etched into her leg.

"What do you think this means?" Maria asked in a near-whisper.

"I don't know." Reid put both hands over his mouth and breathed into them as his mind raced. *Was this done to her? Or did she do it to herself? If she did it, why?* "Maya, can you hear me?"

"Sara," the girl said again.

"Reid, she's barely responsive," said Maria. "We need to get her to a hospital..."

"Train," Maya murmured. "On a train."

"Yes, we're on the train," said Reid quickly. "But where is Sara? Maya, do you know where she is?" He looked down again at the scars cut into her leg. *On a train.* Maya was incredibly smart; if she had been separated from her younger sister but could not do anything about it physically, then she would have found another way. Like leaving hairs behind for forensics to find. Like hiding a message in a toilet tank.

Or carving a message into her own skin, if nothing else was available.

"Is she..." he started. "Maya, is she on a different train?"

His daughter nodded weakly, just once, her chin bobbing only slightly.

Maria sighed. "They put them on two different trains."

"And Maya did this to herself," Reid realized aloud, "to leave a clue." *Pola? Pola. What is Pola?* "Poland," he murmured. "One to Poland."

"But 'red twenty-three'...what is that?" Maria asked.

A color and a number. A train. Train cars. Boxcars...

His mind suddenly flashed onto a memory, one that had happened only a day prior—though now it felt like a lifetime ago. He had stood in Port Jersey, desperately looking for his daughters, surrounded by towering stacks of cargo containers in various colors.

Each one emblazoned with a stenciled number.

"It's a boxcar," he blurted out. "Maya gave us a destination and a location on the train. We have to go. We have to find it."

"What about her?" Maria protested, gesturing at Maya. "We can't take her with us, Kent. Not like this."

"We can," he argued, even though he knew she was right. "We take the chopper, put her in the back..."

"We can't," Maria argued. "I'll stay."

"What?" Reid shook his head. "No, you can't stay. Strickland is on his way, with the Czech police—"

"And probably Interpol," Maria added. "I know. I'll keep her safe until they arrive. I'll make sure she gets to a hospital and that she's taken care of. You go. Get Sara."

"Maria, they'll arrest you."

"Yeah," she said with a small shrug. "They probably will. But if it means that one of your girls is safe and in the right hands..." She rose from her kneeling position and looked him in the eye. "Then it's worth it."

"I won't ask you to do that—"

"You're not. I'm volunteering."

Reid stared at the floor. He looked at his daughter, lying semi-conscious before them. He didn't know what to say; there was nothing he *could* say that would come close to expressing the gratitude he was feeling.

Maria stepped into the corridor and patted down the dead trafficker's pockets, coming up with a cell phone. "Here," she said as she punched in a number. "I know you don't like it, but this is my contact at FIS. Tell them who you are and what's happened. They'll help you."

Reid took the phone. She was right; he did not like the idea of working with her Ukrainians—but if it meant finding his daughter, he would do whatever was necessary.

"Maria, I..."

She took his face in both hands and kissed him. "What did I tell you before? We don't say goodbyes."

"I was just going to say thank you."

She smirked. "I'll take that. Now go. Take the chopper. Make the call. You don't have time to waste."

Reid nodded and grabbed the Uzi. He knelt and kissed Maya's forehead. The sense of gratitude he felt to hold her, to look into her face, was beyond anything he could express.

He felt his eyes well up. And he vowed to never let her out of his sight again.

"I'll be back for you, I promise," he whispered, and kissed her again.

Then he hurried to the door of the passenger car, climbed over the railing into the third and final sleeper car, and pushed the door open.

He staggered to a stop, stunned by what he found. There were four more dead Slavs in the third car, as well as two johns. Maria had cleared the car, and she had done it without the personal investment that he had in this.

She had done it for him, or for his girls, or maybe for both.

Reid stepped over the bodies and exited through the passenger car, hastening toward the waiting chopper. His limbs still ached and the stab wound in his abdomen throbbed, but the pain hardly mattered anymore; he had found Maya, and nothing, not anyone, was going to stand in the way of finding Sara.

CHAPTER THIRTY NINE

Reid piloted the medevac helicopter over the border between the Czech Republic and Poland, heading northeast in the general direction of Warsaw. He kept the lights off and his altitude low, around fifteen hundred feet, maintaining an air speed of about a hundred sixty miles an hour. The radio was off; the last thing he needed was more threats to shoot him out of the sky.

He plugged the cell phone that Maria had given him into the headset interface, but hesitated to press the call button. It was not for fear of betraying the CIA, or his country; US and Ukrainian relations were cordial. Besides, he had been disavowed. He had no one to betray. His hesitation was based on a feeling, the notion that these Ukrainians—if they were really FIS at all—wanted something from him. They had collected information on the traffickers, but done nothing, reported nothing. They had referred to Reid as an "asset."

He hesitated because he did not know their position, and he wasn't sure he wanted to be in their pocket.

Maria's words from earlier, in the black muscle car, flashed through his mind. *A lot of the things you know, or used to know, I also know.* If this was about the conspiracy that he had only begun to uncover, he didn't want their help. And he certainly didn't want to be in anyone's pocket—not the CIA's, not the Ukrainians'... not even Maria's.

He just wanted his girls back. He wanted them to be safe at home with him. *As much as you don't like it,* he told himself, *you have no one else to turn to.*

Reid made the call. The line toned several times. No one answered and no voicemail picked up. Instead, the call simply ended.

Of course they didn't answer. He was calling from an unknown Slovakian phone number.

He continued northeast, frustrated and growing desperate. He considered calling Cartwright again, but he doubted the deputy director would help him a second time. Just putting in the call could tip off the higher-ups that he'd aided them...

The cell phone chimed as a call from an unknown number came through. Reid answered it, but said nothing. Whoever was on the other line was equally silent.

Finally Reid spoke. "This is Kent Steele."

"Ah. Agent Zero." The man's voice was deep and even. He spoke in English, but his accent was heavy. "Is Calendula with you?"

Maria's Ukrainian codename. "No. She's being..." By now Strickland and Czech authorities had surely reached the stopped train. "She's been apprehended."

"I see." There was little remorse in the man's voice; he said it as if Reid had stated a simple fact. "She gave you this number? Told you to inform us?"

"Yes, she did. But there's more." Reid hesitated. "I need information. She told me you would help."

"What sort of information?"

"There's a train, a freight train that crossed the border from Czechia into Poland, probably sometime in the last couple of hours," Reid said quickly. "This train is carrying a red boxcar or cargo container labeled with the number twenty-three. I need to find it, and I need to find it now."

"What of your CIA?" The man sounded almost amused, much to Reid's irritation. "They cannot help you with this intel?"

Reid clenched his jaw. This man very likely already knew that they wouldn't. "No," he said forcefully, "they can't. Can you? Or am I wasting my time?"

"We can locate your train," the man said, his voice smarmy. "However, this information does not come for free. We ask for a favor in return."

Reid scoffed. This was precisely the situation he did not want to find himself in. "What kind of favor?"

"It seems you have much on your mind at the moment. We will not ask this favor now, but sometime in the future—the near future—we will contact you."

"Fine," he said curtly. Of course he would agree to it if it meant finding Sara; besides, he had no idea what might become of him in the near future anyhow. "It's a deal."

"Good. Now this information you give us, it is not much to go on. What else can you tell us about your missing train?"

He shook his head. He didn't have much else to tell them. "It might be owned by Czech Railways." The other trafficker train had been, he reasoned. Then another thought occurred to him. "Wait, you gave us the lead on Filip Varga, right? You've been watching him, building a file on him?"

"Perhaps," the man said vaguely.

"Then you know he's been helping the traffickers move women across the borders. Look into Varga's holdings and see if there's anything associated with freight. It could be that the train, or at least the containers, belongs to something he's got his hands in."

The man on the end of the line chuckled lightly. "She was right. You are astute. Stand by, Agent Zero." The call ended.

Reid scoffed again. He didn't like the situation before he'd made the call, and he liked this man's wheedling, insincere voice even less. But if the means meant that he got to Sara, then he couldn't afford to be picky about his allies, even temporary ones.

A full three minutes passed before the phone rang again.

"We have identified your train," the Ukrainian man told him. "I cannot tell you where it is currently, but I can tell you where it will be. There is a small city called Grodkow, to the west of Opole. You know it?"

"I know it," Reid said, grateful for his thorough knowledge of European history. The city formerly known as Grottkau had been nearly demolished during the Thirty Years' War, one of the most devastating conflicts in human history.

"The train's route will pass just north of there. By our best estimate it will arrive in approximately forty-five minutes' time. I will remit the coordinates. You can get there by then?"

"Yes," Reid told him. He was less than sixty miles from Grodkow; he could get there in roughly twenty minutes, well ahead of the train.

"Good luck, Agent Zero. We will be in touch." The Ukrainian ended the call.

Reid adjusted his tail rotor and pulled the stick back, rising in altitude and accelerating to max airspeed. He did not know what kind of favor they would ask of him, but it hardly mattered now. He had a destination; he just had to get there before anything happened to his daughter.

CHAPTER FORTY

Sara sat on the dirty floor of the boxcar as the train chugged down the tracks. She could see nothing in the darkness, though she was vaguely aware that there were others in there with her. Occasionally she heard a shuffle, a sniffle, the sound of gentle weeping. But none of the girls spoke, least of all Sara.

She had nothing left. There were no more tears to cry; there was no more hope to be had. She had awoken from her stupor when the rough, angry men put her on the train, only to watch her sister torn from her. Only to see the dark-haired girl, the one who tried to help, shot dead in the dirt.

Dad will come for us. That's what Maya had promised. But he hadn't come. No one had. And now Maya was gone too. Sara had nothing left. She had consigned herself to meet whatever fate came to her.

She was not too young or naïve to be ignorant to what these men wanted with her. But the knowledge of it only left her numb.

What could she do that Maya couldn't—or any of the other girls who had been kidnapped and forced onto the train? Her impotence did not even make her angry. It simply drained the strength and fortitude from her small, frail, fourteen-year-old limbs.

Suddenly the brakes squealed beneath her, the train slowing. Wherever they had arrived did not matter to her; she had no idea where they had landed on the cargo plane, or where the van had taken them, or where this train was going. She knew they had traveled far enough and long enough to be in some distant country, some part of the world so far removed from what she knew that she had no hope she could ever find her way back.

The train came to a hissing stop. Without the chugging of the engine, Sara could hear one of the other girls whimpering in the darkness—as if she knew something that Sara didn't. Maybe she did. But no one asked. No one spoke at all.

The door to the boxcar slid aside loudly. Suddenly there was a bright light sweeping the car, the beam of a flashlight in her eyes. She squinted into it.

A man's voice, in the guttural language that she did not understand. He spoke harshly, as if giving an order.

Suddenly there was a hand around her arm. It clamped down hard and yanked her to her feet. She yelped involuntarily as the large, brutish silhouette towered over her, pulling her to the door of the boxcar. Forcing her out into the chilly night air.

Sara was out of the train, but she did not scream for help. She did not try to wrench free from the tight grip. She did not try to run. There was nothing left in her. The train had stopped seemingly in the middle of nowhere; there were only trees and darkness. No lights or signs of people.

She watched the ground, her feet, as she was marched down the length of the train. The man who held her muttered in his language all the while. After several cars he stopped her in front of a long, blue train car with several windows running down the side, each of them darkened by curtains or shades.

He said something gruffly and gestured at the platform. She stepped up onto it as the man slid the door open and shoved her inside.

Sara stood in a hallway, with windows to her right and sliding doors to her left. The windows in the doors were similarly covered from the inside. The train car smelled like a new car, but there were noises from beyond the doors. Noises that made her shiver.

The man pulled her along once again, past the first door. Past the second door. To the third door.

Sara noticed that it was slightly ajar, slid open just a couple of inches. She could not help herself; her eyes glanced inside before she even realized what she was doing.

Her gaze met that of another girl, not much older than Maya. Her face was puffy and red. Her eyes wet with tears. She stared blankly at that narrow opening in the door, back at Sara.

There was a man atop her.

Sara froze. Her legs seemed to stop working. In that brief glance, the girl's face was burned into her mind. Though her expression appeared blank, there was so much more behind her eyes. In that intimate instant, Sara saw fear. Humiliation. Dread. Panic. Complete and utter defeat.

Then the man with the gun grunted and pulled her along, forcing her legs to work again as he led her to the fourth and final door on the left. He slid it open to reveal a tiny, empty cabin. He shoved her in, barked a few unintelligible words, and slammed it closed again.

Sara stood in the center of the small, square space. There was a bed, perfectly made with sheets and a pillow and a blanket. Two silver, lamp-like sconces protruded from the blue wall on either side of a window, a thin shade pulled down over it. A small table was bolted into the floor and wall.

But Sara hardly saw any of that. She saw only that girl's face and everything behind it. She saw the face of the dead girl from the van, the one who had fallen right in front of her, her eyes half-closed and skin chalky white. She saw the face of the dark-haired girl who had tried to help Maya, and been brutally murdered for it.

Three times now Sara had seen her own possible fate at the hands of these men.

Her heartbeat doubled in her chest. She sucked in a deep breath, as if she had just awoken from a coma. Her skin prickled as sensation crept back into her arms and legs, blood rushing at high speeds through her veins.

No.

She no longer felt numb.

That won't be me. I won't let it be me.

The train began moving again, chugging steadily as it pulled itself along the tracks. There were voices out in the corridor—two men speaking. Sara whipped around, looking for something, anything... but there was so little available.

She had shoes, sneakers, from the blonde girl she had exchanged clothes with. She patted down the pockets of the jeans; there was nothing in them. She had a belt...

A belt!

The jeans were cinched with a thin brown leather belt, securing at the front with a gold clasp. Sara tore it off and shoved it underneath the pillow of the bed.

A moment later the door slid open. The man with the gun was there, peering in at her as she stood in the center of the room. There was another man with him—tall, thin, his lanky arms and legs reminding her of a spider. He had dark eyes and long dark hair that hung in his face.

Sara shivered. She did not like the mere sight of him, let alone his reason for being there.

The lanky man entered the cabin, and the door was shut again behind him. In one hand he had a bottle of some sort of liquor; he put it to his lips and took a long sip.

He grinned at her. His teeth were yellow and uneven.

The man said something in a language she didn't understand. It might have been the same language as the traffickers; she couldn't tell. He set his bottle on the small horizontal surface, and then he sat on the edge of the small bed. He patted it, inviting her to sit with him.

Sara slowly lowered herself to a seated position, trying to keep space between them, but the man slid closer to her. He whispered something in his language as he reached up and brushed her hair from her ear.

She did not flinch, but her hands trembled fiercely in her lap. Not from the man's touch; they trembled from the thought of what she might have to do, what she *would* do.

The lanky man with the long hair touched her shoulder. He ran his hand down her arm, and then up her back. Her skin crawled; she wanted nothing more than for him to stop touching her, to leave her alone.

He murmured something and stood, reaching for his bottle again. The man held it out and raised an eyebrow; he was offering it to her. Sara shook her head no.

He shrugged and brought it to his lips.

Sara's hand reached beneath the pillow.

Suddenly she was on her feet. The belt was in her hand. As the bottle was lowered again to the table, she whipped the belt around his neck from behind. She pulled. Teeth gritted.

She could not remember what happened next. It was as if her mind had checked out temporarily while her body did the work. The next thing Sara knew she was kneeling on the floor, breathing hard. Trying to keep herself from sobbing. There were deep red lines in her hands. The belt was on the floor.

So was the lanky man. He wasn't moving. She did not dare look down to see what she had done.

It won't be me.

She climbed to her feet and pulled up the window shade. The train was moving at full speed now; trees flew by in the darkness. Sara tried the latch, but it would not budge. She strained and shoved, but the window didn't move. She cried out in frustration and pounded a fist against the glass.

A harsh voice outside the cabin called out. Though the window in the door was covered, she could see a silhouette on the other side. The man with the gun—he was going to come in and see what she had done.

The latch clicked and the door began to slide open. Sara did not hesitate; she grabbed the lanky man's half-full liquor bottle in an upside-down grip. As the door slid fully open, she let out a primal scream and swung it as hard as she could.

The bottle smashed across the man's face. Glass and potent-smelling liquid flew every which way. The gunman fell back, into the corridor, gasping. There was glass in his face, blood everywhere. Sara instantly felt nauseous.

But she couldn't stop. Not now. Not when there might be others.

Hands shaking, she scrambled over and pulled the man's gun from the strap around his shoulder. She had never shot a gun before. She held it tightly in both hands and, eyes squeezed closed, she pulled the trigger—aiming for the far wall of her cabin.

The gun kicked strongly in her hands, but she held fast. A spray of bullets buffeted the wall and shattered the window. From other cabins came shrieks of panic at the sharp, impossibly loud sound.

Her ears ringing, Sara put both hands on the windowsill. She winced as a shard of glass pierced her hand, but still she pulled herself up.

Chilly air swept through her hair. The ground below was rushing by way too fast. She could be seriously hurt, or worse, in the fall. But behind her she heard another door thrown open, and more angry shouting.

I won't let it be me, she reminded herself. No matter what happened, being outside the train was far preferable to being in it. Sara held her breath as she pushed herself out of the window, end over end. Suddenly her feet were over her head; she somersaulted. Her feet hit the ground first, but only for an instant before they were flung out from under her. Then she was on her elbows, her side, her butt, her knees, tumbling over and over down a dirt hill, smacking painfully into the ground with each roll.

Yet with each roll down the hill she caught just a glimpse of the train above her, like a still photograph, but getting smaller and smaller as she tumbled further from it.

She finally stopped tumbling, coming to rest at the bottom of the hill. She did not move—she wasn't sure she could—as a wispy breath steamed into the night.

CHAPTER FORTY ONE

The helicopter dropped quickly as Reid descended just north of the Polish city of Grodkow, at the precise coordinates the Ukrainian had sent to him. His intention was to land directly on the tracks, just as Maria had done to stop the freight train carrying Maya, but he couldn't see a thing in the darkness below. Reid flicked on the landing lights and intensely bright white beams shone downward, at a slight angle, as he lowered to a thousand feet.

He could only hope that the Ukrainian's information was correct. He could only hope that they had the right train, the right route, and that they hadn't passed through here yet...

Reid sucked in a breath as something rushed past the chopper's windshield, dangerously close and moving so fast he had to adjust the tail rotor to keep from spinning in the object's wake.

What the hell was that? A plane?

He didn't have to wonder long. The flying object slowed not a hundred feet in front of him and perfectly maneuvered around in a circle to face his chopper.

It's a helicopter, he realized. *Not just any—a Eurocopter X4.* The silver helo before him glinted in the glow of his landing lights. It was larger than the medevac, with two wing-like protrusions on either side, each with a vertically aligned propeller.

It was the fastest helicopter in the world, capable of top speeds more than twice that of the red and white chopper Reid was in. And he had little doubt as to who was inside it.

The Eurocopter matched Reid's descent speed, continuing to face him. He had no choice but to land and face this. He couldn't run; the silver X4 could easily overtake him. Besides, there was nowhere for him *to* run. He had to believe that the train carrying Sara would be here soon.

He could only hope that he was still there to catch it.

Reid set the medevac down gently, its skids sinking into soft grass. He powered down the vehicle, watching as the X4's three wheels landed gently, its rotors already slowing. A silver door swung open and a single man emerged. He wore a black T-shirt under a bomber jacket with a wool collar. His dark hair was short, as short as Reid's now was, faded up the sides of his head in a military-style cut.

Agent Strickland stood in front of the X4, awash in the landing lights of the medevac chopper, making no attempt to hide the Glock 19 in his right hand. He stood casually, arms at his sides, waiting.

Reid quickly examined his options. He had the Uzi and the Ruger, both with rounds in them—but there was no way he was simply going to shoot a potentially innocent agent. And if Strickland saw him armed, he might fire first. He could pretend to acquiesce, disarm the younger agent, fight him off… but Strickland was a former Ranger, and Reid was injured. He was in no physical state for another intense showdown.

His only other option was to try to appeal to the agent. Perhaps Strickland would see reason. But, Reid thought, if Strickland was in Riker's corner he would have little chance of seeing things Reid's way. He thought back to Agent Carver, who had attacked and tried to kill him for simply recalling a memory, all on Ashleigh Riker's authority.

I think I'll have to play this one by ear. He left the Uzi in the helicopter but kept the Ruger LC9 tucked in the back of his jeans as he pushed open the door and climbed out of the cockpit.

It was eerily silent in the grassy field, made all the more eerie by the two helicopters sitting dormant, facing each other. Beyond the X4 Reid saw the lights of Grodkow, less than a mile away. But out here, where the trains ran, there was no one but the two of them.

He took slow steps toward the Eurocopter, and Strickland did the same in the opposite direction, neither taking their eyes off the other. The younger agent kept his gun at his side, and he did not seem to be in any rush. His face was passive, his features smooth; he did not look at all concerned to be facing the allegedly legendary Agent Zero.

And that made Reid very nervous, though he didn't let himself show it.

He paused with a span of about twenty feet of foot-tall grass between them, and Strickland did too.

"Agent Steele," he said. Even his voice sounded young; it was not angry or authoritative, but rather casual. "It's a pleasure to finally meet you in person."

"Not 'agent' anymore," Reid corrected. "Just a father looking for his kids."

"That was my job," Strickland replied. "At least at first. It can still be. I can find your other daughter, Steele. I want to. But first…"

"How did you find me?" Reid interjected.

"We caught up with the other train. We found Agent Johansson and your daughter Maya. I saw the message that she…" Strickland trailed off, shaking his head. "She's smart. Obviously strong too. Didn't take us much to decipher it. I was following the train route when I caught you on radar. I saw your landing lights come on."

"Then you know that the train will be passing through here shortly."

"We know," Strickland said.

"And you know that Sara is on it."

"Yes."

"Then let me end this," Reid pleaded. "Let me find her."

"By yourself? Against a train?" Strickland smirked. "I've heard the stories about you, but man, I didn't believe them." His smirk faded. "Look, you've already saved one daughter's life. The Czech police and Interpol are on their way here now. I got here faster. Let us handle this. Step away."

"Can't do that," Reid told him simply.

"You *have* to do that."

"Or what?"

Strickland patted his jacket pocket. "I've got a pair of bracelets here for you. I'm going to put them on you, and you're going to sit in that helo while I take care of this train—with backup. With arrests, not murders. The way it's supposed to be done."

Maria was right; the young agent was, as she said, a loyal Boy Scout. *Not like some of us.*

"You have kids, Strickland?" Reid asked.

"No." He shrugged one shoulder. "I've got a niece. She's seven. There's not much I wouldn't do for her." He looked Reid right in the eye as he added, "But before you ask, no. I wouldn't go rampaging across Europe and shooting at cops. I'd rely on resources. Agencies. The law."

So much for commiseration, Reid thought glumly.

Strickland checked his watch. "That's enough small talk. I know you're armed. I want you to put whatever you've got on the ground, and walk towards me slowly." He raised his Glock 19, leveling it at Reid. Somehow, even in a firing stance the young agent looked calm, relaxed.

There was no way he could draw on him faster than Strickland could fire. Reid slowly reached for the Ruger and pulled it out, holding it aloft by the barrel with two fingers. "This is all I've got." He dropped it in the tall grass. Then he took careful steps forward, wondering just what the hell he could do to avoid being detained.

"That's far enough," Strickland said when Reid was about ten feet away. He reached into his coat pocket, pulled out a pair of handcuffs, and tossed them at Reid. They landed at his feet. "Put these on behind your back."

Reid balked. "You're joking. You want me to cuff myself?"

"I told you, I've heard the stories. I'm not taking any chances."

He shook his head. Strickland was smart, careful, and unruffled. *I'll just have to be smarter—and a whole lot less careful.* Reid stooped and picked up the handcuffs. He clapped one over his left wrist and clicked it shut.

"Now turn around and..."

Before Strickland could finish, Reid clasped the other cuff around the same wrist and locked it shut, wearing both cuffs on his left arm.

Strickland blinked in shock for a moment, seemingly at an utter loss. "Are...are you serious...? What do you think you're doing?"

"Sorry. I'm sure Riker told you, I'm not the best at following orders." It was Reid's turn to smirk—a genuine smirk, the first one in quite a while.

"Son of a bitch," Strickland muttered. "I can't believe you...All right, turn around. Hands on your head."

Reid did as he was told, turning in place and putting both arms up, elbows out. He heard the rustle of grass as Strickland approached behind him.

"I swear to God, Steele, if you try anything, I *will* shoot you."

No you won't. You'll have to holster your gun, because you'll need both hands to unlock the cuffs. He said a small, silent prayer for his body to hold out.

He felt one of Strickland's hands close around his wrist. He heard the jingle of keys.

"By the way," Reid said casually. "You can call me Kent. What's your name?"

One cuff fell away from his wrist as Strickland said, "I really don't think that's—"

Reid spun his body to the right, swinging an elbow backward as he did. It connected with the side of Strickland's face. The young agent grunted as Reid turned fully, raising one leg and planting a solid front kick to the sternum.

Strickland fell into the grass on his back. The keys to the handcuffs jingled again as they flew from his grip. Reid leapt forward, doing his best to ignore the pain in his limbs. He snatched up the Glock 19 and tucked into a roll.

He came up on one knee, both hands around the pistol. Strickland slowly climbed to his feet. He grinned at Reid.

"That was a cheap shot. But what did it get you?"

Reid glanced quickly at the gun and winced. The 19 model was outfitted with Bixby's biometric scanners—the trigger guard was coded to a specific agent's fingerprints. The gun was useless to him.

Strickland reached for his ankle holster. Reid hurled the Glock into the darkness and ran forward, intent on tackling the agent before he could free his backup weapon. But the young agent was bluffing. Instead of pulling his gun, he too surged forward, meeting Reid halfway and tackling him with a shoulder to the abdomen.

Reid howled in pain as his feet left the ground. The stab wound on his stomach burned fiercely, undoubtedly busting open yet again as the young agent drove Reid forward and to the ground. Strickland straddled him and jabbed quickly at Reid's face; try as he might to block the blows, his reactions were too slow. It was all he could do to keep his hands up as he took shot after shot to the jaw and cheeks.

Stars swam in his vision as Strickland grabbed the open cuff and forced Reid's arm into the air. The pressure on his midsection let up slightly as the young agent tried to roll him over, onto his stomach.

Can't let him cuff me. Reid pulled back on his arm as hard as he could, shouting again in pain, but Strickland was stronger and healthy. Reid's right arm was pinned beneath him; his left was being wrenched backward. He couldn't pull free.

But he wouldn't expect me to push.

Reid shoved his cuffed arm forward and curled his fingers into a flat fist. He landed a direct shot into Strickland's throat. A wet choking sound erupted from the young agent as he reeled back.

Reid tugged his right arm free, but it would do him little good. He couldn't fight Strickland one-on-one. He needed some kind of handicap...

The loose cuff rattled, hanging from his left wrist.

Reid grabbed the open cuff and snapped it around Strickland's wrist before he could recover from the blow to his throat. For a moment, Strickland simply stared in disbelief, catching his breath.

Then he swung his available fist toward Reid's chin.

Reid yanked down on his left wrist, throwing Strickland's balance off, and the blow glanced off his shoulder instead.

Balance, Reid realized. *That's my upper hand.*

He quickly pulled his arm up, forcing Strickland's with it, and then back. The young agent was tugged forward. Reid put up a knee and it met with an abdomen. Strickland responded with an upward swinging elbow that caught Reid right in the chin, forcing his head back. He felt an impact to his sternum and doubled over. His left arm was pulled across his own chest as Strickland maneuvered around behind him, snaking an arm around his neck into a sleeper hold.

Reid tucked his chin down before the arm tightened, protecting his neck for a few precious moments. He brought his arm up around his head, and then yanked down, crouching at the same time. The steel cuff bit into his skin, but he didn't stop. Free from the attempted chokehold, Reid spun, forced Strickland's cuffed arm up behind his own back, and wrenched the arm up tight.

Strickland grunted in pain with his arm twisted behind him. Reid kicked at the back of his leg and forced the young agent to the ground, planting a knee firmly into the small of his back.

He reached back with his right arm, keeping the pressure on Strickland's back, and felt for the ankle holster. Reid pulled loose a silver snub-nosed revolver.

He pressed the barrel to the back of the agent's head and thumbed back the hammer, breathing hard. "Stop," he rasped. "Stop, or I will shoot you."

Strickland made a noise that sounded like he was gasping for breath. No, Reid realized—he was chuckling.

"You idiot," Strickland said, laughing bitterly. "What are you going to do, drag my corpse around? I dropped the keys. No matter how this shakes out, you're still my prisoner."

"Not quite." Reid took the gun off of Strickland but kept a knee in his back. With his right hand over his left, he took a deep breath, gritted his teeth, and popped his thumb out of joint.

Pain screamed through his hand, but it was no worse than what he felt in his abdomen or head. He slipped his hand out of the cuff, and then grimaced again as he pushed his thumb back into its socket. It was painful, but it was a trick he'd used at least once before to get out of a bind.

Reid slapped a cuff around Strickland's left wrist, and then twisted the other arm up and clasped that wrist. Then he slowly got to his feet, keeping the revolver trained on the young agent. Strickland rolled over onto his back with a grunt, his hands cuffed in front of him.

"Get up," Reid ordered. He did so, grunting as he climbed to his feet.

"That's a good trick," Strickland said, panting. "What now?"

"I don't want to shoot you," Reid told him.

"I don't want to be shot."

"Then stop. Let me get my daughter. It's all I want."

"Yeah. I see that," Strickland said quietly. "But this is my job. It's my duty. I can't just let you walk."

"I don't know if you noticed, but you're handcuffed and I've got a gun." Reid thought for a moment. "You believe in the law, right? You believe in rules and protocol. But there's a difference between what we consider just, and what's right."

Strickland shook his head. "Right and wrong are subjective. That's why we have laws and rules—"

"And sometimes," Reid countered, "the people that make the laws and rules aren't playing by them. They make them for us. They keep us in line. But these people—the politicians, our leaders, our bosses—they don't always abide by them."

"So…what?" Strickland scoffed. "You can break the law, be above it too? Just like them?"

"Yes," Reid said simply. "If that's what it takes to bring someone down, then yes. Look, you're young. There are things in play that you don't know about and wouldn't understand. I can't tell you about them, because…well, frankly, I don't trust you. But I hope you'll trust *me* when I say that I know things that would change your perspective entirely."

The young man stared at his feet. Reid scrutinized him; he had no reason to believe that Strickland was privy to any information about the conspiracy. If anything, he appeared conflicted as he considered Reid's words.

He sighed. "Coming up through the ranks, you were like a ghost story. You know that? No one believed it. The things you've done. There'd always be someone claiming they were there, that they saw it go down. I still didn't believe it." His gaze slowly lifted to meet Reid's. "I do now. For you to do all this, come all this way, to save your daughter, it's...it's not what I would have done." Strickland shrugged. "But I guess that's why they tell stories about you."

A sound reached Reid's ears in the silence of the grassy field—the chugging engine of a train. *Sara.* "It's coming," he said. "Where's your backup?"

Strickland frowned. "I don't know. They should be here by now..."

"It's just us. Are you going to help me?"

Again he stared down at his feet. "I'm sorry. But no, not like this. I don't execute people. I can't do things your way." He looked up at Reid. "And like I said, I can't just let you walk, either. The moment that gun is off of me, I'm going to come at you again. So you're going to have to do something." Strickland closed his eyes and held his chin high. "You've got me dead to rights. You do what you feel you gotta—"

Reid swung a fist in an arc and connected a solid blow just behind the young man's jaw. Strickland fell limp to the grass, unconscious. Reid shook his hand out; the strike was jarring and painful. When the authorities arrived—if they ever arrived—it would appear that Zero got the drop on him, knocked him out, and cuffed him.

He felt a small pang of remorse for knocking him out; in a strange way, they were kindred spirits, but on opposite sides of the track. He had to admit that he admired the kid's conviction. In another life, they could have worked together, maybe even have been friends...

The train's horn blared suddenly, startling Reid. He spun to see the lights of the freight train barreling down the rails not a hundred yards from him. The horn blared again, sounding ominous in the dark field.

Reid's eyes widened in shock. He hadn't even realized it—and apparently neither had Strickland—but the silver X4 had landed perpendicular right across the train tracks.

Brakes squealed like nails on a chalkboard as the train attempted to stop in time. Sparks flew up from the rails. But it was already too late; there wasn't enough track to stop the momentum.

The freight train plowed through the fourteen-million-dollar helicopter, sending steel and fire exploding around it.

CHAPTER FORTY TWO

Reid leapt into the tall grass and covered his head as the freight train smashed through the Eurocopter. Broken rotors and flaming shards flew over him, showering a fifty-foot radius around the point of impact.

When he dared to look up again, the train was stopped, likely as much from the brakes as the helicopter in its path. It had slowed enough to keep from derailing, but the engine was completely ablaze. The conductor or anyone else in the front-most car was certainly dead.

Reid sprang to his feet, adrenaline pumping in his veins and numbing his pain. Sara was on that train—but so were the traffickers. Emergency personnel would arrive soon from Grodkow, and if he didn't act fast, he did not believe there would be any girls left to find when they got there.

He quickly counted the cars as he sprinted forward. There were twelve, including the inferno that was the engine. Unlike Maya's train, only one was a passenger car. It would seem like the logical place to start…

But then he saw the red boxcar, four cars down from the engine. Stenciled on its side was a large 23.

As he made a beeline for it he was vaguely aware of shouting voices. Men, from inside the train. He kept his eyes open and the revolver in his hands—but as he drew near, a heavy door on the boxcar beside it slid open and a Slavic man jumped out, a machine gun in his hands.

Reid froze immediately, standing stock-still in the grass. The blaze of the engine was not far-reaching enough to show him in the darkness, or so he hoped.

It didn't matter anyway; the trafficker did not even glance in his direction. Instead he hurried to car 23 and threw the door open. He shouted into it in Slovak.

"Out! Come! Now!" The man scrambled up into the boxcar and forced a young woman out—not Sara. Then came a second. Finally the trafficker appeared again, half-dragging a seemingly unconscious girl with him. He lowered her unceremoniously to the dirt and let her fall to her side.

Where is she? Reid thought desperately. *She's here. I know she's here.* Maya left that message for a reason. She *had* to be here.

The trafficker shouted at the girls again, nudging them forward with the barrel of his gun. Reid took careful aim with Strickland's revolver. He was about forty feet out, give or take; not a difficult shot.

He fired once. His shot pulled slightly and struck the Slav in the back left shoulder. The man cried out and fell against the boxcar, spinning with his gun aloft. Reid quickly aimed again and fired, accounting for the pull. The bullet struck the trafficker in the forehead. The two girls he was ushering away fled down the length of the train, vanishing into darkness.

More shouts filled the air as men disembarked from the train.

"Who is shooting?" a voice called out.

"Alexej is down!" someone else called out.

Reid saw shapes emerging and quickly flattened himself in the field again.

"It came from that way! You two, go check! You, get the girls!"

He stayed as still as he could, lying on his stomach in the foot-tall grass. He had to get closer to the train. He had to see for himself into car 23…

A boot crackled over dry grass not ten feet from his location. He dared to glance up enough to see the Slovakian stalking slowly past his position—looking upward, looking for someone standing.

Reid waited until he passed by. Once the man's back was to him, he crept to his feet. In three quick strides he was upon the Slav, his hands reached for his chin and nape. In one quick jerk he broke the trafficker's neck and let him fall limply to the field.

He scooped up the machine gun and turned back to the train. His eyes were adjusting to the darkness; he counted four dark shapes, too large to be girls, scurrying along the train's length, throwing open freight car doors and demanding their cargo come out.

Reid marched forward, the machine gun in hands. *To the left, ten o'clock.* He fired off a short burst and cut down a trafficker with his back turned. *Three o'clock.* Another spun, bringing his weapon up, gunned down before he could get his finger to the trigger.

"Who is shooting?!" someone screamed from inside a boxcar.

"There! I see him!"

Reid threw himself to the ground as soon as he heard the words, just an instant before a barrage of bullets pelted against the side of the closest boxcar. He rolled three times on his side until he was under the car.

"He went under!" the same voice shouted again. "Under the train!"

Reid quickly shimmied forward on his stomach—not out the other side, where the traffickers would expect, but parallel to the length of the car. He groaned as he pulled himself out and onto the coupling between two freight cars, and then scrambled up the rusting ladder mounted on its rear.

He crouched atop the container and waited.

"Dmitri?" a voice called.

"I see no one!" To his right, on the opposite side. Reid leaned over the top of the car and fired straight down, into the top of the trafficker's skull.

"On top now!"

"Who *is* this?!"

"I see him—"

He tracked the voice to his left, leaning over the side and firing down. The trafficker's cry caught in his throat as he fell.

How many left? He had no way to tell. But he had to hold his position until he knew.

"Ivan?" called out a voice. There was no answer, and Reid could not tell where the voice was coming from. He carefully stepped to the right, peering over the side; he saw no one. He approached the left—

Sparks flew as bullets penetrated the boxcar ceiling from beneath his feet. Reid jumped forward, skidding on his elbows. He scrambled to his feet and leapt over the coupling to the next car.

Inside, Reid realized. *He's inside the boxcar.* A wave of dread crashed over him as he realized that the car he had just leapt from was red—the red 23.

"Throw down your gun," the trafficker shouted from inside the car. "And climb off of there. Or I will start killing girls."

Reid gulped. *He's bluffing. There are no girls in that car. The other trafficker, he cleared it already.*

But... what if he hadn't?

"You have until the count of three," the trafficker shouted. "Do not take me for a liar. One!"

What if there was still someone in there?

"Two!"

What if it was Sara?

"Wait!" Reid shouted in Slovak. He threw the machine gun over the side and into the grass. He simply could not take the chance that his daughter was in harm's way. "I'm coming down." He took a deep breath and hopped off the train car. The impact sent a jolting shockwave through both his legs.

The trafficker jumped out of the red car, his SMG pointed at Reid's heart. Through the open door, Reid could see the empty interior of the boxcar; there were no other girls inside it.

The trafficker had been bluffing. And Sara was not there.

The Slav was around his age, with a sharp, angular face and a noticeable scar down his right cheek. He narrowed his eyes angrily as Reid tensed. As long as even one of them was still alive, the nightmare might continue.

"I hear no sirens yet," the trafficker noted in the silence of the night. "You did this? Alone?"

Reid nodded. "Yes."

The Slav frowned. "Who are you?"

"A father."

The man nodded slowly, as if he understood. "You killed many of my friends tonight."

"Your friends were monsters. So are you."

"Yes," he agreed quietly. "Even so, those girls are going to die. You...you are going to die. Someone must pay for this, and it will not be me—"

The trafficker's forehead exploded outward as if a bomb had gone off inside his head. His passive expression never left his face as he fell forward into the grass.

Strickland's hands were still cuffed together, the Glock 19 raised—and now pointed directly at Reid as he stepped forward.

"Clear?" he asked.

Reid slowly put his hands up. "Yes. I think so."

To his astonishment, Strickland lowered his pistol. "Go," he said with a wave of his cuffed hands. "Find your daughter. I'll take care of the other girls until help arrives."

Reid blinked, but he was not about to question it. "Thank you," he said breathlessly. He snatched up the dead Slav's gun, and then he turned and sprinted for the single passenger car on the freight train.

He wrenched open the sliding door and stuck the barrel of the SMG into the corridor. He didn't have to; there was only one man in there, and he appeared to be quite dead. He lay on his back, bleeding from the face and neck. Shards of glass stuck in his skin, and Reid smelled the powerful aroma of cheap whiskey.

He knelt and felt the man's pulse; he was alive, but barely. In minutes he would bleed out—which was just fine by Reid.

But what happened here?

Across from the dying Slav was an open cabin door, and inside it was another apparent mess. A lanky man with long hair was face-down on the floor, a leather belt beside him. Reid approached slowly and prodded the body with the barrel of his gun.

The man suddenly took a rasping breath, startling Reid. He coughed and choked, his face turning from purple to red as he struggled to suck in air.

Someone fought back, Reid realized. This man was a john, and he had been attacked, strangled with the belt. The Slav had been smashed over the face with a bottle. Deep pockmarks littered the far wall in no discernible pattern—bullet holes—and the window had been shot out.

Reid dropped to his knees and rolled the lanky man over. "Who did this?" he insisted. "Who attacked you?"

The man coughed and attempted to speak, but only a gasp escaped his throat.

Reid slapped him with an open palm. "Who did this?!"

"Don't..." the man said in Czech. "Don't hurt me..."

"Who did this to you?" he demanded again in Slovak.

"A girl..."

"A young girl? Blonde hair?"

The man nodded weakly.

"How long ago? Hmm? How long?"

The man's head lolled to the side and he retched. Reid jumped to his feet again. The lanky Czech would be little help; he was likely unconscious and would have no idea how much time had passed.

Reid looked from the dying Slav to the strangled john to the shot-out window. Several shots had been fired into the wall; nearly the whole clip...

The gun.

He snatched up the Agram SMG lying on the floor and felt the barrel. It was still warm; not hot, but warm to the touch.

Sara had escaped the train only minutes before it struck the X4 on the rails.

Reid tore out of the passenger car and leapt into the grass. Further down the train, near the still-burning engine, he saw

Strickland helping girls down from a freight car. But he went the opposite way, down the length of the train in a full-out sprint.

The machine gun bounced against his thigh, hanging from its strap. He tossed it aside. His legs burned with every stride, every flex of muscle. *Pain be damned,* he told himself, panting.

"Sara!" he called out as he ran. "Sara!"

Sirens screamed in the night as emergency vehicles from Grodkow raced toward the crashed train from a road nearby. Overhead, a helicopter thrummed past him.

"Sara!" he screamed.

He ran for more than a mile. He ran until his legs threatened to give out from beneath him, until the pain was almost too much to bear. But he forced himself to keep going. He would find her. He had to find her...

Something crunched beneath Reid's boots and he skidded to a stop. It was glass. He could see it glinting in the moonlight. *The window...*

To his right was a steep embankment. "Sara," he breathed as he started down it, staggering sideways, his feet sliding and sending cascades of loose dirt into his shoes. He reached the bottom and shouted again. "Sara!" *Please be here. You have to be here.* "Sara!"

"Daddy?"

His knees went weak at the sound of her voice. Behind him he saw the small shape of her, lying on her back in the dirt. He dropped beside her, a racking spasm of a sob bubbling up from deep within him.

"Sara. Oh, god. Are you hurt? Are you okay?"

"You came." Her voice was small, nearly a whisper.

"Yeah. I came. Of course I came."

Her face was white in the moonlight, her eyes partially closed in a dreamy stare. "Is Mom with you?"

Reid sniffed, holding back another powerful sob. She was in shock. "No, baby. Mom's... she's not here. Are you hurt?"

"I think so."

"Okay. All right." He wiped his eyes and stood. "I'm so sorry, Sara, this might hurt a bit." He slid his arms under her knees and her neck and hefted her up as gently as he could.

She whimpered slightly and put both arms around his neck as he slowly made his way back up the embankment. It was a struggle, but he was determined. He had found her. Nothing was ever going to hurt her again.

They reached the top and he followed the tracks slowly back to the wreckage site with her in his arms. A light rain began to fall; the chilled water felt good on Reid's face.

"Is Maya okay?" she whispered in his ear.

"Yeah," he told her. "Maya's okay too."

Then she cried, sobbing gently into his shoulder as he carried her toward myriad flashing lights. A dozen emergency vehicles had arrived; the engine fire seemed to be out. Personnel scurried everywhere, shouting orders and corralling the girls from the train.

Only one person was unmoving. Agent Strickland stood near the rearmost car, watching Reid as he approached from the darkness beyond. The young agent nodded once to him.

The handcuffs were off his wrists, dangling open from one hand.

The time had come.

CHAPTER FORTY THREE

Reid sat at Sara's bedside in the small hospital in Grodkow. He held her small right hand in both of his as the sunrise broke on the horizon.

It looked like it was going to be a beautiful morning.

Sara's eyelids fluttered. Her head tilted slightly as she looked at him and smiled faintly. "Good," she murmured. "I was afraid I only dreamed you."

"You didn't. I'm here."

She sighed contentedly as her eyelids drooped again. The doctors had given her a mild sedative so they could reset her broken ulna. She had also suffered a few bruised ribs, and minor contusions and cuts from head to toe.

While the medical staff worked on Sara, a doctor looked Reid over as well; none of his injuries were very threatening. The stab wound in his abdomen was finally stitched up.

But otherwise, he was cleared to be put on a plane.

Sara's eyes opened again suddenly, wider this time. "Wait, where's Maya?"

"Maya is okay," Reid promised. "She's coming here right now. She should be here very soon."

Sara nodded and leaned back, wincing a little as she did.

"Listen," said Reid, trying to keep his voice even. "I want you to know that I'm…" he searched for the right word, "… *devastated*… that you had to go through this."

Sara said nothing in response. She just stared at the white bedspread.

"But...most of all, I'm sorry that I'm going to have to leave."

Sara's eyes widened again, her brow furrowed in confusion. "Leave? Leave where? Why?"

"I..." Reid started, but the door to the hospital room clicked and opened. They both looked up as a slight figure entered the room.

She wore white scrubs, on loan from the hospital to replace her dirty and bloodstained pajamas. There was color again in her cheeks, though one side of her face was still swollen and bruised purple. She limped slightly on one leg as she closed the door again behind her.

Tears welled in Maya's eyes as she looked at him. Words seemed to fail her, but she smiled.

Then she glanced over at her younger sister and her lower lip trembled. "Sara!" she said breathlessly as she hurried to the bedside. "Oh my god. What did they do to you?" She hugged her gently, but Sara still winced slightly. "I'm sorry. Are you okay?"

"I'm okay," she said softly as she hugged her sister with one arm, her other hand still between both of Reid's.

"I'm so glad to see you," Maya gushed. "Both of you."

"Maya," said Sara. "You were right. You were right the whole time."

"I know." Maya laughed a little and wiped the tears from her eyes as she turned to Reid once more. "I knew you would come for us."

Reid stood as his eldest came around the bedside to hug him.

Maya stopped in her tracks, staring in bewilderment at the handcuff chain hanging between his wrists. Sara sat up suddenly, seemingly ignoring the pain in her bruised ribs. She hadn't noticed the cuffs on his wrists as he'd held her hand in his.

"No." Maya shook her head as fresh tears brimmed in her eyes. "No, you just got here. You saved us. They can't..."

"I'm sorry," Reid said, his voice nearly a whisper. He raised his arms high, high enough to slip the handcuff chain over her head so that he could hug his daughter. Maya clung to him; he felt it in the wound in his abdomen, in his aching, sore muscles, but he didn't care. He hugged her back while she cried.

"You two are safe," he told them. "That's all that matters to me. That's all that ever mattered." He had told that to himself so many times during his pursuit of them, and now he knew that he truly meant it. No matter what was going to happen to him, he would accept it, as long as they were safe. "But to get to you, I had to ... do things. And I'm going to have to leave because of that."

"You're not coming home with us?" Sara asked as she too began to cry. "How long will you be gone?"

A sob bubbled from Maya's throat; she understood what Reid meant, even if Sara didn't.

"I won't let them," she said. "I-I'll talk to them. They'll see ..."

"Maya, no ..."

"They'll understand. They *have* to understand why you did what you did—"

"Maya," Reid said firmly. He took one of her hands in his and Sara's in the other, holding them both close. "I knew what would happen to me. I was warned and I did it anyway. I have to face that."

"That's not fair," Maya sobbed. "That's not fair at all. You didn't do anything wrong ..."

Yes, I did.

"Listen to me," he told his daughters. "Before I go, I need to tell you something. You are both so strong. I'm stunned by how strong you both were in the face of what you went through. I am in sheer awe of you for not giving up or giving in. Most importantly ..." His voice broke as he added, "Your mother would be very, very proud of you."

Sara's shoulders heaved as she wept. Maya stared at the floor— or possibly at the hanging handcuff chain—as tears streaked her cheeks. Reid wiped his own eyes.

For the briefest moment, he thought of what he had learned from the assassin about Kate. His daughters deserved to know the truth, just like he had deserved to know. But now was far from the time to mention it. It might never be the time to mention it, he realized.

Maybe Maria had been right. Maybe sometimes ignorance really was bliss. If he could do it over again, he couldn't say for sure that he would want to relearn the truth.

The door to the hospital room opened and Agent Strickland peered in. "Zero," he said gently. "Time to go."

Maya's hand squeezed harder around Reid's. She did not look up at Strickland, barely moved at all as she said, "Please don't take him."

"Hey." Reid hugged her once more. He whispered in her ear so that only she could hear. "You're going to be taken care of. But you need to keep your sister safe, okay? That's your job now. At least until... until I'm back."

"Will we see you again?"

He was quiet for a moment, unsure whether or not to speak the truth. He was quiet for too long. She was smart enough to know the answer from his hesitation.

"I don't know," he told her honestly. He carefully pulled away from her and kissed her forehead. He hugged Sara once more and kissed her goodbye.

"I love you both."

Then he left them there, closing the door behind him as he stepped out into the hall. Agent Strickland leaned against the wall just outside with his hands in his pockets.

"Thank you," Reid murmured. "You didn't have to do that."

"Least I could do," Strickland said with a small shrug. He had been authorized to take Reid to the hospital to have his wounds treated, but it had been the young agent's call to allow him a precious few minutes with his daughters.

Reid sighed and wiped his eyes clear with the back of his hands. "How's your jaw?"

Strickland smiled. "Don't flatter yourself, Zero. I've been hit harder than that before."

They both chuckled, but it was short-lived.

"I know what you're thinking Zero," Strickland said. "You're wondering if it's really safe to leave your girls. You're wondering if you should resist me. Risk it all."

Reid met his eyes. That was exactly what he was thinking—calculating the odds of a confrontation with Strickland. Calculating the risk of personally breaking his daughters out of here, flying them home. Calculating what life would be like, always on the run from the CIA.

Ironically, that sort of life would keep him away from his daughters forever.

Strickland turned to face him, taking his hands from his pockets.

"I promise you," Strickland said, his voice more serious than Reid had ever heard it, "nothing is going to happen to them again. I'm going to see to it personally. I swear by my life."

Reid frowned in confusion.

"You? Why?"

"I've been thinking a lot about what you said—about right and wrong," Strickland admitted. "I didn't think what you did was right... not until I saw their faces. Not until we saw those girls you saved from those trains. Not until I saw you, carrying her down the tracks like you did. I don't think I've seen strength like that before." He shook his head. "So I'm going to make it my personal agenda to make sure those girls are safe and cared for, no matter what. Because it feels right."

"I..." Reid didn't know what to say. Strickland was a veritable stranger, yet when Reid looked into the younger man's eyes, he believed every word of his vow. "Thank you, Strickland."

He nodded. "I'm going to park myself right outside this door until Sara is cleared for discharge. Then I'm going to escort them personally to the airport and we're going to get on a direct flight to LaGuardia. I understand you have a sister-in-law in New York; she's going to meet us at the gate. The girls will be staying with her. I'm also told they'll be chipped—"

"Chipped?" Reid interrupted.

"A very tiny subcutaneous microchip," Strickland explained. "They'll be told it's a flu shot or something similar and it's injected just under the skin, usually in an arm or shoulder. It tracks by satellite. They'll never be lost again."

Three days ago Reid would have argued tooth and nail about the idea of his daughters being microchipped—but that felt like practically another life.

Reid felt his muscles go slack. He felt himself relaxing, embracing the idea of Strickland watching his girls. It allowed him to accept the cuffs on his wrists, to accept his fate.

"What about Maria—Agent Johansson?" he asked. "What's going to happen to her?"

Strickland shook his head. "I don't know."

Reid nodded. *Maybe I'll see her again, if we end up in the same place.* "And … me?"

Strickland sighed evenly through his nose. "There are three agents in the waiting room at the end of the hall. They're going to take you to a plane. Where that plane's going, I have no idea. Sorry, Kent. That's the best I can do."

"No," Reid said. "Watching out for my girls, *that's* the best you can do. And I truly appreciate it."

Strickland raised an eyebrow. "Are you going to?"

"Going to what?"

The young agent gestured toward the end of the hall, where the other agents were waiting. "Go with them?"

Reid smirked lightly. He knew what Strickland was asking; Agent Zero could make a lot of trouble for them if he wanted to, and they knew it. Maybe he could even get away before getting shot.

"Yes," he said. "I'm going to go with them."

Strickland nodded gratefully. He took Reid gently by one elbow and led him down the hall toward the waiting room.

Reid wasn't lying. He was going to go with them. As anxious as he was about his future, as agonizing as it was to leave the girls, and as distressing as it was to be so uncertain about what might happen to those who had helped him, like Maria and Watson, a bizarre calmness overtook him. It was a strange serenity, but he knew its source—his girls were safe. He had done what he set out to do. He believed Strickland when he said he would take care of them. They would never be lost again.

He had no idea what the CIA had planned for him, where they might take him, but at that moment, walking down the hall toward three unfamiliar agents and his fate, it didn't matter. His heart was peaceful and his mind was quiet.

There wasn't much more he could hope for than that.

Now Available!

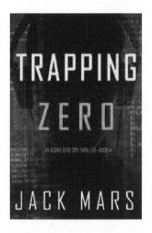

TRAPPING ZERO
(An Agent Zero Spy Thriller—Book #4)

"You will not sleep until you are finished with AGENT ZERO. A superb job creating a set of characters who are fully developed and very much enjoyable. The description of the action scenes transport us into a reality that is almost like sitting in a movie theater with surround sound and 3D (it would make an incredible Hollywood movie). I can hardly wait for the sequel."
—Roberto Mattos, Books and Movie Reviews

In TRAPPING ZERO (Book #4), a terrorist cell in the Mideast gains a new, fanatic leader, one intent on orchestrating what

would be the deadliest attack on American soil. Can Agent Zero uncover the plot and stop him in time?

Although Agent Zero's daughters are home safely, the mental anguish from their experience weighs heavy on their small family. Zero, working to be a good father and to repair the damage, decides the time has come to undergo surgery to regain all of his memories. But will it work?

In the midst of it all, he is again thrust into the line of duty as a U.S. embassy is destroyed in the Mideast and as an experimental new weapon is uncovered. But without his memories, with some of his own CIA allies intent on his destruction, who can he really trust?

TRAPPING ZERO (Book #4) is an un-putdownable espionage thriller that will keep you turning pages late into the night.

"Thriller writing at its best."
—Midwest Book Review (re *Any Means Necessary*)

"One of the best thrillers I have read this year."
—Books and Movie Reviews (*re Any Means Necessary*)

Also available is Jack Mars' #1 bestselling LUKE STONE THRILLER series (7 books), which begins with Any Means Necessary (Book #1), a free download with over 800 five star reviews!

TRAPPING ZERO
(An Agent Zero Spy Thriller—Book #4)